TEMPTED

Torin moved with all the caution of a predatory animal, slow and sinuous in his grace, coming at last to the water's edge. She was even lovelier up close than she had been from afar. He felt his heartbeat quicken as she met him eye to eye. Oh, she was a bold one, this beauty. Most women would be cowering at the thought of even glimpsing a Viking.

"Where are the others?" she asked. "I would be simple-minded to think that ye came alone."

He gestured with his hand. "They are a long way off. Waiting for me on the ship. I wanted to come alone. I'm looking for someone." As he spoke he edged closer.

She looked at him searchingly. "To kill them?" If he was looking for someone because of some kind of vengeance, she wanted to know.

"No. To offer them wealth and power." Her face was now clearly revealed to him and he was struck by a feeling of familiarity. It was as if he had seen her somewhere before. His gaze touched upon her well-formed nose, long lashes, and wide, sensuous mouth. Her cheekbones were high and prominent, adding to her beauty.

"Why, then?"

"I want to take him with me." When she stiffened he said quickly, "His father is a Viking who wants to be reunited with him."

"Reunited . . . ?" He was looking for someone of mixed parentage. Like her.

For one timeless moment they stared at each other across the short distance that separated them. His eyes caressed her with a boldness few had dared—held her, forced her to acknowledge that something was going on between them. An undeniable fascination.

She held her breath in expectation as he reached out. Without a word he caught a fistful of her long silken hair and wrapped it around his hand, drawing her closer. With the tips of his fingers he traced the line of her cheekbones, the shape of her mouth, the line of her brows.

"I'm of a mind to take *you* with me, too, when I go. . . ."

Dear Romance Reader,

In July of 1999, we launched the Ballad line with four new series, and each month we present both new and continuing stories set everywhere from medieval England to the American West—the kind of passionate, romantic stories you love best, written by the most gifted authors. At the back of each book, we tell you when you can find subsequent books in the series that have captured your heart.

Getting this month off to a dazzling start is **Outcast,** the debut story in the passionate new series *The Vikings,* from long-time reader favorite Kathryn Hockett. When a woman proud of her Viking heritage meets the Nordic warrior in search of her father's oldest son, she proves a woman's strength—in battle and love. Next, ever-imaginative Alice Duncan takes us to the 1893 World's Fair in Chicago with her new trilogy, *Meet Me at the Fair.* Everything's **Coming Up Roses** for a trick rider in Buffalo Bill's Wild West Show—until she meets the man who threatens to steal her heart.

Linda Devlin returns this month with **Cash,** the long-awaited sixth installment in the *Rock Creek Six* series, in which a legendary ladies' man—and gunslinger—must face up to his past, and the future he glimpses in the smile of a certain woman. Finally, Corinne Everett ends *Daughters of Liberty* with **Sweet Violet,** as a young Virginia woman determined to find adventure in England discovers danger instead—along with a surprising chance at love.

What a fabulous selection to choose from! Why not read them all? Enjoy!

Kate Duffy
Editorial Director

THE VIKINGS

OUTCAST

KATHRYN HOCKETT

ZEBRA BOOKS
Kensington Publishing Corp.
http://www.kensingtonbooks.com

Author's Note

From the cold North, on ships dancing on the waves, the Norsemen came. For three centuries the Vikings took the world by storm as they searched for land and riches. These brave warriors and explorers set sail from Norway, Sweden, and Denmark, raiding across Europe and voyaging as far as Baghdad. There is proof that they even reached America.

The Vikings loved bright ornaments. Their metal workers were skilled at intricate decoration of jewelry—brooches, necklaces, finger rings, bracelets, and pendants. Wearing gold and silver jewelry was a sign of wealth and prestige. After a successful raid, a jarl might reward a brave warrior or a loved one by giving him a prize piece. Jewelry was also used as a means of protection, a talisman of sorts; some pieces were sculpted to resemble important gods and goddesses.

The Norsemen, as they were called, were shrewd traders, excellent navigators, interesting storytellers, superb craftsmen and shipbuilders. They came at first to raid but later colonized Ireland, Iceland, Greenland, and half of England. Their society was open and democratic, and they were skillful lawgivers and administrators.

Scotland, then called Alba and inhabited by Celts, Picts, and Scots, was also touched by the Vikings. Early writers described these sea raiders as being of two distinct groups: the fair-haired Norsemen and the dark-haired Danes. More than half of Alba was conquered, and by the end of the ninth century the Norsemen were masters of Orkney, Shetland, and the Western Isles. In fact at one period or another, the greater part of Scotland was either surrounded by or in the hands of the Norsemen. With periods of varying success, the Norse occupation continued until about 1264, when they were finally expelled (except from Orkney and Shetland).

The inhabitants of Scotland had a rich oral and written culture and an extraordinarily powerful perception of their racial kinship and blood ties. Their deep attachment to soil and tribe was the emotional foundation of the unique Scottish clan system that was to evolve in which free men pledged their first loyalties to their kith and kin and to their patriarchal leader, even to the death.

Now, from the Hebrides and Ireland to the shores of Iceland, a search is underway to find the three sons of Ragnar Longsword, the daring Viking jarl whose bold raids and conquests of the heart are already legend. To each of his lovers Ragnar has given a jewel from his Viking sword to hang around his sons' necks when they were born. Now those pendants are the only key to his quest.

In Scotland the quest begins, bringing together two brave and determined lovers: a half Viking, half Scots highlander of the clan MacQuarie of Ulva, and a Viking who has been branded as an outcast.

NOTE: The island of Staffa, later to become known for the strange rock formation of Fingal's Cave, which inspired Mendelssohn to write the music for his immortal overture, was at this time part of the territory of the MacQuarie clan. The original name for Fingal's Cave was Gaelic—An Uamh Ehinn, or "the musical cave"—and was derived from the sounds of the sea echoing through its depths.

PART ONE

LEGACY OF FIRE

ONE

Torches flickered and sparked in the *skaalen,* the great hall of Ragnar Longsword. Giant pine logs flamed in the sunken trough in the center of the huge room. The air was clouded with drifting veils of smoke as a huge slab of venison roasted on a spit over the fire for *nadver,* the evening meal. Cauldrons of iron and soapstone, suspended over the flames from a tripod, gave forth a tantalizing aroma from the lamb stew that bubbled within. Wooden tables were laden with freshly baked wheat, barley bread, and bowls of freshly picked berries.

Thralls scurried about lighting soapstone oil lamps that were suspended from the ceiling with iron chains. The fires' reflection glimmered on the shields, axes, and swords hanging on the wall. These weapons made of iron and decorated with silver and copper were Ragnar's most prized possessions, for a beautifully ornamented sword was a sign that the owner was rich and powerful. That same light also sparkled from the silver bracelets, necklaces, gold chains, and brooches of the women meandering about the hall—further proof of the household's wealth.

The air rang with laughter and chatter as men crowded their way into the room, dipping their drinking horns into the large communal mead vat. They amused themselves with drinking contests, board games, and in trying to out-talk each other. A few had set up a target at the far side of the hall and placed wagers on which one of four men hurling axes would hit the mark.

All action stopped, however, as one Viking strode through the door, his shoulders thrust back, his head held up with pride. Dressed in a russet tunic bordered with blue and red embroidery at the sleeves and hem, a brown leather corselet with shoulder straps fastened at the chest with buckles, dun-colored leggings, and silver and gold bracelets arraying his arms, he looked every inch the jarl that he was.

Ragnar Longsword was a big-boned giant of a man in the autumn of his years whose skill at fighting was not to be equaled in all of the Northlands. He was feared all the way from the Hebrides to Kiev. The very glimpse of his Viking ships with their square sails and dragon-headed prows struck fear in the heart of anyone who sighted them on the horizon.

For twenty-seven years Ragnar and his band of men had burst upon the coasts, targeting villages, castles, and monasteries alike in their quest for plunder. The raids had brought Ragnar and his men wealth, land, reputations for being both ruthless and bold, and an armed following to support Ragnar's ambitions at home.

"There are no living men on land or water as bold as we," Ragnar said time and time again. "No one dares to meet us sword to sword. Be we right or wrong, all men yield before us."

Tales had been told and retold of how Ragnar had first embarked with his men in a fleet of dragon-prowed ships. The Viking leader, intelligent as well as strong, had proven himself to be an able administrator in the lands he subjugated. He realized that a man had to be a creator as well as a destroyer, and to reach out to other cultures, to learn from them and absorb outside influences and ideas.

In his youth Ragnar's hair and thick beard had been tawny but now there was far more gray than blond. Lines criss-crossed his high forehead. There were crow's feet at the corner of each eye and a ragged scar across his right cheek. Even so, it was obvious to see from the well-sculpted facial features that once he had been a man who could win any woman's heart as well as any battle. Indeed, he still could turn a woman's head. Looking across the room, Ragnar could see two pretty young women staring at him.

"Gerda and Helga had better beware, or Nissa will have their heads," said a tall man, coming up behind Ragnar, patting him roughly on the shoulder.

"Nissa has no reason to be concerned. I'm growing old. My better days are long since gone," Ragnar replied with a wry smile as he looked across the room at the woman with silver-threaded dark blond hair, his wife.

"Your better days are still ahead of you."

Slowly Ragnar turned, assessing the tall, strikingly handsome man. His name was Torin, the son of Roland. His father had been one of Ragnar's fiercest foes, a man Ragnar had outlawed as a murderer, a coward, and a traitor.

Roland Thorvaldsson had been bloody of heart and bloody of hand. He had been a murderously bad neighbor, a scoundrel on a grand scale—foul-tempered and a heathen to the core. He had disobeyed the law by killing a fellow Viking for a very small offense. There were suspicions that he had not only beaten but murdered his wife; still he refused to make restitution for his transgressions, and to the very end had remained unrepentant. Even so, he had been a threat to Ragnar, for he possessed power and a magnetism that drew people to him so that they would follow him with undying loyalty. Worse yet, he had contested Ragnar's right to rule and had openly challenged him. Ragnar had banished him.

As further punishment he had taken the motherless boy, Torin, from his father's hearth, with the intent of bringing further humiliation upon Roland Thorvaldsson's family. Little did he realize that the quiet, intense, intelligent little boy would slowly steal his affection. He had watched the outcast

Torin Rolandson grow up, had watched him exchange toys for a man's adeptness with weapons. Even as a child Torin was skilled as a theorist, exhibiting an ability to beat even old, seasoned veterans at the board game of *hneftafl*. Ragnar had wisely made use of that expertise when planning his battles, and had to admit that Torin was a born strategist. Slowly through the years Torin had become a valuable asset and an integral part of Ragnar's household and his life.

"You flatter me to say that better days lie ahead for me," Ragnar said, looking him in the eye, "but I know the truth, Torin. One day soon I will be warming my feet at the fire, watching the women spin and weave while the younger men go a-viking."

For a moment there was silence, then Torin shook his head. "That day is a long way off." Or at least that was his hope, for it had been whispered that when Ragnar laid up his sword, Herlaug, Ragnar's younger brother, would take his place. Torin was not anxious for that time to come. Herlaug was his enemy, a cruel man who had constantly reprimanded him for his father's sins, treating him like an underling, taunting him with the name "Outcast."

Seeing Torin's downcast look, Ragnar gave him a nudge. "Come, let's take a seat and talk of more pleasant things."

Thralls passed platters heaped high with food. The sound of smacking lips, gulps, and belches filled the air; spoons and knives scraped across plates as the food was savored. Meals were a time to relax; then, after they had eaten, the Vikings would play games, tell stories, and listen to music. Men of importance had their own poets, called skalds, who entertained guests and praised their patrons. Ragnar was said to have one of the finest skalds for miles around.

Soon after the meal was finished and the dishes pushed away, the skald began his tale about Ragnar and how the noble Viking had lived, loved, explored, and waged war. Already his exploits had taken on the proportion of legend.

Swooping out of the dark sea mists on dragon ships dancing on the waves, Ragnar Longsword came, led by Odin, to fulfill his destiny. Sharp was the clang of sword against shield, shrill the shriek of arrows that flew o'er the field. The warriors from the Hebrides, the men of the Isles, were said to be fierce, but against Longsword's prowess they were tamed, surrounded, then doomed. . . .

When the skald had finished his song, Ragnar made his way to the keg of mead, where he dipped his drinking horn. His head ached and throbbed so much that the skald's droning voice had nearly made him shout aloud to stop. Gripping the hard wooden arms of the chair, he had forced himself to gain control. Now, drinking deeply of the beer made from malted barley and honey, he could only hope that the beverage would numb his senses.

Drinking horns clanked as the men's revelry continued, but there came a time when thirst was assuaged and hunger satisfied. In that moment the Norsemen banged their tankards upon the table in a steady rhythm. "Ragnar! Ragnar! Ragnar!" they chanted, making it known that they wanted to hear him speak.

Ragnar winced, silencing the crowd with his outstretched hand as he stood up. "I fear I am not as poetic as our beloved skald, nor as good with words as my fine friend Torin, but I have something to say that will entrance you nonetheless."

With that he began his own story, holding them spellbound as he talked of things past, things present, and things yet to come. Their journeys were just beginning, he told them, weaving a magical web with his words as he spoke of lands far from their land of snow and ice far out on the horizon near the end of the world. "There are lands still waiting to be explored. Lands only Odin has gazed upon. Lands that . . ." He winced as a sharp stab of pain shot through his head. "Lands that we will claim as our own."

Visibly shaken, Ragnar quickly sat back down, loathing any sign of weakness. His vision was blurred as he looked from man to man, and his head buzzed. As the evening wore on he consumed horn after horn of mead, hoping to soothe the searing pain in his head, but it didn't do any good.

Darkness gathered under the high vaulted roof. The smoking torches hissed, flickered, and died. Shadows loomed tall and menacing. Suddenly the soot-darkened walls seemed to close in on Ragnar. Voices droned in his ears. For just a moment he imagined that he saw Odin standing across the room. Then his father's face floated upon the smoke in the room, motioning to Ragnar as if to beckon him to join him. Join him in what? The afterlife? Valhalla!

Ragnar stood up, looking around him, but all he could see were staring eyes. He felt dizzy, as if the very walls were pushing down on him. His legs felt weak. He fought to steady himself as he took a few steps, but to no avail. The world gradually went blank; the floor rose up to meet him. His long sleeve caught on his drinking vessel, sending it toppling to the floor. With a heavy thump, Ragnar followed, crumpling to the hard, earthen floor as he lost consciousness.

The smoking torches in the great hall hissed as if in warning. The flames from the large fires flickered, sending the shadows of all assembled into an eerie dance. The pine logs sputtered and burned low, but there was enough light for Torin to see the paleness of Ragnar's face as he lay unconscious on the floor. Though the others might think their jarl had passed out from drunkenness, Torin suspected otherwise.

Bending down, he knelt over Ragnar, touching his neck, feeling for the pulsation of life. There was a heartbeat, but it was faint and erratic. Pulling the eyelids open, he gazed into eyes that were like polished stone.

"Ragnar . . . !"

Ragnar blinked but did not answer.

"It is not poison, is it?" Nissa asked, clutching at Torin's arm. Poison was a cruel but efficient way to eliminate a rival. It wouldn't be the first time such a thing had happened in view of all.

"Poison?" Was it? Torin's gaze touched on one face after the other, searching for a guilty expression, but all he could see was the concern that was growing the longer Ragnar lay unmoving.

"Help me to my chair . . ." Opening his eyes, Ragnar issued the command in a shaky voice. When Torin hesitated, he said, "That is the order."

It was a struggle, for Ragnar was a big, heavy man, but Torin helped him to his feet. Pridefully Ragnar insisted on making it the rest of the way on his own. He was determined not to exhibit any sign of weakness.

"Leave us," Torin commanded of the others in the hall. The stern look on his face was enough to make them quickly obey.

For a long moment the only sound was Ragnar's ragged breathing. Then he spoke softly but with conviction. "It won't be long until I'm called to Valhalla." Ragnar revealed that although he had few outward scars, there was something inside his head that had been troubling him for quite a while. "There are times when I think Thor's hammer is inside my head . . . pounding. Pounding!"

Looking into Ragnar's eyes, Torin asked, "Is this the first time you have had such a spell?"

Ragnar shook his head. "No. It is only the first time that I have been unable to hide it." He took a deep breath. "What ails me is not going to go away, though many times I foolishly hoped that it would."

Torin tried to reassure Ragnar, but he was apprehensive. Ragnar had been wounded in the head many times. Had those injuries come back to haunt him?

"My life is coming to an end, Torin, I know it. But I'm

not afraid. I'll go to Valhalla." He did fear, however, that the supremacy he had carved with his sword would crumble when he died, because Nissa, his Viking wife, had not borne him sons, or indeed any children that had survived beyond infancy. It was some kind of a curse.

"You have many brave men who—"

"Who will fight among themselves if I am not there to maintain the peace. That's why you must help me."

Torin grimaced. "You are going to name Herlaug as your successor." He would be expected to help his enemy.

"No."

"Then who?" For a moment Torin held his breath in expectation, thinking perhaps Ragnar would name *him*.

"One of my sons . . ."

"Sons?" For a moment he feared that Ragnar was delusional. "But you have no sons!"

"I do!" Ragnar told him about three magnificent women he had met on his raids—one in the land of the Scots, one in Eire, and one in Britain. In his way, Ragnar said, he had loved all of the women but had been forced to leave them behind when he moved on. Nevertheless, he revealed to Torin, each of the women had given him a child, and he in turn had given each an amulet set with an uncut jewel from the hilt of his Viking sword.

Pride shone in Ragnar's eyes, dulling his pain. "Three sons that I have never seen, but who have been in my heart all this time."

"Sons . . ." Torin didn't know why the revelation should hurt so, but it did.

"I have wanted to see them, wanted to go back, but somehow the years have gone by so quickly." Suddenly he gripped Torin's hand. "Before I die I want to gather my sons together so . . . so that I can choose one of them to take my place as jarl."

"You are sure about these births?" Torin asked Ragnar.

"As certain as I am that I breathe the air of life." Ragnar

smiled. "I knew that my women were true to me. The children born were *my* children, else I would not have given them the pendants to hang around their necks to protect them."

"Pendants . . . ?" Of course, Torin thought. Ragnar had given the gifts for more reasons than just beauty. They had been given as protective talismans.

"There were three pendants."

"One for each of the women."

"No. One for each of my sons." Ragnar had given the necklaces for more than just protection. He had hoped that the pendants would make it easy for him to identify his sons when the time came.

"There is the Raven's Eye, a garnet; the Dragon's Tear, a sapphire; and the Wolf's Shadow, an amber stone."

Ragnar then told Torin that he was sending him on a mission to find his sons by way of the pendants and bring them back to Hafrsfjord.

TWO

A brisk breeze whipped through Torin's hair as he gazed out to sea from the rocky shore. When Ragnar made up his mind, there was little hope of changing it, though Odin himself might deem it a wrongful decision.

"He wants me to find his sons . . ." A simple enough request, except that so many years had passed that it might be difficult to locate the young men, pendants or no pendants. Even if he did find one, two, or all of the sons, there was no guarantee that they would want to come back to Norway with him.

An Englishwoman, a woman from Eire, and one from Alba: All of those lands had been raided by the Vikings at one time or another, which made a warm welcome to his visit unlikely. There was also a possibility that he and those he took with him might be attacked, wounded, or even killed in retaliation for past transgressions. And yet, how could he deny Ragnar's request? Not only was he Torin's leader, he was also his friend. Now that friend was ill, possibly dying. How could he fail in something so important to Ragnar?

Gazing out past the rocky crags to the meadows and grasslands beyond, he pondered what the future held in store for him if Ragnar died. What would it be like to serve another jarl? Torin thought back to the way Ragnar had treated him when he was a boy. At first they'd been at odds, the

Viking jarl's attitude toward him as cold as his ice blue eyes. Indeed he'd been treated like a thrall, kept busy with lowly chores.

All the while, Torin had been only too aware of what had happened to his father. A man declared an outlaw could not fish, trade, join a Viking expedition, or ask assistance in an hour of need, not even from his own family. Permanent out-lawry was tantamount to a sentence of death, for an outcast was fair game for anyone. He could be killed in any fashion at any time.

As a boy Torin had thought about his father often, won-dering where he was and if he was alive. All the while he had been determined that someday he would redeem his family honor. To that purpose he had worked hard at all duties he was assigned, always finding time to watch the men at their mock battles, admiring their skill and prowess. He had even learned the Viking board game, hneftafl, with such skill that he could beat any man he played. Just as in the game that used eight carved game pieces to protect the carved wooden jarl, he would protect Ragnar from the other live and possibly overly ambitious players.

Torin had adored Ragnar and in the end had won him over. Ragnar had taught the boy how to use a sword, and in the obsessive determination to please him, Torin had prac-ticed hard, not only in wielding a sword but also in the thought behind each movement. He would be ready if the need arose, he had told himself.

Because Torin was the son of a man who had been dis-graced, he had to be twice as good at everything he did and twice as smart. In order to prove himself double the worth of anyone else, he had erected a hard shell around himself in his boyhood, for he was more sensitive than he would ever have cared to admit, and loathed it as a weakness.

Then at last on one of the raids, young Torin was given a chance to prove himself. Amid a clattering, clamoring, weapon-thrusting, shouting throng, he had at last come to full manhood. The men of Ragnar's hall, if not fully accepting him, had come to admire him for his strength and leadership, and the young women had granted him their smiles and much, much more. Falling under the spell of his striking male comeliness, they had given him their all-consuming passion and their love. It was a reward Torin accepted as his due.

Now I add one more duty, Torin thought, *finding Ragnar's three sons.* He would begin his journey in the land of the Scots, and would ask his friend Gardar to accompany him. Gardar was loyal and brave and always seemed to understand Torin's moods as no one else could. Gardar, like Torin, was a thinker.

Aye, Gardar, he thought with a smile. Gardar had once been a thrall but had been given his freedom when he saved the life of one of Ragnar's men. More important, Gardar was of Celtic and Pictish origin and understood their ways. Torin had befriended the small, dark-haired man because he, too, knew what it felt like to be an outcast. Under Torin's tutelage and his stern defense, Gardar had at last been fully accepted. In gratitude he had become Torin's friend. That friendship would be a valuable asset on the journey.

So thinking, Torin went inside the hall and back to his chambers. He would try to keep this mission in perspective. He'd seen so much blood and killing that he fully intended to live to the fullest! It was a brutal world, but he could survive if he kept the right attitude. Appreciate each day of life—that would be his motto.

The *Sea Wolf* sailed three days later, her red-and-white sails billowing with the spring winds. Torin had gathered his belongings and made ready for the journey as quickly as he could, which was an easy matter considering the fact that Vikings took very few possessions with them when they sailed. Besides enough water and food for the journey, he and his crew would take only a sword, shield, helmet, and as much as they could carry in a sack one-third their size. The less weight the better. The ship did not have a deck, just open space; there was no place to store unnecessary items.

Despite the fact that Torin had wanted to pick his own crew, Ragnar had given in to his brother Herlaug's promptings to allow him to send some of his own men, a decision that irritated Torin. Herlaug was his enemy and, despite being Ragnar's brother, an instigator of trouble. Torin feared that Herlaug's motives might be rooted in a desire to sabotage the mission, despite his platitudes to Ragnar. A snake was a snake, despite its attempts to prove itself otherwise. As he assessed his crew, Torin had misgivings. There were only a few men he really trusted. He could only hope that all would go well so that their loyalty, or lack thereof, need not be tested.

Standing at the steerboard of the ship like a staunch pillar of strength, Torin tried to put his misgivings aside as he proudly surveyed his long, low ship with its tall, swan-necked prow. Absent was the monstrous dragon figurehead whose main purpose was to instill dread, for Torin's mission was a peaceful one. Instead, Torin had chosen a carved wolf's head to represent cunning.

Torin's vessel, a long ship, was brilliantly designed for commerce and exploration instead of war, with a large square sail in addition to oars. This sail had been unfurled to take full advantage of the newly freshened wind. Built low for speed and ease in handling, the long ship was the most versatile of Viking craft and was used both for raiding and coastal trading.

The body of the ship followed the movement of the sea, the motions of the waves allowing the outside to twist out of line six inches or so and still remain watertight. The sides of Viking ships were built so that the ship could twist and give, thus reducing the danger of its breaking apart under strain and pressure. Because the ship would be sailing close to beaches and land, its rudder had been designed to be lifted from the water when sailing in shallow water.

"I do not envy you," Gardar said, coming up behind Torin. "Halldor is going to be quite a handful to manage. Even now he looks daggers at you."

"That's because he would like to be standing here commanding the crew. Well, as long as I'm alive he'll have to keep his place."

"As long as you are alive?" Gardar patted his friend on the back. "Then I would watch my back if I were you. It wouldn't be the first time that Halldor has acted as Herlaug's executioner."

Torin shrugged. "I'm safe, at least for the moment. Halldor is anxious to count his gold when he returns and Ragnar rewards him." Ragnar had promised to be generous—twice so if the ship returned carrying one of his sons.

"Even so, be careful. . . ."

It was a warning that Torin took to heart, particularly when night fell and he watched Halldor hang the lamps filled with whale oil about the deck. Gardar was right. There was something ominous in the way some of the other Vikings looked at him. As if there might be something sinister afoot.

He would have to watch out.

THREE

The early-morning air was filled with the fragrance of flowers as a breeze blew across the glen. The wisps of fog that had covered the land like a low-hanging cloud had faded, leaving the sky clear and blue. Overhead the sun spread its warmth, shining down upon two combatants fighting a fierce mock battle with wooden swords.

"Geordie, ye move just like a lassie! Hit harder."

"Fight like a lassie, do I? We'll see!" The shorter of the two took the handle of the sword in both hands, striking out furiously.

"Ye are being careless, hinny. Ye must keep a level head on your shoulders. And practice your footwork. Part of being good with a sword is being nimble on your feet, like a dancer." The taller of the two, the one with the fiery hair, demonstrated, dodging in and out, escaping critical blows again and again. "See?"

" 'Tis easy for ye to be graceful. Ye don't have the big feet that I do." The tawny-haired swordsman struck out again, swearing beneath his breath when he missed his target.

"Geordie, temper your aim. Temper your emotions." Moving back and forth, swaying in time to some unheard rhythm, the red-haired fighter circled the opponent, the wooden sword slashing gracefully through the air, weaving a pattern. "See?"

The sound of wood against wood rent the air as the two fought a furious game to show who was the better "man." It was just the sort of test of strength and skill which the fiery-haired Erica thrived on.

"I'm the finest swordsman on all o' Mull and well ye all know it."

"But only with a wooden sword."

"Ach! I'd soon prove to ye all that I'm the best in the Highlands, if I could get my hands on a real sword." With a deep, throaty laugh, the red-haired "swordsman" lashed out, striking her young brother with the flat of her sword to avoid drawing blood. "That is a strike!"

"Oh, it is, is it? Then here is one in answer!" This time it was Geordie who was successful. Even so, it was his opponent who was more adept at keeping their sword fight in perspective.

"Ye cannot win!"

"I can."

"But ye will not."

"Will!"

Geordie was skilled with a sword, but his opponent's lightning-quick agility was more than his match. Again and again Geordie lunged, his anger making him careless. The red-haired combatant blocked each thrust. With a last concentrated effort, she sent her half-brother's sword tumbling to the ground.

"I win this one!"

Geordie made a face. "Ye must promise not to tell the others. I would rather die than have it be known that I was bested by a female."

"And not the first time!" She laughed, reaching out to ruffle his hair with her fingers.

"Aye, not the first time!"

"Now, tie your shoes."

Bending down, Geordie cross-laced his cuarans, which had come undone in the fracas. There was a strange, faraway look as he gazed toward the sea, shading his eyes against the sun's glare. " 'Tis strange to think of how many of our kith and kin have wielded their swords right on this very spot. How many do ye suppose, Erica?"

"I do not know exactly. Hundreds, I would say, and all at odds with the Picts, the English, or the Vikings."

There was always some kind of warfare going on. Was it any wonder that Erica wanted to be prepared to defend herself? First, the warfare had been between the Picts and Scots, for each had their own king and lands and were loath to share. That struggle for supremacy lasted nearly three hundred years, until at last the two became united by marriage, not conquest. Alpin was the son of that union. When he was killed in battle, his son, Ciniod Mac, eventually united the two peoples under one ruler as Kenneth I, king of Alba. Now, however, it was the Norsemen who earned her kinsmen's anger because of their persistent raids and continued threat to the country. Would there never be peace?

Erica looked toward the wild sea lochs that gouged deeply into the land, and breathed a sigh. This land of Mull, Ulva, and the island of Staffa, which she could see in the distance, had been inhabited by her clan since long before she and Geordie were born. The inhabitants of Skye and Mull and other Hebridean islands were of Pictish stock strongly overlaid with Scottish influences.

Erica was proud of her Scots ancestry on her mother's side. The MacQuaries were descended from the second son of Gregor, son of Alpin, and brother of Kenneth the famous king of Scots. Gregor mac Alpin, Siol Alpin, was accepted by all other Highland clans as being one of the most ancient. They had a place of honor in the councils of the lords of the isles. Erica and her half-brothers had listened to the bardic recitals of clan genealogy from their earliest childhood, back to the first man to settle on the land, and beyond.

Erica was also proud of the fact that the blood of noble Vikings coursed in her veins. Her mother had told her that because her father, Ragnar Longsword, was noble and brave, she, Erica, shared in that glory. Although she had never met her father, she dreamed of his valor and good looks. She hoped he was still alive and well and that some day she would have a chance to meet him.

Reaching up, Erica touched the pendant she had always worn. It was a silver raven with a garnet set in its eye, a talisman to keep her safe from harm throughout her life. Most important, it was a gift to Erica from the father she had never seen. Ignoring the taunts of the others of her clan, she took great delight in wearing the pendant, for it made her feel close to her father. Now that her mother was dead, the pendant had taken on an even greater meaning.

Erica pulled the pendant from beneath her gown. Because it bore the shape of a raven, an ill omen for the Scots and a pagan symbol, she kept it hidden beneath her layers of clothing but close to her heart. Now she touched it with reverence. Somehow it made her feel as if her father would always protect her.

"I'm the best of both worlds," she whispered, remembering what her mother had always insisted. It had been her way of soothing her daughter's shattered emotions when she was the subject of taunts and teasing because of her Viking heritage. Erica had found out early in life that it was going to be difficult having Viking blood running in her veins.

Turning her eyes toward the sea, she watched as the foaming waves hit the rocky shore and basalt cliffs with noisy fury. Only the skirl of bagpipes jarred her from her thinking. The pipes, summoning everyone to gather. The sound was unnerving. Shattering.

"What is it?" Geordie voiced his fear.

"It could be many things. . . ." Putting her arm protectively around her brother's shoulder, Erica pretended a bravery she did not really feel. She was just as worried by the sound as Geordie, only she would not allow herself to show it. Instead she whispered sternly, "Come back with me to the hall!" Pulling Geordie by the hand, she led the way over the well-worn pathway.

Pandemonium greeted them as they pushed through the heavy wooden door of the large stone hall. The MacQuarie clan was preparing for a fight. Brandishing their weapons, which reflected the flames ablaze in the hearth, they grumbled in anger as they waited for their chief, Coinneach Mac-Quarie, to enter the hall.

Erica's eyes darted back and forth, searching for the familiar form of her uncle. Where was he? As if her anxiety had conjured him up, he soon pushed through the door of the adjoining room he used as a council chamber. His face was contorted in worry. Pulling at his beard, he strode back and forth before the fire, muttering beneath his breath.

Erica looked at this tall, big-boned man, realizing the responsibility he bore to govern the clan territory for the benefit of the clan. He administered justice in times of peace and led the warriors in time of war. As chief he was responsible for the good of his people, who for their part gave every assistance to him for the mutual good of all members of the clan. Since her mother's death, he had also taken on the responsibility of Erica and her brother.

"What is it?"

"The MacLeods are gathering up arms, no doubt to march against us." A ripple of dread swept throughout the hall.

"The lookouts have spotted them on the horizon, and though it is but a tiny speck in the distance we must be prepared."

Anger buzzed around from man to man. "The MacLeods!" There was boastful talk of how they would easily defeat them, but Erica was dubious. In skirmishes against the MacLeods they had suffered devastating losses of their menfolk and wounds to their pride. Hadn't they learned yet how futile it was to stand alone? Oh, why couldn't they live in peace?

Coinneach silenced the boasting by raising his hand. Though in truth he was but a few inches taller than most of the men, he seemed to tower over them as he pulled back his shoulders and held up his hand. "We have tried to best the MacLeods with swords and we have failed. We must use our heads this time and be canny."

"Och. Our heads have nothing to do with it. We must use our swords!" cried out a voice.

"Do ye forget how they burned our fields, drove off our cattle, and left a trail of blood? We must answer any challenge from those devils, blow for blow, blood for blood." Another man added his opinion.

"Nay, Coinneach is right," called out a third man. "Ye are putting your pride before all else, but we must think of our women and the wee ones. If we fight a battle and lose, they are the ones who will suffer the most, for we will not be here to protect their honor."

"What, then? We cannot just let them march in and take all that we hold dear."

The men argued among themselves, until Iona, Coinneach's daughter and Erica's cousin, pushed her way to her side. "The MacLeods are certainly troublesome," she exclaimed. "They've been a constant source of trouble for Father, nearly as much as the Norsemen have been."

"The *MacLeods* have been a constant source of trouble for us all," Erica retorted. She knew what was coming. Since childhood Iona had never missed an opportunity to remind her scathingly of her Viking kinship.

"Perhaps that doesn't trouble ye. After all, ye are only half MacQuarie. Your loyalties are divided after all."

"Nae. I am as loyal in my heart as ye are." Indeed, the clan was perhaps the most important thing in all their lives. A man's very being, his identity, was bound to the clan. To be driven out, to face exile, was to lose all sense of self-worth. A man alone was as isolated as Staffa, that lonely island she had gazed upon with Geordie.

"As loyal as *I* am!" Iona wrinkled up her nose. "How can ye be, hinny? I am full-blooded Scots, while we all know the story of your birth. Your mother was disgraced. She was taken against her will by that . . . by that . . ."

"Viking!" Erica finished for her. "And it wasn't against her will. She told me time and time again how much she loved my father. He was good to her."

"So good that he left her behind and sailed away."

Erica tossed her head, sending her hair flying in a whirl of dark-tinted flame as she turned to face her enemy. Her cousin's goading had struck home. "Say one more word about my mother or my father and I swear to ye, Iona, I'll tear every hair out of your head. We'll see how bonnie Erskin thinks ye are then!"

"Ye wouldn't!"

"I would!" The menacing tone of Erica's voice and the hard look in her eyes frightened her cousin away, which was just what Erica had intended. She laughed softly to herself at the thought of her haughty cousin being totally bald.

"Would ye really pull out all her hair?" Geordie's eyes were as wide as two coins.

"It would serve her right!" Erica grumbled.

There wasn't time to say more, for once again Erica's uncle held up his hand. "Silence. All this grumbling amongst ourselves will not do any good. Hear me!" All chattering within the hall ceased as all eyes turned toward the chieftain. "We will fight, but we must not fight this battle alone. We must join with others on Mull and do battle together."

"Others . . . ?" Again there was a buzzing of voices.

"We are not the only descendants of Siol Alpin. The MacKinnons, too, not only share this island of Mull but are, like us, one of the branches of the Siol Alpin. We must join with them. To that purpose, I am prepared to marry one of us to one of them."

Though not a word was spoken, the expressions on their faces asked the same question: Who?

Coinneach was likewise silent as he pointed to his daughter, Iona.

"What?" Iona was aghast. "Nae! I will not do it." Moving toward Erica, she shoved her forward. "Take her instead!"

"Me?" Erica shook her head. "Nae. Iona would make a much better choice." She couldn't help but smile as she said, "I snore."

Geordie giggled but Erica soon shushed him.

Coinneach looked first at his daughter, then at Erica with an appraising eye. Both possessed a beauty no man could resist. Their finely chiseled noses, high cheekbones, and enormous dark-fringed eyes were beyond description. Their slender waists and long legs were the envy of all the women; their well-formed breasts and slim hips were a bard's dream.

Erica's eyes were a bit larger, her nose a wee mite shorter, her fiery tresses several shades lighter than Iona's auburn hair. Iona's eyes were brown, Erica's a deep shade of blue. Erica was much taller than her cousin, a mark of her Viking heritage. Coinneach smiled. Neither young woman was what one could call "manageable," but whereas Iona's determination was often termed self-seeking, Erica could be said to be spirited.

They were both dressed in arasaids, a long garment that reached from the head to the ankles, fastened at the breast with a large brooch and at the waist by a belt. Beneath this colorful length of material they wore gowns of thin wool, which clung to their gentle curves. The difference was that Erica's arasaid was haphazardly tied, and her gown had been tucked up to enable her to move around freely. Her long hair was messed up. There was a smudge of dirt on the tip of her nose.

The matter was discussed among the clansmen. Though there were quite a few mumblings, voiced words of disquiet, they at last agreed to their chieftain's proposal.

"But which lass?" Several voices asked the question.

"I have decided on Iona." Coinneach's answer thundered through the room. All eyes looked that young woman's way as she paled. Erica breathed a sigh of relief.

"I will not do it. I will not go!" Iona's breathless protestation was accompanied by tears.

"Ye will do as I say!" Coinneach was visibly angered at his daughter's reaction to his decision.

"Nae!" The trembling girl collapsed in a flood of tears. "I will drown myself in the ocean before I leave here. I will, I swear it!"

Erica gritted her teeth in annoyance. How like Iona to make such a spectacle of herself just for sympathy. The irritating thing was that it seemed to work. One by one, the men assembled clucked their tongues as they looked upon Iona with compassion.

"Ninnies," Erica said beneath her breath. Couldn't they see that she wouldn't really carry out her threat? Drown herself, indeed! Iona was far too much in love with herself, too much a coward, actually to do the deed. Surely Uncle Coinneach could see right through his daughter's tantrum. Or could he?

Her uncle's next words answered that question for her. "Calm yourself, daughter." He sighed, then walking to her, he gently lifted her to her feet. "She will never fare well amongst those who are not of her own blood. I should have known that." He looked at Erica, making her heart skip a beat. "The same is not true of Erica. She is of much stronger mettle; thus, I will send her instead."

Erica couldn't believe her ears. It was so unfair.

"Not Erica. Not my sister!" Geordie was horrified.

It was no use. Coinneach's mind was made up and there was nothing Erica could do.

FOUR

The hall was shrouded in darkness. Everyone was abed except Erica, who prowled about like a sleepwalker. She had spent a sleepless night tossing and turning, going over in her mind the command her uncle had issued. In but a moment, with only a few words, she had been consigned to marriage, a bargain that would take her from this hall and the people she dearly loved.

"Oh, Geordie! What will ye do?" First her mother had died, then her mother's infant son, then her stepfather. Now, in but a few weeks time, she would leave not only her family, friends, and this beloved island of Ulva, but the little brother she had always guarded, adored, and looked after. Worse yet, she would spend the rest of her life with a clan she did not even know.

Her gaze flitted about the room as if to brand a permanent image in her mind for the days ahead when she would be far away from here. Memories. So many memories. Down the center of the hall was a long hearth over which big pots from the evening's meal were still placed. How many stories of fairies, water beasts, witches, and ghosts had she listened to in front of the evening fire? Though her family was Christian, they knew that their lives would always be ruled by older beliefs, too—knew that other beings occupied Ulva and Mull as surely as did those of flesh and blood.

As a child she had listened in awe to such stories and tales of long ago. Before this same hearth she had blissfully enjoyed the music from fiddle, harp, and pipes—riotous songs or soothing songs of reverie that had at last lulled her to sleep. Somehow she had always awakened to find herself in her bed, thinking perhaps the fairies had bewitched her and brought her to her room. Now she was to be carried off, but not by the wee folk.

"Oh, Uncle Coinneach, how could ye?" Was it because of her Viking blood? No. She knew her uncle too well. In his way he loved her; it was just that he loved his daughter more and couldn't bear to see her cry. Perhaps in his way he had thought Erica to be the more logical choice.

A loom and several spindle whorls for spinning of wool stood against the farthest wall. Erica curled her mouth in a bittersweet smile as she recalled how often she had rebelled at joining the women for their daily chores. Cooking, weaving, and sewing bored her. Washing with the harsh lye soap seemed a thankless task. Walking, or hand-shrinking woolen cloth, was a long and laborious process for which she had no fondness. In truth, she had scorned women's work, finding a dozen reasons for avoiding tasks whenever she could. But now, oh, what she wouldn't give to be able to stay among these women instead of women she would not even know. And Geordie. They had shared such closeness, had been like the two halves of a whole. Now they would be parted, never more to engage in mock warfare.

"I will not see him grow up to be a man. . . ." That was the saddest thought of all.

"Oh, Erica, what are ye going to do?" Hearing her brother's voice from out of the shadows, Erica turned around, knowing by the tortured look in his eyes that Geordie was suffering even more than she.

As if he were but a child again, Geordie flew to her arms, furiously dashing tears away with his hand as quickly as they filled his eyes. Erica's eyes were misted, too, but she held her emotions under control. She had to be brave for Geordie's sake.

"Uncle is wrong. He should send Iona away. She is such a troublemaker and—"

"She is his daughter!" She ran her fingers through his long auburn hair. "What was said was said; what was done has been done. Let us hope that some good will come of it. If there will be peace, then it is worth the price." Pulling away, she feigned a bravery she most certainly did not feel. "Besides, I have always craved adventure. To see a side of Mull I've never seen before, the MacKinnons' territory."

"But to marry . . . ?"

"Am I not a match for any man?" Erica sighed as she remembered what she had always said, that she would only love a man if he was as bold as the man her mother had loved.

"Aye, Eri, that you are!" Geordie laughed through his tears.

Holding him at arm's length, she looked into his eyes. "Promise me . . ."

"That I will be the kind of man that ye have taught me to be?" He shook his head. "I promise."

"The kind of man Mother would have made of ye had she lived."

Taking her hand, he led her toward one of the large wooden benches lined against the wall and sat her down beside him. "It's just selfish that I am, Erica. I've always hoped to keep ye near me. Ye are the one who always makes me smile."

"You'll never lose me, hinny." Reaching for his hand, she squeezed it reassuringly. "Wherever I may be, ye will be in my heart and in my thoughts. And I will not have ye worry. The MacKinnons do not intend to harm me."

"They dare not!" He clenched his fists in anger. "If a one of them causes ye pain, they will rue it."

"If only there were another way . . ." She clutched at the

pendant she wore. Her mother had told her that it was called the Raven's Eye and that it would bring her wisdom. Oh, how she needed insight now!

"If the MacLeods would leave us alone, if there was peace, then ye wouldn't have to go."

"Peace . . ." She ran her fingers over the jewel in the pendant, the eye of the silver raven. "What if I could bring peace even before there is any fighting?"

Geordie clutched at the folds of his breacon, a length of cloth wrapped around his waist and draped over his shoulder. "Erica . . ." He was suddenly frightened for his sister as he contemplated what she was thinking.

"I cannot dawdle; I have to hurry." She rose to her feet. "Once assured of the marriage settlement, once Uncle Coinneach hands me over to the MacKinnon; thereafter the contract is unbreakable and I'll have to take a stranger as my groom."

"What are ye going to do?"

"I'm going to seek out the MacLeod chieftain and hope beyond all hope that I can bring about a truce."

"But to travel by boat! Ye might be taken by the *cailleach uisge* and I'd never see ye again."

"Ach, I'm not afraid of the water hag, and besides, I won't be alone. I'll take one of the fishermen's sons with me if I go to their ship." Proving her determination, Erica hurried to her room, gathering up a few necessary items to take with her on the journey, wrapping them in a bundle. A comb, her cuarans to wear along the rocky path, a brooch, a *curraichd* to tie around her head if it was windy.

"Don't go!" Suddenly Geordie was more frightened at the thought of what she was going to do than of losing her to another clan. "Something might go wrong. They might harm ye and I will not see ye again."

"I will not disappear." She tried to sound a lot braver than she felt.

"But what if . . . ?" Geordie clutched his sister's hands.

"I must do something, for the sake of the others even more than myself. Even with the MacKinnons on our side we still might lose the battle."

"But what will Uncle Coinneach say when he finds out ye have gone? He'll come after ye, move heaven and hell to catch up with ye. Ye'll be caught before ye get very far, and a whipping will be your only reward for being so braw!"

"Nothing bad will happen! Ye'll see. Everything will be all right." Bold talk. Forcing a self-confident smile, Erica blew out the candle in her small sleeping chamber, gave Geordie a quick hug, then said, "Now you go back to your own room and get some sleep. Before the sun comes up I'll be gone."

Fumbling around in the dark with her precious bundle, Erica said a silent prayer that she would have no regrets because of her decision.

FIVE

The changing colors of the morning sky lit up the rocky shoreline and cast a glow upon the ship that skimmed through the waters just off the shore of western Alba. It had been a relatively quiet voyage with no troublesome incidents, at least so far.

Gardar was once again at Torin's side, watching over him in case Halldor had devious intentions. He voiced his misgivings with a deep-throated rumble. "I hope we can find him quickly so that we can be on our way. I have learned firsthand that not only Herlaug can be troublesome. The Scots can be fierce."

"Particularly when they are wielding a sword," Torin reflected.

"They may kill you on sight and strangle me for being in your company and then ask questions afterward," Gardar grumbled. "That is the way these quarrelsome Scots are. Always fighting amongst themselves over one thing or another."

Torin knew that Gardar had reason to be bitter. He was the son of a noble Pict family that had been prominent in Alba until they accepted the invitation of Kenneth I to attend a great banquet to discuss his claim to the throne. The guests were plied with food and wine, then late in the evening, when they were sufficiently inebriated, they were attacked and slaughtered by Kenneth's men. The act of treachery had done exactly what had been intended: It had eliminated all remaining competition so that Kenneth could take the throne. It was the first of the events that would put Gardar in the path of the Vikings and slavery.

Torin ran his fingers through his long blond hair. "Let's hope they are distracted by feuding when we arrive. It will make it much easier for us to find Ragnar's son without being stabbed before our quest has even begun."

"Ragnar doesn't know what he asks of you. Why not vanquish these Scots and then seek to find the son?"

"Because we might risk killing or severely wounding him." Torin tapped at his head. "Ragnar is trusting that I can use my cunning and negotiating skill instead of my sword arm to complete this mission."

Gardar flexed his arm. "Before this is over we may have to use everything within our power just to stay alive."

"We'll stay alive, my friend. I consulted a seeress before the journey. The rune stones were favorable." Favorable for Gardar and for him, but not for Ragnar. "I want to return as quickly as I can, for I do not trust Herlaug," he said, more to himself than to Gardar.

Herlaug had assumed that his brother's loss of consciousness had been caused by drunkenness, but what if he found out about Ragnar's spells? If he sensed that Ragnar was vulnerable, he would most likely betray him.

Gardar snorted his indignation, looking toward the uncouth, mead-drinking, boastful men of the crew—half of whom Herlaug had chosen. When not chattering about ships, battles, or how strong they were, they amused themselves by telling jokes or downright lies about the number of women they had taken by force, each trying to outdo the others.

"No doubt they are already conjuring up in their minds the profit they will make from this voyage. Or perhaps they are relishing the thought of pouncing upon any poor women that we come upon," Gardar added.

Torin's expression clouded. "I want no trouble." He fully intended this to be a peaceful mission, not one using warfare. "Nor will I allow any show of brutality." These men had faithfully pledged to follow his orders, to serve and obey him until they were home again. Even if Herlaug had been instrumental in choosing some of the men, Torin was in full charge.

"Then let us hope all will be well," Gardar answered.

Both men squinted toward the shore as they approached. The western coastline of the island appeared to be of solid cream-colored rock and gray granite walls that rose vertically from the sea. Such sea-cliff scenery was awe-inspiring, Torin had to admit. No doubt Ragnar had his eye on claiming it as a fortress once he found his son and gathered him into his confidence. It would be a good stronghold to have when he set out to conquer the Scots.

Torin remembered hearing tales that these islands had wild beasts seldom found elsewhere. The sea was said to be silver with fish. Noisy clouds of wild fowl hung above the coastal waters. Boar rooted in the forestlands. There were even said to be herds of wild cattle with flowing manes like lions, and red deer that roamed in thick herds.

"Look there!" Gardar pointed toward a wooden fortress high on a hill, rising somberly above the rock walls. Torin knew it must be both an observation point and, in times of peril, a place for the Scots to congregate. It was a reminder of the warfare that had raged for years.

"It looks quiet enough. No sign of any Scots guarding the beaches." If they proceeded much farther, however, the ship might be spotted by some of the inhabitants of the thatch-roofed huts that could be seen further down the shore. Gardar looked questioningly at Torin.

"We'll move on. I want this ship to be hidden in the rocks." Nothing more was said as both men concentrated on the boat as it moved toward a fjordlike inlet far below the fortress. Maneuvering the long ship into the inlet, they were soon out of view of anyone down shore.

"Gardar, you will accompany me."

Gardar swore as he hefted a sack filled with gold and silver coins, bracelets and brooches. "I'm coming, bringing Ragnar's 'tribute' with me."

Torin ignored Gardar's complaint, saying, "The rest of you wait here until we come back." Torin hoped that Ragnar's son, Eric, would be receptive to his father's bribery, but there was always the chance that he would not be. He had been raised as a Scot and would have certain loyalties. Would Torin be able to change his mind? Or would Ragnar have to resort to other measures to get his way?

Having seen to the securing of the ship, Torin joined Gardar as he waded ashore. It wasn't long before they reached the rocks and made their way through the tangled seaweed. Several pathways led from the rocks to a valley. Torin consulted the map Ragnar had given him.

"This way." Anxious to reach his destination, he walked at a brisk pace.

Gardar struggled to keep up under the burden of the sack, taking two steps to one of Torin's long strides. At last he stopped, opened the sack, and placed the bracelets on his arm one by one. Next, he pinned the brooches on the front of his tunic. Hefting the now lightened sack over his shoulder again, he grinned. "There, now perhaps I can keep up."

As they moved farther inland they could view the moss- and lichen-covered rocks more closely. The scenery was quite wild. Different. They found the rocks and sand gave rise to an oasis of fertile soil farther inland, however. There was greenery—hazel shrub and bracken—and widespread heaths. The woodland gave way to broad valleys and rich, green land crisscrossed by rivers and streams.

Reaching the summit of a hill, Torin could see a group of men and women working the fields with the *cas-chrom,* or foot plough. The patches of land appeared to be too small for horses to be of use. Farther on, a small herd of shaggy cattle grazed peacefully on the hillside. Wishing to maintain at least a semblance of secrecy about their presence lest there be a terrified outcry at having a Viking in their midst, Torin paused in midstride, retracing his steps toward the forest lands. It seemed a convenient point from which to investigate this island.

Suddenly, a sound behind Gardar startled him. With a loud grunt he drew his sword, fully prepared to defend himself, but it was only a whimbrel, disturbed in the midst of eating its dinner. Voicing a squawking protest, the seabird took flight, joined by others of its kind.

"What if the chieftain of the Scots takes Ragnar's offering with a smile and then cuts our throats?"

"Ragnar is prepared for that possibility," Torin answered, refusing to give in to his own misgivings.

"Well, perhaps Ragnar is prepared, but I'm not sure that I am." Gardar paused to catch his breath, then resumed his trudging along.

A hush had settled over the land as Torin and Gardar walked along, but the years of constant warring had made them both overly cautious. Though the only voices they heard were from a flock of gulls circling overhead, they attuned their ears to catch every sound. Being in foreign territory made them very vulnerable and unwelcome until they had made themselves known and explained their reasons for coming.

Focusing their eyes on the mottled golds, browns, and greens of the land that rolled before them, they kept a lookout for any sign of danger. Even so, Torin was startled as a figure darted out of the foliage several feet away. The well-proportioned figure and long, flowing red hair told him instantly that it was a female.

"A woman!" Gardar's whisper gave voice to the obvious as he pulled Torin with him into the shadows. They watched as she walked slowly over to the edge of a small lake gouged into the land. Silently the two men crept closer.

"We don't want to frighten her," Torin breathed.

She was too deep in thought to be aware of their stares. Captivated and curious, Torin inched closer, close enough to see that she was beautiful.

"Look at her hair! It's like a flame." As the woman threw her head back, the long tresses whipped about her shoulders, catching the rays of the sun, setting her hair ablaze with fiery highlights.

"I know what you are thinking." Gardar had seen that look in Torin's eye before.

Torin shook his head. "You're wrong. I'm not going to forget that I'm here on a peaceful mission. I'll follow the same rules that I set down for the others." That didn't keep him from craning his neck for a better view, however.

Leaving Gardar behind, Torin moved closer, his eyes caressing the mounds of the woman's breasts, then moving to the narrow waist, which he knew he could span with his hands. The gentle swell of her hips and long legs were outlined by her gown, completing the seductive image.

"Give me your cloak."

"What?" Gardar squinted as he realized Torin's intent: He was going to hide his Viking garments under the plain woolen hooded cloak.

"You go on ahead. I'll catch up." Torin exchanged cloaks with Gardar, pulling the hood up so that it hid his face and hair. "I'm going to ask her a few questions. Perhaps she has heard of Ragnar's son."

"And perhaps she has not, but then I don't suppose that really matters." Gardar kicked at the dirt. "Why should I care what happens? I have no love for the Scots, be they men or women." As he put Torin's cloak over his shoulders, he reveled in the feel of the soft cloth beneath his fingers. "Well, I did well on that swap. Let's hope that you do just as well, but be careful, Torin. I know these Scots. If she has a husband and you are caught, you'll be eating your own testicles for your sup—"

Gardar paused in his tirade. Any warning he might utter would be too late. He could only watch as Torin eased out of the shadows, moving toward the red-haired young woman.

SIX

It was beautiful in the place known as the "Fairy Glen." Beautiful and tranquil. The mountains and moorlands sparkled like jewels. A soft whispering breeze caressed Erica's face as she stood by the loch. Glancing about her, she viewed the untamed woodland of tall, slender silver birch trees, marveling at the natural wonderland. The glen was a refuge, with its soft mossy floor that was hidden from view by a drapery woven of hundreds of leaves. Each stone, each tree, every inlet of water that gouged deep into the glens was precious to her. It was a place to which she always came when she wanted to think and be alone.

"There has already been so much bloodshed. I have to do something to bring about peace." But would the MacLeods listen to a woman? Could she convince them that there was far more benefit in maintaining peace than in staining the rocks and sand with more blood? Or were they really as terrible as they were said to be? Setting down her bundled possessions, Erica let the beauty of the scenery calm her uneasiness.

The island of Ulva was a happy, smiling place of wildflowers, waterfalls, and lush green bracken. There were reminders of ancient cataclysms in the gigantic lava terraces of the island and the basalt columns of its neighbor, Staffa.

The familiarity of all the sights and sounds touched Erica's heart.

Despite the many times she felt a spark of adventure and longing to see new places, she felt a sad reverie at the thought that she would have to leave if her uncle married her to a MacKinnon for the sake of an alliance against the MacLeods. Even so, she was resolved to deal with whatever happened. If she was unsuccessful in her plea for peace, if she did have to leave, at least she would have done what she thought was right. Besides, there was no turning back now.

Reaching down the front of her gown, she touched the cool metal of the pendant that rested between her breasts. There were those who scorned her certainty that the image of the raven would protect her. Her cousin Iona had told her that having such heathen superstitions would send her straight to hell, but somehow wearing the ornament had always made Erica feel as if her father was with her. In a way, she could almost imagine that he was.

Flocks of gulls and terns glided overhead. The wild, beautiful music of the inland birds serenaded her as they flew from bough to bough, a melancholy song that fit the mood of her reverie. Staring into the azure depths of the loch, her eyes focused on the water, as if somehow she might read her fate there. Would there be peace in the Highlands? Could she somehow draw upon the wisdom she inherited from her mother and the strength of her father to be a peacemaker? Or would her determination put her in danger's path?

Unaware that she was being watched, she slowly lowered her body in a graceful motion to sit upon a large rock by the lake's edge. Taking off her soft doeskin shoes, she let the water splash over her feet as she closed her eyes. She remembered childhood days when she had come to this hideaway to escape the taunts of her cousin, or when someone had hurt her feelings. Somehow she felt safe here, assured that no one knew of this secret haven. That was why she was surprised to look up and discover that she was not alone.

A man stood silhouetted in the trees, looking in her direction.

"Who are you?" Erica refused to show fear, but she felt it nonetheless. Warily she watched as he stepped out of the shadows.

"Don't be afraid; I won't harm you," he said in a low, husky rumble.

"I'm *not* afraid!" For an instant her eyes betrayed the truth of her boast as she searched for any sign that he had been accompanied, but it seemed he had come alone. That thought comforted her. One man would be easier to deal with.

"All I want to do is talk to you. . . ."

Though he was speaking Gaelic, he had enough of an accent to mark him as a foreigner. "Talk and I'll listen," she said, hoping to figure out where he might be from, "but I do not wish ye to come any closer."

Torin paused for a moment in an effort to reassure her. "Then I won't." At least for the moment, he thought, contenting himself with just looking at her.

Satisfied that his presence did not mean immediate danger, Erica turned to him. "Who are ye?"

Underneath the hooded cloak he was dressed in tight tan trousers, a red tunic embroidered in a colorful design, and leather shoes laced up around his ankles. It was his hair, however, that made her stare. It was not the dark blond that she had seen on her Scots kinsmen, but a pale gold that was worn long and touched his shoulders.

"My name is Torin. . . ." Slowly he moved again through the bracken and trees, not wanting to frighten her, yet unable to resist getting a closer look at the red-haired young beauty. He supposed her to be one of the fishermen's daughters, whose huts he had seen dotting the gently sloping hills. Why else would she be in this deserted spot?

Erica put her hand to her mouth as she gasped. "Ye are

a Norseman!" Her eyes darted this way and that, seeking a way to escape, but he blocked her way.

"I'm not here to destroy; I'm here on a peaceful mission."

"Peaceful? Ha. I know what horror ye have brought to my people. If ye want to talk, let's talk about that."

Torin carefully measured his words. "There is no reason for bloodshed. Fighting only brings one thing: death." As he took another step forward, she took one step back, her hands stretched out as if to push him away were he to come too close. "Besides, fighting is the last thing on my mind when I look at you."

He moved with all the caution of a predatory animal, slow and sinuous in his grace, coming at last to the water's edge. Poised just a few feet from where she stood, he gave his eyes full rein. She was even lovelier up close than she had been from afar. Torin felt his heartbeat quickening as she met him eye to eye. Oh, she was a bold one, this beauty. Most women would be cowering at the thought of even glimpsing a Viking.

The way he was looking at her made shivers run up and down her spine. "Where are the others?" she asked. When he hesitated she said, "I would be simple-minded to think that ye came alone."

He gestured with his hand. "They are a long way off. Waiting for me on the ship. I wanted to come alone. I'm looking for someone." As he spoke he edged closer.

She looked at him searchingly. "To kill them?" If he was looking for someone because of some kind of vengeance, she wanted to know.

"No. To offer them wealth and power." Her face was now clearly revealed to him, and he was struck by a feeling of familiarity. It was as if he had seen her somewhere before. His gaze touched upon her well-formed nose, her long lashes and wide, sensuous mouth. Her cheekbones were high and prominent, adding to her beauty.

"Why, then?"

"I want to take him with me." When she stiffened he said quickly, "His father is a Viking who wants to be reunited with him."

"Reunited . . . ?" He was looking for someone of mixed parentage. Like her. Wordlessly Erica regarded this stranger, just as he was scrutinizing her. This tall, muscular, handsome man was not the kind a woman would ever forget. He had a bold look about him, an impression heightened by the curve of his brows. Brows that shadowed piercing blue eyes. Ah, those eyes haunted her. They were as unfathomable as the sea.

The air crackled with anticipation. For one timeless moment they stared at each other across the short distance that separated them. Strange how just a look could be so exciting. His eyes caressed her with a boldness few had dared—held her, forced her to acknowledge that something was going on between them. An undeniable fascination.

She held her breath in expectation as he reached out. Without a word he caught a fistful of her long silken hair and wrapped it around his hand, drawing her closer. With the tips of his fingers he traced the line of her cheekbones, the shape of her mouth, the line of her brows. He seemed motivated by curiosity, as if to prove beyond a doubt that she was not a dream.

"I'm of a mind to take *you* with me, too, when I go. . . ." His face hovered only inches from her own.

"And ye presume that I would want to go?"

Torin was sure of himself. "If given a chance, I think I could persuade you."

"Persuade me . . ." Vikings didn't need to persuade; they just took what they wanted. Would he carry her to his ship, kicking and screaming, were she to reject his inducement? Most likely. "Abduct me, don't ye mean?"

"No." Gently he traced her jawline with the tip of his finger.

Though Erica knew all the reasons she should run away, she somehow did not. Then all at once it was too late.

At first he simply held her, his hands exerting a gentle pressure to draw her into the warmth of his embrace. Then, before Erica could make a sound, his mouth claimed hers in a gentle kiss, one completely devastating to her senses. She was engulfed in a whirlpool of sensations. Breathless, her head whirling, she allowed herself to be drawn up into the mists of the spell. New sensations clamored within her.

Leaning against the man who held her, Erica savored the feel of his strength; dreamily she gave herself up to the fierce sweetness of his mouth, her lips opening under his as exciting new sensations flooded through her. She was aware of her body as she had never been before, and relished the emotions churning within her.

Torin's lips parted the soft yielding flesh beneath his, searching out the honey of her mouth. With a low moan he thrust his fingers within the soft, silken waterfall of her hair, drawing her ever closer. Desire choked him, all the hungry prompting of his fantasies warring with his reason. His lips grew demanding, changing from gentleness to passion as his hands moved down her shoulders and began to roam at will with increasing familiarity. More than anything in the world he wanted to make love to this young woman. Here. Now.

"Your skin is so smooth . . ." he whispered as he drew his mouth away. The words tickled her ear, making her vibrantly alive and attuned to her senses. Her heart skipped a beat as he brought his head down and traced the bare curve of her shoulder with his lips. A near-madness seized her and she found herself thinking the most dangerous thoughts. She wanted him to keep on touching her this way, wanted to touch him back.

"There is a spark . . . a magic between us. You feel it, too," he was saying. "I want to see your body unclothed, to swim naked with you in the lake, to make love with you until we both . . ."

His words and groping fingers brought her back to reality with a thud. *Naked?* The word reverberated in her ear. What was she doing, allowing a stranger—a Viking—to touch her with such intimacy? What had come over her? She was Ragnar's daughter, not some Viking's concubine!

Erica tried to shake the confusing feelings from her body. What this man wanted—and it was obvious what that was from the look in his eyes—she would not give. So thinking, she jerked back her head and pushed at the hard strength of his chest with her hands.

"Let me be!"

Torin did not take Erica's protest seriously. This time the kiss he gave her was far from gentle, and Erica was mutely aware of the firm muscles of his body as he moved against her. Before she could protest, he had pulled her down with him to the soft woodland grass. This time she was not mesmerized by his touch, however. Indignant fury surged through her. She would let no man take her against her will! That he was a man used to women and therefore potentially dangerous for that knowledge, she sensed now. This was no shy Jamie whom she could frighten away with a scowl or an angry word. He had said that he was a man used to taking what he wanted, and she was what he wanted right now. Arrogant oaf. He would not seduce her.

Locked against him as she was, there was no mistaking his male arousal, and this fueled her temper even more. Oh, she'd heard the women talk, knew what was to follow if she did not keep her head. Well, he would get much more than he bargained for if he tried to ravish her! So much for his talk of being on a peaceful mission.

"Let me go!" she commanded. He did not heed her cry. Instead, he was growing forceful. Determined not to be forced against her will, Erica aimed her knee at his groin, putting an end to his lustful thoughts. She watched as he doubled over in agony.

Disentangling herself from his arms, she stood with her hands upon hips as she assessed him. He was not so sure of himself now. He did, in fact, look most miserable.

"What a temper," Torin managed to say at last. An echo of pain shadowed his face, yet he regarded her with open and somewhat mocking admiration from where he lay in a heap upon the ground. Torin had never been so fiercely upbraided in his life, especially by a woman. He took a deep breath, gratified that the pain at last was subsiding. "But couldn't you just say no?"

She glared at him defiantly, hiding behind a veil of anger. "I did and ye didn't listen."

"Because I didn't want to hear you deny me what we both wanted." He met her gaze for a long moment, unable to look away. *"Still* want. In spite of what you did." As he spoke, his eyes swept over her suggestively.

"That is your misfortune," she said haughtily. He was a smooth-talking, dangerous man. She didn't dare trust him.

"Perhaps the misfortune is yours," Torin answered with a wry smile.

Shielding her eyes, Erica scanned the undulating landscape, looking toward the sea. She didn't see any sign of his ship or ships. "Where are your ships?" Hidden? Or had they sailed up the coastline, bringing terror in their wake?

"I told you that I have come in peace and I meant it." Slowly Torin stood up, boldly feasting his eyes on her for several moments longer.

His arrogance was not to be borne. "Ye have come lusting after Scottish women." Vikings seemed to be a lusty lot. She had heard about the way they treated women. Only her father had been different. He had been gentle and loving with her mother. "Ye are not my father," she said beneath her breath.

"For which I am thankful at the moment."

Torin had heard that there were hundreds of pretty young

women in the Highlands, yet somehow at this moment she was the only one he wanted. He started to move toward her; then, remembering the pain she had dealt him, the physical comeuppance, he backed away.

Erica smiled as she realized that her well-aimed knee to his groin had made him wary of her. But what of the other Vikings? How fearsome would they be? "How many ships are there?" If this was to be a full scale invasion, she wanted to know so that she could warn the others.

"Why don't you come with me and I'll show you," he taunted.

"Come with ye, ye say?" What if he abducted her? How would she help the others then? "Nae, I think I will find out the answer for myself."

Disappointment rankled him as he realized she meant exactly what she said. She wanted nothing to do with him. Strange how her determination only seemed to make him more intrigued with her. He hated to lose at anything.

"Find the ships then if you can," he said angrily. "I'll waste no more time on you."

"Good. It is my wish never to see ye again."

The finality of her tone stung him. Even so, his last look was a wistful one before he turned to walk away. He knew the image of her would be etched in his memory for a very long time.

SEVEN

The *Sea Wolf* bobbed up and down on the water. From the deck three pairs of eyes scrutinized each jagged rock, tree, shrub, and every patch of land. Though Torin had come with peaceful intentions, there were those aboard the ship who did not share his thoughts.

"I say we strike and strike now before the Scots are forewarned," Halldor declared.

"And I say not yet!" Audun, a more cautious Viking, grumbled. "Herlaug was specific in the orders he gave us. We are to let Torin lead us to Ragnar's son."

A big, hulking Viking named Bolli, who had been eavesdropping, quickly spoke his mind. "Let him lead us to them, and then with one fell swoop"—he brought his fist down on his muscular thigh—"we'll kill Torin." He grinned. "I've long wanted to kill the outcast. He always looks at me as if I'm a thrall and he Odin's own son."

"Ragnar listens to him and that gives him power," Audun answered. The bearded, big-boned giant was at the steerboard, having taken Torin's place at command while he was away. He and Halldor had had more than one spat or two over who was actually in charge of the voyage in Torin's absence.

"Don't be a fool. I agree that Torin holds himself above us despite his father's treachery, but we can't kill Torin, because he is going to lead us to the others. First one son and then another . . ."

Bolli laughed aloud, holding up his fingers one at a time. "One . . . two . . . and—and—uh—"

"Three!" Halldor Snorrason replied with a shake of his head at the other Viking's stupidity. "Ha, it is no wonder Torin beats you at every game."

"Because he cheats!" Bolli's smile turned into a frown.

"No, because he is cunning. But we will be more so this time," Audun said. "And when we return, Herlaug will reward us richly."

"But why can't we kill some Scots while we wait?" Halldor gritted his teeth. "They aren't as rich as the English or the Irish monks, but there might be something of value."

"No!" Audun was adamant.

Halldor persisted. "It has been a long time since our last raid. Too long!" He ran his fingers down his chest to the stomach that was gathering a bit of a bulge. "A man can go soft if he does not keep up on his fighting skills."

"We wait!" So far, Audun had his way and the men had agreed to be patient, but he could tell that some of them were itching to go ashore in search of plunder. "That is what Herlaug would want us to do."

"So you tell us, but what if *I* don't listen?" Halldor's eyes touched quickly over the assembled men, wondering which ones were loyal to him, which to Audun, and which were loyal to Torin.

"If you do not listen you will suffer the consequences." If he had to club Halldor over the head and tie him hand and foot, Audun was determined to maintain control of the men.

Halldor gave in. "All right, I will listen to you. We will wait, but only for a time. In the meantime, Torin didn't say we couldn't hunt."

The two principal commodities that brought the most money were furs and slaves. Halldor quickly took note of the possibilities. This area that was rich in wildlife promised a plentiful cargo. Audun gave in. "No, he didn't say that."

"Then let's go." A rowdy laugh passed from man to man as they gathered up their weapons. Bolli was the first to leave the ship. Halldor and nine others soon joined him as he waded ashore, leaving Audun and the others behind.

Erica had crept out on a rock ledge, then hidden herself when she saw the long ship. Now she watched uneasily as the Norsemen left the large vessel. She counted them apprehensively. Only eleven. The rest were staying behind. Nevertheless, she feared what even eleven could do.

She could hear them talking but was too far away to understand what they said. She only knew that their voices were harsh and unpleasant. Not at all like the other Viking's voice. Nor were these Norsemen pleasing to the eye. They were big, hairy, and oafish-looking.

"Uncle Coinneach is right. They are heathens!"

She heard one of the Vikings curse and she shivered, crossing herself hastily. Moving along the ledge, high above the ship, she stared down at them as they pushed through the trees and shrubbery. Just the sight of them made her curse her Norse blood for the first time in her life.

Shadows from the clouds moved across the sky, putting the Vikings in darkness for just a heartbeat. It seemed to be some kind of bad omen. "I must tell Uncle Coinneach. . . ."

Wind stirred the heather. A deer ran out of the trees, only to be felled by a hastily thrown axe—further warning about the skill the Vikings had with weapons when they wanted to kill. What if one of those axes struck someone she loved?

"Geordie . . . !" Fearful that her cry could be heard, she muffled her mouth with her hand.

Erica watched one of the men take off his helmet. His light-brown hair was unruly, his beard unkempt, his face crisscrossed by scars. Somehow, she sensed that this was a man of no loyalty except to himself. A dangerous man.

"They are all dangerous. . . ." Even the Viking she had met at the lake had thought nothing amiss in taking what he wanted.

For a long time Erica watched, pushing back the bright strands of hair that whipped at her face and blew into her eyes. The brown-haired man was standing tautly with legs apart, his fists clenched, his head thrown back in an attitude of utter defiance as he looked back toward the ship.

The Viking at the lake claimed that they have come in peace. Having caught sight of these men, her hopes for any kind of peaceful coexistence were shattered. They were just the kind of heathens she had always been told they were. But what about her father? What kind of a man was he? Had he been a heathen, too? *Did ye lie to me, Mother?*

Was Iona right? Had her mother been taken against her will? Had Ragnar ruined her mother's life? Or had he loved her? Heathen or hero: which one had her father been?

More than at any other time in her life, Erica regretted the passing of her mother. She needed to ask her so many questions that had just sprung into her head, but there was no one who would be able to answer. No one! Whatever decisions she made, she would have to make on her own.

If I tell Uncle Coinneach about the Vikings, he will attack them without question and bloodshed will be of a certainty. But if I do not tell him and the Viking by the lake lied to me and he is here to pillage and loot, then we will be taken unaware. . . .

Could she trust the word of a Viking?

Taking one last look at the Viking ship, Erica sprang up from the rock. She would go her secret way, up the face of the rock and through the forest. Once she had reached the hall, she would make her decision.

EIGHT

Torin caught up with Gardar at the edge of the glen. "Here so soon, Tor?" Sitting on a rock, Gardar had taken off his shoes and was rubbing his blistered feet. "Either the woman did not have much to . . . uh . . . say or you have lost your touch."

Torin's ego had been bruised, and he hated to admit that he had been scorned. "Ragnar sent me on a quest to find his sons, not to lust after a woman, no matter how lovely she is."

Frustration surged through him. He'd known a hundred women who were by all measures beautiful, and yet when he'd looked into those blue eyes he'd been lost, caught up in a fascination he couldn't explain. It was totally unusual for him to feel such a sudden, compelling physical attraction, and yet he had. And he'd sensed that for one moment there had been a mutual attraction. *Perhaps I gave up too easily,* he thought.

"She rejected you." Gardar smirked. He had always laughingly prophesied that one day Torin would meet his match. It seemed to have come to pass much sooner than he had expected. But would Torin admit it? Never!

Torin's jaw tensed. "I changed my mind. She was too tall and too bad-tempered."

"Bad-tempered? The perfect woman for you." He started to comment further, but Torin interrupted him.

"I don't want to talk about it. I intend to forget, and you had best do the same." Forget her? How could he when even now her face hovered in his mind's eye? He could still remember her firm breasts pressed against his chest, could still taste her lips.

Gardar stood up and put on his leather shoes. "Let's get going. I'm anxious to get this over with so we can return and you can make good on your promise to see that I get my own ship."

"A small one," Torin chided.

Gardar quirked his brow. "How small?"

"I ask that Ragnar give you a knorr so that you can become a trader. If we survive our meetings with the Scots, that is."

Gardar shrugged. "Once we give them the silver arm rings, coins, and brooches we brought with us and promise them gold coins from Ragnar's own chests, I think they will be willing to listen to our offer of peace." With a grunt he slung the bag of coins over his shoulder. I hope Ragnar is ready to pay."

"He is."

They walked in silence the rest of the way. At last Torin could see the MacQuarie stronghold from afar. The roughly hewn broch was high on the hillside overlooking the entire valley. Standing strong and defiant amid woods of beech and oak, the tower looked like a guardian. No doubt it had been built as a lookout after the Vikings started raiding the shores several years ago.

The motte on which the broch stood was a steep-sided, flattened cone formed by nature from hard-packed earth and rock—a perilous climb, which Torin maneuvered quite well. At the base of the mound was a trench, hacked out of the hard dirt, the stone being used to form the high wall that enclosed the entire area.

Buildings below the motte and dun were also of stone with thatched roofs and lay within the safety of the wall, with a guard gate limiting access. It had been easy to find his way, but Torin knew that finding the stronghold was just the beginning. Now came the hard part—maintaining peaceful relations with the Scots just long enough to find Ragnar's son.

Ragnar and Torin had differed in their ideas of how best to find Eric. Ragnar had wanted to use force; Torin had preferred to try diplomacy. Ragnar had opted to kidnap his son from under the Scots' very noses, but Torin had realized how difficult that would be, never having set eyes on the young man. Now, however, as Torin prepared to put his life on the line, he had second thoughts. He could not really be certain that he wouldn't be killed the moment he was seen. Nevertheless, he had decided to take the risk.

"Come. . . ."

The castle was of rugged gray granite, a three-storied structure with a semicircular tower on the west side overlooking Loch Tuath. It obviously had been built to withstand seaborne invading forces, and looked sturdy enough to frustrate any intruder. Square- and oblong-cut windows high above ground level gave proof that the castle could be amply protected with swords and arrows. Its size and strength made it appear impressive, nearly impenetrable, though as Torin came closer he could see that it was much smaller than he had supposed. Even so, as he viewed the structure he envisioned the possibilities for expansion that existed here if the Vikings settled on the land.

Suddenly the air whistled as an arrow flew by his ear. From out of the shadows a hulking figure appeared above the guard gate. Torin came cautiously closer. "Do not be coming any nearer." The voice was gruff.

Careful to avoid touching his weapons, Torin raised both his hands, palms up. A gesture of peace. "I've come a long distance to see your chieftain. I've come in peace."

"Peace? A Viking? What kind of trick is this?"

"No trickery."

"Ye come alone?" This time the voice did not sound as harsh. A lone Norseman did not seem too intimidating.

"I was accompanied by a companion. A dark-haired man much smaller than I." As Torin spoke, Gardar stepped out of the shadows.

"A Pict!"

"His name is Gardar and my name is Torin Rolandson. Ragnar Longsword sent us with gifts." Reaching into Gardar's sack, he lifted up a handful of gold coins that sparkled in the sun as Gardar preened about, holding up his bracelet-covered arms.

There was a rattling of chains and a groan of wood as the gate was raised. Beyond the wall, within the enclosure, were storage facilities, cattle pens, small garden plots, and a variety of stone buildings.Unfriendly glances challenged Torin, though not one threat was spoken. Did these Scots then adhere to the laws of hospitality? Just in case they did not, he touched the dagger beneath his cloak reassuringly. If the need arose, he could defend himself.

"I'll take this." The guard grabbed the sack Gardar was carrying. "And these . . ." One by one he stripped the arm rings off Gardar's arms.

"Greedy isn't he?" Gardar's mind was on his stomach. He'd sniffed a pot of porridge bubbling in a cauldron over the hearth as the guard led them past the kitchen, and he was determined to have a taste.

Torin took hold of his tunic and pulled him back. "Later."

The kitchen rang with sound—pots clanking, spoons rattling. Torin viewed the scene stoically, thinking how similar it was to any Viking kitchen. There were cauldrons bubbling, and foodstuffs in barrels and sacks, and the ever-present aroma of food cooking. In some ways all people were very much the same.

He let his eyes roam freely about the larger room, critically assessing it. Ragnar always said that a man could tell much from another man's abode. What was this man Coinneach like?

Just as in Ragnar's hall, the walls were lined with benches, but these were covered in padded wool cushions with embroidered designs, not bare wood. The lofty hammer-beamed ceiling was hung with brightly colored banners, including those of scarlet and black. Even the floor was lavishly decorated with curly sheepskin rugs. The wooden walls here were adorned with a gaudy display of shields and weapons—massive two-handed claymores as well as axes, spears, dirks, and long, tautly strung bows. Torin wondered if these men had the skill to use them to advantage.

"I wish I could take some of these women with us," Gardar said, pointing toward several young women who were helping to prepare the food. Some kind of grain, it looked like. "What would Ragnar do if I abducted the lot of them and took them back to our own stronghold?"

"He'd have your head. We are here for another purpose. Besides, we have enough of our own women." Torin tensed as he remembered the invitation he had given to take the red-haired young woman back with him. Well, what did it matter? He'd never see her again. At least, he thought not. That was why he thought he imagined it when he heard a woman's voice cry out.

"You lied to me!" Erica was out of breath. She had run all the way.

Torin's jaw dropped open in surprise as he turned around. "What are *you* doing here?" With her flaming hair tumbling wildly about her shoulders and falling into her eyes, she looked wild and beautiful.

"My uncle, Coinneach, is chieftain of this hall." Because of her anger she was anxious for the arrogant Viking to be humbled.

He hid his surprise, but he was stunned by the information. "Then you can lead me to him." He brushed at his tunic and stared at her as she ran her fingers through her tousled hair. "We have much to talk about, he and I."

"Och, I'm certain that ye have a great deal to explain," she said, putting her hands on her hips. "Such as why your companions are armed to the teeth as they crawl like maggots over our shores!"

Torin damned Audun and Halldor beneath his breath. He had clearly told them to stay hidden and not cause any alarm. "The weapons we carry are for protection. We have no plans to attack."

"I don't believe you!" She motioned to two tall men in the corner. "Take him to Coinneach!"

Torin was roughly ushered inside the great hall and pushed into a heap before a large carved chair. His anger at being so ill treated knew no bounds. He had come with peaceful intentions. It was the Scots who had started trouble. "Is this a measure of Scottish hospitality?" he cried out, fighting the arms that held him. They'd soon be begging his pardon when Ragnar learned how he had been treated.

The commotion could be heard all through the hall. Standing in the doorway, Coinneach scowled as he looked upon the scene. "What's going on?"

"We've caught a Viking," one of the Scotsmen who had manhandled him answered.

Torin swore beneath his breath. "I wasn't caught. I came here to talk with the chieftain of the MacQuaries." He could see that the man addressing him was wearing two of the silver arm rings that they had brought—gifts from Ragnar.

"That would be I!"

Coinneach motioned for the Scotsmen to move away. "It appears that we have not shown ye courtesy. For that I apologize."

"Courtesy?" Erica was horrified. "Do you usually give courtesy to those who plan our doom?"

Turning to Erica, Coinneach spoke in an angry tone. "And do ye usually go running off to escape your duty?"

He scowled. "Ye gave us cause to worry, slipping away as ye did."

"I meant well." Erica put her hands upon her hips. She would not back down on this. "I'll not marry a man I have not laid eyes on. I will not marry the MacKinnon laddie. There has to be another way." She turned toward Torin, hoping he would not notice the tremor in her voice. Seeing him again had shaken her to the core.

"Ye'll do as I say."

"Nae, a woman should have some say in who she spends her life with. But that is not why I left."

"I know." Coinneach's expression softened. "I'd see to your punishment for such a rash action, but Geordie told us what ye planned and why. Ye could have been harmed, hinny. The MacLeods are nearly as bad as the Vikings."

"But I wasn't harmed. I didn't have time to do as I planned." Erica turned her attention back to Torin, looking at him accusingly. "But I'm glad I went, for I saw them with my own eyes. Big, ugly Vikings are even now wandering about our shores and up to no good, I would say. That's why I came back so quickly. I had to warn ye." She took several steps toward Torin. "Ye said that ye came in peace."

"And I did! The men have been given strict orders not to cause any trouble." He looked toward Coinneach then back at Erica again. "I did not come to plunder but to search for someone. I am looking for a young man. I have been sent to take him back with me."

"Who?" Coinneach asked warily.

"His name is Eric; his father's name was Ragnar Longsword and his mother's name was Flora, nic Dugald."

Erica gasped. "What did you say?" In all her wildest imaginings she had never foreseen this.

"I'm looking for Eric Ragnarsson," Torin said again. "He is part Scots and part Viking. And the son of a jarl. It is time he took his rightful place."

"Eric Ragnarsson?"

Coinneach was stunned, but not half as surprised as Erica. Her whole body quivered. For a moment she was speechless. He was looking for her! He assumed that her mother had borne a male child. She tried to speak, to tell him of his mistake and that Ragnar was *her* father, but Coinneach stood in front of her.

"Ye have come to the right place. Flora, daughter of Dugald, was my sister. I am uncle to whom ye seek."

"Then my journey is over." Torin felt relieved. It had been so easy. "I must see him. I have a message from his father."

A message! Erica started to speak again, but she felt her uncle squeeze her arm in warning. Her eyes met his questioningly, but she did not say a word.

NINE

Erica ran up the circular stone staircase to her bedchamber so fast that she almost flew. Once inside, she plundered her large wooden trunk, pulled several items of clothing from pegs on the wall, and stuffed what she deemed necessary into a large sack. She was determined that now that she finally had a chance to see her father, no one would stand in the way. Not even her uncle Coinneach. She had dreamed of this moment for too long.

I'll leave with the Viking come morn whether or not uncle wants me to go with him! It is my only chance to meet my father.

Even if she had to stow away she would not miss this opportunity. If she was sent to the MacKinnon household, it would be too late. She might never get the chance to see her father.

I am Ragnar's daughter. She wondered what that arrogant Viking would think when he found out.

The Viking! Oh, how he infuriated her with his attitude of male superiority. As if by being born a female she was somehow inferior. He seemed to have little interest in women at all and had preferred "man talk," except of course when he had been interested in seducing some lowly fisherman's daughter by a lake.

Clenching her hands into fists, she remembered the

heated look in his eyes at the lake and the passionate kiss they had shared. How different that was from the look on his face when she had announced to him that her uncle was the chieftain. That, however, would be nothing compared to how surprised he would be when she revealed her parentage.

Oh, how I want to see him grovel when I tell him that I am the one he is seeking. Not Ragnar's son but Ragnar's daughter! She felt a fierce burst of pride as she said it again aloud. "Ragnar's daughter."

Erica had wanted to tell the Viking who she was the moment he had announced that he had come with a message from Ragnar Longsword, but her uncle had silenced her, at least for the moment. Meanwhile, Coinneach had promised the Viking that he would meet Ragnar's "offspring" very soon.

Though her uncle's behavior had surprised and puzzled her, Erica had kept silent. *The truth cannot be kept secret for long!*

Though usually careless in her dress, Erica carefully chose a russet undertunic and a dun-colored arasaid striped with a rainbow of colors, the one her mother had woven for her on the large loom in the ladies' hall. She would pin it with a large gold brooch. Several gold arm bracelets would complete her outfit. Carefully she laid the items on the bed that stood in the middle of the room.

Suitable for a jarl's daughter, she decided.

Erica had always scoffed at Iona's frivolity in using sweet-smelling herbs in her bath, but now she had second thoughts. If she was going to be on a ship there might not be another chance to bathe for a while. She had best take advantage of the fact that it was the third day of the week and thus the women's turn to bathe. She grabbed an old woolen tartan to serve as a towel, but before she could head toward the bath-house a knock sounded at her door.

"Erica. Erica . . ." Her uncle's voice sounded insistent. Erica quickly opened the door. There were several things she wanted to discuss with him. His coming to see her was timely.

"Why did ye silence me down there?" she blurted. "I'm proud of who I am. I wanted to shout it to the stars."

Coinneach's eyes were drawn immediately to the large bundle of clothing on her bed. "And just where do ye think ye are going?"

"I think ye know." A surge of excitement swept through her. "I think ye have always known that someday I would seek out my father. Now the opportunity has come right up to the door, and it is he who seeks me out."

"Ragnar Longsword is looking for his *son!*" The words exploded from his lips. If they were meant to wound her, they did.

"What are ye saying? That just because I was not born a male that he doesn't care about me?" She didn't wait for him to answer. "Just because I was not born with a 'sword' between my legs doesn't mean that I am not worthy."

"Ye are a very braw lassie!" Coinneach said. "Ye have all the fine qualities of a man. Ye hunt, swear, fight and have a will of yer own. There isn't anything that ye cannot do." He shrugged. "Except become jarl," he said matter-of-factly.

His words struck her like a blow. Slowly the truth seeped into her brain. Her father wasn't looking for his child with Flora out of any kind of love or because he wanted to make up for the years they had been apart. Her father was looking for a successor. That and that alone was what had suddenly thrust him back into her life.

"Why didn't ye want me to tell the Viking?" Her eyes demanded the truth. "And why didn't my father already know that I was born a female? What kind of deception was carried out, and why?"

"No deception." He reached up and patted her on the head as if she were still a child. "Ragnar didn't know his bairn was a lassie. He and his band of Vikings left Alba and my sister before the child—*you*—were born."

"He left before the birth?" Erica was confused. That was not the story her mother had told her. Her mother had always told her how proud her father had been of her and how tenderly he had held her in his arms. Now she knew that, for good or for ill, her mother had lied. Her father had never even seen her. "He left . . ."

"Aye. He slipped away without even telling her good-bye." There was an edge to Coinneach's voice. "She heard no word."

"Mother told me that he always meant to return," Erica said quickly, fighting tears, "but that there was unrest and fighting in the Northland."

Coinneach shook his head. "He struck at us like a viper, took all that we had, including my sister's virtue, then, when it suited his selfish interests, he left without even glancing back. Even now he sends another to do his bidding." Reaching out, he brushed her cheek with his fingers, wiping away her sudden tears. "I have tried to be like a father to ye. The father that ye never had."

"And you have done so." Gently she laid her hand on his arm. "The death of my mother was a catastrophe for my brother and me. Somehow she had always held out the hope that one day my father would come back. Now I can only suppose that he never intended to return, at least until he needed someone to follow in his footsteps as a Viking!" At that moment she hated them all. Especially Ragnar. He had broken her mother's heart without even a second thought, and now he had broken hers.

"I thought that it was better that Ragnar not find out about his daughter. Not that there is anything wrong in having sired such a lovely lass, but because I wanted to protect ye, hinny. I didn't want him to use ye as a pawn and marry ye off to some brutal pagan who doesn't even worship God."

Ah, but you would marry me off to a man I don't even

know just because Iona doesn't want to go, she thought but did not say.

"Besides, as long as he"—He paused, cleared his throat, then continued—"he thinks that his son is in the Highlands, we have had a respite from his raids."

And ye think the raids will begin again because he finds out I am female born, she thought, but said instead, "The Viking will find out and tell Ragnar when he returns to the Northland."

Coinneach shook his head. "Not if we use our heads."

Erica read the answer in his eyes and knew what her uncle was planning. "He will not be going back."

"Nae, he will not."

She thought a moment. "What of his crew?"

Coinneach's eyes glittered. "They will have to be destroyed. Kill or be killed, Erica. Do ye understand?"

She nodded but asked, "What will my father think when they do not return?"

Coinneach grasped her shoulders, forcing her to look him in the eye. "Ships get lost at sea all the time. . . ."

What her uncle planned was ominous, and it deeply troubled Erica as she at last made her way to the bathhouse. Pushing open the thick wooden portal, she was grateful to see that all of the six large wooden tubs that studded the rush-strewn floor were empty. She would have the seldom-granted opportunity of privacy. A well for washing or drinking water was available at the central drawing point; she busied herself with procuring a plentiful supply. She filled the buckets and heated the water in the large iron pots that were perched over an open fire. Careful not to burn herself, she carried the large pot to one of the tubs, completing the job of filling her bath. The hot water would soothe her and help her to wipe out the thoughts that were swirling around in her mind. Turning around, she stripped off her tunic and lifted the skirts of her undertunic to disrobe, but paused as she heard the door creak.

The sudden unwelcome feeling that someone was staring at her crept over her. Whirling around, she was startled to find herself face to face with *him* again. "You!" She said the word like a curse.

He shut the door behind him. "It seems I'm always finding you perched by the water."

"And I always seem to have ye sneaking up behind me," she snapped, holding the tartan protectively up to her bosom to hide the outline of her breasts and the pendant beneath the thin linen.

The soft glow of the flickering torchlight illuminated the room and gave her a clear view of his manly form. He had obviously readied himself to bathe, for he was naked to the waist, wearing only his tight-fitting Viking trousers. Out of the corner of her eye she appraised his broad shoulders, muscled arms, and wide chest and had to admit to herself that he looked very virile—and so alive! For just a moment it was as if a fist clutched at her heart.

"It appears we had the same idea," Torin whispered.

To her mortification Erica realized he had caught her staring. "What are ye doing here anyway? 'Tis the women's turn to bathe," she said peevishly, angry at herself for giving him even a cursory glance. He and all Vikings were her enemies. She knew that beyond a doubt now.

"The women's turn?" Torin had felt so grimy and dirtied from the journey that the very first thing upon his mind, after being offered the MacQuarie hospitality, had been a bath. "I didn't know. . . ."

Erica conceded the point. He wouldn't have known their customs and the bathhouse schedule. "There was no harm done." At least she hadn't had time to disrobe fully before he rushed in. She could not say the same for him. He was perilously close to being naked. Moreover, he didn't seem to mind. He seemed to be flaunting his masculinity, in fact.

In the silence that pervaded the room, each was intensely conscious of the other. The attraction they felt was nearly tangible. Erica was aware of him in every nerve, pore, and bone in her body. Torin felt a physical urge to reach out and touch her, an impulse that he only narrowly held under control. The very air pulsated with a primitive, sensual tension that was undeniable.

"I must go. I cannot be alone with ye like this," Erica said at last, fearful of her own emotions. She was perilously close to feeling sorry for him and for what had to happen. But it was the way of things. Kill or be killed, her uncle had said. She had to put aside any sympathies and think of what danger the Vikings posed to her kith and kin. She turned her back on him.

"No, don't leave." Torin took a step forward.

"Ye can have the bathhouse all to yourself." She took a step back. Hastily she rearranged her clothes.

There was so much that he wanted to say to her, but all he could whisper was, "I do not blame you for being apprehensive after the way I acted at the lake."

His voice was so soft and caressing that it was almost as if he had kissed her again. She felt the same pulsating warmth spread over her. "Ye made no secret of what ye wanted."

"I didn't know who you were then." But he did now. Torin's eyes were drawn to the outline of her breasts beneath the linen. No fisherman's daughter, but the niece of the MacQuarie chieftain. He must remember that.

"And just who is that?" Erica said petulantly. "Not the son ye thought ye would find," she said beneath her breath.

"You are a woman it seems I was destined to meet," Torin answered, speaking from his heart. "A lovely and spirited woman."

"And ye are a man good with words. Now, ye may leave. . . ." She pressed her lips together tightly as she pointed toward the door. If he thought there was going to be any dallying just because he'd flattered her, she would let him know he was wrong.

"I'll leave, but first I do want to soothe the ill will between us. It's still there despite your words." His eyes focused on hers, his gaze intent as he walked the short distance that separated them. "Let us have peace."

Erica started to turn away, but just at that moment he reached out and captured her hand. Just the feel of his hand seemed to sear her flesh, awakening that same flutter in her stomach she'd felt at the lake. She found herself remembering the pressure of those warm, knowing lips against hers. Though it was her hand he touched, her heart pulsated as rapidly as the wings of a trapped bird.

She tried to ignore the sensations, but somehow his look revealed his sincerity, and she felt sorry for the fate that she knew awaited him. But any feeling that might have sparked between them was all for naught. The Viking was a doomed man, and she was equally doomed if she allowed herself to care even one whit about him. In a gesture of defiance she pulled her hand away.

The soft material of her tunic tightened across her firm breasts. Tearing his gaze away, he merely said, "I'll go and leave you to your bath, but I know in my heart that we will meet again and again."

The wavering torchlight danced on his strong cheekbones, and Erica stared, fascinated at the way the flames played across his boldly carved nose and hard jawline. In that moment she regretted with all her heart what her uncle Coinneach had planned.

TEN

Torin looked out the window at the flower-covered hills and forests of the MacQuarie lands. From the window of the bedchamber Coinneach MacQuarie had given him for his stay, he was afforded a magnificent view. There were blue ribbons of water winding a path over the hills, and trees raising their branches to the sky. It was a far cry from the rocky shores and rough terrain that he was used to.

"No wonder Ragnar fell in love with this land," he said as his gaze swept over the greenery. "What surprises me is why he would leave."

"Because the Scots are difficult to deal with," Gardar said petulantly. He joined Torin at the window. "I think we should grab Ragnar's son and go. Quickly. Before we are stabbed in the back."

Torin disagreed. "Ragnar wants to establish trade with the Scots. That the young man is both Scots and Viking will help him seal the bargain." He smiled. "Besides, I like it here. A few days spent will not matter."

"A few days smiling at the tall red-haired Scotswoman and hoping to get her in your bed, you mean," Gardar grumbled beneath his breath. "I'm telling you, Torin. One of these days your lust is going to get us both killed. And this just could be that time."

"It's not lust!" He had other, unfamiliar feelings for the

young woman. He tried to change the subject. "Coinneach was friendly. There was no hostility shown by him."

"Perhaps not by him, but you should have seen the way the others looked at you." Seeing a bug on the floor, he stepped on it with a thud. "There, that is what they will do to you if you do not listen to me."

Torin turned away from the window and began unpacking his belongings from his traveling bag. Inside he had a change of clothing, his favorite tankard, a silver mirror, two dragon-headed silver brooches for securing his cloak, several bracelets, coins, a dagger that he used mainly for shaving, a bag filled with ivory and amber carved game pieces, and most important of all, his wooden game board, which had a different game on each side.

"Coinneach MacQuarie would never betray the law of hospitality. Highland custom forbids killing a man when he has been offered hospitality within a Highlander's home. It is like the law of sanctuary in a Christian church."

"Which of course we have recognized," Gardar said dryly, thinking of all the monks and priests who had been dragged out of their sanctuaries by their hair.

Torin stiffened. "Ragnar has always abhorred acting like a heathen. He has never acted like the others. Nor have I!"

Gardar began to unpack his bag also. They were to share the chamber, although Torin would get the bed and he would have to sleep on the hard, cold floor. "The Scots will not know the difference. To them a Viking is a Viking. Besides, you can not trust Halldor for very long. He will get into mischief if given half a chance. Again I tell you, we must grab Ragnar's son and go!"

Turning his head, Gardar grimaced as he saw that Torin was carefully scraping his stubbled face as he looked into his silver hand mirror. Although most Vikings preferred letting their stubble grow into full-fledged beards, Torin shaved his face, a habit he had learned from Ragnar, who was likewise vain.

"We are staying! A curse on that red-haired girl. She has blinded you to the truth and turned a wise man into a fool."

"Gar—!" Though Torin wanted to protest, he choked on his words. Gardar was right. He did hope that he could change the young woman's mind about him.

"I only wish that I could call upon my ancestors for their magical powers so that I could save you when the time comes. And it will come!"

Resigned to staying, Gardar emptied his bag. Inside he had a change of garments, a wooden mug, several colored wooden balls that he used for juggling, coins, and most important of all, a flute carved from a sheep's leg bone. Picking it up, he put his fingers over the holes carved in the bottom, put his mouth at the top, and filled the air with a mournful but beautiful song.

As she stood in the doorway of the hall, Erica's gaze touched upon her clansmen and women as they went about their morning chores. The inner courtyard rang with the sound of women's laughter and the chatter of the men as they went about the preparations for the day's events. They were happy, content. As for Erica, although she tried to put out of her mind all that her Uncle Coinneach had told her, it darkened her mood like a thundercloud.

"After all these years my father . . ."

Acutely conscious of the fact that the Viking and his companion had been given a sleeping chamber just down the hall from her own, she had listened to each and every sound outside their room, hoping to learn more about this quest he had been sent on to find Ragnar's son, hoping to learn something that could avert a catastrophe. Alas, except for playing a lovely, sad song on some kind of flute, they had been silent.

Why does my uncle insist on such subterfuge? Why can't I come forth and tell the Viking who I am? Why does my uncle think that we must use violence? Hasn't there been enough bloodshed already?

"Get a hold on yourself, lassie," she scolded herself aloud, still caught up in the turmoil of her emotions. "Stop thinking about what is going to happen. He's a Viking, not one of your own. He's done his share of killing."

What was done was done. The decision had been made. It was over and done with. Although she didn't know the when, where, or why her uncle was going to strike, she knew that the Viking's life would soon be forfeit. And for all intents and purposes, all chances to be reunited with her father would die with him.

"And I will have to marry the MacKinnon whether it be my choice or not, for that is the way of things."

The sound of happy chatter filled the air. A dozen or more smiling faces greeted Erica as she walked through the door. Though she was not in a particularly good mood, everyone else was, and the gaiety was infectious, soon wiping away her frown.

It was not a feudal society here; there were no serfs to do the work. All were of the same kin and willingly did whatever chores were necessary. Even a chieftain's daughter, she thought, looking toward Iona. Everyone was busily working at some task or other, and Erica took her place beside the women preparing the food.

Breakfast was to be simple—porridge and fruit and fish, for the men were eager to be about the day's activities. Erica filled a cauldron with water from a wooden bucket, anxious for her chores to be done so that she could hurry back to the glen. Perhaps the beauty there would take her mind off her troubles.

She brought the water to a boil and let the oatmeal trickle into it. From the corner of her eye she scanned the room as the men filed in. And there he was, the Viking. Though he didn't make any attempt to attract attention, he stood out nonetheless because he was taller, lighter-haired, and broader of shoulder, and he had an aura of masculinity that was overpowering and very appealing.

The other men wore breacans of bright red-and-black plaid, the long ends draped over their left shoulders and pinned in place with a brooch. They looked colorful, while the Viking was dressed in somber earth tones. His tunic was brown, his trousers beige, yet despite the muted colors, all eyes were drawn to him, including hers.

"He's a fine-looking man," she thought. Even though the room was noisy and crowded, she was aware of him and he was equally aware of her. Over and over again she could feel his eyes on her as she worked.

With a shiver she remembered their meeting in the glen. If the Vikings were so violent, then why hadn't he forced himself upon her? He could have. But he hadn't. Nor had he led his Viking band in an attack upon the MacQuarie stronghold. Why, then, did her uncle think he deserved to die? Because of what might be?

It's so unjust. And troubling.

Stirring the pot constantly with a spurtle—a wooden stick about a foot long—she glanced the Viking's way from time to time, trying to assess the kind of man he was, but she hastily averted his gaze the moment he glanced back.

What is he thinking? Does he sense at all that he is in danger? Or does he trust my uncle's gesture of hospitality? And what about me? Does he sense that I am more drawn to him than I will admit?

She let the porridge cook steadily for a half hour, all the while contemplating the matter as she stirred and watched for lumps. But though she was determined not to scorch the porridge, she nearly did. And all because of his presence in the room. He was distracting!

This must be how my mother felt when she first laid eyes on Ragnar! He, too, must have made the other men look plain by comparison. Was it his broad shoulders? His long legs? The curve of his mouth? His hair, so golden as it hung down to his shoulders? Realizing that she was staring again, she hastily looked away.

Breakfast was eaten standing. Erica ate her oatmeal with fresh goat's milk, sugar, and salt, adding wild berries and curds. The Viking ate his plain with only a few raspberries on top and drank the tankard of goat's milk intended to be used sparingly on the porridge. Obviously he was unaware that it was to be shared with others.

Erica watched from a distance as Iona hurried to refill the tankard, smiling at the Viking all the while. Though she would not admit it to herself, Erica felt a twinge of jealousy.

"The next thing ye know she'll be asking Uncle Coinneach to let her keep him as a pet!" She could almost imagine Iona putting a rope around the Viking and leading him from room to room. Then suddenly she remembered. The Viking was going to die, and by Iona's father's own hand. The reminder suddenly spoiled her appetite.

"Good morning." Geordie's cheerful greeting startled her.

"Ye know that Uncle has declared that anyone who isn't at breakfast promptly will not get his share." She winked at him as she spooned out a large portion of porridge. "But if ye will not tell, then neither will I."

"I had a reason to be late." Geordie puffed out his chest proudly. "Uncle Coinneach wants me to spy on the Viking and his friend."

"Spy?"

"He wants to know how many Viking ships there are before he . . . before he . . ."

"Murders him?" she asked harshly. She didn't like Geordie involved in any way with such things. He was still a boy.

"Aye." Geordie stared at the Viking. "I've never seen a Viking before. I thought they were supposed to have horns!"

"That's only a tale, hinny, because when the priests first laid eyes on them they thought that they were devils. Though he's a mite bigger, he doesn't look that much different from you or me."

"Oh, but he does. . . ." Curiosity toward the stranger in their midst prompted Geordie to move closer. Erica followed. "I thought all Vikings had beards!"

"This one must be overly proud of his handsomeness," she answered as her eyes explored his face. She liked the shape of his brows. They weren't bushy like those of some of the MacQuarries. And his nose. It looked as if it had been carved from wood. And his mouth . . . Once again she hastily looked away, for the sight of his mouth always made her think of his kisses.

"I wonder if the Norsemen play shinnie?" It was a simple game using curved sticks and a ball.

Before Erica could answer Geordie, he had boldly moved across the room and was asking him. Erica could see the Viking laugh as he seemingly accepted Geordie's challenge. Anxious to humble the Viking, the men in the hall immediately chose sides.

It was a dangerous sport, one said to be the fastest ball game in the Highlands and beyond. To play it a man needed to possess extraordinary athletic abilities—a quick eye, a ready hand, and a strong arm—and be an excellent runner and wrestler as well. Erica was not one to sit idle like the other women and watch the event. Hiking up the hem of her gown, she elbowed her way among the players to join in, just as she had done since childhood. Plucking up a stick, she aligned herself with the players.

The field had the appearance of a battle scene. That she found herself on the opposite side from the Viking spurred her on to win. So he had come to find Ragnar's son. Well, she would show him what Ragnar's daughter could do. With that thought in mind she threw herself into the fracas, pleased when at last she caught the look of surprise merged with admiration on his face.

Torin was amazed by her concentration and determination. "You play as well as your men."

"And ye learn quickly, Viking," she answered.

"Perhaps not quickly enough." He had not been wrong about her. She was intriguing. "Do all the women of Alba play as furiously as you?"

"Nay, they prefer to watch, but I . . . I've always liked the feeling that I get from winning." She gripped her stick.

"And do you always win?"

She laughed. "Usually."

Torin couldn't let a woman beat him; he preened his skills before her. He was quick and strong and ran with easy grace, cutting back and forth across the pasture with his stick. Fighting the others for the ball with a reckless ferocity, he strove as always to prove to all those who scorned him that he could do anything.

Grudgingly Erica had to admire him. Though she was more than a match for Geordie, Malcolm, and even Jamie, she discovered that the Viking swung his stick as powerfully as her uncle wielded his sword. Surely he and the men who came with him would be menacing. Was that the reason that her uncle was going to kill him as well as the others? It was something to think about as she continued to play the game—which might have been why her side lost.

Erica gritted her teeth. If only they could play again she would redeem herself.

"You played a good game." Huffing and puffing, the Viking tried to catch his breath, surprised that a woman of beauty could also possess skill and strength.

"If I had played such a good game I would have won."

She wanted to say much more, but they were interrupted by Geordie. "Did ye see the way he played, Erica? And he didn't even know the game." It was obvious that Geordie was beginning to like the Norseman.

"I learn quickly." Torin patted the boy on the shoulder. "A man needs to be strong, but he also needs to use his head. How would you like to learn a new game?"

"A game?" Geordie was intrigued. "What kind of a game?"

"We Vikings like to play board games," he answered. "You would like *hneftafl*. One player uses his eight carved pieces to protect the king from the other player, who has sixteen pieces. Very challenging." He looked at Erica. "Would you care to learn?"

She started to say yes, then thought better of it. If she was smart, she would stay away from the Viking and not put herself in the path of temptation. "I have work to do and so does Geordie!"

Geordie tugged playfully at her hair. "I can do my chores first and then play, can't I, Erica?"

Reluctantly she said yes, though she muttered beneath her breath that even Vikings must have better things to do. Still, in curiosity she followed them back to the hall, watching as the Viking sat down at a corner table. He put down a wooden board cut with forty-nine holes. It had a carved human head at the top and a carved wolf's head at the bottom. He opened a small sack and poured what looked like miniature carved statues into his hand.

"Are you sure you don't want to learn?" Torin asked, reaching out to touch her hand.

Startled by the shivers that went up and down her spine as he touched her, Erica pulled away. "I told ye no! I must be about my work." She pretended that she did not have any interest in the game, yet from time to time she cast a longing glance at him over her shoulder as she cut up the vegetables for the stoves for the noon meal.

A hundred times she had imagined what it would be like to find herself in his arms. He was handsome, so undeniably handsome. Surely no Scots warrior could have had arms as strong, a face so wonderfully chiseled, or hair that shone like gold in the sun.

Only when his gaze met her eye did she realize how intensely she was staring. Hastily she looked away, but not before she witnessed the smile that curved his lips.

Erica gasped as she accidentally nicked her thumb with

the knife. Resigning herself to keep her mind on what she was doing, she nonetheless found it impossible. She just couldn't keep her eyes from roaming to where the Viking sat slumped on his bench, intent on the pieces he was moving around on the board.

"I wonder what Vikings are like in bed?" questioned a voice behind her.

Turning, Erica saw one of the married women staring at the Viking as he adroitly moved the carved pieces. "Ye be brazen to say such a thing!"

"Brazen because ye have set your sights on him? Ye be not alone. There must be at least half a dozen with the same thought in mind. Ha, I'd even say there are some of the married ones who would shove their husbands aside to have the Norseman in their bed." She giggled suggestively. "Ye know what they say about a tall man. . . ."

Erica did, and she blushed to the roots of her hair. She had heard the women talking, discussing what went on between a woman and a man. They had even been so bold as to talk about marital secrets, comparing their husbands' love-making. Some had been said to be ample; others were found wanting. Now she could not help but wonder about the Viking's prowess in bed, and as she did so, primitive desires swept over her with a fever that shocked her. She felt an intense need to get a breath of fresh air.

Wind whipped at Erica's hair, sending the strands flying about her shoulders as she stepped out the door. Carefully she adjusted her arasaid to cover her head like a shawl. Suddenly she had a feeling that she wasn't alone.

"Are you all right?" His voice startled her, for she had not seen him nor heard his footstep as he approached.

Despite her heart's prodding, words failed her and all she could do was look into the depths of his sea blue eyes. Nervously she tugged at the fabric of her blue arasaid. The Viking pulled it down, leaving her hair to blow wildly in the wind.

"I like your hair flying free. It reminds me of fire." The warmth of his fingers gently caressed her hand. "I wish . . ." His voice was low.

"Wish what?" Somehow she found her voice, but it came out in a croaked whisper.

"That you did not see me as an enemy, for I swear to you that I am not!"

Grasping her shoulders, he pulled her toward him. Then, before she could pull away, he cupped her chin in his hand, bent his head, and claimed her mouth in an ardent kiss.

Closing her eyes, Erica gave herself up to the sensations that swept through her, all the while realizing that she might never have another chance to kiss him before her uncle carried out his plan.

"No!" she murmured, then reaching up, she wound her arms around his neck, holding him closer, never wanting to let go. But in the midst of her kiss, heartache engulfed her. She didn't want him to die!

Pulling violently away, she ran, hardly even caring where she was going. She ran back toward the hall, stumbling along. Somehow she had to save the Viking's life. Somehow she had to change her uncle's mind.

ELEVEN

The stairs leading to her uncle's chambers were drafty, but that was not the reason Erica felt chilled. It was because of the quandary she found herself in. She was loyal to her clan and equally so to her uncle, and yet she could not stand by and see the Viking struck down.

For a moment she stood as still as a statue in front of her uncle's door. He would accuse her of being disloyal. He would throw her Viking lineage in her face. He would bluster. He would rage. Raising her hand to the wood, she started to knock, then changed her mind.

"Ye cannot do this, Uncle Coinneach!" she blurted out, sweeping into the room. "Ye cannot do this, I say."

His furrowed brows showed his impatience at being disturbed, as Coinneach MacQuarie sat up from his position on the ground. To her dismay, Erica saw that his plaid was laid on the ground and gathered into folds in the center. Her uncle had lain down on top of it and gathered the loose ends across his stomach, as the men did when dressing in their breacans. He now fastened it with a belt as he stood up.

"Can a man have no privacy!" His short kilt did not quite reach his plump knees. Swearing beneath his breath, he fastened the long length of material that hung from the belt with a large metal brooch and threw it over his shoulder.

"I'm sorry."

He grunted. "I cannot do what?"

"Kill the Viking." Though once she might have cowered, Erica let her rising tide of anger consume her.

"And who is there to stop me?" Coinneach was defiant as he stood up, facing her squarely. The years had threaded his hair with gray, but he was still an imposing man—one who knew his word was law.

"Your conscience!"

His face turned red; he balled his hands into fists but did not say a word.

"Ye know yourself the force of the absolute law of hospitality." If any person was admitted to a Highlander's dwelling and sought and was offered protection, he was not to be disturbed or harmed. There was no obligation to give shelter or to offer protection, but once given, the rule was absolute and binding. "You cannot kill him within the castle's walls."

"So," Coinneach said, "we will kill him out of doors."

Reaching out, she gripped her uncle's shoulder, digging her fingers into the firm, muscled flesh with bruising strength. "What ye plan is vile, a sin against both man and God. And just because ye have a grudge against my father." There, she had said it.

"Aye, I have a grudge! Against heathens who crawl across another man's land like a plague of insects bringing death and destruction in their wake." The blue eyes beneath the thick brows were slits of anger, an anger that had never dimmed throughout the years. "I will not allow any Viking, even if he is your father, to gobble up our rightful land as they did in Shetland and the Hebrides!" He forced himself to be calm. "Ye are young and a woman and ye do not understand!"

"I'm old beyond my years; I understand the things of men and I do understand," she countered.

"I'm the father and the people of the clan are like my children." The Highlanders called themselves "families" for they were children of the chieftain. "I have to do what I think best, and it is not for ye to be arguing. And that is that." Grabbing her by the shoulders, he maneuvered her toward the door, pushed her outside, then slammed the door in her face.

Later in the day Erica stared out the window, watching as a small hunting party led by her uncle left the stronghold. Taking note that the Viking was with them, she remembered what her uncle had said: "Then we will kill him out of doors."

"Not if I can help it!" Stubbornly she decided that perhaps the Viking needed help if he was going to stay alive. She hurriedly dressed in an old gown and arasaid. Usually Erica went barefoot in spring and summer, but today she wore brogs—laced shoes with deerskin worn with the hairy side outward—as she followed after the men. Just in case she needed to walk a long distance.

For the hunt the men would use bows and arrows, though some took their swords and dirks with them. It would be a perfect opportunity for an accident, she thought. She would have to think quickly if she was going to intercede in the Viking's behalf.

Erica ran until she thought her lungs would burst, but at last she reached the tail end of the line of horses. The shaggy-haired mares were equipped with keisans, woven baskets slung over a horse's back to carry back any small game or birds. The horses' harnesses were of twisted withies, rods of hazel; the saddle was a piece of goatskin. It seemed an ominous sign that while most of her clansmen were riding, the Viking was walking. It was as if he were intended only to travel one way.

Torin smiled as she caught up. He was surprised to see the red-haired woman armed with a bow. "A woman going hunting?" he asked. Some of the Viking women went falconing, but he'd seldom been in the company of a woman skilled in bringing down animals. "After meeting you, my impression of Scottish women sitting docilely at their sewing has been shattered forever."

"I've been hunting since I was no higher than my step-father's knee," she answered tartly, misunderstanding his words to be criticism. She offered him a word of warning. "If I were you, Viking, I would watch that you do not become the hunted."

What a lovely sight she made, he thought. Wearing that short garment similar to a man's, her shapely, long legs were plainly visible beneath the hem of the plaid, drawing his stare again and again.

Ulva was much like a flat, terraced cone, composed of mountaintops and stark, naked volcanic rock. The ground was porous, and bracken grew rampant. Several kinds of trees grew in the alkaline soil or out of the rock. There were green, even terraces with occasional gullies. Truly a beautiful landscape, Torin thought as he walked along.

"The hunting here will be a mite different from what ye are used to," Coinneach MacQuarie declared proudly, coming up beside Torin. Was it Torin's imagination, or was he looking daggers at his niece? "Our animals include the Rhum mouse, brown rat, pygmy shrew, pipistrelle bat, gray seal, common seal, otter. Besides the red deer there are feral goats, lizards, and palmate newts. Make your choice. Ulva is a wonderland of fish and wildlife."

He explained that salmon was rare, brown and sea trout abundant, and eels common. Edible crab was fished off the rocky coasts. "Oysters are present in the Outer Hebrides, sometimes twenty horse loads of them on the sand."

"Oysters! A welcome delicacy. Perhaps we can come to an agreement. Ragnar would like to open up trade negotiations. . . ." Coinneach wasn't listening. "What is that island?" Torin asked Erica.

"Staffa." She pointed toward the hexagonal columns rising up abruptly from the sea. "MacQuarie territory, too, though no one has visited the island in a long while. It's said to be haunted."

"Staffa? I've heard of it." Torin didn't believe in ghosts.

"Surely you are not going to tell me that Ragnar's son lives there."

"Ragnar's son?" She looked at him questioningly.

"Every time I ask your uncle when I am going to meet this elusive nephew of his, he changes the subject or promises me that I will meet him tomorrow. I was just thinking that perhaps young Eric is a ghost. Is he?"

Erica wanted to tell him the truth right there and then, but as if sensing her thoughts, her uncle cast her a surly frown. Riding close to her he said, "If you tell him I will strike him down!"

A dark shroud of clouds was gathering near the coastline. Ominous. Torin wondered how long it would be before Thor, the god of thunder, threw down his lighting bolts on the sea.

"Looks as if there is going to be a storm over there," he pointed.

"I hope your ships are well anchored," Coinneach said casually. "How many ships are there? One, two, three . . . or more . . . ?"

Torin was reluctant to say, for he did not totally trust the Scots chieftain. He would let him think he had more ships than there were just for safety's sake. "I've lost count."

"Lost count, or is it that ye will not say?" Coinneach blustered, then motioned for the party to move on. "Ye had best hurry," he called over his shoulder sharply.

Walking side by side with the young red-haired woman, they came to the forest. Coinneach's huge russet wolfhounds were leading the way, hot on the scent. Their eager racket of barking echoed through the lonely forest as they sighted their prey across a large burn. Bows were raised as the clan chieftain gave the signal. A whir of arrows stung the air, bringing down a large red deer.

"He's down!" came Coinneach MacQuarie's triumphant cry, accompanied by a thunder of hooves and a splash as the hunters forded the water. Torin, however, did not follow. He'd sighted his own target, a deer larger than this one. To his surprise he saw that Erica had spotted it, too, for she managed to beat him in reacting to the prize. In a flash of red and green she ran by him.

It was a predominantly oak forest, Torin noticed. Some pine and birch. Much of the ground was high with a lot of bare rock and scrub—difficult to travel through. On such ground there was no animal better adapted than the red deer.

"You're laggin' behind. . . ." Despite the danger, she was enjoying herself and the look of surprise on the Viking's face.

"I'm not used to such rocky ground!" he shouted out. "But even so, I'll give you a contest if that's what you are after."

"I do not want ye to get lost." Her red hair blew into her eyes, giving her the appearance of a warrior woman as she ran through the trees. Torin kept his eyes upon her, wondering what she was thinking. She looked troubled, as if the weight of the world were on her shoulders.

"Is something wrong?"

Clutching her bow, Erica took off in search of the red deer that had disappeared into the forest. Her intention was to lead Torin as far away as possible from the others. Then, when all was safe, she would take him back to the stronghold. In that way she would thwart her uncle, at least for the time being.

Stealthily following the trail of the deer, she could see that the tracks led down the steep embankment. Torin followed down the narrow trail. Once again he felt the allure of being in her company. Though they didn't touch, there was an underlying current of tension.

"What a beautiful world it is. Your uncle should be proud of his land."

"He is. And determined to fend off any attackers." She was all too aware that she was devastatingly drawn to him. It was a feeling that unnerved her. She'd always had complete control over her emotions before, but now it seemed whenever he was near, her heart fluttered like a bird's wing.

That knowledge prompted her to be curt with him, to avert her eyes whenever he looked her way.

Torin was tired. Pausing by the bank of a small pool, he sat down, nodding for her to sit beside him on a large, smooth rock. "It is not my intention to lead an armed band of raiders against you. When I told you that I came in peace I told the truth. Ragnar has sent me on a quest to find Eric, though I must admit that my patience is waning."

"It's a big island. Eric has been fostered out, as is our custom. It will take some time but he will come," she said softly. She sensed his presence beside her with every fiber of her being. How could she think or breathe when he was so close to her? His very masculinity gave her cause for foreboding, particularly when she remembered the other times they'd been alone together.

"If you tell me that he is soon to come, then I will be patient, for I trust you," he said softly. In a gesture of gentleness, Torin reached out to touch her face, to brush away the red hair that tumbled into her eyes.

Trust. The word gnawed at her heart. If he knew that she had just lied, would he trust her then?

Every time Torin had asked her name, she had refused to tell him, explaining that it was against her uncle's wishes for them to become too familiar with each other, particularly since she was promised to the son of the MacKinnon. Now, however, Torin was determined to find out.

"Is it Glenna? Jeanne? Shona?" Her silence was daunting. "My name is Torin! Say it. Just once call me something other than 'Viking.' "

"That is what you are!" she exclaimed, but the words died in her throat as she heard the whir of an arrow. Reacting instinctively, she pushed the Viking aside, but not quickly enough. She screamed as she saw him fall.

TWELVE

Erica bent over the crumpled figure lying on the ground. "Viking!" His eyes were closed. He looked frighteningly still. Bending over him, she whispered a fervent prayer as she looked for any sign of a wound. Please let him be alive! Seemingly, her plea was answered, for as she put her head to his chest she could hear a heartbeat.

His breathing was even, though his face looked ashen. Though the arrow hadn't struck him, Erica realized that he had somehow struck his head on a rock when she pushed him out of the way. She gently wiped the blood away with her fingertips.

Someone is out there aiming for the Viking. Whoever it was will try again unless I get him to safety. For a long moment she stared down, mesmerized by how vulnerable he appeared. An all-consuming sense of protectiveness surged through her, an emotion she'd only felt before for Geordie. Now the urge to safeguard him, to shield him, consumed her. She knew she had to get him to one of the black crofts nearby. Somehow, despite his bulk, she did.

It was a tiny dwelling of thatched wattle and daub with a floor of beaten earth, a crofter's hut. It was a blessing now. It would keep them dry if the skies opened up and poured down rain.

The walls of the cottage were cracked in several places.

Broken pottery, pieces of wood and straw littered the earthen floor. The interior was covered with a thick coating of dust that caused Erica to cough as she pushed her way inside. As she scanned the small one-room dwelling, she caught sight of a straw mattress in the corner. Gently she placed the Viking upon it.

Gently she brushed his hair aside to examine his head. A knot the size of a goose egg. No wonder he was still deeply asleep, she thought. She'd had experience tending the wounded, and knew a cold, damp cloth would bring some relief. Tearing off a strip of her arasaid, she dipped it in a rain barrel outside the door, laid it on his forehead, and sat back to wait, all the while ignoring her own discomfort.

"There, ye will be all right." But he would not have been if the arrow had hit its mark. Loyalty to her clan warred with her feelings for the Viking. How could she warn him and still maintain her loyalty to her clan? And what of her uncle? What if she warned the Viking and, instead of running, he decided to *fight* her uncle?

Confused by her feelings, torn by her allegiances, she let her eyes move tenderly over him in a caress, lingering on the rise and fall of his chest. For just a moment she gave in to temptation and kissed his soft warm mouth. A parting kiss, she thought. A sad tribute to what might have been. *Oh, Mother, at last I understand what you really felt and why you risked so much to love your Viking.* But the longing that she felt would forever remain unfulfilled. No doubt her uncle was scouring the whole countryside for the Viking.

Suddenly he stirred, putting his hand to his temple. "Mmmmm. My head," he moaned. Instinctively he reached out, feeling disoriented, clinging to her, needing stability in a turbulent, whirling world.

The closeness of her softly curving flesh was nearly Torin's undoing. The brush of their bodies wove a cocoon of warm intimacy that he relished. The feel of her body pressed against his was pure torture that was only relieved when she pulled away.

"What a pleasant surprise . . ."

"You hit your head."

"I'd do it again and again if it meant that we would be together like this." Despite her silence, her fingers were strokes of softness as she touched him, making him feel warm and tingly inside. Pretending that he was still dizzy, he nestled closer, his face buried against her soft breasts.

"Ohhhhh."

"You hit your head on a rock."

He seemed to remember now that she had kissed him. Had she? His thoughts were hazy; his head throbbed painfully as he sat up.

They stared at each other, two silent, shadowy figures in the dimly lit hut, each achingly aware of the other. The very air pulsated with expectancy. Erica could not help but wonder what he was going to say, what he was going to do. Sitting like a stone figure, her eyes never once left him as he moved forward.

"I asked you by the lake if you would come with me when I went back to the Northland. I still want you to go." The tone of sincerity in his voice deeply touched her.

"As your concubine?"

"As my wife." He sat up, causing the mattress to sag under his muscular weight. This time when he reached out to touch her face, she didn't pull away. Slowly Torin bent his head, cherishing her lips in a kiss.

Her lips parted in an invitation for him to drink more deeply of her mouth. He did, igniting a warmth that engulfed her from head to toe. Breathlessly she returned his kisses, tingling with pleasure when he began hungrily to probe the inner warmth. Following his lead, she returned his kiss, tentatively at first, then passionately, tangling her fingers in the thick gold of his hair.

Their kiss was his undoing. All he could think about was

the pounding of his heart as he relished the warmth of her body. He had wanted her the first moment he met her. And now she was here. How could he let her go?

Capturing her slender shoulders, he pulled her up against him as his mouth moved hungrily against hers. Her head was thrown back, the masses of her fiery hair tumbling in a thick cascade over his arm, tickling his neck.

A hot ache of desire coiled within Erica. Fear warred with excitement in her veins. Fighting against her own desire was more difficult than she could ever have anticipated. How could she push him away? How could she ignore the heated insistence in her blood? There was a weakening readiness at his kiss, a longing she couldn't explain but which prompted her to push closer to him, relishing the warmth of his hands as he outlined the swell of her breasts beneath her gown. When he drew his mouth away, she tugged his head down, seeking his lips eagerly.

Erica didn't understand this all-consuming need to be near him; she only knew that he alone aroused an urgent need within her, a longing to embrace him. She craved his kisses, his touch, and wanted to be in his arms forever. Dear God, she was helpless against this powerful tide that raised gooseflesh down her arms, up her legs.

"Torin." She moaned his name into his hair as his lips left her mouth. Soft sobs of pleasure echoed through the hut's silence, and she was surprised to find that they came from her own throat. Her senses were filled with a languid heat that made her head spin. She closed her eyes, giving herself up to the dream of his nearness.

Agonizingly gently he traced a path from her jaw to her ear to the slim line of her throat. Dear God, she tasted so sweet. He was mesmerized by her, by how right it felt to hold her in his arms, his hip touching her stomach, his chest cradling the softness of her breasts. The longing to make furious love to her overpowered him. Kissing was not enough to satisfy the blazing hunger that raged through him.

She was too tempting, and the delicious fact that she was responding to him made him cast all caution aside. Compulsively his fingers savored the softness of her breasts as he bent his mouth to kiss her again, gently lowering her onto her back.

She stared up at him, watching as he studied her, and the look of desire she saw branded on his face alarmed her. Her woman's body craved the maleness of him, but her logical mind screamed at her to make him stop. She arched up against him. Through the haze of her pleasure, she felt his hands roaming more intimately and struggled to push him away. What was she doing? If she allowed his hands total freedom he would find the pendant and the Raven's Eye. If he did, if he realized who she was and said something to her uncle, then all was lost!

He shifted his position, reaching out to smooth the tangled strands of hair away from her face, then tracing her jawline again, all the way to the opening of her gown.

She jerked violently away, forcing herself to say, "Leave me be! Take your hands away," even though there was a part of her that didn't really want him to stop. "I am a Christian and you are a heathen. Did ye really think that I would want to go with ye?"

"What?" He frowned, looking down at her.

"I said get your hands off me, Viking!"

He rolled away from her, coming to his feet, standing with his legs apart, his arms crossed over his chest. His head still hurt; his breathing was deep as he struggled to get control of himself and his emotions. He swore a violent oath.

"You took a long time to tell me no, as usual." Clenching and unclenching his hands, he sought to put his thoughts in order. By Odin's chin, why was she glaring at him as if he and he alone were responsible for what happened between them? He had meant to pull away but she had clung to him.

Wordlessly they regarded each other again for a long time until Erica looked away. The pulse at the base of her throat fluttered wildly; her heart beat so frantically she thought it would burst.

"I'm to be married. To a man of the MacKinnon clan." A possibility that she regretted with all her heart.

"Married . . ." The truth stung him. "Why didn't you tell me right from the first that there was someone else?"

"Because there wasn't. Not in the way that ye mean. My uncle is marrying me to the MacKinnon lad for the sake of the clan."

"Like a sacrificial offering." He scoffed. "And you called me a heathen! Well, at least a Viking woman can choose her own husband. They aren't treated like . . . like . . ."

"Ha! Scottish women are well treated. I would not have ye think otherwise. My mother always used to say that running of the clan was always a man's affair but the running of a man was a woman's affair." She tried to smile.

"Viking women are respected. Enough so that they have to step into their husband's shoes when he is away."

"Frightening the priests in the monasteries?" She had no idea why she had said that.

"I see that your uncle has talked in your ear. But were you to know the truth, you would see that the Norsemen are not as bad as you have heard."

Nevertheless, her flashing eyes made further accusations, though a part of her wanted to tell him that she was half Viking. What would he think then? How would he react if he knew that she was the daughter of the man who had sent him to Alba?

He leaned so close that she could feel his breath stirring her hair. It thrilled her, yet frightened her too. "Come with me. Don't let your uncle marry you off to someone you do not love, for I think if given the chance you could love me."

The effect this man had over her was unnerving. She wanted to melt into his arms, give herself up to the strange feelings he inspired. Instead, she again sought haven in sharp words.

"I will not say yea to ye, Viking. Now or ever." She swallowed the lump that rose in her throat, certain it matched the one on his head for size. The truth was, she wanted to go with him. Wanted it more than anything in the world.

A muscle in his jaw ticked warningly, but she took no heed. All she knew was that she felt safer—from herself, her own emotions—when they were arguing.

"Then I shall cease asking. Even Vikings have pride."

She wanted to reach out to him, to beg him not to go away, to tell him she had wanted him, but the realization that their love was doomed kept her from speaking. How strange that this man she hardly knew could so complicate her feelings.

Without even a backward look, he kicked open the door. Realizing that she dare not leave him alone for fear of his being killed in the forest, she hurried after him.

THIRTEEN

Bell heather grew in tufts among cairns and rocks, sparkling now like jewels as the moisture from the rain caught the glow of the late-afternoon sun. Somehow the lush beauty soothed Torin's mood, and he paused to watch a plump reddish-brown grouse feed upon the leaves of the purplish-pink flowers. Though most of the low ground was covered with willow scrub, heather grew so well and so thick here that he supposed regular burning was necessary if a good crop of young heather was to be kept going for sheep and wild fowl.

"Hurry, we cannot linger here!" Erica prodded, looking behind her. So far, there was no sign that they were being followed. Still, she was anxious to get him back to the safety of her uncle's stronghold.

Before they had gone halfway, however, they were intercepted by three crofters, who recognized Torin as a Viking at a glance. Their arrows were pointed his way.

"Are ye lost, Viking?" One of the most fearsome of the crofters bared his teeth, showing his animosity.

"No! I—we . . . were out hunting." Torin took a step forward but decided against too much show of bravado.

"He looks lost to me, Ian." The second crofter quickly cut in, snickering openly. "And as helpless as a bairn. He is not armed."

"He will not get a stag with his bare hands," another taunted. The three men guffawed, but as Erica stepped forward, threatening them with her uncle's anger, they stepped back and let them pass.

"Quick, we must hurry," she cautioned again.

Though he wanted to argue, Torin matched her pace. Only when they arrived back at the gates did Erica slow her stride. "My uncle . . . he's here." She laughed softly. She had been so afraid of his following them, and yet he had arrived before her. She could see that a tally was being made of the kill: six rabbits, four red deer, a roebuck, and several birds.

"But they cannot add the Viking to their count," she thought proudly. She had saved his life. She knew it, but the Viking did not. Somehow, however, she sensed that her uncle did, for his expression was as sour as spoiled milk, despite the fact that since he had felled a buck at 170 yards he was being heartily congratulated. Bending down, he joined the others in dividing up the meat. The scent of blood drove the two russet wolfhounds into a frenzy of barking. Coinneach quieted them by throwing them the animal's entrails.

Coinneach then stood motionless, his eyes like two glowing coals as he gazed intently at Torin. The unwavering stare seemed to scorch him. "Where were ye, Viking? Dallying with my niece, I would declare."

"Nay." Erica quickly explained that he had fallen on a rock and hit his head.

"Och, ye must be careful of accidents," Coinneach said pleasantly.

"My head hurts a bit, but that is all. I have suffered far worse wounds many a time." Though she had told him she would never go off to the Northland with him, Torin still couldn't help watching her as she made her way toward the other women. "Would you ever consider changing your mind and marrying your niece off to a Viking for the sake of peace, instead of a rival clansman?" he asked.

"Marry her off to a Viking," Coinneach stated. "I would

just as soon die." He patted Torin on the back as if he had been joking.

"And what about Ragnar's son, Eric. Would you just as soon die as have him return to his father's hearth? Or will you allow him to make his own choice?" That he was losing patience was evident in Torin's tone.

"Eric?" Coinneach grinned. "Why, you will meet Eric tonight. He will be at our feast." He gestured toward the bounty of wildlife that had been taken. "Let's hope that your men are just as fortunate."

"My men?" Torin stiffened. He had been so caught up in the day's activities that he had forgotten the men who sailed on the *Sea Wolf*, but now he remembered them vividly. He hoped they had finished their hunting and were on board the ship, waiting to set sail, for he fully intended to depart for Alba once they had Eric Ragnarsson in tow.

The sound of laughter echoed through the courtyard as Erica entered through the gate. It was washing day. She had forgotten. It was a time she usually enjoyed, but today it was just another chore. Tucking her long skirts up above her knees, she stepped into the huge low tub of water to join Jeanne and Iona. Several other young Scotswomen were in other adjoining tubs, all washing the laundry by trampling on it with their bare feet. Usually the laundry was done inside the bathhouse, but since the rain had stopped and the sun was out again, they had dragged the tubs outside.

"Where have ye been, Erica?" Iona looked at Erica askance, her lips curling up in a sarcastic smile. "Or should I guess?"

Erica shook her head, averting the other young woman's eyes. "Are ye my keeper, Iona?"

Iona snorted in ire. "It seems someone should be, or ye wouldn't ever do your part."

"Erica hates women's work. Perhaps she wants to sail with the Viking."

"Perhaps your words are truer than ye know," Erica retorted peevishly. Kicking at a submerged sodden shirt, she vented her frustration.

"Then perhaps my father ought to lock ye in your chamber," Iona exclaimed.

Erica tried to maintain her calm. "I'm sure that ye would take great delight in that if he did," she answered.

Though Erica joined in to sing a rousing song, though she moved her feet and danced about just as playfully as the others, her heart was not in it now. She had to think what to do.

Her tranquil mood broken, she was silent, giving free rein to the thoughts stampeding about in her brain. She should have warned the Viking—Torin—today when she had the chance. As long as he stayed here, he was in danger. But how was she going to let him know without betraying her uncle and the others?

"Father says that he found out the Viking has only one ship," Iona said suddenly as if she had read Erica's mind.

"One ship?" Her cousin's words startled her. Erica slipped and nearly lost her balance. Only Jeanne's strong arm kept her from a bath in the warm water.

"Ye had best watch yer step, hinny!" the bold woman advised.

"I . . . I will." She concentrated on where she placed her feet, trampling the dirty garments furiously in her zest to get them clean.

"Erica! Erica, what do ye think on the matter?"

"What?" Erica looked up to see Jeanne looking at her.

"About that old woman who lives in the cottage on the hill." Her voice lowered and she crossed herself. "They say she's a witch!"

"A witch?"

"She's been seen crossing Loch Tuath in an eggshell, a

sure sign of a witch. And Jamie himself says he saw her transform herself into a hare," Iona said. She hastily made the sign of the cross with her hand.

"Foolishness." Erica didn't believe in witches, though she did believe in ghosts, elves, and water sprites.

"Perhaps she's a good witch," Jeanne relented, "but a witch just the same. Jamie says she gave him a potion to chase away his shyness." Jeanne grinned knowingly, "and believe me, it worked."

"She gave my father a potion," Iona said for all to hear.

Erica pricked up her ears, but no more was said. "A potion of poison?"

The soap from lye made with wood ash stung Erica's feet, thus she was the first from the tub. As she wrung out the garments and laid them to dry on the grass, she envisioned the Viking in her mind: the proud way he always tilted his chin, his smile, his eyes. He had a way of looking directly into another's eyes when talking, as if everything he said was the truth. Was it? And what of her uncle? Now that he had been thwarted today, would he honor his offer of hospitality, or was he determined that the Viking must die?

FOURTEEN

The leader of the Scots had gone all out to impress him, Torin thought as he looked around. Rushes and herbs—basil, chamomile, costmary, and cowslip—were freshly strewn on the floor. There was an abundance of food, including what had been killed at the hunt: wild duck and roast grouse with sprigs of heather, venison, boiled goose eggs, beet root salad, curds, wild carrots, honey cakes, and wild raspberries.

Barley broth bubbled noisily in a cauldron over the fire, its steam giving off an aroma that heightened his appetite. The smell of roasting meat permeated the air. Platters were artfully arrayed with a variety of fruits and vegetables.

A raised dais of stone ran the full length of the hall, across from the fireplace, and it was there that Coinneach Mac-Quarie sat, in a massive chair that made it very evident that he was the man who held the most importance. Torin wondered which of the young men sitting on that same dais was Coinneach's nephew and Ragnar's son. Was it the tawny-haired youth with the large overbite who seemed to be talking all the time? Torin hoped not. Or the overly tall red-haired young man with a seemingly eternal scowl? Or was it perchance the dark-haired Scot who looked upon Coinneach as if he were some sort of god? He found himself hoping that it was none of them, for not one of the three seemed of the stuff that jarls were made of.

"I think it's the frowning one," Gardar said, noticing his glance.

"You're wrong! Something deep inside me tells me that Ragnar's son isn't here at all. And if he is not, then what kind of game is our fine Scots chieftain playing?" Coinneach had insisted that tonight at supper Torin would at last know the identity of Ragnar's son.

"Maybe he doesn't trust you. Maybe he is going to put you through some kind of a test before he reveals the identity of his nephew."

"A test?"

Gardar nodded. "You must remember that Ragnar's son is not only important to us, but to the Scots as well. Unlike Vikings, those of Celtic blood put great importance on the mother's bloodline. Coinneach's people are part Pict, and theirs was a matriarchal system. Young Eric might well be in line to follow in the Scots chieftain's shoes, as well as being in line to become Ragnar's successor."

"The mother's line, you say." Torin sat pensively sipping his cup of barley brew, contemplating what Gardar had said. If he were right it would answer a few nagging questions. "Ragnar assumed that it would be easy to slip away from Alba with his son now that it is his desire, but what if Coinneach has other ideas? What if he has plans for Ragnar's son?"

He decided to put such reasoning out of his thoughts, at least for the time being, and enjoy himself. He had to admit that it promised to be a fine supper. No man or woman here would go away hungry. Unlike some areas of Alba that had been heavily hit by Viking raids, both Norse and Dane, there had been few raids here. Ragnar had tried to spare the MacQuarie's lands in most of his attacks on Ulva and Mull.

Relaxing in his chair, Torin drank and supped, but he looked at the door from time to time, hoping for sight of the red-haired young woman despite the quarrel they had at the woodland hut. At last he caught sight of her across the room, strangely isolated from the others. She looked troubled, and Torin found himself wanting to comfort her. Instead he contented himself just looking at her, wondering what she was thinking as she raised her eyes and met his stare.

Erica felt as if the weight of the world were on her shoulders. Looking at the pale-haired Viking, she could only wonder what was going to happen to him tonight. Would he be poisoned? Had her uncle been given a potion by the witch? Despite the law of hospitality, would he be stabbed in the dark of the night? Would he be drowned in the same loch where they had shared a kiss? Or worse yet, would he be imprisoned in the darkest dungeon with only the rats and the mice, never to be heard from again?

Her uncle had made his intentions very clear. He did not want the Viking or his friend, the Pict, to be reunited with the Viking crew. As to the Vikings aboard the ship, he intended to use their love of hunting to pick them off one by one while they were on land. *His* land. Then the ship would be burned and Ragnar need not know what had happened. He would undoubtedly think that the ship had been lost at sea. Or better yet, he might assume that they had been attacked by the Danes. He had laughed to think that if the Danes and Norsemen came to blows he would rid himself of two enemies at one time.

The Viking's smiling at me, little realizing that all is not as it seems, she thought. Could she sit calmly by and watch his demise? Yes, she told herself. She must! Her uncle was doing what must be done for the good of the clan.

"He's my enemy!" She wondered how many Scots this Viking had killed, maimed, or stolen from. Ten? Twenty? A hundred? Perhaps more? "But he has come in peace this time." And he had been sent by her father. . . .

The reminder of her father and her Viking heritage troubled her. Although she did not want to have divided loyalties in this situation, she could not help the sense of deep regret she felt at the thought of the Viking's demise. When he smiled across the room at her, the sadness worsened. She was waging a tug-of-war with her conscience.

Usually Erica had a hearty appetite and ate her fill at the evening meal, but tonight she wasn't hungry. She found herself meeting Torin's gaze time and time again. Stoically she appraised him. Just what kind of man was he? What thoughts whirled inside his head? What emotions were buried in his heart?

Erica tensed as she watched Geordie approach the Viking, buzzing around him like a curious bee. Strange, but her half-brother wasn't afraid of him. Instead he was asking him a dozen questions and even sharing some sort of story with him. Their laughter could be heard clear across the room. The sound softened her thoughts and her heart. When Torin bent down, however, and picked up one of the children, carrying him on his shoulders, she was totally lost.

There has to be another way to keep the clan safe besides marrying me off to a MacKinnon and harming him, she thought. Oh why couldn't men learn to live in peace?

Turning, Erica saw Iona standing behind her waiting to pounce, like a cat on a mouse. "You have eyes for the Norseman!"

"I don't!" Oh, but she did. What's more, she suddenly worried that everyone would know it. Hastily she looked away, refusing to look at Torin again. For the first time in her life she sincerely wished she could make herself invisible—flee the hall before her expressions gave her true feelings away.

"Father says I must stay away from him, that he is dangerous, but he doesn't look dangerous to me." Iona laughed. "Just virile!"

"I hadn't noticed."

Iona wasn't fooled. "Oh, I think that ye have. What is more, I think ye are wondering what it would be like to lie with him." Iona started to leave, but before she did, she taunted, "Like mother, like daughter . . ."

Leave it to Iona to know just how to goad her, Erica thought. The truth of it was, Erica *was* wondering many things that an unmarried young woman should put out of her thoughts. It was true, her woman's body craved the male-ness of him no matter how much her logical mind rejected such desires. Though she had tried to put what happened at the crofter's hut out of her thoughts, the memory and the feel of his kiss seemed to be branded on her emotions. Some-how, deep inside, she knew she had to save his life without betraying her people and leading them into danger. But how?

Focusing her attention for a moment on her uncle, she stared into his deep-blue eyes, wishing she could read his mind. Was he going to strike quickly or would he take his time deciding the fate of the Viking? Nervously she tugged at the Raven's Eye pendant, wishing that somehow the pro-tection it offered her could be transferred to the man named Torin, at least until he was out of jeopardy.

Nae. The pendant will not save him. . . . In that moment Erica realized that she, and she alone, was the Viking's only hope.

Smoke puffed up like a cloud; flames licked at the night sky, illuminating the faces of the Vikings as they sat around their fire drinking ale and tallying up the pelts in the pile beside them.

"We have killed and skinned enough animals to make our coming here profitable. Now it is time to turn our at-tention to the Scots," Bolli said, and licked the tip of his index finger, then touched the blade of his axe. "Still sharp enough to slice through a few of their hides."

"It is not time yet," Audun answered. "We have not heard from Torin."

"Bah, maybe we won't hear from him. Maybe the Scots have killed him," Halldor sputtered.

"Let's hope not or we will not find Ragnar's sons. Ragnar will be furious if we do not find them!" Bolli took a long swig of his ale.

"And Herlaug would be even more angry. We can't kill them if we don't know where they are," Halldor added.

Audun picked up a clump of dirt and threw it into the fire. "Ragnar was a fool to think they would welcome Torin into their midst like a friend."

The other eight Vikings, all loyal to Halldor, had remained silent. Now Ulf No-nose spoke up. "Torin isn't dead. He's eating and drinking his fill in the hall of the Scots without even giving a second thought to the likes of us."

Bolli grinned. "He wouldn't even know if we cut a few of the Scots' throats while we are waiting."

"He'd know!" Audun shot Bolli a murderous look. Folding his arms across his chest, Audin made himself appear formidable. "Until we know for certain that something has happened to Torin, we wait!"

With a shrug Bolli turned away, occupying himself in gathering up his furs in a pile.

"Wait? I hate waiting." Halldor rose to his feet and started to pace up and down in front of the fire.

"What's wrong with waiting?" Round-faced Gundi, the most jovial of the Vikings, asked. "It isn't so bad here. There is fresh water in the streams nearby, berries, plenty of fish, birds, and wild game. Why be in such a hurry?"

"Because we will soon run out of ale," Ulf guffawed.

"And when we do we will have to remedy that," Halldor said, staring Audin down. "The Scots undoubtedly have a plentiful supply and—"

There was a stirring in the thicket behind them. Then a rustling and a twittering. Hurriedly they reached for their swords, but it was only an animal. Nevertheless, it was decided that while the other Vikings slept, Ulf would stand watch.

FIFTEEN

The firelight illuminated the face of the MacQuarie bard as he fingered the strings of his harp. Erica listened as he sang a droning account of the MacQuarie ancestry and a lavish praise of the clan. Guarai was a second son of Kenneth MacAlpin, he recounted, one of the chiefs of Ulva. Looking at Torin from time to time to see if he was properly impressed, he told of how the MacQuaries held a place of honor as a tribe in the councils of the Lords of the Isles. He told a tale of voyages across the sea and migration to the Isles. He talked of the heroes of Caledonia, the favorite of these being Cormac, surnamed Mor, who had joined with his followers and three biorlins of sixteen oars each in the great expedition against the inhabitants of the Isles under Norse rule.

Although Erica usually enjoyed hearing the story, she didn't pay attention to it tonight. Nor did she have much interest as the Pict did his best to keep the group entertained. With a smile he showed them magic tricks that he insisted came naturally to one of his heritage. He joked about being an elf, then made the children laugh by first standing on his head, then leaping and rolling about.

Erica held her breath, certain he would fall and harm himself, but he managed it with grace. Turning somersaults and handsprings with arms and legs extended, like the turning of a wheel, he soon had a cluster of children around him, as well as those of more mature years. Even the Viking was caught up in the spell.

"Surely he is brownie or fairy folk," Jeanne giggled. Always one to have eyes for any man, she asked behind her hand if the little man would be as agile and skilled in bed.

"Fie! Ye are brazen even to ponder!" Erica heard Iona say, blushing a deep red.

Gardar tossed a few eggs up into the air—one, two, three, and four—keeping them all suspended, juggling them with such deftness that even the most sullen clansman applauded. Erica waited for the little man to drop them, but he managed to collect them all, turning them over to the cook for the evening's meal.

Despite the little Pict's antics, an atmosphere of anxiety hovered about, a tense feeling of anticipation. The second song the bard sang seemed to be equally ponderous. It was a tragic tale of the handsome lad with whom the wife of Fingal fell in love. In revenge, the song said, Fingal challenged Diarmaid to slay the wild boar that harried the neighborhood, and then to measure its carcass against the lie of its bristles with his bare feet. A bristle pierced Diarmaid's vulnerable spot on his foot, and Fingal heartlessly refused him a draught of his healing cup as Diarmaid lay dying.

Fingal? Erica remembered hearing other tales of him. Marauding Norsemen had been wary of landing their boats on Staffa because Fingal had used the island as his base in warfare against the sea raiders so long ago. One of the caves on Staffa was named for the ancient hero.

Erica quickly turned her attention back to the Viking. Would her uncle use poison? Although Erica doubted that he would use a method that so blatantly betrayed the Scots' law of hospitality, she couldn't be certain. Her uncle had once said that the Vikings were a law unto themselves and therefore excluded from the law of the Scots. Because she was unsure of what was going to happen, she kept watch from afar, taking note of what Torin ate and drank to see if others partook of it as well.

"Am I imagining it or did Hamich put something in the ale?" Not willing to take a chance, Erica moved stealthily toward the Viking before he had a chance to take a drink.

Raising his head from his full trencher, Torin sat upright in his chair, looking toward Erica again and again. He wondered why she was so tense. "Look at her, Gardar," Torin said as his friend returned to his chair. "She is as edgy as a fish out of water."

"She looks as if she knows something is about to happen." Gardar patted the dirk hidden beneath his tunic. "Whatever is wrong, she is coming our way."

Erica purposefully bumped into Torin, spilling the entire contents of his tankard as he started to take a drink. "I'm sorry," she whispered.

"I'm not." Reaching out, Torin brushed her fingers with his hand as she reached out to grab hold of the overturned mug. "I have been looking at you all night, and now you are near me. No matter what you said at the crofter's hut, I think you care about me more than you will admit."

"Nay. Ye are wrong."

"Then why do you keep looking my way?"

The aroma of fruit-decorated *bannocks* wafted in the air as they were passed right under their noses, but Erica waved them away. No one else was eating any, and that made her suspicious.

"Aren't you hungry?" Torin's tone was teasing as he smiled at her, but he declined one also. Now that she was here, he was too preoccupied to think of food. She was so lovely tonight in the candlelight. He wanted to touch her again as he had in the crofter's hut. Instead, she was the one who touched him as she picked up the corner of the tablecloth and dabbed at the spilled ale on his tunic.

Erica stared into the deep-blue eyes that regarded her so intently, wishing she could read his mind. He'd said there was a special magic between them and he was right. So very, very right. Even now she felt it—a potent current that hovered in the very air when she was near him. She knew she couldn't bear to see him killed.

Iona is right, she thought. *I'm drawn to him like a wanderer to the North Star.* She admired his strength, his courage, and the loyalty it took to put his life in danger for the sake of a promise and a vow. More than that, however, was the gentleness he had displayed toward Geordie and the other children. Surprising for a Norseman. Would he be as gentle with a woman or would he be a rough and uncouth lover?

Ye will not find out, she scolded herself silently. Quickly she shook her head to clear such thoughts away. If he was fortunate enough to escape, he would sail away and she would never see him again. It was just as well.

The room became silent as Coinneach MacQuarie stood up. "Time for the dancing." His eyes touched on Erica as if to censor her proximity to Torin, and she felt his annoyance as if it were tangible. His expression gave her a warning to keep silent. Erica nodded that she understood.

The empty goblets, tankards, and platters were cleared away on the far side of the room. Benches were pushed back, the trestle tables folded and placed against the wall. Erica started to move away, but Torin grabbed her hand and held it firmly. Now that she was here, he wasn't going to let her get away.

Erica felt lightheaded. Though she knew it was just in her imagination, she could feel the heat of his gaze. It was as if he were making love to her with his eyes. She shivered, then felt strangely warm all over as she looked into his eyes.

He leaned closer. "I wish we were alone," he whispered.

Erica didn't answer, but in her heart she was glad there were people around. There was safety in numbers. She felt certain that as long as there were people in the hall the Viking was safe. Her uncle Coinneach would not have him stabbed or strong-armed in front of a large group of people. Once the others left, however, the Viking would be vulnerable. She had to warn him.

Suddenly the pipes began their keening. The dancing had started. First the men danced alone, a rousing dance of high-kicking feet. Then the women joined in, choosing partners for a spirited reel. The hall soon hummed with the drone of skirling pipes and the thumping feet of the dancers. Torin's blood surged wildly in his veins, his heart seemed to beat in rhythm with the steps of the dance. He had always told himself that women were as plentiful as waves in the sea. But that was before he met *her*.

"Why won't you tell me your name?" he said, moving closer so that she could hear him above the din of the music.

"It's not important. . . ." Erica stiffened as she felt the heat of her uncle's eyes. Quickly she yanked her hand from his grasp. Turning, she noted that Coinneach was frowning at her. Seeing Iona prattling in his ear, she could imagine why. Leave it to her cousin to get her into trouble. "Listen to me, ye must leave," she whispered.

"Leave?" He looked deep into her eyes, trying to fathom why she was so breathless.

"I cannot explain, but ye must trust me."

He was confused. "Leave the hall, leave the castle, leave Alba . . . ?"

"Leave Alba," she explained.

He looked at her as if she had suddenly lost her mind. "I can't leave. I must wait until I meet with Ragnar's son. It is my sworn duty to . . ."

"Fie! Ye will not speak with him!" There, she had said it.

Torin was jolted by what she said and the way she had said it. As if she was positive. "What are you telling me?"

"That you will not find him." Oh, why did he have to be so difficult. Why didn't he just do what she told him to do before it was too late?

"Why?"

"He doesn't exist," she answered, knowing she had said too much.

Torin didn't understand what she meant. "Is he dead?" If he had died, then why hadn't Coinneach told him?

Erica paled. She had to be careful. "I cannot tell ye more. All I can do is to tell ye to leave as soon as ye can. Get out of here. Run. Run as far as ye can and never look back."

He forced her to look at him. "What are you trying to tell me?"

"That we are in some kind of danger here," Gardar answered for her.

Torin looked around the hall. Was it his imagination or was there a sense of macabre expectation in the room, at least from those around Coinneach? "So much for hospitality," he grumbled.

"There are too many for us to fight," Gardar rasped. "We will have to use our heads."

Torin cursed himself for a fool. "I should have known. I should have sensed that something was wrong when Coinneach did not take us to Ragnar's son right away." Looking back at Erica he asked, "What is going on?"

Torin didn't suspect the truth, but Gardar did. "I think Ragnar misjudged the gender of his child," he blurted. "And I think you should look critically at the woman you are so besotted with. If you look closely at her you will see what I mean."

"What?"

Gardar was exasperated. "Look at her!"

Torin did look, but it took a long time for him to come to grips with the truth. There were certain things about the red-haired beauty—the profile, the eyes, the shape of her mouth—that branded her as Ragnar's offspring. Why hadn't he realized it? How could he have been either so blind or such a fool?

"*You*. You're Ragnar's daughter." Torin's voice was raspy

and sounded strange even to his own ears, yet he struggled to keep his composure.

Erica's eyes shown with pride. She wasn't going to lie. "I am."

Torin's gaze was unfaltering as he stared at Erica, seeing her through different eyes. Now he knew why she had looked so familiar right from the first. He had seen the resemblance, but he had refused to believe his eyes.

Taking on an attitude of deference, forcing himself to forget that he found her alluring and that he had lusted after her, he sought to fulfill his mission. "Your father sent me to find his son, Eric. The son he had with Flora, nic Dugald. He made no mention of also having a daughter."

"He didn't know. He left Alba and my mother before I was born."

Torin jumped to the conclusion that Ragnar must have had two offspring by the Scottish woman. A son *and* a daughter. Ragnar had been emphatic about his son and his plans for him.

His eyes were drawn to the lovely flame-haired young woman. "My ship is waiting to take both you and your brother to Hafrsfjord. Ragnar's son is in line to be his successor when the time comes." He looked toward Geordie. "Will you come with me?"

"Nae!" Fear for Geordie surged through her. She had to make the Viking understand. "Geordie is not who ye seek! The laddie is full-blooded Scots. Sired by a kinsman of my mother. A cousin. He was handfasted to her a year after your Viking chieftain, my father, sailed away."

The full realization of what had happened hit Torin full force. There was no son of Ragnar's loins in Alba. Perhaps Ragnar's wish for a son had caused him to assume it. "There is no son!"

A tidal wave of silence consumed them. For the first time in his life, Torin did not know what to say. It couldn't be.

"Your name . . . *Erica*. . . . No coincidence. . . ."

"Nae!"

Ragnar had a daughter and not a son. There was no Eric, but there was *Erica*. He didn't believe it. Loki the god of mischief was playing some sort of cruel joke.

The flames engulfing the huge logs in the hearth sputtered and sparked in time to the music. Although the music and dancers were lively, however, it seemed to Torin as if they moved in slow motion. And all the while one thought kept whirling about in Torin's mind: The woman that he lusted after was Ragnar's daughter.

A yearning surged through him. He wanted her so much! If only they could go away together, give free expression to the passion that sparked between them, he knew they could be happy. But that was a madman's wish. If Ragnar didn't have his head, then her uncle would stir up a hornet's nest. Impossible dream—that's what loving her would be.

"Gardar and I must do as you said and go!" It was a perfect time to leave. Everyone was either exhausted from dancing or in their cups from drinking too much ale. Even Coinneach looked more than a bit tipsy.

"I'll guide ye!" Erica didn't want to take a chance that the Viking might get lost in the maze of corridors and become trapped.

Although Torin wanted to say no, he knew he needed Erica's help. "Only to the outer gate, then Gardar and I will have to fend for ourselves."

Erica searched the room with her eyes and sensed that now was the time to make a move. Her uncle had joined in the dancing and was preoccupied.

Gardar had a plan. He would pretend to pass out cold, and Torin would sling him over his shoulder and act as if he were taking him somewhere to sleep it off. Erica was to meet them at the bathhouse.

More than one unwary guard received a painful crack to

the head as Torin frantically sought to maintain his freedom.
Slowly but surely, he and Gardar worked their way to the
bathhouse. Joining Erica, they moved stealthily across the
inner bailey, hiding in the shadows. At last they reached the
outer door and pulled it open. Torin clasped Erica's hand so
tightly that she winced.

"I'll remember what you did for us. I'll never forget
you!"

Torin felt a shiver convulse her slim frame and wrapped
his arms around her, shielding her from the cool air with
his cloak. An unpremeditated act, but one that most defi-
nitely felt right. She belonged in his arms.

"Erica. . . ." Torin's mouth hovered only inches from her
own. Giving in to his longing, he moved swiftly to claim
her lips before she could turn away.

She was not prepared to feel the jolt of sweet, honeyed
fire that swept through her at the touch of his lips, but when
it came she welcomed it as if she had been waiting for this
kiss all her life. Gone was any anger she had felt. Giddily
conscious of the warmth emanating from him, she reached
up and drew him closer. Stunned and shaken by the potent
reaction to each other, they clung together in the shadows
until Gardar's indignant snort reminded them of the danger.

"Odin's breath, Torin, have you taken leave of your
senses? The Scots will be down upon our heads at any moment, and you take time for a kiss!"

Erica knew the little man was right. Quickly she broke
away from their embrace. "Ye must hurry. My uncle is no
fool. He will have started to search for ye the moment ye
left the hall."

The creak of the door was a welcome sound as Gardar
opened it wider, though Torin watched it with anxiety. What
would be Erica's punishment for aiding him? he wondered,
knowing any similar betrayal of Ragnar would not be taken
lightly.

"Come with me," he said softly.

Erica felt as if she were in the midst of a dream. She had wanted to go to the land of the Norsemen to be reunited with her father for as long as she could remember. Before she could answer, however, the dream turned into a nightmare as four of her kinsmen stepped out of the shadows. With loud grunts they grabbed Torin and Gardar and pinned their arms behind their backs. Giving Erica a shove, one of them commanded, "Take them away!"

SIXTEEN

The musty stench of the dungeon hit Torin full force as he was shoved down inside. "So much for the law of hospitality," he muttered, his eyes darting back and forth for any means of escape. There was none. Worse yet, he and Gardar had been separated and put in different dungeons, which made him feel utterly alone. "At least you haven't killed me," he said to the man guarding him.

"Not yet!" Dangling the keys in front of Torin's nose, he dared him to reach for them, but Torin was much too smart to play that kind of game.

It was a tiny, cramped cell, more cellar than prison, with a stone-and-iron barred trapdoor that was locked from above. Torin was familiar with the dungeon, for it was similar to some he'd seen in other parts of Alba and Eire. There was no way of escape; of that he was certain. Even if he could crawl up the wall, there was no way he could remove the stone from the hole. He was completely at Coinneach MacQuarie's mercy.

"My father and uncle were killed by Vikings." Calling down to him, the guard's voice was ominous. "Ye cannot know how it irked me and the others to see ye come sweeping into our hall after all the years ye have robbed us and carried off our women."

"I came in peace."

"Ye do not know the meaning of the word!"

"Nor do you, or so it seems!" Torin could see that it was useless to argue or to tell the Scotsman that there came a time when all men wanted to settle down and put the wrongs of the past behind them. Instead, he hunkered down, listening to the rattle of the keys and the heavy tread of footsteps as the appointed guard kept watch.

Torin seemed to lose track of time as he languished in the cell-like room. It was dismal, uncomfortable, and humiliating. It was a disgusting hellhole. The walls of dirt were infested with all kinds of vermin: spiders, worms, and bugs of unknown origin. He thanked Odin for his cloak, for it was long and thick enough to serve as a warm blanket to shield him from the damp cold.

It was dark in the tiny dungeon. Only the glow of torchlight from above cast a faint flicker of light through the iron grate, illuminating the dismal prison. Torin huddled in the folds of his cloak, trying to fend off the chill.

"Gardar! Gardar, can you hear me?" Was it his imagination, or did he hear a muffled string of curses in answer? "What kind of men are these Scots? And to think that they call *us* heathens!"

Rising from the ground, Torin paced back and forth across the cubicle's hard earthen floor, feeling like a trapped rodent. He had to get out! If he or Gardar didn't return to the ship, Audun, Halldor, Bolli, and the others would know something was wrong. They would come to find him, and when they did they would bring death and destruction in their wake. He had to do something to divert the disaster that he knew was going to ensue.

Gripping the dirt walls, forcing a foothold, he tried to climb up the side of the hole he'd been flung into, only to slide back down each time he was within an arm's length of the top. His only reward was blistered and bleeding fingers.

Taking off his leather belt, he tried another approach, looping it through the bars of the iron grating. Again he failed, watching in abject frustration as the belt missed its mark again and again. It was as if the walls were closing in on him. Never had Torin felt so totally powerless.

"Like being gelded," he swore aloud. "Coinneach knows well the way to torture a man." What was happening up there? "Erica!" Above all, he wanted to make certain that she was safe.

Erica was roughly ushered inside the great hall and pushed into a heap before her uncle's large carved chair. Rising from the floor, she brushed at her gown and ran her fingers through her hair. No matter what happened, she was determined to keep her dignity.

"I had hoped that Iona was wrong, but ye proved her right." With an outraged oath Coinneach vented his anger, overturning a chair. "Ye seem to have a fondness for our enemies, so much so that ye boldly crossed me, girl."

"I didn't want ye to kill him!"

"And do ye not think that he would kill under like circumstances?"

Erica thought hard on the matter. "All I can say is that I think he is a man of his word."

"Bah!" Coinneach's face reddened and his cheeks puffed out with indignity. "All Vikings are rogues at heart, sailing up and down the coasts as they please, taking anything they want without a care for the consequences." He stamped his foot. "Well, this Viking will not have ye. He will not! Ye will stay here where ye belong, not go traipsing off with the likes of him."

Waiting until he had finished his tirade, she said, "Not even if it would bring about peace?"

Coinneach was adamant. "Not even then."

Erica knew that there was no use in arguing, at least not at the moment. She would have to handle things another way. Still, she had to ask, "What are you going to do with him?"

"Keep him locked up until he is an old man."

Relief surged through her. He hadn't said that he was going to kill him. As long as Torin was alive there was hope.

"If ye try to interfere again it will go hard on him, do ye understand? I will seek punishment on *him.*"

Erica paled. "I understand!"

"That means if ye go to see him, talk to him, or if ye even so much as sneeze, I will. . . ." He made a slicing gesture at his throat.

Erica knew her uncle well enough to know that he would carry out his threat if he felt that she had betrayed him. And yet, she couldn't let Torin rot away in the dungeons. It was cold, damp, and depressing. Few men condemned to be locked up there had stayed alive long. Most had died of lung fever from the dampness; a few had lost their minds; one had killed himself. She couldn't let that happen to Torin.

Something or someone was watching them from the undergrowth. "There is danger in being here," Halldor said to Bolli. "How else can you explain that we have lost three men?"

"Not lost." Bolli shook his head. "They must have run off into the woods and gotten turned around, or maybe they are on the trail of one of the animals we saw earlier. What do we care. It makes fewer men to share in our bounty."

"And fewer men for fighting if the time comes." Halldor shook his head. "I do not like it. Worse yet, we have had no word from Torin, or even Gardar. They too have disappeared. They might even be dead."

"Never! Torin isn't dead!" Ingemund was perhaps the staunchest ally of Torin. "He'll come. He said he would and he always keeps his word."

"I say he is dead, which is what all of us will be if we don't go back to the ship and sail away."

"Sail away. You mean run with our tails between our legs because a few men have deserted us?" Audun sensed he was losing control and tried to say something that would help him regain it. "I say we wait." He was certain that Torin was at this very moment searching for them with equal fervor.

"Sail away!" Bolli proclaimed.

"Wait," Audun insisted. It looked as if a full-blown fight might ensue. At last, however, it was decided that they would wait two days, and that if at the end of that time Torin had not joined them, then they would sail back to Norway.

SEVENTEEN

Erica sat on the edge of her bed staring at the floor. The very thought of Torin's predicament sent a chill up her spine. Would her uncle show at least a shred of mercy, or would Torin be left in that torturous hole to starve, die, and then rot?

She shuddered at the thought. "How can he talk about the cruelty of the Norsemen and still show such savagery himself?"

And yet there was nothing she could do about it. She couldn't protect him, for if she tried and her uncle found out, he might carry out his threat and kill Torin in retaliation for her disobedience.

Erica braced her legs against the cold wooden floor. If only she could see him just for a moment, so that she could make certain that he was not suffering too much down in that horrid, rat-infested hole. Just an instant . . .

Closing her eyes, she was tortured by the image that danced before her; of Torin so thin that she could see his bones. He looked up at her and the look of agony on his face caused her to cry out. Touching her fingers to her face, she felt moisture and knew that she was crying. Crying for him. Crying for herself. Crying for what might have been, had things been different.

"Erica?" Geordie's voice startled her, even though it was little more than a whisper. "What's wrong, hinny?"

"They have thrown the Viking laddie in that hellhole." She gasped the story between sobs. "I—I—didn't want to see him killed."

"But ye went against Uncle Coinneach for the sake of an enemy," Geordie scolded gently. "Oh, how could ye have done it?"

"I had to do what I thought was right." Anger chased her sorrow away. "He came in peace. He didn't come here to raid us. He came to find someone. He came here to find me!" It was the truth, in a manner of speaking. "He was offered hospitality and then vilely betrayed."

"Uncle Coinneach did what he thought was best." Geordie was anxious to uphold his uncle's actions, yet at the same time, his expression showed how he was also wrestling with the affection and admiration he felt for his sister.

"Uncle Coinneach can be a stubborn old goat," Erica rasped, dashing her tears away.

Geordie giggled. "He can be that, all right."

"But I didn't realize how unmerciful he could be." Erica continued the story, telling Geordie how she had been forbidden even to set eyes on the Viking lest there be consequences. "So, I will not even know if he is suffering." Putting her hands up to her face, she started to cry again.

Moved by her tears, Geordie scurried to her bed, hugging his sister tightly. "Hush, now! Dry your tears. It will be all right."

"Not if they . . . they kill him. I will not be able to forgive Uncle Coinneach."

He gently patted her on the back, just as she did to him when he was upset and she wanted to quiet him. "Ye'll forgive him and carry on with your life and soon forget."

She shook her head. "Nae. I'll never forgive or forget because . . ."

The truth came to Geordie in a flash. "Because ye care about him. Deeply. Just like Mother cared about her Viking."

Although Erica staunchly denied having any tender feelings for Torin, though she tried to convince Geordie that she was merely being stoic about the matter, it did little good. Geordie knew her much too well.

"Ye do. Ye cannot pretend otherwise."

Loosening his hold on his sister, Geordie plopped back on the pillows, crossing his arms behind his head as he gave the matter considerable thought.

"It won't do to fuss. Uncle Coinneach will be expecting that. He will only stand his ground all the more firmly. Ye know how he can be. He'll lock ye in your room and ye'll be the one to suffer nearly as much as the Viking."

"I know." She dabbed at her eyes with the back of her hand. "All I want to do is make certain that he is being fed and tended to. I couldn't wish more than that."

"That is all?"

Erica knew her little brother was weakening. "Geordie . . . hinny . . . ye could do it for me. Ye could look in on him from time to time and—"

"Nae!" He sat up. "I cannot turn against my own." And yet he could not stand by and watch Erica feel such pain.

"I wouldn't ask ye to turn against Uncle Coinneach or the others. Only to take Torin a bit of food and clean water now and again." When he didn't answer, she turned and looked him in the eye. "Please, Geordie!"

He grinned. "Torin, is it? I see ye are on familiar terms with the man." He shrugged. "I cannot lie. There is something about your Torin that made me like him, too."

Erica blinked through her tears. "Then ye will help me to help him?"

He folded his arms across his chest. "I might, and then again I might not. What will ye give me if I say yes?"

Erica knew that he was teasing her. "I'll give ye my fine

comb." She ruffled his hair. "It looks to me as if ye could use one now and again."

He stuck out his lower lip. "I do not want yer comb. I wouldn't use it anyway."

"My hand-carved tankard with the boar's head?"

Geordie shook his head. "Nae." She started to speak, but he held up his hand. "I will not take anything. I'll look to your Viking because of the love that I feel for ye, and because of the love ye have always shown me!" Taking the edge of the coverlet, he dried his sister's tears. "And somehow I'll find a way to persuade Uncle to change his mind about the Viking."

It was dark. Dark and silent. Depressing. The gloominess enveloped Torin in spirit as well as in body. He worried for his sanity. Would he lose his mind? Or his life? "I've been thrust in here without a measure of decency. To suffer and . . ." To die? No, Torin couldn't believe that it was the end for him. Or at least, he didn't want to believe, and yet . . .

What day was it? Time moved so slowly in the darkness that he had seemed to loose all track of it. Calculating in his mind from the time he and Gardar had first been incarcerated, he estimated that nearly two days had gone by. It must be night again. His stomach rumbling its hunger seemed to affirm that conclusion, and he wondered how long he could go without food.

Something tickled his ear and he hastily brushed it away. A spider? He hoped it wasn't a poisonous one, but perhaps it was better not to know. Odin's teeth! How he hated the chilling darkness! It was nearly enough to drive a man mad—that and the foul-smelling moisture that wafted in the air. His nostrils flared as he tried to accustom himself to the stench of the dungeons. The stench of death and decay.

He could hear the faint trickle of water. There was water

nearby, but not a drop for him. Licking his lips, he was determined not to think about his hunger or his thirst.

"I'll get out of here somehow . . . some way. Audun and Halldor . . ." Would do what? Torin's distrust of the two men twisted in his stomach, making him ill. Would they even try and rescue him if they knew where he was? Or would they take advantage of his misfortune for their own betterment?

Torin was frustrated. More than that, however, he hated the feeling that he had lost control of his destiny. He loathed being at the mercy of someone else. But then, wasn't that the very idea? Well, he wouldn't give the stubborn Scot that satisfaction. Somehow, he would get free.

Suddenly he stiffened. A soft noise disturbed his solitude. The faint moan of faraway bagpipes cut through the stillness. Bagpipes! Torin held his breath, atuning his ears to the wail.

"Gardar! Gardar, can you hear me?"

A muffled voice called back to him through the thick wall of dirt.

"What are the pipes for? What do they mean?"

He thought he could hear Gardar say something about celebrating. Were the Scots celebrating? He supposed the answer was yes, and cursed when he determined that the cause of celebration had something to do with him and his imprisonment.

Gripping the dirt walls once again, forcing a foothold, he tried for the hundredth time to climb up the side of the dungeon, only to slide back down each time he was within an arm's length of the top. Still, he wasn't yet ready to declare his actions an impossibility, and he said so to himself out loud. His words seemed to be punctuated by a noise above him.

A sound! What was it? Torin looked up, expecting to see the familiar ugly face of the abusive guard, but saw instead another face looking down at him. One without even the first sign of a beard. It was a boy.

He yelled at the top of his lungs, "Get me out of here!"

"Shhhhhhh! We do not want to stir up an alarm. At least not yet." The boy grinned. "I've come at the plea of Erica to help ye."

"Help me? Get free?" His heart took flight.

"Nae, I couldn't go against my uncle, but I can give ye food and something to quench your thirst."

It was enough for the moment. "Then I will express my gratitude with words now, and with actions if I am fortunate to be freed soon."

"I promised my sister that I would talk with my uncle about securing your release." As he spoke, Geordie lowered a tankard of ale tied to a long length of rope down through the opening in the grate, and followed it with a few scraps of venison tied up in a leather pouch.

Torin watched as Geordie carefully guided the precious cargo, hoping with all his heart that they would not spill. They did not. A bladder filled with water was next.

"Erica . . . how is she?" Torin wanted to ask more questions, but he was ravenous. He stuffed the venison into his mouth, swallowing it with little chewing. Reaching for the pig's bladder, he washed the meat down with water. Next, he was treated to a sack filled with berries, which he devoured nearly as quickly as the venison. He decided to save the ale for that time when he wanted to blur his senses.

"Erica would have come herself, but she has been given an ultimatum. If she comes near ye it will cause yer doom."

"My doom?"

Geordie recounted all that he had heard. "If she tries to help ye in any way, my uncle has threatened to kill ye."

"So she sent you." Torin was warmed by the thought that she had not forgotten him.

"Aye, that she did. I came because I never could abide her tears and . . . and because I do not think ye are bad, laddie— for a Viking that is." There was a pause before Geordie added. "I do not think ye are like the ones I saw in the forest."

"The ones you saw in the forest?" Torin stopped eating.

"The ones that were stalking our animals and skinning them. Erica saw them too. The big, hairy, ugly ones."

"My men." Torin was relieved. At least Audun and the others were still there. They hadn't attacked the Scots or sailed away. Even so, he knew that could all change in a heartbeat. Particularly when he heard Geordie's next words.

"Uncle Coinneach is going to get rid of them."

"Get rid of them?" If he did, Torin felt certain that he would be doomed, for then he would be totally at the mercy of the Scots.

Realizing that he had said too much, Geordie pulled away from the grate.

"Boy . . . come back!" There was a long moment of silence, but then his face suddenly returned to the grate, peering down at Torin. "Coinneach—is he going to attack my men?"

Although Geordie didn't deny or affirm the question, Torin's deduction was that Coinneach was going to corner them into battle soon. What then? Though he was angered at the Scots, he didn't want to see it come to that.

"Boy, do you think you could find them in the woods again? Do you think you could give them a message for me? A message to sail down the coast and wait for me there until I can get free?"

Geordie was adamant. "Nae! I will not betray my kin, nor talk with Vikings. Unlike my sister, I am not in love with ye." Without another word he scurried away, leaving Torin alone but at least well fed.

The boy's words rang in Torin's ears. *"Unlike my sister I am not in love with ye,"* he had said. *"Love."* The word echoed over and over again in Torin's brain, and despite the fact that he was imprisoned, he smiled.

EIGHTEEN

Storm clouds and sunlight competed over the green valley. Opening the shutter of her small bedchamber window, Erica peered out through the slits, gazing at the sky. Another day, seemingly no different from any other. Except that, while she was fortunate to move about freely in the light, Torin was condemned to languish in the darkness. Was it any wonder that she hadn't slept a wink last night? She'd tossed and turned tormented by what was happening to him.

"Uncle Coinneach! How can ye be so stubborn, unrelenting, and cruel?" In anger she stripped off her sleeping tunic and, after getting dressed, flung it across the room. A comb and the pillow followed.

"Fie, sister, ye would have the room in a shambles." Geordie's voice was teasing as he breezed into the room. "Mother always did say ye had more than a wee bit of temper."

Seeing her younger brother, Erica's bad mood softened. "In this case it is justified."

Geordie bent to the task of picking up Erica's things. When he was finished he looked up at her. "I think perhaps your mood will lighten when I tell ye that your Viking is alive. I gave him food and drink just like ye asked me to."

"Ye saw him." Erica felt relief sweep over her. Torin was alive, and thanks to Geordie he had eaten.

"I fed him last night and this morning. He asked me to give the little Pict he was with half of his share."

"Was he . . . was he . . . ?"

"He's strong." Geordie's admiration glowed in his eyes. "And he's canny. He'll survive."

"Did anyone see ye?"

"Nae. Ye know how I can make myself invisible when I want to." Geordie waved his hand up and down. "Just like the Pict who came with the Viking. It's the Pictish blood in me, too, I suppose. That's why the Vikings didn't see me."

"Vikings?"

Geordie realized that he had said too much. He shrugged. "Don't worry. They didn't even know that I was watching them." He wrinkled his nose. "Ye were right. They are big and they are hairy!"

"And dangerous!" All of Erica's protective instincts were on alert. Grabbing Geordie by the shoulders, she looked him in the eye. "I don't want ye to ever go near them again."

"But Erica . . ." He looked down at his shoes. "I'm not a bairn anymore."

Oh, but he *was*. It would be some time yet before he would even be able to grow a beard. He was in that in-between stage. A boy growing into a man. "Geordie . . ."

He knew what she was going to say. "I'm a man. I can take care of myself."

"Nae. Ye are no match for them. The Vikings are a hand-ful, even for our fiercest fighting men." She was adamant. If anything happened to Geordie, she couldn't bear it. "Promise me ye will not take such a risk again."

"But Erica . . . Uncle Coinneach wanted . . ." Besides, he had to know what the Vikings were planning. Thoughts of becoming a hero and proving his manhood once and for all danced in his brain. Besides, it was interesting and ex-citing watching them from the security of the bushes. It was like viewing another world.

"I don't care what Uncle Coinneach wants. Promise me!"

Hoping to avoid making such a promise, Geordie walked to the window. Looking at the crags and hills, he tried to change the direction of their conversation to other things. "Uncle Coinneach says I can have a real sword now."

"Ach, did he?"

"He said that since he has no sons that I am in line to be tanist."

Once again the sting of being passed over because she had been born female pricked her pride. "So he's bribing ye now, is that it?"

"I cannot be bribed. First and foremost my loyalty is always to you," he answered.

He was of a mind to prove it, and found himself standing before his uncle later in the day to plead for the Viking.

"I want to talk with ye, Uncle Coinneach," he announced, not even masking his nervousness. Something about Coinneach always made him feel as if he were somehow growing smaller.

"Oh?" Sitting in his favorite chair, his feet perched on the table, Coinneach didn't even bother to look up. "And just what is it ye want to say, laddie?"

Geordie blurted it out. "Ye cannot do this, Uncle Coinneach. Ye cannot keep the Viking locked up!"

"Arghhh!" Bounding to his feet, Coinneach looked like an angry bear. "I can and I will, and no half-grown pup is going to tell me nae."

"But he didn't do us any harm. He came in peace—and—and he's brave—and—and I—I—like him."

The dark eyes beneath Coinneach's thick brows were slits of anger. "Your sister put ye up to this!"

Geordie fiercely shook his head, but his uncle was not fooled.

"She did. Because he is in her heart."

Geordie repeated, "I like him."

"Do ye like the man so much that ye want to see your sister go sailing off with him? Are ye prepared to cut her out of your life and never see her again because she is one of them? Or do ye want to see her pine away for love of a man who gets her with child, then leaves her without even a blink of the eye?" Coinneach looked Geordie in the eye. "What I do, I do for the love that I bear your sister. I'm protecting her from herself. If that means that the Norseman has to be sacrificed, well . . . so be it."

A tight knot formed in Geordie's stomach. He knew he had lost the argument. He didn't want Erica to leave Alba, nor did he want her to pine away as his mother had. But did the Viking really have to die in order to protect his sister? There were times when right must overpower wrong no matter what the price. True, Coinneach was the chieftain and his uncle, to whom he had sworn loyalty, but kin or not, he was grievously unjust in what he was doing.

Leaving the room, he took the stairs two at a time. It would be a traitorous act to follow the urging of his conscience, he thought. Even so, he knew there was no other choice. He didn't want to see the Viking suffer an agonizing, demeaning death. It would break his sister's heart.

"Perhaps there is another way. . . ."

The Vikings had chosen to make camp on the bank of a small stream so that there would be water to drink and where they might have the good fortune of spearing a fish or two. Boasting that he could catch enough to feed them all, Halldor had taken on fishing as his duty. Bolli busied himself collecting firewood, Einar searching for edible berries or roots.

It was foggy. The haze blocked out the sun. There was hardly any light between the branches of the thick trees although it was still early afternoon. Dense and seemingly impenetrable forest wilderness met Audun and the other Vikings in all directions—except in the direction of the ocean.

"I say we either attack the Scots now or turn around and go home," Halldor grumbled.

"And tell Herlaug what?" Audun asked with derision in his tone.

"To jump into the ocean," Bolli cut in. "If he wanted to capture Ragnar's sons he should have come himself."

"Ja! Never send a fool on a fool's errand," Einar replied, belying his usually meek manner. He nodded in Bolli's direction.

"Who are you calling a fool?" Baring his teeth, Bolli picked up his axe.

"You, that is who! Wasn't it you who wanted to disobey Torin's orders and go ashore?"

"Maybe it was and maybe it wasn't. But what if it was?" Bolli lunged in Einar's direction.

"Enough!" Striking out with his sword, Audun knocked the axe from Bolli's hand. "Leave it be. I will not have you fight amongst yourselves." Angrily he looked first at Einar then at Bolli, as if he blamed them both.

Retrieving his axe from the ground, Bolli hacked at the thick foliage that rose up to block his path. "How could you expect that we would not quarrel? Torin said to wait, but he has not come back. Does he expect us to wait for him forever?"

"Something must have happened. Not even Gardar has sought us out. That can only mean one thing!"

"Torin is dead!"

It didn't take long for that idea to catch on. Soon it was the consensus that Torin had either betrayed them and joined up with the Scots, or been killed and taken to Valhalla by the Valkyries, the warrior maidens who attended Odin, ruler of the gods.

"And we will soon be dead, too, or disappear in the night

like the others if we do not go back!" Einar was not afraid to speak his mind even if it did anger Bolli.

"Go back and let the Scots call us weak behind our backs?" Bolli spat on the ground to prove the very idea was distasteful. "No. I say we attack as fiercely as Arm, the hound of Hell, and not only kill the Scots but scatter their bones."

"Attack? Don't be a fool. We are outnumbered." Audun tapped at his forehead with his finger. "For once use your head, Bolli."

"Stay."

"Attack."

"Go back."

The Vikings grumbled among themselves, their voices growing louder and louder until it sounded like thunder. Cautiously coming closer, Geordie winced at the violence of their anger. He had come to spy on them again to make certain of their whereabouts. Before he released Erica's Viking from the dungeon, he had to make certain that Torin would have transport home. Now he knew it was much more than just a mission to save his sister from heartache. Hearing these heathens quarrel, he knew it was imperative that they leave Alba's shores before their brutality touched the people he loved.

"Perhaps Uncle Coinneach is right. Perhaps they should all be destroyed."

The very thought was numbing, yet remembering his sister, he knew that at least one Viking must be spared. As for the others, he had no compunction about seeing to their demise as quickly as possible. Perhaps then the Viking would stay in Alba and live happily ever after with his sister.

I will not let him take her back to the Northland. Not now. Not ever! She and the Viking could be happy together if given half a chance, Georgie thought. And surely Torin would get used to living in Alba.

Stealthily Geordie moved closer. The Vikings' harsh, guttural voices battered his ears as they argued. When Torin spoke the language it sounded pleasant, but their voices were as ugly as they were, he thought. He wrinkled his nose in disgust.

Their strange words were difficult for Geordie to understand, but one thing was certain: Torin's name was spoken over and over again. Clearly he was an integral part of what they had planned.

"I wish I could just make them disappear," he murmured. But how could he thwart them? He couldn't fight them single-handedly. Or could he? Closing his eyes, Geordie gave in to a daydream wherein he slew the terrible Vikings one by one. He would be a hero! There would be feasting in his honor; the bards would write stories about his valor; there would be . . .

"What . . . ?" Audun thought he heard a sound. He signaled for the others to be quiet.

Geordie froze. He had been careless. Stepping backward, he had bumped into a bush, frightening a nesting bird. Squawking and scolding, the bird flapped its wings.

Quickly the Vikings reached for their swords, but Audun laughed. "Are you so fierce that you need to make war on the birds?"

"Are you so certain that it is a bird?" Halldor was more cautious. "It wasn't a bird that stole some of our men away," he said, gripping his weapon tightly and moving in the direction of the sound. "Someone is there."

"It's a bird!" Audun scoffed.

"We'll soon see!"

They had seen him! Geordie panicked. Darting out of the bushes, he ran as fast as he could.

"Get him!" Halldor watched as the tall, thin figure seemed to skim over the ground; then he gave chase.

Geordie ran so fast that his feet hardly seemed to touch the earth, floating on the salty breeze of the sea. Breathing heavily, Halldor and the others followed, though at a slower pace. Weaving in and out of the trees, circling around, pushing through the undergrowth, they tried their best to keep up.

"We have to catch him! He was spying on us."

It was more easily said than done. Geordie led them on a frantic chase, then disappeared into the trees. "Ha! Clumsy Norse, they are no match for a Scots—" He cursed as his shin hit a fallen log and he went flying. Hitting the ground with a thud, he was winded and helplessly immobile for just a moment, but long enough for the Vikings to catch up with him.

"We've got him!" Bolli whooped with glee. "But what are we going to do with him?" He grabbed Geordie by his hair.

"Kill him!" Halldor said with a shrug. "Isn't that what we should do with all Scots?"

Bolli lifted his axe.

Hurriedly crossing himself, Geordie prepared to meet his death. He closed his eyes, hoping that it would be quick. The blow never came. Looking up, he saw that one of the Vikings had grabbed his assailant's wrist.

"Kill, kill, kill. Is that all you know?" Audun tried to control his anger. "Dead he is of no use to us. Alive he may be valuable."

Bolli put his face to within an inch of Geordie's, nearly suffocating him with his foul breath. "How? He's much too skinny to be of any use if you ask me."

"I didn't ask you."

Geordie gasped, trying to catch his breath as another quarrel broke out. He tried to tell himself that everything was going to be all right, but the strange look in the Vikings' eyes gave him an ominous feeling. In that moment he knew that his life may have been saved, but that these ugly Norsemen were not going to let him go.

NINETEEN

Oh, how she hated women's work, Erica thought as she worked diligently at the loom, a simple rectangular frame made of wood. Today it seemed even more of a drudgery. She swore beneath her breath as she looked down and realized that she had made a mistake. The last three rows would have to be redone. It was difficult to concentrate on weaving when her thoughts were on Torin.

She couldn't help worrying about him! He filled her thoughts by day and her dreams by night, haunting her like a ghost. Was it damp down in that horrible hole of a dungeon? Would he take a chill? And Geordie—was he taking Torin enough food to feed two?

Smiling, she remembered that Geordie had told her that Torin had shared his meager fare with his friend, the Pict. "Say what ye might about Vikings, he's a generous man."

And handsome. And brave!

"What did ye say, Erica?"

Looking up, Erica saw her cousin staring at her from across the room. She flushed as she realized she had spoken aloud. "I said, say what ye might about weaving, it's necessary to do it again and again, if it's any of your business, Iona, dear." She couldn't hide the anger in her voice. It would be a long while before she forgave Iona her part in Torin's misfortune.

Torin. She'd never realized how quickly a man could invade one's heart, nor that she could be so miserable not seeing him. Over and over again she conjured him up, reliving that last moment when he had kissed her and thanked her for giving him warning and helping him escape. But his gratitude had come much too quickly. Now, as he languished down below, did he understand why she had not come to see him? Had Geordie explained?

"Erica! Be careful. You're tangling the threads." Iona's whining voice sounded a warning.

"I know. I can see that with my own eyes," Erica said peevishly. Plucking at the wool, she hastily rectified the situation, untwisting the thread, then passing it more cautiously back and forth, interlacing the weft through the warp threads with her shuttle. "There. It will not happen again!"

"I wouldn't be so sure." Iona's smug expression irritated Erica to the core. Worse yet, it was true. When it came to weaving, Erica was often all thumbs.

Erica focused her attention on the loom, watching as the other women rolled up an end of the finished cloth to make way for a new length of weaving. They unwound the spindle and measured off the vertical threads in roughly equal lengths. The threads would be the warp of the extended length of cloth. Setting the loom upright again, tilted against the wall, they let the warp threads go taut, hanging down vertically across the wooden frame.

"No doubt ye are all thumbs thinking about your upcoming wedding with the MacKinnon laddie," Iona said with mock sweetness.

"There will be no wedding!" Erica said between gritted teeth. At least not if she could help it. She had heard that Malcolm MacKinnon had a foul temper, and that he was knock-kneed and overly fond of his whiskey.

"That's not what I heard. My father said that we still need an alliance and that even though the MacLeods are so concerned with the threat of the Vikings that they have laid low, they could still sweep over the hill at any moment."

Erica turned her head. "If ye are so worried about an alliance, why don't ye marry the MacKinnon yourself, cousin, dear. As I recall, if it had not been for your whining, ye were first in line."

"And as I recall, my father has made ye promise to behave or else he might remember how angry he is at ye." Iona knew she had struck a nerve.

For a long time Erica sat looking at her hands; then, determined not to let her cousin bother her, she set her mind to the task at hand. She would weave a perfect row if it killed her!

"Where's Geordie?" Jeanne's sudden question disturbed Erica's concentration, causing her to tangle the threads again.

"Aye. Where is he?" Iona looked at Jeanne and winked, giving evidence of a conspiracy.

Erica wondered if Geordie was down in the dungeons giving Torin his breakfast. Yes, that was where he was. Ignoring the question, she was silent as she pretended to have an unwavering interest in the *maide dalbh,* the pattern sticks that served as a guide for the weaving.

Iona asked again. "Where is Geordie?"

Erica shrugged. "He must be with the other men, which is where he should be."

Iona looked toward the door as if expecting him to be there, then at Erica. "I agree that's where he should be, but usually he's hovering about ye as if ye shared some kind of secret."

Erica dropped her spindle, then quickly picked it up. Did Iona suspect something, or was she just chattering? "There is no secret. My little laddie is quickly becoming a man and his life is changing to reflect it."

"He is, but that doesn't seem to keep him from clinging

to your skirts," Iona said. "Or conspiring with ye for some misdeed or other."

Erica grew tense. What was Iona talking about. Did she know about Geordie's trips to the dungeons? "What do ye mean?"

Iona lowered her voice as if she didn't want the other women in the room to hear. "My cousin had the gall to tell Father that he should free the Viking. Now who do ye think put him up to that?" She grinned maliciously.

All eyes turned toward Erica, accusingly, waiting for her to deny Iona's allegation. She did not. How could she?

"The Viking's been wronged. I will not say differently. Geordie thinks so, too. There is no wrong in saying what ye think. Nor in asking for mercy."

"Mercy for a Viking?" Jeanne clenched her hands into fists. "Did they show mercy when they killed my husband?"

"Or my son?" Jeanne demanded. "An eye for an eye and a tooth for a tooth, or so it is said."

Erica's nerves were on edge. Iona had accomplished what she had set out to do—cause trouble. "That is the old way of thinkin', or so I've been told," she blurted. "It would seem to me that if we followed such a path it wouldn't take long until we were all blind and gumming our food." Rising from the chair, Erica set down her spindle and walked away.

"No doubt she's anxious to leave," she heard Iona say. "It must make her feel guilty siding with the enemy. But then, perhaps she cannot help it, seeing as how her own blood is tainted."

The barb hit home as intended. Now more than at any other time in her life, Erica needed to be alone. Not because of what Iona had said, but because there were thoughts and emotions surging through her and she needed to sort them out. She wanted to be away from the stifling air and the walls surrounding her.

Making her way across the room, she stepped out into the fresh air, feeling soothed by the soft breeze that caressed her face ever so gently. Standing stock-still as if in the midst of a trance, she let the gentle wind blow her long tresses about her shoulders. Even from here she could hear the chirping of the birds, and for a moment she contented herself with listening to the sound. In that moment she longed for Torin to be by her side, sharing the music of the birds with her.

I've been a coward. So afraid of my uncle's wrath that I have done nothing to save him. That was soon going to change. Though Erica knew that she risked severe punishment for her actions, she made her way to the staircase. If she couldn't be happy with Torin, at least she could have peace of mind knowing that he was safe and back in his homeland where he belonged.

How was she going to free him without being seen? And if she did, how was she going to make certain he got away without being followed? And what about the other Vikings? Could she be certain that they were still waiting for him? It didn't matter. Somehow he would find a way if only he had the chance.

Hearing the chattering of several women, she quickly put her musings aside and ducked deeper into the shadows. Waiting until the way was clear, she entered the nearby storeroom to obtain a small digging tool and a rope ladder before heading toward the dungeons.

It was deathly quiet in the tiny dungeon—so quiet that Torin could hear his stomach growl. Where was Erica's brother? Why hadn't he come? Sagging to the ground, he grasped his knees, hugging them with his arms. For the first time in his life, Torin felt a total sense of devastation, a longing for what might have been.

Staring into the gloom surrounding him, he watched his thoughts run in futile circles. He had met a woman he could love, only to lose her. Now, here he was, imprisoned in a hole in the ground without any hope of escape. And there was no way of changing his ill fortune. Odin and all the other gods had seemingly deserted him.

Ragnar's daughter. Whoever would have guessed?

Drawing his legs tightly to his chest, resting his head on his knees, Torin allowed his thoughts to linger on the flame-haired young woman who had come into his world by a strange turn of fate. She had intrigued him. Not just her beauty but her daring, her grace, her intellect.

"Erica . . ." Her eyes haunted him, her voice seemed to whisper in his ear.

"Torin!" It *was* Erica's voice; he had not imagined it.

"Erica, it is you." Somehow, deep in his heart he had felt that she would not let him down.

"Shhhhhhh! There are still two guards in the passageway. They could come in at any time."

"Can you get the key?"

"Nae. I think my uncle has it with him. I fear I'm going to have to dig ye out, loosen the dirt around the grate." The staccato noise above his head told Torin that Erica was doing just that. Soon a circle of light appeared above his head as the grate was opened. He stood up, reaching up as if to caress the face he saw hovering above his head.

"Erica!" He blinked against the bright light.

Lowering a rope ladder, she stretched out her fingers and brushed his with the poignancy of a kiss. "I'm sorry that I didn't come sooner. Will ye forgive me?"

"What is there to forgive? You are here now!" His eyes met hers in a tender caress. Then Torin put aside his feelings and concentrated on getting out of the hole.

Winding her arms around his neck, Erica welcomed him to freedom, then she kissed him, much too quickly, but with such a tender show of emotion that he was deeply touched. "We have to hurry," she said against his mouth.

"Gardar. I can't go and leave him behind!"

"I didn't think that ye could." Picking up the rope ladder

and digging tool, Erica and Torin hastened to Gardar's cell nearby. Tugging at the grate, then lowering the ladder, they had soon freed him from his prison.

"Hurry," Torin said, patting his friend on the back.

They slipped into a dark corridor, fearful of lighting even a tiny candle. Torin stumbled along, blindly following, trusting. When they came to a bell tower, Erica drew aside a wood panel to reveal a cavernous opening.

"My secret. Mine and Geordie's. It was through this panel that my father came to my mother." Her expression grew melancholy. "And left her for the final time."

"I would never leave you." Torin felt the need to tell her that. "Come with me!" He gathered her into his arms and felt a shiver convulse her slim frame. She belonged in his embrace.

A yearning surged through her. She wanted to be with him, wanted it more than anything else in the world, but she could never leave Geordie. "I can't."

"Then this will be good. . . ."

His mouth muffled any other words. Erica felt a jolt of sweet, honeyed fire sweep through her at the touch of his lips. It made parting all the more difficult. Giddily, conscious of the warmth emanating from him, she reached up and drew him closer, savoring their gentle embrace. They clung together in the shadows for a long, aching moment. She let the darkness of the dungeons hide her tears. Burying her face against his shoulder, she nuzzled against him as she said a last good-bye. Then they parted. Erica watched as the shadowy figures of Torin and Gardar disappeared.

TWENTY

He missed her! He hadn't even gone a quarter of a mile, and yet Torin was thinking of her, remembering the fragrance of her hair, the softness of her lips, and the warmth of her body next to his. He had been a fool to give her up so easily. Now he was having second thoughts about leaving her behind.

"What's the matter? Why are you moving so slowly?" Gardar motioned to Torin to quicken his pace. "It's more dangerous making an escape in the light of the day. The lookouts might see us. We have to hurry."

Torin paused and looked over his shoulder, squinting his eyes as he tried to catch sight of Erica's retreating form. "The Scots won't be expecting us to walk out of the dungeon right under their very noses in broad daylight."

Gardar quickly noted the direction of Torin's intent gaze. "But they will find out that we are gone and give chase. We want to be halfway to Norway by then." With a grunt he poked Torin in the ribs.

Torin walked faster, then paused to look back one last time. "Do you think they will suspect her of being the one to free us?

Gardar was noncommittal. "Maybe yes. Maybe no. Come on!"

Torin had a gut feeling that they would know immediately. Coinneach MacQuarie was no fool. He would sense that Erica was involved in his prisoners' disappearance. Who else would free them? "They'll know." What then? What reprisals would there be? What would happen to her? What would be the penalty for going against her kinsmen?

"So-o-o-o-o, they will know. We're free. That's all that matters now." He nudged Torin in the ribs again to get him moving.

Torin kept to the shadows, darting in and out among the trees as he followed after Gardar, but as he ran he could not force Erica from his thoughts. He could envision her now, her dark-red hair flying around her shoulders like a shawl of living flame. She was beautiful and she was proud. But how proud would she be when she was punished?

He imagined her being surrounded by a throng of Highland warriors, heard her cry out as she was humiliated, dragged to the dungeons by her hair, then pushed down into the same dungeon that she had freed him from. It was a daydream that left him shaken to the core and sick to his stomach.

They wouldn't! Or would they? What did he know about the Scots? "Wait!" Torin stopped in his tracks.

Gardar was exasperated. "Wait? Are you crazed? We must keep moving."

Torin pushed Gardar along the path. "You go on. Tell Audun and the others to get ready to sail."

Gardar didn't even ask why there was a change in plans. He knew. "You're going back for her."

"I am!" Torin knew he had no other choice. He just could not leave her. Despite the circumstances, he smiled as the idea flitted before his eyes of throwing her over his shoulder and sweeping her from her uncle's hall. What would the MacQuaries think of that? It would surely be the subject of the bards for quite a while.

"Torin . . ." Gardar sighed. He knew there was no use in arguing the matter.

"I'll meet you at the ship."

"If you have not lost your head, you mean."

"I'm not afraid!"

"Then I will be afraid for you." Gardar made one last plea. "Go about Ragnar's errand and then come back for her. If she cares for you she'll be waiting."

"You don't understand." How could he? How could he feel what Torin was feeling? For so long he had been an outcast because of what his father had done. He had felt that he needed to prove himself, but with her he had felt as if he knew where he belonged. He belonged with her. "Even if I have to carry her off, I won't leave Alba without her."

"Argh! Men think they rule the world, but they are wrong. It is women!" Mumbling beneath his breath that it served Torin right if he ended right back in the dungeon, Gardar took his leave.

Erica's heart was heavy as she opened the door. She had stood atop the hill, watching protectively to make certain that Torin and Gardar had not been pursued.

"He's safe. No one followed . . ." He was gone. And already she missed him. More so than she had ever thought it possible to miss another human being.

She felt more alone than ever. Life could be unfair, fate a bitter draught. Something had been missing from her life until she had looked into Torin's eyes, until he had kissed her. Now whatever might have been would never be.

"Torin . . ." The sound of his name on her tongue brought an agonizing torment. She would never see him again. He would sail to his own homeland and never think about her, while she would be haunted by his presence in her heart forever.

"There ye are!" Iona's high-pitched voice was like a slap in the face, startling her from her thoughts. "Is Geordie with ye?"

"Geordie?" Erica shook her head fiercely. When it was found out that she had freed the two Vikings, she didn't want her brother involved in any way. "I have not seen him all morning!"

"Neither has anyone else." Despite her usual smugness, Iona seemed to be sincerely worried. "Usually he is such a little pest! But though we have looked for him, it's as if he has disappeared."

"Uncle. . . ?"

"Has not seen him either. Nor has any of the men."

"Geordie!" Some inner instinct, a touch of the fey, perhaps, told Erica that something was amiss. It wasn't like Geordie to wander off. Hurriedly she rushed off to search for him, but though she looked everywhere, Geordie could not be found.

Erica knew a moment of blind panic as she remembered her conversation with her brother earlier in the day, when he had innocently revealed to her that he had been watching the Vikings from the bushes. She had made him promise never to go near them again, but had he kept that promise? The fear that he had not gnawed at her heart.

Geordie found himself looking into the piercing blue eyes of more than fifty men. He was surrounded. Worse yet, he was on the Vikings' ship. There could be only one reason for that. They were going to sell him as a slave!

"No-o-o-o-o-o-o-o!" The ear-shattering scream tore from his throat as he realized what was going to happen.

Reason fled his mind as he fought wildly against the two Vikings who held his wrists. Pulling free, he made his way to the ship's stern. Looking down at the foaming waters, he closed his eyes, preparing to jump. He wouldn't stay among these warlike, ruthless heathens one moment longer.

"Get him!" Halldor's strong arms reached out just in time to keep Geordie from a watery grave. The force of his pursuit sent Geordie sprawling to the wooden deck of the ship.

"Let me go! Let me go!" he cried, forgetting for the moment that most Vikings did not understand Gaelic. But he understood them! His mother had taught both her children the strange Norse tongue.

"Shall we kill him?" Bolli as always was anxious to shed blood. "Herlaug said that we could—"

"No! We need him."

Needed him? For what? Geordie wondered, quieting as he realized that his life wasn't in danger, at least for the moment.

"Ragnar wishes to have his son. . . ."

The ugliest of the Vikings pushed forward. "That's Ragnar's son? He looks too puny." A cacophony of arguing broke out as each of the Vikings seemed to want to have his say.

"Silence!" The Viking who acted as if he were the leader held up his hand. "He is Ragnar's son if we say he is!"

"Ragnar's son?" Geordie gasped.

Audun grinned. "For once, Halldor and I are in agreement." His eyes met those of one of the other Vikings and he winked. Then he forced his expression to be more somber. "Torin is dead. The Scots killed him."

There was another outburst as some of the Vikings shouted out their anger at the news. Threats of vengeance against the Scots horrified Geordie, but the Viking leader soon quieted them again.

"Torin is dead, but not before he led us to young Eric." He winked at the other Viking again.

"But I'm not . . ." Geordie started to blurt the truth, then thought better of it. Those two Vikings knew perfectly well that he wasn't really Ragnar's son, but it didn't matter to them. Why? Because they were going to pretend. *And as long as I play along with the game I will stay alive!* The truth was chilling, yet it gave Geordie hope. Somehow Erica would find out what had happened to him. She would free Torin and they would come to rescue him.

TWENTY-ONE

Erica paced the hall, hoping with all her heart that she was wrong about Geordie. She wanted to believe that he had listened to her warning and stayed far away from the Vikings, but despite her search for him he remained unaccounted for, and thus she had begun to fear that her instincts were right.

"Iona, sound the alarm. Tell everyone ye see that my brother is missing."

"Missing or hiding?" Iona put her hands on her hips and her voice took on a tone of scolding. "Ye have spoiled the boy, Erica. He is willful."

"He is spirited and has a mind of his own; that is all." Erica was quick to defend her brother as usual. Besides, Geordie and she were kindred spirits.

"Spoiled. Spirited. One and the same. I can tell ye that if he is hiding for whatever reason, I will see that he gets a beating for causing us to fear for him. I will!"

"Geordie is too old to play childish games. Something has happened." When Iona hesitated, Erica shouted, "Go!"

Erica ran toward the woods, to the spot where Geordie had told her he had spied upon the Vikings. Cupping her hands around her mouth, she cried out his name again and again, but her voice was lost in the wind and thus there was no answer.

"He couldn't have just disappeared unless . . ."

She gasped as she saw a bright piece of red hanging from a branch. Hurrying to the spot, she tugged at it out of the tree and examined it. It was a piece of red cloth with thin crisscrossed stripes of green and black running through it. Erica recognized the imperfect plaid. She had woven it. It was Geordie's breacan.

"No!" There was a sign of a struggle and a torn piece of leather on the ground a short distance from the tree. For a moment Erica feared the worst. What if Geordie had been caught spying on the Vikings? What if they had killed him in anger? What if . . . ?

Taking a deep breath, she forced herself to calm down. There wasn't any blood, or anything to make her think that a murder had been committed. She had to keep calm and think things out. Assuming the worst would do no good at all. She must take things one at a time. First, she had to find out if the Viking ship was still in the cove or if it had sailed. What she did next would depend on that.

Arming herself with a sword, Erica chose a pathway through the forest that was rarely used. Climbing in an area of steep banks and rough stones, she steadily made her way up the face of the rock and through the trees, heading in the direction of the ocean.

It was a grueling climb that yielded her nothing. Worse yet, it was dangerous. A storm was brewing. The wind tore at her face and blew strands of her hair into her eyes. Looking down she winced as she saw that the cliff upon which she was perched dropped away to the sea. The ocean pounded, frothing and foaming. One false step and she would fall to her death. Even so, she had chanced it, hoping beyond hope that from this vantage point she might see something, anything, that would help her find Geordie.

Shielding her eyes from the sun with her hand, Erica looked out at the ocean, feeling a fist clutch at her heart as she at last spied the Vikings' vessel. On the slow surge of the ocean it dipped and pitched as seagulls circled and screamed from above.

"The ship!"

Feeling a sense of helplessness, Erica watched it sail away from the shore. Was Geordie aboard? She clutched at the sword in desperation. She might never know.

"I'm too late . . ." What was she going to do now? Who would help her? Surely not her uncle Coinneach. When he found out that his two prisoners were gone, he would be furious, and that anger would surpass his fear for Geordie. He would punish her, possibly imprison her, and then she would never be able to help her brother. She was on her own.

"Geordie!" Hastily she crossed herself; then she moved cautiously across the ledge, moving with the wind so that it helped, not hindered her.

At the foot of the cliff, the path veered away from the rocks, twisting into the forest. Pausing, Erica took a long, hard look at the terrain below, hoping beyond hope that she had been wrong and that she would see her younger brother walking up the hill. Though she did not see Geordie, she saw another familiar form that made her heart skip a beat.

"Torin!" He had not gone toward the ocean; he was coming back toward the glen. "Torin!"

Engrossed in staring at him from afar, she lost her footing, sending a rock down the face of the cliff and into the sea. Letting out a shriek, she clutched at a tree for dear life.

Torin heard a scream and looked up. A woman was in trouble. Hurriedly he ran in the direction of the sound. As he came closer he could clearly see long, red hair whipping in the breeze as a young woman struggled to keep her balance on the ledge.

"Erica!" Climbing up the steep face of the rocky hill, he ignored the danger to himself and thought only of saving her.

* * *

The wind was cold. Geordie sat curled up on a thick pile of furs near the sternpost and watched as the ship swayed up and down. Trembling, he pulled one of the furs up to his chin, using it to shield him from the wind.

What is going to become of me? Whatever the Vikings planned it boded no good. Geordie knew that his only hope was to enlist the help of those Vikings who were against the three ugly ones. Perhaps if he used his wits and if he didn't act too hastily, he could play upon the ill will between the Vikings. Then they might help him.

He could hear the rhythmic thrashing of the long oars as they swept through the water. The Vikings were intoning some old melodic chant, perhaps to one of their pagan gods. Their song brought Geordie a sense of melancholy, for it was just another reminder of how different they were from the Scots.

Geordie reached up and brushed a strand of hair from his eyes. It was sticky from the sea spray, a strong reminder that this was not a nightmare but reality. When he awakened tomorrow he would find himself still on the ship, among the very men who were his clan's enemies.

"Oh . . . Erica . . ." Rising to his feet, he walked to the side of the ship and looked toward the shoreline. His eyes were drawn to a small, dark-haired man who was running along the shoreline as if trying to catch up with the ship. Geordie recognized him in an instant. It was the short Pict who had accompanied Torin on his journey.

Seeing Gardar gave Geordie a faint flicker of hope. He had to let someone know what had happened to him, for only then could he be rescued.

His breacan had been ripped apart in his struggle with the Vikings. Now Geordie purposefully tore a piece of cloth from that garment and used it like a flag to signal the dark-haired little man.

* * *

Erica was certain that she was going to fall to her death. Looking down, she could see that the drop to the ground below might very well either kill her or break her bones. If that happened, what would happen to her brother?

"I will not fall!" Stubbornness had always been her downfall, yet she used it now as she fought to regain her footing on the ledge. "I can do it!" She was agile and strong. Years of climbing trees as a girl would be a godsend.

"Erica!"

The sound of Torin's voice was the catalyst that prodded her to survive. Although for a moment she was certain that she was going to tumble to her death, she somehow managed to grasp his outstretched hand and put both feet securely on the ledge.

"Don't look down!" Torin disobeyed his own advice and nearly fell himself. There was a loud splash as his foot dislodged a loose rock. Though he had meant to be the rescuer, he ended up being rescued.

"It's all right. I have ye!" Erica tugged at his belt, holding him until he too had regained his footing.

Torin moved toward her, pulling her against him. His mouth came down on hers, engulfing Erica in all the familiar sensations his lips always brought forth. Pressing her body closer to his, she sought the safety and the passion of his embrace. For just a moment, she felt warm, safe, and loved. But the moment couldn't last.

"My brother is missing. We cannot find him anywhere," she said, wrapping her arms around his neck and pressing against him. "I fear that he is on the ship sailing out to sea." She looked in that direction.

"The ship . . . ?" Torin stared at the ship upon the horizon and swore beneath his breath. "Damn Audun. I told him to wait for me." He was angered to think that he had been disobeyed. But the anger turned to surprise as he realized what Erica was saying. "You think Geordie is on that ship?"

"I do." As quickly as she could, she told him about Geordie's spying. "I found evidence of a struggle. And . . . and I have a feeling in my heart that he was abducted. It wouldn't be the first time."

"Then it seems the only thing we can do is to follow." But how could they? Ships did not just appear out of thin air. "It is much too far to swim. We would never catch up.'

"I know where there is a boat! Much smaller than your Viking ship, but a boat nonetheless. Come." She took him by the hand.

Erica and Torin ran for what seemed an eternity. Reaching the ocean, she led him up the rocky beach to a spot that was secluded. There, hidden in a thicket of trees, was a small vessel that Erica called a *curach,* a boat constructed with a wicker frame and covered with hides.

It was much smaller than Torin had anticipated, but still it was all that they had. Taking her hand he helped her into the boat, then took his place at the helm. "There's going to be a storm. We must hurry and catch up with them before the waves get too dangerous."

Erica felt in her heart that everything was going to be all right. They would catch up to Torin's ship, he would take his place at the helm, and that would be the end of that. Geordie would be safe. The Viking would have saved him. How, then, could her uncle Coinneach do anything other than put aside his anger.

As the familiar shores of Ulva fell away, however, Erica's optimism gave way to an unnerving sense of wariness. Since childhood she'd heard tales of sea people: water horses and water bulls that enticed unwary travelers. *Nuckelavee. Glastig.* Were these creatures even now lying in wait to snatch the boat as it bounced on the waves in pursuit of the Viking ship? Scolding herself for having such pagan thoughts, Erica hastily crossed herself.

"Are you afraid?"

"No," she lied, though the truth of her fear was in her eyes.

She looked over her shoulder from time to time, watching the waves warily for any sign of such a beastie. And yet she could not turn back. Not until she knew whether Geordie was on the Viking ship. As the boat skimmed the rough waves, she fought her inner turmoil and bolstered her courage.

Up and down, back and forth, the boat rocked unendingly. Erica and Torin traveled over the ocean until a dusting of powdery stars dotted the sky, fading into clouds of mist above the horizon. At last she had to admit that it was not as easy to catch up with the Viking ship as she had supposed.

"We've lost them!"

"No!" Erica wouldn't accept defeat. Taking the oars herself, she rowed frantically, stopping only when her arms ached so badly that she could not move them. Tears filled her eyes, but Torin reached out and brushed them away.

"All is not lost. Geordie will be safe, at least for a while." Torin looked for the familiar constellations to get his bearings. "I think that they believe he is you."

"Me?"

Torin damned Audun for his greed. Instead of obeying orders, he had been only too ready to make the most of his chance encounter with Erica's brother. "When they came upon Geordie, they must have jumped to the conclusion that he is Ragnar's son."

"And so they are taking him to my father!"

"Yes." Torin wasn't really certain that it was as simple a matter as that, but there was nothing they could do at the moment. "Remember, I was sent on a peaceful mission to bring Ragnar's son back to him," he said.

"But what will happen when they find out that he isn't Ragnar's son?" She shivered at the thought.

"Perhaps they will bring him back." His voice held more confidence than he felt, but above all he didn't want her to worry. It was something that went far beyond her control, or even his.

Torin suspected that when Audun discovered his mistake, when Geordie lost any usefulness for them, they would sell him as a slave, but he would save her the heartache of telling her that.

"What if they don't?"

Torin cupped her face with his hands. "I promise you that we will get him back." It was a promise he hoped that he could keep. "There is a Norse colony in the Hebrides. We'll sail there and get a ship and a crew and go after Geordie."

Torin's words calmed Erica's fears. Pulling the oars into the boat, she nestled into his embrace and contented herself with counting stars, thankful that the wind had died down. It was so peaceful.

Introducing Ballad,
A LINE OF HISTORICAL ROMANCES

*A*s a lover of historical romance, you'll adore Ballad Romances. Written by today's most popular romance authors, every book in the Ballad line is not only an individual story, but part of a two to six book series as well. You can look forward to 4 new titles each month – each taking place at a different time and place in history.

But don't take our word for how wonderful these stories are! Accept our introductory shipment of 4 Ballad Romance novels – a $23.96 value – ABSOLUTELY FREE – and see for yourself!

*O*nce you've experienced your first 4 Ballad Romances, we're sure you'll want to continue receiving these wonderful historical romance novels each month – without ever having to leave your home – using our convenient and inexpensive home subscription service. Here's what you get for joining:

- *4 BRAND NEW Ballad Romances delivered to your door each month*
- *30% off the cover price with your home subscription.*
- *A FREE monthly newsletter filled with author interviews, book previews, special offers, and more!*
- *No risk or obligation...you're free to cancel whenever you wish... no questions asked.*

*T*o start your membership, simply complete and return the card provided. You'll receive your Introductory Shipment of 4 FREE Ballad Romances. Then, each month, as long as your account is in good standing, you will receive the 4 newest Ballad Romances. Each shipment will be yours to examine for 10 days. If you decide to keep the books, you'll pay the preferred home subscriber's price – a savings of 30% off the cover price! (plus shipping & handling) If you want us to stop sending books, just say the word...it's that simple.

**Passion–
Adventure–
Excitement–
Romance–
Ballad!**

Get 4 Ballad Historical Romance Novels FREE! ❖

$12.50 value — **FREE!** No obligation to buy anything — ever.

4 FREE BOOKS are waiting for you! Just mail in the certificate below!

BOOK CERTIFICATE

Yes! Please send me 4 Ballad Romances ABSOLUTELY FREE! After my introductory shipment, I will receive 4 new Ballad Romances each month to preview FREE for 10 days (as long as my account is in good standing). If I decide to keep the books, I will pay the money-saving preferred publisher's price plus shipping and handling. That's 30% off the cover price. I may return the shipment within 10 days and owe nothing, and I may cancel my subscription at any time. The 4 FREE books will be mine to keep in any case.

Name _____

Address _____ Apt. _____

City _____ State _____ Zip _____

Telephone (___) _____

Signature _____

(If under 18, parent or guardian must sign)

All orders subject to approval by Zebra Home Subscription Service.
Terms and prices subject to change. Offer valid only in the U.S.

DN022A

If the certificate is missing below, write to:

**Ballad Romances,
c/o Zebra Home
Subscription Service Inc.**

P.O. Box 5214,
Clifton, New Jersey
07015-5214

OR call TOLL FREE
1-800-770-1963

Passion...
Adventure...
Excitement...
Romance...

PLACE
STAMP
HERE

ll..I..l.llll....l.ll.l.l.I.l.l..lll.l.I.I..l..lll..l

BALLAD ROMANCES
Zebra Home Subscription Service, Inc.
P.O. Box 5214
Clifton NJ 07015-5214

TWENTY-TWO

Darkness brought a cold, heavy, mist but Erica and Torin did not care. Locked in each other's arms beneath Torin's heavy cloak, basking in the warmth of each other's bodies, they did not even notice the slight chill of the night.

"When I saw you on the ledge, you will never know how lost and helpless I felt," he whispered, tightening his fingers around her shoulders as if to reassure himself she was really there. "If I hadn't realized it before, I realized then how much you mean to me."

"When you left, I saw my life stretching out before me, a lonely existence without you." She closed her eyes to the pain that memory evoked.

"I couldn't leave without you. I had to come back. I would have taken you with me even if I had to carry you off."

She couldn't help but smile at the thought. "Ye really would have carried me off?"

His eyes turned from bright blue to a darker, smokier hue, mirroring his desire. Erica's heart hammered at the glitter of desire she saw. "Can you doubt it?" He tickled her ear with his tongue, sending shivers of fire up her spine. Reaching out, she clung to him as his lips nuzzled against the side of her throat.

"How can a fighting man be so tender?" The roaring of

her blood was deafening in her ears. There was no ignoring the flicker of arousal that spread to the core of her body.

"Because you inspire me."

"Do I, now . . . ?" Twining her hands around his neck, she clutched him to her, pressing her body eagerly against his chest. She could feel the heat and power and growing desire of him with every breath. Slowly, leisurely, she reached out to touch him, admiring his strength.

He uttered a moan as her hands moved over the smoothly corded muscles of his shoulders. Burying his face in the silky strands of her hair, he breathed in the fragrant scent and was lost to any other thought.

"Torin . . ." Closing her eyes, Erica awaited his kiss, her mouth opening to him like the soft petals of a flower as he caressed her lips with all the passionate hunger they both yearned for. Erica loved the taste of him, the tender urgency of his mouth. Her lips opened to him for a seemingly endless passionate onslaught of kisses. It was as if they were breathing one breath, living at that moment just for each other.

Desire that had been coiling within Erica for so long only to be unfulfilled, sparked to renewed fire. She could feel his passion likewise building, searing her with its heat. They shared a joy of touching and caressing, arms against arms, legs touching legs, fingers entwining and exploring.

Mutual hunger brought their lips back together time after time. She craved his kisses and returned them with trembling pleasure, exploring the inner softness of his mouth. The wickerwork and leather of the boat was hard against her back, yet at the moment she hardly noticed. All she was aware of was his tall, muscled length straining against her.

"Erica . . . !" Desire writhed almost painfully within his loins. He had never wanted anything or anyone as much as he did her at this moment. It was like an unfulfilled dream just waiting to come true.

Pushing her *tonnag* aside, Torin's palm, firm and warm, slipped down the front of her gown, cupping the full curve of her breast. Lightly he stroked until the peaks sprang to life under his touch, the once soft flesh now taunt and aching. Then his hands were at her shoulders, tugging at the gown until her breasts were bare.

His breath caught in his throat as his blue eyes savored her. "Beautiful!"

And indeed she was, he thought, pausing to feast his eyes on the lush contours of her breasts. Between her breasts was a silver figure of a raven with a large garnet eye. That huge eye seemed suddenly to be staring at him as if chastising him.

"The Raven's Eye . . ." For just a moment it hypnotized him. He pulled his hands away, remembering why he had come. "Ragnar . . ." How could he have so easily forgotten that she was his daughter?

"Ragnar is my father, a man of flesh and blood with desires, too. Were he not, I would not be here." Taking his hands, she placed them on her breasts. "I cannot believe that he would begrudge us our happiness."

"Nor can I." Bending down he worshipped her with his mouth, his lips traveling from one breast to the other in tender fascination. His tongue curled around the taunt peaks, his teeth lightly grazing until she writhed beneath him. He savored the expressions that chased across her face, the wanting and the passion for him that were so clearly revealed.

Her hands crept around Torin's neck, her fingers tangling and tousling the thick waves of his tawny hair as she breathed a husky sigh. How wonderful it was to be loved!

The night air caressed Erica's skin as Torin undressed her, slipping her gown over her head. She caught fire wherever he touched her, burning with an all-consuming need. She shivered in his arms, and fearing it was from the night air, he gathered her closer, covering her body even more tightly with his to keep out the chill. With tender concern he tugged at his cloak, giving her the larger portion, tucking it beneath the firm curve of her buttocks.

"I'm not cold!" she whispered. "It's just that I want you so . . ." Now she knew how he had felt. If she had known then what she knew now, she would never have pushed him away.

"Erica!"

A shudder racked through him as he pushed her away. Just for a moment. Quickly he stripped away his own clothes and Erica took her turn to appraise him. The image of broad, bronzed shoulders, wide chest, flat belly, and well-formed legs would forever be branded in her mind. Reaching out, she touched him, her hands sliding over the hard smoothness of his shoulders, moving to the crisp hair of his chest. Torin had two scars, and she lightly traced each one with her finger.

"Battle scars?" She wondered if he got them fighting the Scots.

"Constant reminders that I have to be quicker and stronger than my opponents." He seemed to read her mind. "I got them fighting the Danes."

"Danes . . ." She was glad it wasn't any of her kindred.

His fingers entwined themselves in her flaming hair, pulling her face closer. His teeth nipped gently at her lip. "But come, let us put fighting out of minds for the moment. . . ." He pulled her closer, rolling her over until they were lying side by side, and she felt a great pleasure in the warmth and power of the firmly muscled body straining so hungrily against hers.

He kissed her again, his knowing, seeking lips moving with tender urgency across hers, his tongue finding again the inner warmth and sweetness of her mouth. His large body covered hers with a blanket of warmth. Erica felt the rasp of his chest hair against her breasts and answered his kiss with sweet, aching desire. But kisses weren't enough. . . .

"Torin . . . love me," she breathed.

"In due time . . ." His hands caressed her, warming her with their heat. They took sheer delight in the texture and pressure of each other's bodies. Sensuously he undulated his hips between her legs, and every time their bodies caressed, each experienced a shock of raw desire that encompassed them in fiery, pulsating sensations. Then his hands were between their bodies, sliding down the velvety flesh of her belly, moving to that place between her thighs that ached for his entry. His gentle probing brought sweet fire, curling deep inside her with spirals of pulsating sensations. Then his hands left her to be replaced by the hardness she had glimpsed before, entering her just a little, then pausing. Every inch of her tingled with an intense, arousing awareness of his body.

Bending his head to kiss her again, he moved his body forward just as a wave rocked the boat. The surge of the water pushed him deep within her, fusing their bodies. There was only a brief moment of pain, but the other sensations pushed it away. Erica was conscious only of the hard length of him creating unbearable sensations as he began to move within her. Capturing the firm flesh of her hips, he caressed her in the most intimate of embraces. His rhythmic plunges aroused a tingling fire, like nothing she had ever imagined. The rocking of the boat coincided with their own pulsations, and she arched herself up to him, fully expressing her love.

Torin groaned softly, the blood pounding thickly in his head. His hold on her hips tightened as the throbbing shaft of his maleness possessed her again and again, moving up and down with the waves. Instinctively Erica tightened her legs around him, certain she could never withstand the ecstasy that was engulfing her body. It was as if the night shattered into a thousand stars, bursting within her. Arching her hips, she rode the storm with him. As spasms overtook her, she dug her nails into the skin of his back.

A sweet shaft of ecstasy shot through Torin and he closed his eyes, whispering her name. Even when the intensity of their passion was spent, they still clung to each other, unable to let this magical moment end. They touched each other gently, wonderingly.

"Are all Scots so passionate?" He nibbled playfully at her ear.

"Aye. 'Tis something about our red hair. Makes us fiery."

Torin laughed softly. No wonder Ragnar had spoken about Erica's mother with such ardor. If she was anything at all like her daughter, she must have been a sensual woman who was more than Ragnar's equal in passion—the perfect mate.

Erica shivered again, but this time it was from the cold. A chilling fog was slowly engulfing the curach. She smiled as Torin massaged her body with slow, lingering movements, bringing warmth with his touch. It promised to arouse them to each other again, but he shook his head regretfully, pulling her gown over her head, helping her into her garments.

"I had better pay attention to where we are going." Tilting his head, he looked up at the sky. "By Odin's beard, the wind is coming back. I had hoped to get all the way to the Hebrides before the sea got rough again, but we are not to be so lucky." He kissed her lips gently, then hurriedly dressed himself. Bundling her in the warmth of his cloak he held her close. "You aren't afraid, are you?"

"No. Particularly when I am with you." She picked up an oar. "How can I help?"

He gently pulled it from her hand. "You can't. At least not at the moment. But I might have to call upon you when the storm hits. Until then, try to get some sleep."

"Sleep?" They were out in the ocean in a boat with a storm coming, and he expected her to drift off as if she were in her bed? "I cannot." She touched his lips in a smiling kiss. "I'd rather make love with ye again."

He was tempted, but realized that he had to keep his wits about him. "After the storm is over and we reach the Hebrides . . ." His eyes roamed up and down her body, remembering the pleasure he had found there. An incredibly tender expression crossed his face. "Once this is all over and we have found your brother, I want you to share my bed, my name, my life. I want to give you the chain of keys to my house, my sheds, and my heart. The keys that proclaim you to be my wife."

"Keys?"

"A Viking custom which you soon will understand." He gathered her close against him, shuddering as their bodies embraced, but then he pulled away. "Now, do not tempt me."

Erica lay down in the boat. The curach gently rocked back and forth. She closed her eyes for what she thought was just a fleeting moment, but soon she was fast asleep.

Torin contented himself with watching her for a long while, feeling an aching tenderness.

A cold spray of ocean mist splashed into Erica's face, awakening her, and she stirred, stretching her arms and legs in slow, easy motions. Feeling warmth against her flesh, she opened her eyes, remembering all that had happened. *Torin* was with her. Her heart quickened as she turned her eyes in his direction.

"I . . . I thought perhaps I had been dreaming."

"No, it was real. You are here with me and I will never let you go!" Bending forward, grasping her shoulders, he kissed her long and lingeringly, running his hands through her hair.

"Where are we?" Sitting up, she stared out at the sea mist that engulfed them, a blinding swirl of white.

"I wish I knew. Somewhere off Mull, I believe." He tried to keep the tone of his voice calm, for more than the fog concerned him. The wind was starting to blow, and though it would push out the fog, he didn't like it. The coming storm threatened to be even more violent than he had first supposed, which wouldn't have bothered him if he had been in a ship and not in a Scottish boat. He could read it in the churning of the sea, smell it in the air. Instinctively he gathered her into his arms, as if to protect her from what was to come.

"Torin, what is it? Ye are worried."

"There is going to be quite a gale. We'll have to brace ourselves, that's all." He stroked her hair again, remembering their lovemaking. No matter what happened to him he would protect Erica.

"I hate storms! When I was a child my mother told me that they were caused by huge sea beasties growling. And yet when I am in your arms I have no fear." Reaching up, she touched his cheek with her fingers. "I feel safe with ye, my love."

"Erica!" He cupped her face in his hand, kissing her soft open lips. Like a flower opening to sunshine, she moved her mouth upon his, feeling again the wondrous enchantment of the night before.

Lifting her arms, she encircled his neck and wound her fingers in his damp, tawny hair, clinging to him, wanting him to love her again. " 'Tis too bad that it is so chilled this morning, for I long so to be naked in your arms again."

"Oh?" Torin's hand reached out to caress her, sliding his fingers over the soft mounds of her breasts. Her body, pressed so tightly against his, drove him beyond all thought, all reasoning. "The cold should be no problem to those in love. I'll show you." Lifting up his shirt and her gown, he caressed her bared flesh against his own. His hand moved over her body from shoulder to thigh, caressing the flat plain of her belly, then moved to cup her breast. "I can keep you warm. See?" The warm safety of his arms was a blissful haven from the storm.

"Aye." Oh, how she loved the feel of her bare breasts against his chest. She arched against him in sensual pleasure. He had initiated a hunger in her that she had never even known existed, a desire only for him that couldn't seem to be appeased now that she knew what it was like to be with him. Her whole world was Torin, now and forever more. She closed her eyes, sighing as he took her mouth in a hard, deep kiss. For a long time she relished being close to him, just being held by him.

"Oh, my dear one, I love you so much!" he whispered huskily. The words trailed off as his mouth traced a pattern of fire on hers. Their lips caught and clung, smiled against each other as they held each other tightly.

Torin's hand moved down her stomach and into the soft hair between her thighs. Tremors shot through her in pulsating waves. She lifted her hips, seeking him. The whole world seemed to be rocking crazily, like an enormous wave crashing over her. Only the harsh recognition that it was indeed the sea and not her desire causing the tumult brought her back to reality.

Torin pulled away and looked around him, peering out at the ocean, straining his eyes for any sight of land. The storm! He damned himself for letting his attention wander from the boat for even a moment when he had known a storm was coming. But Erica had been so tempting.

"Are the water beasties angry?" She tried to laugh but couldn't hide her apprehension.

"Angry and threatening. We're going to have to weather out the storm, Erica. Whatever happens, no matter what, hold on to the side of the boat. Do you hear me?"

"Aye!" Her heart lurched in her breast as she realized fully the danger they were in.

"Even if—if something should happen to me, do not let go. Do you understand? You will be safe as long as you stay inside. The curach is sturdy. It will float. Remember!" What he didn't want to tell her was that if she didn't hold on, if she fell into the ocean, she was doomed. And so would he be without her!

Erica nodded, holding on to Torin as tightly as she could,

praying that the fearful gusts of wind and turbulent waves would soon abate. Oh, how she suddenly wanted to be on land again. Never would Ulva and the MacQuarie side of Mull seem so dear.

The small boat rocked from side to side as the ocean pounded viciously against the stern. Torin looked nervously over his shoulder. "Odin be with me," he said. Pulling away from her, he picked up the oars that lay in the bottom of the boat.

"What is it? Tell me, what is wrong?" Alarm rang through her, hurrying her heart, jangling her nerves and stretching her courage to its limit.

He confided in her, counting on her bravery. "We are off course and heading ashore. I have got to stabilize our course."

"Ashore?" The dark-gray basalt rocks up ahead seemed to be drawing them, pulling them. Staffa! Erica knew the danger of capsizing upon the jagged rocks. Staffa was an island to be avoided at all costs. "What can I do to help?"

"Just sit quiet!"

"I will not just sit by and be swallowed by the waves! Tell me, Torin." She crept cautiously toward him on hands and knees, intending to help him at the oars. A violent wave sent her sprawling, unbalancing the boat as she hit the side.

"Erica!" On both sides of the boat, the treacherous sea flung itself in massive crests, the spray whistling into the air. The rumble of the water was so loud it caused the boat to vibrate. "Are you all right?"

"Aye! Oh, Torin, what are we going to do?"

"Stay clear of the rocks," Torin shouted. "Perhaps I can steer the boat . . ." The roar of another wave drowned out his words.

Suddenly the boat capsized, and Erica was hurled into the air by a giant wave. A scream tore from her throat as she felt herself hit the water. She was engulfed in icy blackness. "Torin!" she cried silently. Blindly floundering about, she searched for him in the watery prison. No! This could not be happening. "Torin!" She choked out his name between mouthfuls of seawater. Where was he?

Taking a deep breath, she plunged into the water's depths, searching beneath the boat. There was no sign of Torin. In agonized fear for him she cried out his name.

Frantically fighting the water, Erica renewed her search, but he had vanished. He had been worried about her, but he was the one who was gone. "Torin!"

The watery prison seemed almost endless as she put one arm before the other, fighting for survival. Somehow, she had to hope that Torin was struggling just as hard, that he was even now swimming for the shore. She didn't want to believe that death had been his fate. *No! Oh, please let that be the answer.* He was struggling toward the shore just as she was now.

She fought the strength of the ocean but as a large wave tugged her under, Erica choked and swallowed some of the salty water. *Oh, please!* She had so much to live for. *Blessed Saint Michael!* Her life was still ahead of her. And Torin! She could not exist without him. *Please, dear God!*

As if in answer to her prayers, the flow of the water changed direction and rose to aid her. She found herself drifting toward the shore. From childhood Erica had known how to swim; it was something she always enjoyed. But that was in lochs and burns, not in such threatening water. Still, she knew, if only she could reserve her strength and let the sea carry her to land, she might survive. Trying to control her breathing, to relax despite her fear of the icy ocean, she determined that she, not the icy sea, would be the victor. She was strong. She was half MacQuarie and half Viking! With that in mind, when the next huge waves appeared she rode with them, and when they ceased, paddled in the direction of the land.

The ocean seemed to go on forever, the tall monoliths of Staffa were large, ominous specks in the distance. The longer she struggled, the more hopeless the situation seemed. The icy water robbed her of her stamina. Her strength was wavering. She was weary. Despite her resolve, she was just too tired to go on. If there were any sea fairies to aid her, she needed them now. Opening her mouth, she whispered a plea for herself and for Torin.

A rock struck her foot, and she realized that all was not lost. Not yet. Just a little farther and she could make it. Somehow she had to find the courage and the physical prowess to stay alive! Fight. She must survive the waters. She would not give up.

Hands reached out for her, grabbing her, pulling her ashore. Torin? The salt water stung her eyes so she could not see. "Torin!" A hazy figure loomed in front of her. With a final effort, she shook her head and squinted her eyes. Though half blind, she saw an ominous shadow.

Instinct told her to run. Run. Nimbly escaping the grasping hands she sprang to her feet and sprinted across the rocks as fast as her weary legs would carry her. It was not fast enough. The shadow had closed the distance. With a shriek of despair, Erica gave in to the darkness that swirled before her eyes, and fell unconscious to the ground.

TWENTY-THREE

An eerie song as breathless as the wind whispered in the darkness. It echoed over and over. Haunting. Chilling. Erica struggled to open her eyes. "Please. Help me," she murmured.

It was as if she were walking down a long, dark tunnel, groping about, struggling to come into the light. A figure waited for her at the tunnel's end and she reached out. Torin? She whispered his name over and over, needing him, wanting him, but the fearsome mourning song was like a moaning wail, driving him away. That howling song!

Sea witches! They were singing! Erica gasped raggedly for air, trying to scream. But no sound came. Her throat burned like fire. *"Glastig!"* she tried to say, but her throat constricted; she was choking. Sea fairies! Singing their song. A frightening image of the deceiving crones, part seductive woman, part goat, hovered in her mind.

She remembered seeing a figure, a shadow. *Run! Get away!* Kicking and thrashing, she tried to move but was helpless. She was hot, burning up. The sea witch was trying to smother her, roast her alive.

The eerie song moaned again, and Erica put her hands over her ears in an attempt to block it out. The sea fairies always sang, trying to entice a human mate, luring men into the sea. *Torin!* "Nae, he is mine!" she croaked, tossing her head from side to side. Visions swirled through her mind: Torin lying on the rocks as a swarm of unearthly beings chanted over him.

Blindly, uncontrollably, she struck out like a wild thing at the figures. She would never see Torin again. They would hold him captive. "Please . . . !" Opening her eyes to slits, she saw a figure bending over her.

"Sleep!" a voice said, touching her with fingers that were strangely gentle, like a soft summer breeze. Again warmth surrounded her, but this time she didn't struggle. Unconsciously she reached out, touching warm flesh, grasping tightly with her hands. "Ye will be all right!" It sounded like a promise. Again the whispering song. Despite her fear it lulled her to sleep.

When Erica awoke she was lying on her back, swathed in soft wool. Opening her eyes, she gasped at the sight of the man holding vigil by her side. He was a bearded man whose pale face held a look of kindness. "Who . . . ?"

"Hush. You must get back your strength."

Erica took a deep breath and slowly appraised the man. The dark-blond hair was streaked with gray and hung wildly about his shoulders. He had a prominent nose and high cheekbones. There were tiny lines at the corners of his eyes and mouth.

"Where . . . where am I?" Erica whispered, trying to focus her eyes in the dimly lighted room.

"My island!"

"Your island?" Erica shivered as her gaze roamed over her surroundings. Not a room at all, but a yawning cavern of dark rock, lit only by torchlight.

"I have claimed it as mine." He noticed her confusion. "I pulled you from the ocean and brought you here to care for you."

"Aye!" Erica remembered everything clearly now. He was the frightening shadow. "My throat . . . my . . . my chest. . . ."

"You swallowed part of the sea. I had to push it out of your lungs." Opening a small leather bag, he drew forth a gnarled root, mortar, and pestle. "I'll fix you something that will soothe the soreness of your throat."

Erica shook her head. She didn't trust him entirely; besides, she didn't want to take a chance that it might be a sleeping potion. "Nae! My—my throat feels much better and I—I . . ." Pausing, she listened. "That song!" Erica shuddered. "It . . . it sounds like . . . like ghosts."

"It's the sea singing. It echoes through the caves like a chant. *Am Uamh Ehinn.* The musical cave. The song soothes me, but then I've grown used to it." Rising to his feet, the man walked slowly across the cave and poked about the embers of a fire. "Are you cold?"

"Aye." Erica tried to sit up, but the whirling inside her head caused her to lie back down. She was so dizzy, so weary. Tears stung her eyes as she remembered Torin. "Was there . . . was there a man with me?" The man shook his head. "No sign of him?" He was lost to her, then. To have had such happiness only to lose it. "Oh, Torin!" Why had *she* been saved and not him? The thought of being without him unleashed a flood of tears. Turning over on her side, she gave vent to her pain in great, gulping sobs.

The man tried to comfort Erica, but her torrent of weeping was uncontrollable.

"He is gone!" Mumbling through her tears, Erica told her story of losing Torin in the storm. "I cannot live without him."

"Stop that!" Hunkering down, the man reached out and shook Erica by her shoulders. "Weeping will do no good. Believe me, I know. I have cried an ocean full of tears, but they can not soothe *my* pain."

"Your pain?" Erica wiped her eyes. There was something so mournful in the man's expression. He reminded Erica of a lost soul. "Tell me. . . ."

Wearily the man shook his head.

"Are ye mourning someone? Ye seem so lonely. . . ." The sudden tensing of the man's body, the look of utter despair mirrored in his eyes, answered Erica's question. Something had happened to this man, but she wouldn't press him for answers, at least not yet. He had saved her life. She would grant him his privacy in return.

The waters swirling around Torin were freezing, debilitating. Trying to ignore his discomfort, he strained against the waves, searching for Erica. He had seen her go over the side, buffeted by a huge, handlike wave when the curach turned over. Then it was as if she had just disappeared! Though he had gone below the surface of the ocean again and again, he had not been able to find her. Even so, he had been determined not to give up. Erica had very quickly become his heart, his soul.

Taking a deep breath, Torin dove deep within the sea, stubborn in his resolve. He stayed under until his lungs were screaming for air, then surfaced. Treading water, he continued his search, but at last he had to admit defeat. He was winded; his strength was giving out.

Keeping his head above water, Torin looked around him, taking note of the huge, dark shape looming in front of him. The strange-looking stone formations looked much like the massive trunks of forest trees bundled together. It seemed as tall as a castle. An island of sorts.

"An island!" he gasped. An island meant people and boats. He'd procure the aid of the fishermen who surely inhabited the land mass. Aye, he'd get help in finding Erica. Then once they were reunited, they'd sail to the Hebrides just as he had promised.

How long he had been in the water, Torin did not know. He only knew that his arms ached, his legs were numb, his breath was coming far too hard. He had to face the possibility that the icy water might very well be his grave. He was sinking beneath the surface, but the memory of Erica gave him new resolve. No! He would *not* give in to death. He would challenge the water. He would live to find Erica! He would win! If he could only manage to survive, make the short distance to shore. That thought gave him renewed strength and he struck out again, arm over arm, legs propelling his body through the water until something hard scraped his feet. He could feel solid ground beneath the water.

With a final surge of strength, he fought his way through the last few feet of water and pulled himself up. Stumbling upon the shore, crawling across the slippery rocks, Torin fought for breath, then glanced in the direction of the ocean. The tide was going out, and if he wasn't careful he could be swept back out into the sea again.

"I can't stop now," he wheezed, scrambling over the slimy seaweed and jagged rocks. He had to find help. Had to initiate a renewed search for Erica. That thought drove him on to the point of total, unrelenting exhaustion. Black splotches danced before his eyes as he walked endlessly, but he refused to succumb to unconsciousness. He hadn't come this far to give up now. With determination he stayed on his feet, wandering about.

Rock. Nothing but rock. Huge basalt columns that rose up to the sky, crags and caverns. There was no sign of life. No boats. No cottages. No vegetation. The longer he walked, the more certain Torin was that there were no people. An uninhabited island. A never-ending acreage of nothingness. He was marooned with no visible way of getting off except throwing himself into the sea to swim endlessly. He had hoped . . .

Collapsing to the rocky ground, Torin realized he could not take another step. He was tired. So tired. Disappointment and disillusionment had taken a toll of his stamina, and he felt as feeble as a newborn lamb. With a deep sigh, he ceased his struggle.

Surely he must have lost his mind, for in the silence he

seemed to hear music. He struggled with such an illogical thought. It was impossible. If he'd had the strength, he might have laughed. Music! Eerie voices, muffled by the wind, groaning. Was it a portent of something evil?

Am I dead? Wearily he lifted his head. Surely this was not Valhalla. The realm of the goddess, Hell, then? All the stories he'd heard of such things came back to haunt him. "No!" He forced himself to calm. His head ached. The dead felt no pain.

He strained to hear the strange sound again, to discern its direction. To the left? The right? Ahead of him or behind? He peered into the misty darkness, hoping to see at least a silhouette, but he could only see the dark water and gray, swirling fog. Closing his eyes, he let the seductive darkness enfold him.

Erica sat upon the cold, damp rocks, gazing solemnly into the swirling waters. Hugging her arms around her knees, she breathed deeply of the sea air, remembering so vividly the moment Torin had held her in his arms and made love to her. How strange that the ocean should yield such happy memories and yet such tragedy as well.

The wind swirled around her, whipping thick strands of her flaming hair into her face. Reaching up, she brushed the silken threads away, not at all surprised to find her cheeks wet with a mixture of salt spray and tears. Erica had spent the past few days in a haze of grief, haunted by tortured visions of that tragic moment when her happiness had been shattered upon the crest of a violent wave.

Oh, Torin! Never had she felt such overwhelming despair, an emptiness, as if a part of her soul had died. And what of Geordie? How could she help him now? *The two I loved the most, now gone . . .*

Turning her face toward the sea, she watched as the foaming waves hit the stone cliffs with noisy fury. The expanse of water was an awesome reminder of her helplessness and her grief. Oh, how she wanted to get off this sullen, deserted island as soon as possible, to go back home, but she was trapped by the same waves that had so tumultuously brought her here. She was marooned with a strange, silent man whom she was not at all certain she trusted.

Apprehension for that man gnawed at her, for she didn't know his motives. He had saved her life, of this she was certain, yet there were times when he acted very strangely, murmuring to himself, exhibiting an obsessive fascination with the raven-shaped pendant she wore around her neck. Coupled with the fact that he was evasive about his own identity and enshrouded himself within a shell of secrecy, it was unnerving and very puzzling. Yet if not for this man, Erica knew she might well be dead. He had shared his cave, given her food, and tried to soothe her grief with mumbled words of comfort. There were times when he seemed a congenial companion, sympathetic, gentle, kind, but at other times his change of mood was frightening.

There were times when he hovered by Erica's elbow and other times when he just seemed to vanish. But no, he had not disappeared after all. She could see him gathering driftwood for the fire, bending and stooping as if each little stick were a rare treasure. He was so self-reliant, not depending on anyone or anything for his comfort except his own skills, and yet Erica was struck by how lonely it must be not to have a family. No clan! Who or what was he? And what had drawn him here?

Over and over again, Erica had tried to learn the story of what had brought the man to Staffa, but all she had gotten for her efforts was silence. The man refused to talk about himself, preferring instead to ask her questions.

"I'm called Erica," she had answered, "and I have a brother who was taken from me and I must find him."

Strange how Erica had babbled so much about her childhood. The pranks she and Geordie had played, the love they shared for their mother. Erica had noticed a smile trembling at the corners of the man's mouth. When she had revealed her love for a Viking, and how she had boldly freed him, the man had seemed to cheer inwardly. It was only when she had mentioned the name *Ragnar* that the man had turned quite pale, as if that name held terror for him. But though Erica had tried to find out why, it had been useless. He had seemed again to enter into his own private world, and Erica had wondered what thoughts tortured the poor soul.

Seeing the familiar form of the man coming her way now, Erica got to her feet and walked to meet him, granting him a semblance of friendship. "Here, let me have a bit of that. It looks like a heavy load."

"Not so heavy, but cumbersome." Thankfully he gave up half the pieces to Erica. "There are some fine clams. I saw them. Just as soon as I have started a fire I'll go get us a few. It will be a welcome change from fish and seaweed."

"Aye." Oh, what Erica would not have given for a slice of venison. Fish, fish, fish, that's all she ate now, and yet she scolded herself for her ungratefulness. Without this man she might well have gone hungry. "I'll give ye a hand gathering the clams. My uncle used to say I might have been a fine fisherman were I not a lass."

The man smiled sadly, as if somehow Erica's conversation brought to mind his own memories. Thoughtfully he spread the pieces of driftwood on the rocks to dry. Erica did the same. When she looked up, however, she could see that he was staring. Reaching up, she touched the pendant.

"Ye seem to be interested in this," she said, coming right to the point. "Why?"

"It is curious that you wear the Celtic symbol of misfortune and death around your neck, yet from what you have said, I know that you are a Christian."

"I've told ye. My father was a Viking. 'Twas he who gave this to my mother to place around my neck." She sighed, remembering all the times she had been chided by Iona and her uncle for insisting on wearing the pendant. "According to Viking legend the raven is a symbol of wisdom." Immediately her mother came to mind and she remembered her story of how the Viking god, Odin, had two ravens that sat on his shoulder and whispered every scrap of news they saw or heard of.

"Wisdom . . ." A strange look came over the hermit's face.

"I remember my mother telling me that Huginn is thought and Muninn is memory. Odin's ravens."

At the name of the Viking god, the hermit crossed himself in the same manner she had seen one of the priests do when warding off evil. Then he continued to stare at the pendant.

"What is it? Why are you so interested in the amulet that I wear?"

His eyes held a faraway look for just a moment, as if he was remembering. "I have seen another such pendant, once long ago."

"A raven?" Now it was Erica who was interested.

"A wolf. It had a yellow stone. I saw it at the monastery."

"Monastery? Where?"

"In Eire." The man stiffened. As if to put an end to the conversation, he hurried on ahead of Erica, making his way to the cave. There he busied himself with stoking the small fire that kept them warm.

No, Erica thought. *I am not going to let him keep evading me this way.* Her curiosity was much too fierce to pretend that she just didn't care about this man's identity. If he was a priest, if he had committed some kind of sin, if that was why he was so fiercely secretive, then Erica wanted to know.

Coming up behind the man, she laid a gentle hand on his shoulder. "Tell me, please. Are ye . . . are ye a holy man?"

The man drew back, looking this way and that as if he wanted to run. Sensing his intent, Erica blocked his way. "Please, don't run away. I won't hurt ye. I want to be yer friend. Tell me."

Never had Erica seen so much pain reflected in anyone's eyes as she did now. "What once was is gone forever. There is no use in talking about it. I am dead to some and it is best that I remain that way."

"But ye must have a family, kin who will be mourning ye. . . ."

Nervously the man brushed the matted hair from his face, shaking his head as if to clear it of unpleasant memories. "There is no one."

"I'm sorry." Her heart grieved for him, for she sensed that he had been greatly wronged in some way. Driven from the bosom of his clan, perhaps, but why? There were many reasons for being exiled: disobedience, going against the good of the clan, harm to another clan member. The system of clan justice was administered by a *brieve,* who apportioned fines and imposed punishment for offenses. Had he been sentenced for a crime? What had this poor man done?

"Don't be sorry for me. I am content in my own way."

"But perhaps I can help ye. I owe ye a debt of gratitude for pulling me out of the sea."

Eyes like those of a wounded animal looked back at Erica. "I told you. I can't go back, child."

He had called her "child." Once again Erica had the feeling that a long time ago this man had been in some kind of religious order. A priest? A monk? Erica tried to piece together what might have happened. Had he fallen in love with a woman and given up his vows? Had something happened to that woman? Her blue eyes widened as the man put a hand up, as if to ward off evil.

"No! Go away. I don't want you here. Go!"

Erica followed the line of the man's vision, fearful suddenly of what she might see. A ghost? Stiffening her shoulders she prepared herself for the most unearthly of sights.

Even so, she was totally stunned by the person who stood before her. If it was a ghost, it was one whose presence she welcomed. Rising slowly to her feet, she moved toward him, choking out his name. "Torin!"

TWENTY-FOUR

Torin's breath caught in his throat as he stared at Erica. Had he gone mad? Was she *here*? He dared not blink for fear she might vanish into the misty haze that enshrouded the island. "Erica?" Realization that she was real was like an elixir, giving him renewed strength. He had cursed this barren isle and the fate that had brought him here; now he blessed it. "Erica . . ."

She looked like a red-haired goddess standing there in the early-morning sunlight, her hair hanging down her back in glistening, flaming strands. Reverently he worshipped her with his eyes, the slim curve of her neck, her profile with the haughty uptilt of her nose, the soft swell of her breasts as they strained against the finely woven wool of her gown.

"Blessed Saint Michael, I thought ye were . . ." Erica's throat went dry as she stared at him, mesmerized by the potency of his gaze. In his face she read her own longing, and her heart gave a crazy leap as he moved toward her. Then he was sweeping her up in his arms in an embrace that crushed the breath from her, but she didn't care. For the moment, nothing mattered except that somehow she was being given a second chance at happiness. Perhaps, then, Staffa was magical after all. It had given her back her love.

"When I saw you go over the side, when I couldn't find

you I thought . . ." He buried his face in her hair, content for the moment just to hold her.

"I died a hundred times thinking . . ." She clung to him fiercely. Forgetting for a moment that they were not alone on the isle, she slipped her hands inside the neck of his shirt, shuddering at the warmth of his skin. She lifted her face for Torin's kiss, but the rasping sound of indrawn breath behind her reminded Erica of the hermit's presence.

"A Viking. Are there others?" A look of consternation etched the hermit's face. It was obvious that Torin's presence frightened him.

"Who is he?" Torin asked, eyeing the man warily, in much the same manner Erica had upon first seeing him. He allowed his eyes to drop to the tattered garments, the hair spilling over the man's shoulders in wild disarray.

"I don't know exactly, but whoever he is, the man saved my life and for that I am grateful." Pulling free of Torin's embrace, Erica hovered over Staffa's guardian as if to give credence to her words. "He pulled me from the ocean and breathed new life into my lungs."

Torin breathed a deep sigh. "Then if that is true, if I can thank him for finding you here, then I am deeply grateful." He bowed gallantly. "Torin Rolandsson at your service."

"Torin . . . Roland . . . Ragnar!" He gasped the names like omens of evil, then taking to his heels, fled the cave as if he'd just come face to face with the devil.

"Catch him, Torin! Don't let him go!" Erica followed Torin in pursuit of the frightened man, who led them a merry chase up and down over slippery rocks, across a small burn indented in the rock, past the singing cave. Only when he stumbled and fell was Torin able to catch up with him. Grabbing him by the leg, he fell to the ground, tangled in his long arms and legs.

"No! No! Don't kill me! Don't kill me!" His shrieks were pitiful, frightened cries. By his terror it was obvious that he really did think that Torin meant him harm.

"Kill you? By Odin's sword, I swear that I will not; only cease your floundering." Such a pathetic creature, Torin thought. Seemingly mad. "I swear I will show you nothing but kindness, for I owe you a debt of gratitude for the kindness you have shown the woman I love."

"You won't hurt me?"

"No!" To prove his good intentions, Torin loosened his hold on him. "There, you see? You have nothing to be afraid of."

Shakily he got to his knees. "I—I thought for a moment that you had come for revenge."

"Revenge?" Torin had not really looked closely at the hermit before, but now he did? "Who are you?"

"Just a man who seeks peace and solitude," he answered evasively. His eyes darted this way and that, nervously looking for a means of escape and finding none. "Please, let me be. I haven't done harm to anyone."

"Then why speak of revenge?" He eyed the man suspiciously.

Tears welled up in the man's blue eyes. "I have suffered much these years. Memories I seek to forget in my wandering. Perhaps I speak of God's revenge."

"God's revenge?" Erica was horrified. "God does not seek revenge. He is forgiving and loving, but ye should know that." Erica knelt down to the man, putting her arm around his shoulders. "Please tell me what happened and why ye grieve so. Perhaps in the telling ye will be absolved of that which is tearing at your heart."

The hermit's eyes clouded, and for a moment he seemed to be in his own private world of memories. "Once I was a priest at a monastery in Eire. Armagh by name. I was young and foolish in my pride and my ambition." He sighed. "I thought that the world was mine, with little thought to the God I was supposed to serve. I thought that I could live two lives, one for myself and one for God. I . . . I met a woman." His eyes closed and he seemed to be remembering her face.

"A woman. You loved her." Torin clenched his jaw. He could never understand the Christian way of some men being forced to be celibate. It wasn't that way with his belief. Odin, Frey, Thor, and Loki enjoyed the softness and warmth of women and likewise wanted their followers to enjoy love-making. "I do not see any harm in that."

The hermit opened his eyes wide. "She was married."

Torin stiffened. "She belonged to some other man." That she had a husband made this a far different matter, for often death was the punishment among the Vikings for adultery.

"She belonged to a cruel man who would beat my lovely Colleen just for the fun it gave him."

"The beast!" Erica gasped. "She should have fought him. That's what I would have done."

"She was too sweet and too gentle; that's what made it so terrible." It seemed that now that he had started, the hermit couldn't stop. "One night he nearly killed her with his brutality, and I stilled his life with my bare hands." His eyes closed again as he recalled that day so long ago.

Torin patted him on the shoulder. "I would have done the same if anyone harmed Erica. You have no reason to feel shame."

"But that is not all. I fled from the monastery and from Eire in fear of retribution, thinking only of myself and my reputation. A year later I learned that my beautiful Colleen had been found guilty and put to death. No one believed her plea that she had not killed her husband. Thus, my cowardice and selfishness caused the death of the one person in this world that I truly loved."

"And that is what brought you here . . ." Erica was saddened by the hermit's story.

"I stripped myself of my priestly trappings and retired to this island in an effort to punish myself, and so I committed another sin. I was not there when the Vikings invaded the monastery and killed my fellow priests. I was not there to protect . . ." Fearing that he had revealed too much, he quieted.

"Go on." Erica wanted to hear the whole story.

"No." The hermit was wary as he looked at Torin. It was as if he somehow blamed him partly for what had happened.

Erica pushed on. "Ye said that ye had seen someone with a pendant just like mine. Was that . . . was that the one ye were supposed to protect?" Taking hold of her necklace she held it out for the hermit priest to see.

"Pendant? Like yours?" Torin stepped in front of Erica. He had to know about the pendant, and whether it was one of the pendants that Ragnar had spoken of. A pendant that might lead him to one of Ragnar's sons. "Tell me."

"No-o-o-o-o-o-o."

Putting his hands to his ears, he sought to block his questions out, but Torin gently pulled his hands away. "The pendant . . . Was it a dragon? With a blue stone?"

Now it was Erica who wanted to know about the pendant. "What are you talking about, Torin?"

The hermit shook his head. "No . . . no dragon."

Torin had only one thing on his mind. "A wolf, then. A wolf with amber eyes." Though the hermit didn't answer, the look in his eyes spoke for him. "It was! The second pendant!"

"Second pendant?" Erica's eyes widened. In her mind she had already made the connection to the pendant that hung around her neck. "My—my father—Ragnar." It had to be! There was no other explanation.

Torin regretted that he had not told her sooner. "There are two other pendants, Erica. Your father gave one to each of his children."

The truth hit her hard. She was not her father's only child. Her mother had not been his only love. "Sons?" So, her father had his precious male children after all. "Why didn't ye tell me?" She focused her anger on Torin.

"In my way I was trying to protect you."

"Protect me? From the truth?" Erica's eyes met Torin's accusingly.

"Erica!" Torin tried to put his arms around her, but she pulled violently away.

"Nae, do not touch me!" Her anger flashed in her eyes. "Would ye just have sailed away in secret and not let me know?"

Turning her back on Torin, she sought her own solitude. The pieces of a long-ago puzzle were slowly being fitted into place, and this hermit who had once been a priest was an integral fragment.

Torin kept his distance from Erica so that her anger at him would cool down. Meanwhile, he spent time with the hermit, whose name he learned was John. A change had come over the hermit since Torin and Erica had landed on Staffa. He was not as withdrawn. The fear had melted from his eyes. It was as if, by talking about what had happened, he had come to terms with it. Now a camaraderie had sprung up between him and Torin.

John had confided to Torin that he knew where there was an old Viking ship. Not a long ship, but a much smaller *knorr*, or trading vessel. With John's help, Torin hoped to make the ship seaworthy so that he and Erica could sail in search of Geordie. Once they found Erica's brother, Torin planned to sail to the monastery of Armagh in search of the amber pendant John had spoken of. With luck, that pendant would be around the neck of its rightful owner.

"It must have been a fine ship," Torin said to John as he pulled at a few of the old nails in the ship, trying to straighten them out. "How did it come to be here?"

John's usually pale face grew flushed. "It was a ship used to transport pilfered goods taken from Alba and Eire back to the northland."

Torin had worked up a sweat. He wiped the perspiration from his brow. "What happened to the occupants?"

"Dead!" John stopped hammering to look at his handiwork. "We will have to gather some pitchy logs to tighten the seams."

"How did they die?"

"The tar will work wonders and make the ship watertight."

"How did they die?" Torin had to know.

"They were killed by their own kind." John told of how he had seen the sea battle from afar. "All the treasures aboard the ship were taken after the men were killed and the ship was set afloat. I swam out and brought the ship here, just in case I should ever need it." For the first time since Torin had set eyes on the hermit priest, John smiled. "And now I'm glad that I did, for I am able to give it to you."

"But you might need it."

John shook his head. "I'll take the little curach in trade. It's all I'll need." Picking up a chisel, he began to work at the splintered oar holes.

"Are you certain you don't want to come with us?"

"I can't. I promised the Lord that I would stay here in penance for my great sin."

"A sin that happened a long time ago. Doesn't your God give a man a second chance?" Torin turned his attention to fixing the sail, but as he looked at John out of the corner of his eye he could see that the hermit was contemplating his words.

"Perhaps some day I will leave Staffa, but not now." He looked toward Erica, who was occupied with cooking fish for their supper. "Besides, it would seem to me that my coming along would be an intrusion."

Torin's gaze touched first upon Erica, then focused on the sea. "Even when we are at odds I love her more than I ever thought possible. You Christians speak of heaven, but to me heaven would be to hold her in my arms throughout eternity."

John smiled for the second time. "Then perhaps that is the way it will be, my son. My prayer for you and for her is that you will grow old together, enjoy great happiness, and then sail into Heaven together on a ship such as this one."

PART TWO

JOURNEY OF THE
HEART

TWENTY-FIVE

The refurbished merchant ship glided over the waves, leaving the Isle of Staffa far behind. Erica stood as unmoving and silent as a statue, ignoring Torin as she relished the wind that blew across her face and raked its fingers through her hair.

"How long are you going to stay angry?" Torin said at last.

Slowly Erica turned her head. "Were ye going to keep my brothers a secret from me? Had ye planned to soothe your desires, then leave me behind while ye sailed off to God knows where so ye could please my father?"

"No!" That hadn't exactly been his plan. "I would have told you eventually."

"When? After ye had presented my father with his precious heir and earned your eagerly sought-after reward?"

Torin shook his head. "I would have told you when we set sail from Staffa."

She ignored his answer. "How much is my father paying ye to sail all the way to the edges of the earth to seek his fine sons? How much?"

Torin's jaw tensed and he spoke in a mumble. "There is no coinage changing hands. I'm not a mercenary. I admire your father and I am honoring his request."

Once, she had honored Ragnar also. Too much. Now she

felt a surge of disappointment at the betrayal. Her mother had been but one of many. Was it any wonder, then, that her father had forgotten her for all those years? At least until he wanted to assure that his progeny would keep his name alive. Sons. He had wanted sons!

"Erica . . ."

For just a fleeting moment she looked at him, seemed to react to what he had said, and then without a word turned her head, concentrating on the open ship. The sides were nicked with small, square holes from which oars protruded. The oar ports were in the fore and aft parts of the ship with six rowing benches. Rising from the center was a sturdy, smooth pole that held the sail—a black wolf silhouetted on a square cloth of gold—and cross-beam. In the center of the ship the Vikings would have stashed their treasures. There were also round wooden casks of what Torin called "mead," and water as well as other provisions for the short journey.

"I'm on a Viking ship; I'm going to the Northland, but it's not at all the way that I dreamed. . . ."

"I'm deeply sorry for what happened, Erica, and the way it happened." Gently he touched her shoulder, willing her to love him again. "But I'm not sorry that I came to Alba, nor that I met you. Whether you will believe me or not, I know in my own heart that meeting you has changed my life and made me understand the importance of love."

Wanting to make her comfortable, Torin grabbed a pelt from the cargo hold and held it out to her like an offering.

Erica took the fur but didn't look at him. Her anger was beginning to wane. "I thank ye. . . ." There was something in the tone of his voice when he spoke to her that cooled her anger.

"I never thought it possible to find a perfect woman, and yet I did. We were happy in those all-too-brief moments when we were together, Erica. Now, deep in my heart I fear that our chance for happiness may be gone because of a misunderstanding."

"Our happiness was just an illusion," she said softly. She was tired, the fur coverlet was inviting, and the gentle rocking of the ship upon the ocean was making her sleepy.

"No. It was real." And he would do everything in his power to prove it to her.

"Not real . . . just a dream," she murmured, bending down first to sit, then lie on the fur coverlet.

Up and down, back and forth, the ship rocked unendingly, lulling her to sleep. Deep in her dreams she was conscious only of the motion of the ship and the sound of the water. Her mind drifted from one fantasy to another, imagining the expression on her father's face when he found out that he had a daughter. But she wouldn't let him crush her spirits; she would walk brazenly into her father's hall. She would not be some shrinking maiden. No, not she! She would prove herself worthy of sharing her father's blood. She would save Geordie and take him right out from under the very noses of his captors if need be, even if one of those captors proved to be Ragnar himself!

Torin looked down at Erica, then out at the waves. Water surrounded them as far as the eye could see in a never-ending blur of white foam and murky blue ocean. Though Torin and his men were excellent navigators on the open sea, there was no sign of land to guide him, no maps or charts, nothing but the stars and his own wits.

Rays of sunlight shone on Erica's face as she lay on her thick bed of furs. Stretching her arms and legs, she opened her eyes, then buried her body in the soft thickness of her makeshift bed. Sun and fur, nothing could compare to the feel of either one upon the skin. Except for the touch of Torin's hands. For a moment she imagined his hands stroking her, his lips beginning a journey at her neck, exploring all her secrets, then traveling back again.

"Torin . . ."

With a sigh she relished the fresh smell of sea air, inhaling deeply. Rolling over on her back, she forgot for a moment that they were sailing in pursuit of her young brother, but quickly it all came back to her. Poor Geordie! They had to find him.

Erica looked around her. The ship, completely surrounded by water, brought forth an eerie feeling within her, as if she were being swallowed up by the ocean. Nor were the storms at all reassuring. When huge waves lashed out at the ship, Erica had prepared herself for death, but somehow Torin had managed to keep the craft under control until the fury passed.

At times the ship seemed to be such a fragile vessel that she wondered how it kept afloat; at other moments she marveled at the strength it displayed, just like the man who stood upon its deck. Several times she had feared that they were lost, but Torin had a keen sense of the ocean that was nothing short of amazing.

Torin. With the sun dancing on his hair, his blue eyes glittering with excitement, his stance wide as he balanced on the deck, he looked arrogant and strong.

"Are you hungry?" Torin spoke so softly that at first she didn't hear, but when he asked again she looked up at him and shook her head. "You aren't seasick, are you?"

"No." Several times she had felt queasy in her stomach, but she had fought against it. She wouldn't be weak.

"Then eat! You have to keep up your strength." Food was dried fish and meat with unleavened bread. Hardly appetizing fare.

"At least eat some of the bread." His voice was commanding, much harsher than he intended. "Please . . ." he amended, holding it out to her.

For a moment their eyes met and held; then Erica looked away, but she did take the food and she did eat, asking between mouthfuls, "How much longer will it be until we reach the Hebrides?"

"Not long." She shivered as a gust of wind swept over the deck. Torin took off his cloak and draped it over her shoulders in a show of tender concern, his hand brushing hers as he did so.

She ached with memories of how it felt to have her bare breasts pressed against the hair on his chest. He had opened up a whole new world of beauty and emotions to her. His mouth on hers had sparked a fire within her. Under his touch she had known greater delights than she could have ever imagined.

Could she ever forget those moments when their bodies and spirits had joined together? No. Nor did she really want to. But just to quell the emotions rising within her, she was determined to keep him at arm's length, at least until her brother was found. Oh, but there were times when she would have liked nothing more than to sleep against his chest. Without his arms around her she felt so lonely.

He cupped her face in his hand, looking deep into her eyes. "We'll find Geordie and when we do we'll take him back to Alba."

Though she knew Torin had no part in what had taken place, what had happened had changed her forever and, in changing her, had complicated her emotions. She needed time. As if sensing this, Torin gently kissed her brow, then left her to return to his duties navigating the ship.

The sail of the knorr was up, rippling full and taunt as gusts of wind puffed at it. Erica gazed up at the sail, wishing that she could do something to make the ship move faster.

The breathtaking rocky grandeur of the Hebrides hovered before Geordie's eyes. At least he was still in Alba, though so far away from his home that he felt a twinge of home-sickness.

"We'll sell the furs here for coinage. Herlaug won't have

to share in any of our spoils if we don't tell him," he heard the ugliest of the Vikings say.

"Why don't we sell the boy as well?"

"Cut out your tongue before you say that again, Bolli. I don't want to have to keep repeating my plan. We are going to take him to Herlaug to do with as he pleases. If he is gullible, as I think he will be, then we will take our reward and go in search of Ragnar's next "son.""

"But . . . but Torin is dead and he is the only one who knows how to find the others. . . ."

Without even a warning, Halldor slapped Bolli in the head. "You oaf! I don't really intend to search for Ragnar's true sons. We'll just find two young men of about the same age as Ragnar's sons and bring them back to Herlaug."

"Ohhhhhh!" Bolli laughed.

"In the meantime, all we have is this little bear cub!" He reached out and tugged roughly at Geordie's hair.

So that was their game, Geordie thought. They weren't satisfied with him, but then perhaps he could make use of their greed.

The jagged coastline went on for miles, making the ship's landing harrowing as it swept ashore. Nonetheless, the man named Audun artfully steered the ship in close and found sand for a smooth beaching.

Geordie followed the others, fighting to get his sea legs under control. The cramped position had weakened his muscles somewhat, but not his brain. He knew that Erica would come after him when she found out what had happened; therefore, he knew that he had to leave a trail for her to follow.

TWENTY-SIX

The knorr skimmed through the waters of the North Atlantic. Now that Torin knew the territory and where he was going, the journey was more rapid and far less harrowing. Torin's eyes narrowed into slits as he strained for sight of the familiar landmarks. He had sailed this route once or twice when coming home from raids on Eire and Alba—a truth he kept from Erica.

"Odin be praised, we are almost there!" he exclaimed. "We'll be at Stornoway within a shake of a dragon's tail." He planned to sail to the northernmost island of the Hebridean chain, which was occupied by Norsemen. They would stop there to replenish the food supply, then sail onward through the North Sea.

The sky seemed bluer, the water clearer, and the land in the distance greener as the merchant ship journeyed onward. The sky was alive with birds. Small islands jetted out here and there. Erica concentrated upon the coastline scenery, feeling a newfound sense of calm. She had a feeling in her heart that they would find her brother alive and well. With Torin's help they would free Geordie and send him safely home. But what then? What about her? Did she want to go back to Alba with Geordie, or on to the Northland with Torin? She was emotionally torn in two directions, for the truth of the matter was, she loved them both. As if somehow the foaming waves could help her decide, she looked out at the sea.

Torin's attention was focused on Erica, though he took great pains not to show it. He tried to keep from looking at her, but he couldn't help glancing at her from time to time out of the corner of his eye.His heart jumped every time she glanced his way, and he felt a familiar stirring in his loins. He knew now how she looked in the throes of passion, and it was haunting him. He had vivid, hot memories of her body squeezed tightly to his, of her legs wrapped around him.

Why was he tormenting himself? Why didn't he just take her? Make love to her? *You could have her, were you to reach out and make your claim,* he thought. But no, he wouldn't do that. Having been gifted with her love, he didn't want to take a chance on losing it. Together out on the ocean with no one else around, it was inevitable that any anger she might have would subside. If he was patient, he knew he would reclaim her affection.

"It won't be long until Geordie is back home where he belongs," he said softly, "and all your heartache will be but a dream."

"Will it?" She wanted to think that was true. "They will not harm him?"

"No. He is much more valuable to them alive than dead, else they would have harmed him while they were in Alba." He knew Halldor's way of thinking. Somehow he had to figure out a way to make a profit on the boy.

"I keep thinking that the poor wee laddie must be so afraid. . . ."

Without really thinking, Torin reached out and took her hand. Putting it to his mouth, he pressed his lips gently to the flesh of her palm, then pressed it to his cheek. It was a gesture of compassion and love that totally stunned her and left her speechless. Who would ever have thought that a Viking would be capable of such tenderness?

"I'll do everything within my power to bring him back safely."

"I know." Looking up, she stared deep into his eyes. "I am not angry with ye any longer. I realize that my father sent ye to find his sons, and ye went to fulfill your duty."

Torin knew that he had to tell her the whole story. She deserved to know. "Your father is ill, Erica. He wants to make certain that everything he has done won't crumble if . . . if something happens to him."

"He is ill?" She was crushed by the revelation. It was as if she had lost him before she had even found him. "No!"

Torin tried to soften the blow. "He has been having dizzy spells. We do not know if the spells are life-threatening." An ominous boom of thunder rumbled high above them, punctuating his sentence. Erica looked up at the sky. A swiftly moving thunderstorm was sweeping over them.

"Take cover. It's going to be a downpour," Torin rasped. The only refuge was the small cloth canopy in the middle of the ship. He pulled her toward it.

It was a hard, driving rain that pelted the canvas above them with a fierceness that was frightening. Only by sitting tightly together could they have any hope of staying dry. Was it any wonder that Torin was thankful for the rain?

Huddled so close together, he could feel the heat of her body; he could smell the freshness of her skin. His whole body tensed as tightly as a coiled spring. Never in all his life had Torin been as tempted by a woman as he was now. Desire slammed into him as swift as the lightning lashed through the sky, but it was much more than passion. Another emotion swept through him as he reached out and touched her cheek.

"Are those tears or is it the rain?" he asked gently.

"Both," she answered truthfully. She was crying for her father and for what might have been. "I . . . I want to see him."

Wordlessly he gathered her closer into his embrace, marveling at how right it felt to have her cradled in his arms. It was as if that was where she was supposed to be forever and ever.

The rain stopped as swiftly as it had begun, leaving only the drip, drip of water cascading down the canopy to the wooden deck below. Once again the sun shone on the wet landscape, making the raindrops sparkle like gemstones. Erica could feel the heat of the sun through the canvas and smiled sadly. Perhaps the sun was an omen, she thought. A sign of better things to come, and of a turning point in her relationship with Torin.

"I forgot that so much water could come so quickly out of the sky," Torin whispered, looking down to where their hips and legs were still touching so intimately as they knelt together. For a long time Erica remained in limbo, not wanting to move away, glorying in his hard, solid frame.

"Torin . . ."

Her voice was drowned out by the eerie sound of a horn in the distance—a noise that sent chills up Erica's spine.

"We've arrived."

Torin picked up a long, curled horn, inhaled deeply, and put it to his lips. He blew three mighty blasts that were echoed from the land. "Just to let them know we are friendly."

The ship had been spotted on the horizon by a lookout. Men, women, and children ran down to the landing to greet the returning heroes. At their heels were several dogs following after their masters and mistresses. A ship was exciting. A merchant ship carrying goods even more so.

"They don't know that our cargo hold is empty," Torin said with a smile, "or they would not be so excited."

With the expertise of one who has sailed many times before, Torin guided the ship up the peninsula, toward the shore. "Come."

He saw her stiffen. He touched the tip of her nose, imagining her in a silk dress that would complement the pendant she always wore around her neck. "I will get something for you while we are here. And for me. We both need a change of garments."

"A present?" Erica couldn't wait. Her eyes were wide as she asked, "What?"

"A dress made from cloth that is smooth to the touch and shimmers like the sun and is so light that it feels as if you have nothing on. It is called silk."

Erica quickly looked down to assess her appearance. Although she had tried to tidy up, she knew she must be a sight.

Her hair was windblown, and though she tried to subdue the wild, thick red mane into orderly waves, the salt air had wreaked its havoc. She rubbed at the dark circles beneath her eyes, wishing now that she had gotten more sleep.

"I will shame you dressed like this, it is true."

"Shame me?" Suddenly he realized that he had unwillingly hurt her feelings. "Never, Erica!" With her large, expressive blue eyes, her long red hair flowing over her shoulders, and her nose held high in the air, she would put every other woman to shame. Even in her begrimed garments she was beautiful.

Torin drew her close to his chest. She could feel his heart beating rapidly. Then he kissed her, with all the passion of that moment in the curach. For a long moment they held tightly to each other; then Torin said again, "Come."

Throwing back her shoulders, lifting her chin, Erica put on a facade of bravery she certainly did not feel. The thought of being surrounded by Vikings was unsettling. How she forced her feet to move, she'd never know, but somehow she was following Torin as he threw down the plank, then walked ashore.

Torin was proud of the way she was handling herself, with nearly as much courage as he. She had guts, that he had to admit. Even when they were immediately surrounded by bearded Norsemen, she didn't flinch.

"It's good to be on land again."

Erica did not share in Torin's excitement at arriving in this strange place. To her it was noisy, crowded, and filthy, with the smell of fish heavy in the air. Even from far away she could see that several of the inhabitants were looking in her direction. Likewise she gazed at them, soothed to see that there were several red-haired men and women—obviously Scots. This place was so unfamiliar, so strangely different from what she was used to.

Affectionately he brushed her red locks from her face and reached out to hold on to her arm. Then he grinned at her as he led her to a stack of barrels. "At least here we can be alone."

But not for long. Soon they were joined by a man even larger than Torin. The man was dark-skinned. His head was shaved completely bare. From his upper lip hung hair that had been molded to perfect points at each side. It was his eyes, however, that frightened her. Small, piercing black eyes that resembled a snake's. Thick muscles bulged from his bare arms.

"Muhar!"

"Torin, what are you doing here?"

"Trying to find my ship and my men," Torin answered dryly.

"They have disappeared?" Muhar scratched his head.

"It is a long story." Hoping that Muhar could help, he described Geordie. "Have you seen him?"

Muhar shook his head. "If I know Halldor, he will sell him for gold."

Erica winced at the reply. The very thought of Geordie being sold as a slave made her shudder. She wondered if Muhar the Bald was a slave trader.

As if sensing Erica's feelings, Torin took her by the arm and hastened off without another word to Muhar. They were both silent as they wove in and out among the walls and merchants' tents at Stornoway.

True to his word, Torin purchased an emerald silk dress, a tunic, a tan woolen dress, a brown cloak, and shoes for Erica, then used his talents in bartering to buy his own garments.

"Torin. Torin, is it you?" Turning around, Torin came face to face with a man who had sailed with him to Eire and back again.

"Lief."

There was a great deal of backslapping, jovial laughter, and man talk. It didn't take Torin long to convince Lief to sail with him to Kaupang in pursuit of Audun and the others. Lief knew of five other men who could be counted on to sail with them.

Erica felt ill at ease, for every now and then she caught the man named Lief staring at her. At last he asked, "who is the woman?"

Putting his arm protectively around her, Torin answered, "Her name is Erica."

"A red-haired beauty." He took a step toward her, but Torin pushed him back.

"She is a Scot—and Ragnar's daughter."

"Ragnar!" The man bowed his head with all the deference of one meeting a queen.

"She is the sister of the boy I am searching for." Seeing Lief's puzzled look, he said, "It's a long story. I will explain it all once we are out to sea." Torin felt relieved and optimistic. It had been much easier to gather up a crew than he had imagined. He turned to Erica, hoping to put his optimism into words, but the words died in his throat. Her face had paled; her eyes were wide. Raising her arm, she pointed.

"That piece of wool."

Torin followed her line of vision to where a scrap of red wool, hung high on a tree, billowed in the breeze.

* * *

The longer he was among the Vikings, the more Geordie loathed them. They were greedy, stupid, and cruel, particularly the one named Bolli. Boasting was their favorite pastime. Now, as he touched the iron collar they had put around his neck to lead him like a puppy, he truly hated them.

"We don't want you to get away," Audun explained, giving the chain at the end of the collar a tug. "As soon as we are back aboard the ship we'll take it off."

If they were going to treat him like an animal, he would act like an animal, Geordie thought. Then let them try to pass him off as the Viking jarl's son. He would make fools of them all.

"What is he doing?" Halldor was furious. Taking the chain from Audun, he yanked it hard.

Geordie got down on his hands and knees.

"He is making fun of us!" Audun gestured for Halldor to stop tugging.

"We can't pass him off as Ragnar's son if he acts like a dog."

Brandishing his sword, Bolli stepped forward. "We ought to chop off his head."

Audun pushed the big Viking away. "You'll get your chance soon enough. After Herlaug has given us our reward." He patted Geordie on the head. "I'll take off the collar if you promise not to run away. Do you promise?"

Geordie glared at him, but he nodded his head. All the while he was imagining what Torin would do to this Viking if he knew the way they were treating him.

"Please find me. . . ."

All during the sea voyage Geordie had anxiously looked behind, waiting for Torin and Gardar to catch up, hoping to see another Viking ship on the horizon. With that hope he had left pieces of his breacan at various places along the way. Hoping. Always hoping. Now he was starting to lose hope.

"Find me. Please find me."

Erica had always said that if you thought very hard, you could transport thoughts. Now Geordie mentally tried to guide Torin to Kaupang.

TWENTY-SEVEN

Once again the ship glided over the waves, only this time it was manned by six muscular Vikings. Though Erica was unnerved at first by their intrusion and missed the intimacy she and Torin had shared, she had to admit that the shaggy-bearded Norsemen added power and speed to their journey. More important, these were Vikings that Torin trusted.

"Lief saved my life more times than I can count," he had told her. "When the others shunned me and treated me as an outcast because of my father, he offered his hand in friendship."

"Then, if he has treated ye kindly I will do the same for him," Erica had answered. Now she watched as they stood at the prow, huddled together like two lads awaiting adventure.

Torin was insistent that they sail to Kaupang, a Norse port, for it was there that traders came with their cargoes of furs, skins, walrus ivory, and slaves. Torin suspected that Audun, Halldor, and the others would stop there before returning to Hafrsfjord.

"Something strange is afoot," he confided to Lief. "I suspect that Audun thinks to worm himself into Ragnar's favor by bringing him the boy."

"No doubt he thinks the Scots killed you. Who, therefore, is left who can reveal his lie?"

"The boy! I fear his life may be in danger when Audun has no more use for him. We must find him!"

Lief nodded in Erica's direction. "And what then? What will you do with your flame-haired beauty? Surely not take her back."

"I want to make her my wife."

Lief raised his brows. "And what if Ragnar has other plans for his new-found daughter."

Torin clenched his jaw. "I will marry her with or without Ragnar's approval," he said. "I have served him well these past years. She is the only reward I ask for."

The ship traced the upper coastline of the area inhabited by the Scots and Picts, then rounded the southeastern tip toward their destination, a land of steep mountains and tundra to the west and pasturelands to the east.

"Erica . . . ?" Torin moved toward her, his eyes caressing her. She was wearing the bright blue underdress and tan overtunic that he had bought for her. It was a stunning contrast to her flaming hair. Around her waist was a thin leather belt that made her small waist look even narrower than it was.

"We're coming to Normannaland." He pointed toward the shore, taking note of the immense rocky cliffs.

Erica could sense a change in the air. The wind tickling her face was much colder than it had been on Ulva. The skies seemed cloudier. Shadows crept along the deck. She shivered.

"Don't be afraid." Reaching out, he gently moved his hand up and down her spine.

"I have no fear for myself, but for Geordie." Closing her eyes, she tried to block out the image of her brother's fearful expression, but still it danced beneath her eyelids.

"He is alive. You wouldn't have found that piece of cloth if he were not."

"He's trying so hard to guide us, but he must be terrified. My poor Geordie . . ." Could Torin understand her feelings?

She was Geordie's sister. She had always protected him, but now he was all alone and there was nothing she could do.

He felt her shiver again and quickly covered her with his cloak. "It is colder here than where you come from," he said, trying to take her mind off her brother.

"Colder . . ." she whispered. And so very barren.

Steep, solid cliffs rose on both sides of the ship like rock walls—mountains that sprang up abruptly from steep-sided, long, narrow waterways, extending inland for many miles. *Fjords,* she had heard them called.

As they sailed farther, she saw that it was desolate, sparsely populated, almost treeless, and cold. Erica supposed that the scant forests were due to the many huge canoes that rode the waters. Boats that were similar to Torin's, only much larger.

"That is Kaupang that you see way over there."

Kaupang lay on the shores of a bay where island, shoals, and narrow channels made the approaches slow and hazardous for marauding strangers. It effectively prevented surprise attacks. It was used only as a summer marketplace, Torin told her. It was in Kaupang that merchants would peddle their wares from turf-walled, roofless booths that were sometimes covered over with woolen sailcloth from the Vikings' ships.

The settlement of Kaupang, which meant *market-place,* was situated on the west side of the entrance to the Oslofjord. On the west side of the small bay was a complex of houses and workshops with wells attached and placed by the waterside. It was known for its metalwork in iron, silver, and bronze. Kaupang was an important center for one of the most popular of Norse products: soapstone used for bowls, cooking ware, lamps, and loom weights. It could be shaped in much the same way that wood was carved.

Once they were on land, Torin took her hand and pushed through the cluster of onlookers. The mists of early morning hung over the city like a shroud. It was damp as well as cold, and the air was heavy. The smells of the city floated on the breeze and Erica wrinkled her nose. The odors of unwashed human flesh and plant and animal waste filled the air.

As they drew closer Erica could see animals and humans surging through the narrow streets, clattering over the wooden walkway. Unlike the other, sparsely populated village they had passed, Kaupang was crowded. She had never seen so many animals and people crowded into such a small space. There were people of every shape, color, and size, from Vikings with their fair skin and blond hair to men and women whose skin was as dark as the night.

There were men dressed in cloaks like Torin's, with neck chains hanging across their chests, men in furs and tall hats, men in Viking helmets carrying large swords. Women, dressed as Erica now was in Viking-style linen underdresses and woolen overtunics, freely associated with women who wore dresses made of colorful cloth that sparkled. Erica stared hard at every face, hoping against hope that she would find Geordie, but to no avail.

"If he is here he will have left another scrap of cloth behind!" Torin told Lief and the other Vikings to search all of Kaupang if necessary to find any shred of a red woolen breacon. Meanwhile, Erica and Torin went toward the center of town, asking everyone they met if they had seen a boy of Geordie's description.

"There are some here looking at ye with unfriendly eyes," Erica whispered. "Are ye sure they can be trusted?"

"No, but we have no other choice. We have to find your brother if he is here, before the ship sails again."

It was a chaotic scene of buyers and sellers haggling in at least a dozen languages. People, mostly men, thronged the timber boardwalks and jostled each other in the dirt streets. A lot of people, yet none had seen a young Scot.

Torin spent the morning searching, questioning everyone he came to. Just as he was about to give up and gather the others to return to the ship, he was accosted by an old woman.

"I saw the child." She held out her hand as if to say her information was not free.

Torin hesitated. He had bartered everything he owned to buy garments for himself and Erica in Stornoway. All he had was a ring given to him by his father. "You are sure you saw the boy?"

"I know."

Torin looked at the woman, then at Erica, then at the woman again. His father's ring, yet he had to make the sacrifice for her. "Here." He handed the ring to the old woman. "But know well, old woman, that if you play me false I will hunt you down and pull it from your finger by force if need be."

The woman took the ring with a satisfied smile. "You will have no need to take it back." She put the ring on her thumb. "I saw the child not long ago. He had a collar around his neck and he was being dragged through town like a slave or a dog."

"Dragged!" Erica was horrified. She stifled a sob with her fist.

"Where were they? Lead me to the spot."

The old woman was slow. Once or twice as they walked, Torin gave her a slight push to hurry her along. At last they came to a row of stalls that specialized in clothing for wealthier Vikings. There were fine linens, fur-trimmed hats, and warm woolen cloaks.

"Look!" Erica's hands trembled as she pointed to the tattered piece of red woolen that was stuck on the tip of a sword.

"I was right. They did come here." Torin searched the area; then, climbing up a hill, he looked down at the ocean. "There!"

Erica ran up behind him and gasped at what she saw. "Geordie!" From a distance they could see her brother. His hands were tied behind his back and he had an iron collar around his neck. A big, hulking Viking was leading him back toward a ship.

"Bolli!" Torin's heart pounded. His anger rose to a boiling point. Without even thinking of the danger of loose rocks, he climbed down the hill and ran in pursuit of the boy and his captors.

From a distance Erica could see the fierce fight that ensued. Torin and one of the Vikings rolled over and over on the ground, but Torin's anger gave him superhuman strength. It looked as if Torin was going to be the victor, until other Vikings joined in the melee. The tallest of the Vikings caught Torin from behind while another put his fingers around his throat and squeezed tightly. Erica watched in horror as Torin slumped to the ground.

Putting his hands up to his neck as he gasped for breath, Torin looked up at Geordie, feeling helpless and foolish. He had rushed in to rescue him but now it was he who needed rescuing. So much for being a hero. Still, he wouldn't give up trying.

"Ye came to rescue me, Tor. Just as I knew ye would!" Geordie's eyes shown with admiration.

"Let the boy go, Audun," Torin ordered, buoyed up by the young Scot's adoration. "He hasn't done any harm to you."

Audun snorted. "It is not revenge that goaded me to take him, but profit."

"You have made a mistake. He is not Ragnar's son!"

Throwing back his head, Halldor laughed. "No, you are the one who has made a mistake if you think that it matters."

So he was right, Torin thought. They were going to make use of Geordie to promote a lie. "Ragnar is no fool. He will know the boy's age and realize he is too young to be his son."

"Ha, Ragnar hasn't anything to do with it," Bolli cut in.

"Then what . . . ?" Torin shook his head, trying to clear a sudden wave of dizziness.

"What a shame that the Scots didn't kill you. It would have saved me the trouble," Audun hissed ominously. He motioned for Bolli. "Kill him!"

Bolli came at him with his sword but stopped in midair as Torin stood up, spread his feet apart, and took the stance of a man willing to fight. "I'm unarmed. If you kill me, Bolli, it will bode ill for you. There are severe penalties for killing a man who is Viking-born. That's why Audun and Halldor are leaving it up to you to kill me."

"Huh?" Bolli put down his sword. He wrinkled his nose and squinted his eyes as he tried to think.

"Viking-born, ha." Halldor was scornful. "He is like his father, an outcast." He shouted out, "Kill him!"

"Kill me and you will pay with your life, Bolli," Torin exclaimed. "Look!"

Erica had rounded up the other Vikings. Now they were making their way down the hillside with swords upraised to aid Torin. At the sight of Lief and the others, Bolli ran.

Now that he had comrades-in-arms, Torin rasped, "Give me the boy, my ship, and my men!"

"Think again, Torin. The men are mine now, not yours. They will do as I command them." Now Audun commanded them to return to the ship and set sail.

Torin glanced about him, wondering how many of these men would fight on his side. One. Two. Three. Four. Five men deserted Audun and joined with Torin. Forming a living wall, they moved forward to block Audun's retreat, but Audun and his band were fleet of foot. Torin gave chase as they ran, swam, and climbed back to the ship. Angrily he watched them set sail.

TWENTY-EIGHT

The gold sails of the knorr billowed in the wind as it sailed in pursuit of Torin's long ship. The frigid waters of the North Sea buffeted the merchant ship, causing her to bob up and down through the angry waves like a child's toy.

Torin shouted out commands to his now-larger crew as they hustled about with poles and rope. A terrible storm was brewing. He could tell from the changes in the wind and wave patterns as well as from the cloud formations. Reaching down into his shirt, he brought forth the sunstone tied around his neck to guide them. When held at right angles to the plane of light from the sun, the mineral crystal changed from yellow to dark blue, so that a navigator in midocean could locate the exact position of the sun and thus calculate the ship's position.

Beneath his breath Torin swore. The storm would make it more difficult to catch up with the other ship, which had gotten a head start. Worse yet, he had questioned the four Vikings who had sailed with Audun and had learned the ship's destination. Halldor and Audun were not taking Geordie to Ragnar, as he had first thought but to Herlaug, Ragnar's devious brother.

Audun, Halldor, and Herlaug—what a dangerous combination. But Torin was determined that they would not triumph. He would get back the boy and see that they all paid for what they had done to him! He owed that to Erica, to Geordie, and to himself.

"I hate storms." Erica cringed as she remembered the storm that had upended the curach and left them stranded on Staffa.

Torin cursed Aegir, god of the sea, in his heart for the timing of the gale. At the same time he tried to comfort Erica. "Don't worr—"

A giant wave lashed out like a hand, throwing their bodies together with such force that Erica was winded. She gasped and choked, trying to catch her breath as another wave drenched them with its fingers. Grasping desperately at Torin's arm, she clung to him. Her breasts pressed into his chest, and in spite of the danger, he was aroused. Once Geordie was safe and they were alone, he was going to make love to her again and again to make up for lost time.

"It will be all right," he whispered in her ear. "Everything will be all right." He only hoped that he could keep his promise.

Reaching for a length of rope and picking Erica up in his arms, Torin made his way to the nearest crutch, a rising beam of wood, and draped the rope around her waist. "I'm going to tie you to the beam. That way you will not be swept overboard."

"Tie me . . . ?"

Once Erica might have argued, but she trusted Torin now. Trusted him with her life. Though the rope cut into her flesh, she did not cry out as he tied her to the wood of the T-shaped crutch, then returned to his men.

Suddenly it was as if the ocean were a live being, tossing the ship to and fro. Erica watched as the ship's small crew struggled desperately to survive. Loose rigging snapped and slashed in the savage winds, and she was certain that at any moment the ship would turn facedown in the churning water. She clung to the pole until her hands were numb, thankful that Torin had been wise enough to secure her to the pole.

Erica's eyes were riveted on Torin. He didn't show any fear as he moved about the ship, taking his place at the stern. Even when the rains came, pouring down upon the ship like water from a barrel, he didn't even flinch. When one of the Vikings fell overboard, Torin kept his self-control. He ordered his crew to throw several ropes into the sea so that the Viking could be rescued.

If only my uncle could see Torin now, he would realize how strong and brave he is. Perhaps then he would understand why I love him and why I cannot let him go, even if it means that I will be banished from Alba forever.

Erica watched now as the other Vikings helped the fallen Viking back on board, then slapped each other on the back in congratulations. Seeing Torin among his own gave her a new perspective on the man she cared so deeply about.

When the storm was over he untied the ropes that bound her and gathered her into his arms, pushing back the hair from her face. "Not even the ocean can stop us. We'll find Geordie."

"Aye, I believe that we will." Erica clung to him, overwhelmed by the feelings that stirred within her at his touch. He was an amazing man. She felt a newfound appreciation of his wisdom and ability to read the signs in nature, such as the pattern of the flight of birds, the rising and setting of the sun—even the way the wind played upon the waves. He could determine the path and follow a straight line toward his destination.

Erica clung to the crutch of the ship and to the shreds of her courage, staring out to sea. They were almost *there.* Though she tried to smile bravely, she was ill at ease and apprehensive. What if all of Torin's good intentions were for naught? What if they couldn't reach Geordie in time? What if . . . ?

She shook her head. All of the what-if's whirling through

her mind were giving her a headache. She had to be patient; she had to believe and to trust that right would overpower wrong. And she had to believe in and trust Torin.

She watched as he strode about, preparing the ship for a smooth entry, a process which took a great deal of skill and maneuvering, considering the elongated rocks that rose up from the waters.

Erica watched as the knorr moved up the fjord. The rocks soon faded out of sight. The view of the coast changed from rough, barren, rocky cliffs to an area with trees that looked as if it had been hacked out of the mountain. Apparently it was a village, for she could see clusters of large longhouses emerging through the clouds.

The sail was furled, the rowers positioned at the oars. At the stern, Torin raised the curled horn to his lips and blew three loud blasts as a signal that the ship was friendly and intended no harm. The three notes were answered by another horn high atop the hill in a reverberating sign of welcome. As the ship pulled to the shore, a crowd of people soon appeared to greet it, just as they had in Stornoway and Kaupang, but here they were louder in their welcome and seemed friendlier.

"We're home."

"Home." Erica whispered. This cold land wasn't home for her. She was apprehensive about what she would find here, but at the same time anxious to put her feet once again upon dry land.

She watched as the knorr stopped not more than a few feet from shore. Anxious to familiarize herself with this new land, she looked around. Just as in Alba, she could see fishermen. *Fish must be the main source of food here,* she thought. The ocean seemed to be very important to the Vikings. They drew their food from it, traveled in ships upon it, and even built their lodges overlooking the ocean. She spotted a dwelling balancing on the bank of the waterside,

another nearly touching the mountain slope, and even dwell-
ings perched on ledges high above the water.

"You Vikings must be sure-footed," she exclaimed as Torin's arm encircled her waist.

He laughed. "As sure-footed as goats!" As the ship came
to shore, his hold on her tightened. "Hang on!" With a
hearty yell he swept her with him onto the dry land.

Because of the large throng of people, it took Torin a long
time to lead Erica through the crowd. She could tell by the
reaction his people had toward him that he was respected,
for the men clasped him on the shoulder, laughing and talking, and the women looked upon him with sparkling eyes
that left no doubt as to how much they admired him. And
yet, despite all the adulation, there was an aloofness about
Torin. As if he had once had to shield himself from hurt.
Had these same people once shunned him?

Taking her hand, motioning for the others to follow, he
pushed through the cluster of onlookers and walked up the
shoreline, searching for sight of the long ship. Trying to
adjust her sea legs to land, Erica added her eyes to the search.

"They have to be somewhere. They couldn't have just
disappeared unless . . ." Torin didn't want to even think
about the possibility that he had been wrong in supposing
that Audun would bring Geordie here, but the nagging
thought intruded nonetheless. What if Geordie had been
taken to Hedeby to be sold as a slave?

"Torin. There. I see it!" Lief clutched at his sword.

Erica squinted her eyes. She saw the ship, too. Ignoring
Torin's command that she stay behind where it was safe, she
followed as he and his band of Vikings ran toward an out-
cropping of buildings.

Geordie was pushed and pulled toward a group of large
wooden buildings that he heard one of the Vikings refer to
as outbuildings. There was a byre for housing animals in the

cold days of the winter, barns to store their fodder, a stable, a small smithy, and a bathhouse.

"Let's get this over, get our reward, and sail away," Halldor grumbled. "If I know Torin, he will be close behind us, anxious to spoil everything."

"Come inside," Audun said. He led Geordie to the largest building, which he said was the central dwelling house, the *skaalen,* or hall where cooking, eating, feasting, and gaming were done.

Geordie stood in the shadows. He was petrified. What would happen when it was found out that he was not half Viking, not the son of the jarl. What then? "How strange. . . ."

His eyes touched on the large fireplace in the largest room of the dwelling. Big pots hung over the fire on chains from beams in the ceiling of the gabled roof. Was it true what he had heard, that Vikings boiled their enemies in oil? He hoped not. Then he saw the big, blond, scar-faced Viking standing in the shadows, and he feared the worst.

"You wanted the sons of Ragnar," Audun proclaimed, giving Geordie a push. "Here is one of them. A half-Scots, half-Viking bastard!"

"Ragnar's son?" Herlaug looked Geordie in the face, pressing his nose right against the boy's nose. Then he grunted. "He's a runt! Smaller than I thought he would be."

Though Audun and Halldor had bought expensive garments for Geordie and padded them to make him appear more muscular, his face still held the innocence of youth.

"Because he is the youngest." Halldor was obviously nervous, for he paced up and down as he spoke. "We followed Torin, though he wanted us to stay on the ship. Once we realized who the boy was, we snatched him up and of course brought him to you."

Herlaug tugged at his beard. "I wanted all three."

Audun stepped between Herlaug and Halldor. "And you

shall have them, one at a time." He held out his hand. "Pay us for this one and we will return with the others in tow."

Herlaug grunted. "Why do I feel as if I am being cheated?"

"Cheated?" Halldor gave Geordie another push. "How could that be, when we risked our lives to aid you in your quest to follow in your brother's footsteps as jarl?"

"What about Torin?"

"He is dead," Halldor lied. "Bolli killed him." Making eye contact with Audun, he urged him to hurry up the transactions somehow so that they could be safely on their way out to sea before the falsehood was discovered.

"Dead?" Herlaug freely displayed his displeasure. "You fools. I told you to kill him *after* you found out where the others were."

"Which we did," Audun assured him. "That is why we will set sail for the eastern coast of Britain just as soon as we collect our reward." He held out his hand and was rewarded when Herlaug plopped a small sack of gold coins on his upturned palm. Halldor and Bolli were likewise rewarded. As an afterthought Audun asked, "What are you going to do with the boy?"

Herlaug answered without a second thought. "Kill him!" He motioned for Bolli to do the deed.

"Nay!" Now that he knew exactly what his fate was to be, Geordie spoke up. At least if he was going to die, he would reveal the truth. "I am not the son of Ragnar!" he declared, speaking the Vikings' own strange language.

Halldor was stunned. All along the sea journey the boy had kept quiet except for a word or two. They had not realized that he could speak their language so well.

"I am not related to him at all," Geordie continued. "They are lying to ye just to get rich."

"Lying?" Herlaug raised his thick brows in question, then turned to Halldor. "Is that true?"

Audun answered, "He is Ragnar's son. I swear it!"

Bolli raised his sword.

"I am not! I am too young. Ask Ragnar himself when his sons were sired and ye will clearly see the terrible lie that is being told here."

Herlaug looked at Audun, then at Halldor, and finally at Bolli. Something in their eyes revealed that what the boy was saying was true. Without saying another word, Herlaug took the sword from Bolli's upraised hand. Without a word he raised it high, then sent it downward in a crushing blow that severed Halldor's hand. With a gruesome thud, the hand and coin pouch fell to the hard earthen floor. Without even a blink, Herlaug turned to Audun.

"I should and could have killed him."

He didn't have time to say anything more. The sound of broken wood shattered the air. Geordie saw the gleam of upraised swords, saw Torin's face, and shouted out in relief.

"Bastards!" Torin cried out. He hurled himself forward, lashing out wildly. Seeing Bolli move forward, he met him head on, swinging and slashing. The air was rent with the sound of steel on steel. Seeing Audun fall, Torin picked up his limp body and threw it at Bolli, knocking him to the ground. Picking up a discarded sword, Erica joined in the fighting.

"Hold!" Putting up his right hand, Herlaug gestured for an end to the fighting. Hesitantly Torin complied, though he clutched his sword so that he would be ready in case there was any foul play.

From the corner, Halldor clutched at the stump where his hand had once been. He didn't have time even to cry out before Herlaug impaled him on his sword. Herlaug then moved to Bolli and to Audun with the swift finality of an executioner.

"You killed them!" Torin was angered, for he knew that Herlaug had murdered them to make certain that his own perfidy was not revealed.

Herlaug pointed to the bloodied hand that had been

knocked into the corner of the room. "I punished them for what they have done. My brother will commend me. They were traitors. They brought me this poor boy, trying to pawn him off as Ragnar's son."

Running forward, Erica quickly freed Geordie from his bonds and gathered him into a hug that was so tight he could hardly breathe. All the while she whispered endearments in his ear and stroked his long hair. She had feared that she would never see him again, and yet thanks to Torin they had been reunited.

"Geordie . . . Geordie . . ." She crooned.

"How do you know he is not Ragnar's son?" Torin asked through clenched teeth.

"I heard the truth from the boy himself," Herlaug hissed. Though he tried to act as if Torin was in his favor, the flicker of anger in his eyes could not be disguised. In truth, Erica suspected that he hated him.

"He spoke the truth. He is not Ragnar's son, but what if he had been? What then, Herlaug?" Torin knew the answer. Herlaug would have killed him. The trouble was, how was he going to convince Ragnar of that?

"I would have welcomed the boy with open arms. After all, that would make me his uncle, Torin."

Erica started to speak, but Torin hurried to her side and gripped her arm to warn her to keep silent. Though he knew that she would want to tell Ragnar that she was his daughter, Torin feared for her fate if her identity came to light. He knew that Herlaug could not be trusted. Not now. Not ever.

"Who is the woman, Torin?" Now that the excitement was over, Herlaug quickly took note of the woman in their midst.

"She is Geordie's sister and the woman I have brought here to be my wife!"

TWENTY-NINE

Torin could see that all eyes followed the stunning vision in emerald green silk as they entered Ragnar's hall. Herlaug had the tongue of a gossip, he thought. It had not taken long for the word to be spread that he had brought back a woman to marry. No doubt she would be the topic of conversation in every household, which was just what Torin wanted. The more people who were curious about her, the more eyes would be watching and the harder it would be for Herlaug to do her any harm.

If the Vikings were looking at her, then Erica was equally intrigued with them, particularly the women. She could not help comparing their dress with those of the Scots. The Viking women attired themselves in long, trailing garments of bright colors—yellow, blue, green, and brown, some finely pleated with short sleeves, others with no sleeves at all. None as beautiful as the dress Torin had given her. The colors for the dyes had been selected from nature's plant life, just as they were at home. Their garments were closed at the neck with a drawstring. Over this was a woolen tunic, held in place by a matched pair of oval bronze brooches. From this oval jewelry hung chains that held knives, needles, combs, and strange objects.

Some wore cloaks. Sometimes the young unmarried Scottish women would pull their long skirts up between their knees in order to make dancing easier. She smiled as she thought of how some visitors at home approved and others thought the practice absolutely pagan. Instead of letting their hair flow free, it was pulled back and covered by an ugly piece of cloth tied at the back of the head. Erica had insisted that her hair remain long and flowing. She had always been independent in thought, and when she returned home she would remain so.

Just as she was beginning to feel a little overwhelmed by all she was observing, Torin came to her rescue. He had a way of anticipating her moods. Taking her hand, Torin pushed through the cluster of onlookers, ignoring their questions of who she was and where she came from. "There will be time for talk later," he exclaimed.

"But how I wish there were time for talk now," Erica replied, ill at ease about not telling her father who she was and why she had come to the Northland. "What of Geordie?"

Torin sought out a quiet corner. "Geordie is just fine. Lief has taken a liking to the boy. He took him with him to the bathhouse and he is going to give him one of his older son's garments to wear until we can get him garments of his own. Then he is going to teach him some Viking games."

Erica squeezed his arm. "What about my father? Why can't we tell him who I am?" She had imagined their meeting a thousand times in her dreams. "It has been so many years. . . ."

It seemed they were having the same conversation for the hundredth time. "Because if we tell him you are his daughter he will tell Herlaug, and we can't take the chance of your treacherous uncle finding out. At least not until we know why he was interested in finding Ragnar's offspring and we are certain of his intentions."

She smiled playfully. "Oh, so ye are telling me that perhaps Herlaug would worry about a woman *if* she was Ragnar's daughter. And here I thought ye didn't think me important."

"You are important to me. More so than anything or anyone in the world." He nuzzled her neck, then made a wide sweep of the hall with his hand, feeling very proud of his homeland and hoping that perhaps she might feel comfortable here and want to stay—forever, if he had his way.

Down the center of the room was a long hearth on a raised platform, from which glowed several fires. Both side walls of the hall were lined with indoor benches that were used either for sitting or sleeping. There were several tables which could either be pushed aside to make more room or used for dining when there were guests.

"Those tables remind me of food."

"Are you as hungry as I am?"

"I am famished!" Besides, people were far more amiable when their stomachs were being fed, she had always found.

"I would imagine that since the word has gone out that I have come back with a potential bride, it should be quite a crowd."

"Bride?" She folded her arms across her waist. "I cannot seem to remember that ye asked me to marry."

For just a moment he feared that he had been too presumptuous. What if she said no? "But I thought—I hoped—"

She put her arms around his neck. "That I would say yes! I will marry ye."

He kissed her on the forehead. "I love you! I want everyone for miles around to see you and know that you are mine." Including Ragnar, he thought, wondering what the consequences of his actions would be. No doubt Ragnar would be furious.

A loom and several spindle whorls for the spinning of wool stood against the farthest wall, and Torin could nearly imagine Erica sitting there, making cloth for the family he was anxious to sire. Toward the far wall was a chair, much higher than the benches around it. It was heavily carved with geometric and floral designs that were representations of the Nordic gods. Erica examined the chair as he told her which gods the carvings represented.

"Odin is our chief god, then there is Thor, who caused thunder with his hammer, and Loki the mischievous god, and Frey and Freyja . . ."

For just a moment a frown creased her brow as she was reminded that Torin worshipped pagan gods. Could she resign herself to that and love him for the man that he was without trying to dictate how he should think, feel, and believe? Would she be happy to let him be the man that he was? Her mother had given Ragnar total freedom. She knew she would have to do the same or all was lost.

"This is your father's chair." The words were hardly out of his mouth when Ragnar swept into the room like a raging thunderstorm.

"So, here you are! Why did you sneak into the village like a thief without first coming to see me? And where is the son you were supposed to bring back with you?"

The loud, booming voice startled Erica. Hurriedly she shrank deep into the shadows, watching as the powerfully built, though haggard, blond man strode toward Torin, standing but an arm's length away. Like the rest of the others, he had a hairy face and strong features that had been etched by the march of time. His heavy mane of tawny hair was streaked with gray, and as he turned to face her, Erica could see a resemblance between herself and him that was staggering.

"My father . . ." she whispered to herself.

She had pictured him so many times in her mind, but he had been so much younger, without the lines of worry etched on his forehead, or the bags under his eyes. Or the sadness in his eyes. Even so, it was a beloved face. How she wanted him to reach out to her and gather her into his arms. Instead, he merely cast her a cursory glance as he asked Torin who she was.

"She is from Alba," he answered evasively.

Ragnar grimaced. "I guessed as much, but who is she?"

"She is the sister of the young man . . . the boy . . . who was abducted from Alba and brought here by Audun, Halldor, and Bolli." As if further explanation were needed he said, "They stole my ship while I was held a prisoner. This brave young woman freed me."

"She did." Now Ragnar was more interested. Slowly he walked around her, looking her up and down, then nodding in approval. "You have chosen well. She is pretty, looks strong, and has the hips of a good breeder. What's more, I remember my woman from Alba. She was passionate. . . ." His eyes held a faraway look, as if he were remembering a special time with her. "You have chosen well."

"I know." Torin cupped her face in his hand and bent forward to kiss her. "I know," he said again.

Ragnar treated Erica with the deference befitting a guest. "Sit beside me. I would hear of Alba so that I can refresh my mind."

Possessively Torin took a seat on the other side of her. "Now that I have recovered my ship and my crew, I will sail again. I met a priest who remembers seeing the amber pendant. In Eire."

"The wolf," Ragnar sighed. "So long ago." He took Erica's hand in his, and she couldn't help noticing that he had long, slim fingers so like her own. He squeezed gently. "Tell me, where in Alba are you from?" She could hardly keep from blurting out the truth.

"Ulva!"

"Ulva. I should have known. That is where I sent Torin on a quest to find the raven." She swallowed hard to keep the tears from flowing at the mention of the precious raven pendant. He turned toward her, staring deep into her eyes. His eyes were so magnetic, Erica waited for him to show recognition, but he merely smiled. "Once I loved a woman from Ulva. It is a long story."

"Perhaps you can tell me some time."

"I will, some time." Ragnar squeezed her hand again, and Erica squeezed back, feeling the warmth of her affection for him fill her heart. He seemed so warm, so gentle and understanding. Hardly a heathen.

Massive pine logs flamed in the sunken trough in the center of the great hall. The air was clouded with drifting veils of smoke as a huge slab of venison roasted on a spit over the fire. Cauldrons made of iron and soapstone were suspended over the flames from a tripod in which bubbled broth and meat stew.

The air rang with laughter and chatter. Already the throng of male guests were elbowing each other for a seat close to where Ragnar sat. They were obviously hoping to eavesdrop so that they could hear firsthand what had happened to Torin across the sea.

Erica took note of the men and women dressed in undyed wool of somber colors, moving back and forth in the large room of the lodge. It seemed that only some of the Vikings worked, for there were several males and females who seemed to do little more than sit while they were waited upon. It was something that would never have occurred in Alba. Laziness was severely frowned upon there.

Ragnar motioned to the skald who picked up his harp. His nimble fingers moved across the instrument, plucking the muted strings as he sang about the days so long ago and never-forgotten heroes. Proud, adventurous, with a yearning for glory, these men had excelled in battle and scorned death to venerate the very name *Viking*. When he devised a melodic tale about their victories over the Scots, the entire hall cheered—except for Erica—who was horrified.

"I'm a fool. I had forgotten that these people are the enemies of my own," she whispered softly to herself.

Seeing the horror in her eyes when the Scots were mentioned, once again Ragnar took her hand and squeezed her fingers as if to offer her comfort, "Fighting is a necessity, but it can have good consequences if at the end there is peace. That is what I want. Peace."

He sounded so sincere that Erica could not help but believe him. "The Scots want peace also," she whispered. "My unc—" Remembering that she was supposed to keep silent about her identity, she hastily picked up the tankard in front of her and took a sip.

Oh, how she hated the secrecy. She wanted to blurt out the truth and tell Ragnar how she had longed all of her life to see him, touch him, hear from his own lips that he had cared about her mother and that he now cared very deeply about her. She wanted to tell him of her exploits, show him how well she could handle a sword, prove her bravery, and in all ways make him proud of her. But most of all she wanted him to cradle her in his arms while they talked with each other and tried to make up for all the lost years.

She watched Ragnar out of the corner of her eye, smiling as she noticed so many things about him that were so like her: the way he wrinkled his nose when he laughed; the way he cocked his head when someone intrigued him; the proud way he carried himself. She had his eyes, his nose, his forehead, even his ears.

In so many ways it was as if all the years between her birth and their first meeting had melted away. Her heart warmed with affection and with a longing for him to care.

"So, you think you want to become a Viking wife," Ragnar said, nodding his head in the direction of the women of the household.

"I want to become Torin's wife," she answered, tensing as he motioned two of the women over to where they sat. She learned that one of the women was his sister and one his wife.

"This is Nissa."

The woman with graying blond hair was a scowling, big-boned woman who soon made it clear that she considered Erica an interloper and a nuisance of whom she wanted no part. Displaying her displeasure with silence, she merely nodded.

Torin whispered in Erica's ear, "Do not feel hurt by her actions. She does not like any other woman. Her beauty has long since faded and she fears that Ragnar's eyes will turn to younger women. She views you as a rival."

"A rival," Erica sighed. "She does not know that she has nothing to fear."

Ragnar rapped sharply upon the table with his knife. It was a signal that the meal had officially begun.

Torin whispered, "The patriarch also signals when the food is to be cleared away. Anyone who has not finished eating will find his food removed before his eyes. Therefore, eat quickly."

Ragnar laughed at that. In fact he seemed to be in a jovial mood, Erica thought. It soothed her concern for him. Torin had said that Ragnar was ill, but he did not look ill tonight— just very, very tired.

"Eat!" Like a stern father Ragnar pointed to her plate.

Erica found mealtime among the Vikings to be a happy and noisy event with a lot of laughter, boasting, and story-telling. But remembering Torin's words to her, she ate hastily in silence. There was a great variety of food in addition to the venison: chicken, goose, rabbit, and fish, as well as cheese and barley porridge.

She was so intent upon eating that Erica did not notice the eyes burning through her until Torin gently nudged her in the arm.

"Beware of that man," he cautioned. "That is Herlaug."

Herlaug, she thought quickly, looking in his direction. She saw a powerful man with a broad chest and muscles of iron. The scars that were visible on his arms, face, and chest were marks of a man used to violence.

My uncle, she thought. And the man to whom the Vikings had taken Geordie. "Herlaug," she whispered. She would remember that name.

THIRTY

Darkness gathered under the high vaulted roof. Shadows loomed tall and menacing. Erica lay on the lumpy straw mattress in the small sleeping area that had been given to her. Built at right angles to the main hall, the bed closet was tiny, just big enough for a bed. She looked at the thin door that led to the hall, longing for Torin to walk through it. Then suddenly, he did.

"Erica . . ." His voice was soft.

She longed to throw herself into his arms, tell him that she loved him, but instead she remained silent. She would let him come to her.

Torin brushed his fingers against her hair. It was as soft as silken threads. Everything about her was softness, tempered with the strength of determination, Torin thought as he studied her in the dim light. She inspired a maelstrom of emotions within him. Passion mixed with tenderness.

He wanted to tell her how he felt, but as he looked down at her he saw that she had fallen asleep. She had been through such a stressful day. Giving in to his yearning, he lay down beside her. Positioning her head on his shoulder, he closed his eyes.

An all-consuming sense of protectiveness surged through him, an emotion he'd never felt for a woman before. He let his eyes move tenderly over her in a caress, lingering on the rise and fall of her breasts. He was entranced by the way the silver moonlight played across her curves, creating tantalizing shadows and reminding him of how beautiful her body was.

He felt an aching tenderness, a tightening inside. He could feel the heat of her body, smell the freshness of her hair. The brush of their bodies wove a cocoon of warm intimacy that he relished, yet his passion was tempered with a more tender feeling. He longed to clasp her in his arms in a close embrace and stay that way forever.

"You don't know how long I have wanted to . . ."

Reaching out, he touched her face, relishing the softness of her skin, like velvet or the petals of a rose. Night scents surrounded him, the smell of leaves, earth, and flowers. Was there anything as peaceful?

"I wish we could be frozen in time," he whispered.

"So do I." She opened her eyes.

They studied each other, two silent, shadowy figures, each achingly aware of the other. The very air pulsated with expectancy. Erica could only anticipate what he was going to say, what he was going to do. She lay like a stone figure, her eyes never once leaving him as he moved forward.

He cupped her face in his hand and brought his mouth down to hers. The pressure of his lips forced hers to part. His lips felt warm, soft, moist, and coaxingly gentle.

Torin's fingers were on her face, stroking her cheek, smoothing her hair back from her temples, touching her eyelids lightly. First one and then the other. Like a flower opening to sunshine, she moved her mouth upon his, feeling the wondrous enchantment.

When at last he broke away he was smiling. "It seems that you have made an impression on Ragnar. All he could do was talk about you." His voice was incredibly tender and husky. Lowering his head, he pressed his mouth to the tender flesh below her ear.

"And he has made an impression on me." She smiled. "He is one of two Vikings that I love."

"And who is the other?"

She moved closer to him, moaning his name into his hair as his lips gently explored that sensitive place. Soft sobs of pleasure echoed through the silence, and she was surprised to find that they came from her own throat. Her senses were filled with a languid heat that made her head spin. She closed her eyes, giving herself up to his nearness.

Lifting her arms, she encircled his neck and wound her fingers in his blond hair, clinging to him, wanting him to love her.

Slowly Torin bent his head, cherishing her lips in another kiss. A much different kind of kiss than he had given her before. Bolder. More demanding. Her lips parted in an invitation for him to drink more deeply of her mouth.

His long, hard kiss ignited a warmth that engulfed her from head to toe. Breathlessly she returned his kisses, tingling with pleasure when he began hungrily to probe the inner warmth. Wishing to bring him as close as possible, she tangled her fingers in his hair and drew him even closer.

All he could think about was the pounding of his heart as he relished the warmth of her body. Capturing her slender shoulders, he pulled her up against him as his mouth moved hungrily against hers. Her head was thrown back, the masses of her flaming hair tumbling in a thick cascade over his arm, tickling his neck.

"I love you," he breathed against her lips. His teeth lightly nipped at her lower lip. His only thought was to bring her pleasure.

A hot ache of desire coiled within Erica. There was a weakening sensation at his kiss, a longing that prompted her to push closer to him, relishing the warmth of his hands as he outlined the swell of her breasts.

His lips nuzzled against the side of her throat. He uttered a moan as her hands moved over the smoothly corded muscles of his shoulders. "Ah, how I love you to touch me. . . ." Once more he brought his lips to hers. Burying his face in the silky strands of her hair, he breathed in the fragrant scent and was lost to any other thought.

Closing her eyes, Erica awaited another kiss, her mouth opening to him like the soft petals of a flower as he caressed her lips with a passionate hunger they both felt. Erica loved the taste of him, the tender urgency of his mouth. Her lips opened to him for a seemingly endless onslaught of kisses. It was if they were breathing one breath, living at that moment just for each other.

The desire that had been growing within Erica for so long only to be unfulfilled, sparked to renewed fire, and she could feel his passion likewise building, searing her with its heat. They shared a joy of touching and caressing, arms against arms, legs touching legs, fingers entwining and wandering to explore.

Desire writhed almost painfully within Torin's loins. He had never wanted anything or anyone as much as he did her at this moment. It was like an unfulfilled dream just waiting to come true. But he didn't want to hurry.

Pushing her clothing aside, Torin slipped his hand down the front of her gown, cupping the full curve of her breast. Then his hands were at her shoulders, tugging at her clothing until her breasts were bare. Lightly he stroked in gentle, circular motions until the peaks sprang to life under his touch, the once soft flesh now taut and aching.

Erica caught her breath as a tremor shot through her. Under his gentle massaging, her breasts seemed to have a life of their own. Swelling. Warming.

His breath caught in his throat as his eyes savored her. "Lovely!" And indeed she was, he thought, pausing to feast his eyes on the lush contours of her breasts. Bending down, he worshipped her with his mouth, his lips traveling from one to the other in tender fascination. His tongue curled around the taut peaks, his teeth lightly grazing until she writhed beneath him.

Torin's hand reached out to caress her, sliding his fingers over the soft mounds of her breasts. Her body, pressed so tightly against his, drove him beyond all thought, all reasoning. He caressed her bared flesh against his own, shivering as her hardened nipples made contact with his chest.

Oh, how she loved the feel of him. She arched against him in sensual pleasure. He had initiated a hunger in her, a desire for him that ached to be appeased.

His hand moved over her body from shoulder to thigh. His fingers caressed the flat plain of her abdomen, moving lower and lower.

"Oh, Torin . . ." At this moment her whole world was him, now and forever more.

Torin's hand moved down her stomach and into the soft hair between her thighs. Tremors shot through her in pulsating waves. She closed her eyes, sighing as he took her mouth, this time in a hard, deep kiss that coincided with his exploration of the softness between her legs. She lifted her hips, seeking him. The whole world seemed to be rocking, like an enormous wave crashing over her. For a long time she relished being close to him, just being held by him.

Torin closed his eyes, lost in her nearness, her softness. Passion tempered by love washed over him and through him. Their lips caught and clung as they held each other tightly.

The cool night air caressed Erica's skin as Torin undressed her. She caught fire wherever he touched her, burning with an all-consuming need.

"Erica!" A shudder racked through him as he pushed her away. Just for a moment. Quickly he stripped away his own clothes and Erica took her turn to appraise him. The image of broad, bronzed shoulders, wide chest, flat belly, and well-formed legs would forever be branded in her mind. Reaching out, she touched him, her hands sliding over the hard smoothness of his shoulders, moving to the thick hair of his chest.

His fingers entwined themselves in her hair, pulling her face closer. He rolled her over until they were lying side by side, and she felt a great pleasure in the warmth and power of the firmly muscled body straining so hungrily against hers. He wanted to know every intimate part of her, wanted her to feel every part of him, wanted to renew the joy they had found in each other that magical time in the curach.

Erica felt the rasp of his chest hair against her breasts and felt herself spinning out of control with sweet, aching desire. "Torin . . . love me," she breathed.

His hands caressed her, warming her with their heat. Torin and Erica took sheer delight in the texture and pressure of each other's body. Sensuously he undulated his hips between her legs, and every time their bodies caressed, each experienced a shock of raw desire that encompassed them in fiery, pulsating sensations. Then his hands were between their bodies, sliding down the velvety flesh of her belly again, moving to that place between her thighs that ached for his entry. His gentle probing brought sweet fire, curling deep inside her with spirals of pulsating sensation. Then his hands left her, replaced by the hardness she had glimpsed before, entering her just a little, then pausing.

Bending his head to kiss her again, he moved his body forward. Erica was conscious of the hard length of him creating unbearable sensations within her as he began to move. Capturing the firm flesh of her hips, he caressed her in the most intimate of embraces.It started as a spark of heat deep within her, then flared slowly. She seemed to break free of the earth and rise up through the flames that flickered behind her closed eyelids. His rhythmic plunges aroused a tingling fire, like nothing she had ever imagined. The heat seemed to fill her until she could not bear it any longer. Then, when she thought surely she must die of the pleasure, it burst within her.

Torin groaned softly, the blood pounding thickly in his head. She was so tight. So moist. So hot. His hold on her hips tightened as the throbbing shaft of his maleness possessed her again and again, moving up and down. Instinctively Erica tightened her legs around him, certain she could never withstand the ecstasy that was engulfing her body. It was as if the night shattered into a thousand stars, bursting within her. Arching her hips, she rode the storm with him. As the spasms overtook her, she dug her nails into the skin of his back.

A sweet shaft of ecstasy shot through Torin, and he closed his eyes whispering her name. It had never been like this. His heart was thundering, his breath coming in a tight rasp. Even when the intensity of their passion was spent, they still clung to each other, unable to let this magical moment end. They touched each other gently, wonderingly. Erica smiled as Torin massaged her body with slow, lingering movements.

Sooner than she might have thought, she settled into a deep sleep, welcoming the warmth of Torin's arms as he gathered her close again.

THIRTY-ONE

Erica realized that a whole new world had opened up to her. While at first she had felt as if she was not really welcome in Ragnar's hall, she soon found that living among these people might not be as difficult or unpleasant as she had always heard it would be.

First and foremost, she learned that the Norsemen were people much like those she had lived among. They were different from her and the Scots in looks and in the manner in which they did everyday things, but as her mother had always said, people were very much the same. Nor were they as brutal as she had first thought. They were polite to each other, loyal to their families, and if they showed little mercy for their enemies, she now understood that side of their nature. The Scots were likewise brutal to rival clans.

The land was harsh and barren, not green and lush like Alba. She heard that the winters were long and cold. The Viking way of life was rough, and Erica realized that was one reason that led them to wander in their ships seeking out a better life. Here, as in Alba, it was important for people to be strong. They had to be survivors, thus they showed little patience for weaklings. Erica made up her mind quickly that she was going to prove to them that she was courageous, proud, and strong. She too was a survivor.

During the next few days Erica's life quickly settled into

a pattern. Just as she had in her uncle's hall, she aided in the cooking and the cleaning. It seemed that there was no getting away from women's work no matter where one traveled.

There was always work to be done. Household tasks were fitted around the meal preparation twice daily, morning and night. The Vikings were not as disciplined as the Scots, Erica mused. There was no formal sitting down around the fire, nor the dedication of the first piece of meat to the chieftain. Everyone seemed to eat when they were hungry unless there was a special feast, in which case they sat on benches or chairs around the huge table.

"Come here, Erica, I'll show you how to make something that's delicious." Gerda crooked her finger to motion her forward.

Erica was shown how to put unleavened bread into flat cakes upon a rock to bake. As soon as that was done, she was given another chore by one of the women—cutting up several different kinds of vegetables and placing them in a large cooking pot. The Vikings preferred to boil rather than roast their meat; therefore Erica concocted a tasty dish by using the broth left from the boiled meat, cutting up small pieces and ladling it into the pots of vegetables. It made the broth more palatable to her and reminded her of the kind of food she had eaten at home. When the other women started doing the same, she felt complimented.

"Putting the meat and vegetables together into one pot. What a good idea!" Gerda praised, taking a taste of the stew. "I like it."

Erica was given the task of spooning great chunks of honeycomb into smaller bowls that would be set on the table.

"So that it could be spread on bread," Gerda informed her when her puzzled expression asked the question. Taking a piece of bread from the table, she covered it in honey and held it out for Erica to taste. Indeed the Vikings were very fond of honey. They even fermented it into a beverage like the Scots' barley brew.

Erica finished each task only to be given another and then another, but instead of feeling put upon or unhappy it made her feel useful. She could hear the guttural chatter of the women as they worked.

During a great part of the day, Erica made herself useful, helping the other women at their chores. It was a comfort to have the other women around her. While they worked they sang, and Erica was soon humming the tune of their song.

The rich smell of freshly baked bread drifted through the halls and chambers, mingling with the aroma of the bubbling stew Erica was cooking in a large iron cauldron. But she was not finished with her work. More flour had to be ground from a rotary hand quern, and dough kneaded in a wooden trough so that it could be baked on the long-handled iron plates over the open fire as soon as the other bread was done. Grinding and baking was a daily chore, for unleavened barley bread needed to be eaten while it was hot or it would soon turn hard and stale.

Little by little, Erica became more comfortable among the Vikings. The more she opened herself up to them, the more she found that although she was not fully accepted, at least she was now being kindly tolerated. At first when Torin had introduced her to the women of the household, their names had been nothing but a confused blur of strange sounds. Now she began to remember them, and to place a name with each face.

"Strange, but I am beginning to feel as if this is home," she whispered.

Now that she had been among the Vikings for a while, Erica understood that each prominent male held dominance in his own wooden longhouse as head of the household. While he held sway over the subordinate males, his wife or another designated female ranked above the other women and was responsible for seeing that the duties of the household ran smoothly.

The men and women had such different tasks that the two groups seldom came together except when it was time to eat, thus there was little time in which to seek Torin out. Men sat at one end of the table and the women at the other, so Erica had little contact with Torin during the morning or evening mealtime; but at night when they were together and making love, the loneliness of those other times was well worth the wait.

Except for her hair color, Erica now looked a great deal like the other women. She wore a chemise of linen and over that a long dress of lightweight wool decorated with colorful braid and two ornamental brass buckles that caressed her breasts as she moved about. Torin had a large stock of linen and woolen cloth from their merchanting, and she had made several garments: two long chemises, a tunic, and a cloak. There were also luxurious silks from the East, but Erica was saving that cloth for something special. There was no use wasting it by dirtying it with household dirt.

Nissa, however, never wore anything but silk, and preened herself before the others every chance she got. As if fearful of having her treasured possessions stolen, Nissa always wore twin gold brooches from which hung several chains. At the end dangled scissors, keys, a comb, and a silver box in which she kept her smaller treasures. She wore on her bosom a little box made of silver. Attached to this box was a ring carrying her knife and several gold rings. Nissa had so many that she couldn't put them all on her fingers, and she wore so many that Erica wondered how she could even lift her hands.

Nissa wasn't alone in appreciating finery. Erica was quickly coming to understand that the dress and belongings of the Vikings was used to display their wealth, for riches— not deeds and bravery—seemed to be the measure of their status and success.

Even their many gods seemed overly desirous of displaying their possessions. Odin was said to have a hall, Valhalla, with 640 doors and a throne from which he could survey all creation. Thor, the god of thunder and rain, always drove a chariot drawn by goats across the sky, hurling a golden hammer that the Vikings believed caused the lightning. The goddess Freyja rode a chariot drawn through the air by cats and wore a magic cloak of feathers that gave her the power to fly. It was Freyja who accompanied Odin into battle, for she had the right to bring back to her own hall half the warriors killed. Now Erica understood why Torin had mistaken her for the goddess that day and why he had shown such fear.

A shrill shriek interrupted Erica's thoughts as she kneaded her last roll of dough. Nissa had a nasty temper that she only displayed when Ragnar was absent. She yelled out orders, screamed at the thralls, and beat all those who did not instantly obey. She was openly critical of the other females of the household, whom she chastised for their slovenly habits. This time it was a young servant named Breena who was suffering under her scorn.

"She reminds me more and more of Loki's daughter, Hel, with her shrewish tongue," Rhianna whispered, coming up behind.

Erica had recently learned that Hel was the ruler of the realm of the dead. She was said to be half alive and half decayed. Her face, neck, shoulders, breasts, arms, and back were of flesh, but from the hips down every inch of her skin was shriveled like that on a decaying corpse. Comparing Nissa to her was far from a compliment. Though the men of the hall did not fear an honorable death, many of them lived in fear that they would die ignobly and thus be doomed to Hel's evil kingdom of the dead.

"Listen to her!" Breena put her hands over her ears as Nissa's tirade continued. "Oh, why don't they just put her out. Why doesn't Ragnar banish her! Why do the other women let her rule here?" Nissa had mastered the art of intimidation and it was working masterfully.

Erica shrugged, thinking of what her mother might have said. "Perhaps it is easier not to argue." Only Breena and Gerda ever stood up to the other woman. One by one the women were drawing away from Nissa, who was haughty, stingy, spiteful, and obsessed with always being in the right.

Even Herlaug was becoming a bit annoyed with her. Signe laughed when she revealed that in a fit of temper he once threatened to gag Ragnar's wife.

Knowing the language aided Erica in developing a strong friendship with two of the women, Morga and Rhianna, reader of rune stones. Rhianna had a fierce sense of protectiveness toward Geordie and had taken it upon herself to watch over him.

Erica's mother had told her the power of the small, square stones with symbols, which Rhianna always carried with her. Rhianna brought forth thoughts of Erica's own mother. The seeress adamantly insisted on consulting them about the coming events of Erica's life. She called the stones an ancient oracle.

"I was given the gift of reading the future by how the stones fall," Rhianna said. "Merged with my wisdom, they make it possible for me to know what is going to happen. I want to help you by *seeing* what is to come," she emphasized by repeating it again and again.

"Seeing?" Erica wasn't certain that she really wanted to know, for such foresight seemed to go against her Christian teachings. "I'm not sure I like these stones," she said, eyeing them warily.

Rhianna's blue eyes opened wide, as if just by looking into Erica's eyes she could change her mind. "Next to the gift of fire the runes are the most precious," she said solemnly. "The runes are Odin's sacred gift."

Erica had heard Torin speak of Odin, the most powerful

of Norse gods. "His name means *wind and spirit,*" Rhianna explained.

As the god of war it was Odin who directed battle and decided who was to live and who was to die. He was a being who held a frightening power.

"For nine nights he hung on the Yggdrasil, the Tree of the World, wounded by his own blade, tormented by hunger, pain, and thirst. He was alone but he saw the runes from afar and, gathering all his strength, seized them. Now I have learned how to make use of them so that I will be valuable to those who think to be my masters," Rhianna said more to herself than to Erica.

The runes were important to the Vikings; Erica could see that. Runes were carved on amulets, drinking cups, battle spears, and onto the prows of Viking ships. Scratching the symbol that looked like the horn of a deer, which she had seen carved on one Torin's amulets, she asked Rhianna what it was.

"Algiz. The protector. The protection of the warriors is like the curved horns of the elk."

"Protector."

Erica watched as Rhianna scattered the stones onto a white cloth, mumbling beneath her breath as she did so. Then, one at a time, she selected three runes and placed them in order of selection from right to left, blank sides up. The magical number three was important.

One by one Rhianna turned the stones over, muttering in dissatisfaction all the while. "I do not like it! One rune in particular seemed to worry her. The stone she called the Hagalaz which signaled disruptive forces. Clucking her tongue, she shook her head in a way that made Erica shiver. "You see this blank stone? It is called the rune of destiny. Its meaning is unknowable, unforeseeable at least at the moment, but I feel in my heart it bodes ill." She pointed to another stone. "This is the Nauthiz. It signifies constraint, necessity, and pain. Not good. Your life will not be easy here." Closing her eyes, she mumbled again, "There is a man, a man who means danger for you. Beware! Beware!"

Even though she wasn't certain she believed in the power of the runes, it was a warning that chilled Erica to the bone.

THIRTY-TWO

Geordie picked listlessly at the food on his plate as he sat across from Erica at the morning meal. "I want to go home."

Reaching out, Erica gently squeezed his hand. "We will. Have patience. Torin is gathering up a crew—one that won't betray him this time. And he is making repairs to the ship and stocking it with food."

"Are ye going, too?"

The question took her by surprise. "Of . . . of course I am going, hinny. I wouldn't let ye travel all that way by yourself."

Geordie stared into her eyes. "But are ye staying? Or are ye going to come back here with him when he returns?"

It was a question that Erica had asked herself over and over again. She had been torn between her love for her little brother and her love for Torin. Having been raised as a Mac-Quarie, she had a fierce sense of loyalty to her clan, yet at the same time she was just beginning to get to know her father and wanted to spend time with him. Then last night's lovemaking had tipped the scales, and she had realized how empty her life would be without the warmth of Torin's love. She couldn't imagine being married to anyone else. If she stayed in Alba her uncle might marry her off to the MacKinnon for the sake of the clan.

"I love ye, Geordie."

"But ye love him more." There was a tone of jealousy in his voice.

"I love ye both with all my heart, but it's a different kind of love." She tried to explain. "It's as though he and I are two halves of a whole and . . . and we are better together than apart. Do ye understand?"

He bit his lower lip. "Ye promised that ye would never leave me. Ye said that we would always be together, that ye would watch over me."

"Sometimes promises have to be broken." Ragnar's voice was strangely gentle as he spoke. "Particularly when it comes to matters of the heart." He patted Geordie on the shoulder. "Some day you will realize."

"I won't because I won't ever let myself fall in love," Geordie answered, shrugging off Ragnar's hand. "It causes too much trouble."

Ragnar laughed. "It does, boy, but the happy times make it worthwhile."

"Not if Torin breaks her heart and leaves her the way that—"

Erica nudged her brother in the ribs, silencing him "Enough! We will talk later."

"Later. How I hate that word." Geordie wrinkled up his nose. "Ye remind me of mother when ye say it." He sighed. "I miss her so much sometimes."

"She must be a fine woman—if one is to judge her by her offspring, that is," Ragnar declared. "What is she like?"

Erica answered quickly before Geordie had a chance. "Beautiful, kind, gentle, and very, very wise."

Cupping Erica's face in his hand, Ragnar turned her face this way and that. "If she looks like her daughter, then she must have made Freyja bitter with envy."

Once again Geordie spoke right up. "She didn't look like Erica; she looked like me! My mother once said that was the way it was. Boys are like their mothers and girls like their fathers."

Ragnar ruffled Geordie's hair. "Then your mother must be all spit and vinegar." He looked him right in the eye; then, as if something he saw in Geordie's face bothered him, he looked away. "Strange. There is something about your eyes that haunts me." As if trying to change the subject he asked, "Have you ever walked on water, boy?"

"Walked on water?"

"On ice. We tie antlers or horns to our boots. We call it skating." He motioned to Lief's son. "Olaf, why don't you take him up to the lake and show him? Though the ice is thawing, there still should be a spot thick enough to hold your weight."

Olaf was happy to oblige, and Geordie was anxious to try something that sounded fascinating. Together the two boys ran out of the hall.

"You love that boy."

"Very much. I've looked after him since he was a baby. I've always protected him." She stared in the direction of the door as if she could see Geordie through the wood. "That's what makes it so hard to take him back to Alba only to leave him behind when I go."

"So, you have decided to marry Torin. That is good." Ragnar sat down beside her. "The boy is growing to manhood, and though he will always love you he will need you less and less. It is time for you to find happiness and make a life for yourself here with us in the Northland." Seeing the corners of her mouth turn down in a frown, he asked, "You do care for Torin, do you not?"

"I do. I love him with all my heart; it's just that I am a stranger here. I am not used to certain things." Her eyes focused on the Viking women as she said, "I feel so much like an outsider."

He reached for her hand and gave it a gentle squeeze. "Then we will just have to make you feel more at home."

"Ye already have," she answered, feeling a genuine affection for him.

"Has Torin told you about his father?"

"Not a word."

"He was banished for his misdeeds. Torin felt the brunt of that punishment as a child. He too felt like an outsider, though he was Viking-born. To my regret I took out my anger on the boy, that is, until I grew to love him. Perhaps that is why I am so thankful to the goddess Freyja that he has found you!"

He stood, lifting her up with him. "Come. I have something to show you that should bring a smile to your face." He led her up a pathway where houses dotted the green and brown fields. "Look there."

Erica's eyes were drawn toward three men who were occupied in building a wooden house, a small replica of Ragnar's abode. The layout seemed much the same as those all over the Viking world. A long, open hearth would burn wood in the center of the hall, and the smoke would escape through a smoke hole in the ceiling. There would be a small area for cooking and one for spinning on either side of the main hall. A small building nearby would be used as a workshop.

Around the building was a planked wooden walkway, which led up to one of the two entryways. Like the other houses it would have a turf roof.

"My wedding present to Torin and to you."

"Our house!" Without even thinking, she threw her arms around Ragnar and hugged him. It seemed a natural thing to hug her father, at least until she remembered that he had no idea of who she was. Hastily she pulled away, lest he misunderstand.

"That's all right." He smiled. "I don't think Torin will be jealous, though once when I was in my prime he might have had reason to think that I would steal you away." Grabbing her arm, he steadied himself.

"Are you all right?" Erica sensed that he was feeling

dizzy. Torin had told her about her father's headaches and fainting spells.

Ragnar pridefully forced himself to act as though he felt just fine, but his expression was that of a man in pain. "The sun got into my eyes," he said by way of explanation.

"And into mine," she said softly, leading him back toward the central dwelling house. Along the way she spotted some catnip and peppermint growing wild and stopped down to pick a large quantity of it, using her apron as a bag. "When we get back I'll put some of these leaves in boiling water. I want you to drink the potion I make. It will help your head." When he started to protest, she looked him in the eye. "Please, it will help you." Catnip and peppermint soothed headaches and were used in Alba for maladies affecting the head.

For a moment it looked as if Ragnor would argue, but then he nodded. "If it will please you, then I will try this potion of yours." They walked a few steps; then he paused. "Perhaps it's because you too are from Alba, but you make me think of someone."

"Who?" She held her breath in expectation.

"Many years ago, when I was still young and impulsive, I met a beautiful woman from your land with auburn hair and green eyes and a smile that could melt the hardest of hearts."

Erica wanted to ask him so many things about the past, but spying Herlaug out of the corner of her eye, she remembered Torin's warning and kept silent.

"Like you, her chieftain had promised to marry her to the son of another chieftain to strengthen the clan in times of battle. And indeed, she might have been married, but Odin willed that I meet this woman, even though I already had a wife at home." He had a faraway look in his eyes as he was swept back in time. "At first she fought me, but we soon had a deep love between us, and in time she gave me a son."

"You had a wife?" Erica was stunned and heartsick at

the implication, for it corroborated the story that Iona had told her again and again.

"A woman I did not love and who did not love me." He shrugged. "It did not matter to me, for we Vikings can take several wives." Pointing to Herlaug he said, "My brother has three, and still he has spread his seed all over the land. I am different. I have loved only three women in my life, and in my way I was true to every one of them."

"Three women?" Her mother had been only one of them, while Ragnar had been her only love. It deeply troubled her, yet she asked, "And did you—did you have children with these women?"

Ragnar winced as if in pain. "Each bore me a son, and fool that I was, I left them all behind to sail the seas and explore. But now with the aid of Torin I want to make amends."

As if you could ever right such a wrong, Erica thought bitterly. Still, as her father swayed on his feet, she put her arm around his waist to steady him. He was growing old and he was sick. How could she help but forgive him?

"Torin told me of his quest." Oh, father, she thought. *Look at me and see the truth! Look at me and love me! Maybe it is not too late to form a bond between us despite all those years apart.*

"A quest that keeps me young with anticipation even though I am in the autumn of my years." He gazed up at the sky as if seeing something in the clouds. "One of the Valkyries riding her chariot across the sky. One day soon she will come for me and take me to Valhalla."

"Not for many years to come. Ye are still strong." The thought of him dying before they had really come to know each other prodded her to tell him the truth. "Ragnar . . . there is something I want to tell ye. I . . . I . . ."

"A ship! A merchant ship!" Nissa came through the door, her voice as excited as a child's as she ran to her husband. Pushing in between Erica and Ragnar, she wiped the flour from her hands on her apron and led him down the steep, narrow path toward the sea.

The sound of horns, the answering blasts, the brightly colored sails billowing in the wind created a feeling of excitement that was contagious. Erica felt it, too, and followed them down to the ocean, watching as the ship was run ashore. As the crew carefully secured the ship, then waded through the water to unload the many casks and chests, Erica shielded her eyes from the sun to see if there was anything aboard that they would need for their voyage back to Alba.

"Gardar?" For a moment she imagined that she could see his familiar form. Then, all at once she was certain of it. "Gardar!"

With a shout of delight to see him safe and sound, she ran toward him. "Erica?" If she was surprised to see him, he was flabbergasted to see her standing on the rocks across the sea from where he last had seen her. "What are you doing here?"

"We followed after Geordie. Torin's Vikings took him."

He wrung his hands. "I know. I know. I saw him waving to me from the ship as it sailed past me. I swam to catch up, but the water was so cold that it took my breath away. So I stole horses and boats along the way until I made my way to the Hebrides, where I used one of Ragnar's peace offerings to bribe the merchant who owns that boat to let me sail with them." He looked around. "Where is Torin?"

"Making the ship ready to sail."

"To go in search of the boy?" He looked so genuinely concerned for Geordie's welfare that she wanted to hug him, but there had been enough hugging for one day.

"Geordie is here." As quickly as she could, she told Gardar the whole story, asking him when she was finished, "Will ye come with us when we take Geordie back?"

"To Alba?" His expression seemed to say that he had had enough of the Scots to last him a lifetime.

"Torin is going to take Geordie back. Surely my uncle

will be so relieved that he will have no more thoughts of warfare, at least for a while. If he does, then I'm certain that the Vikings who accompany us will quickly change his mind."

"Going back, you say." Gardar thought a moment. "Whether he knows it or not, Torin needs me. Besides, I met a woman there. A Pict like me. Maybe when we leave we can take her with us."

They made their way to the great hall. Gardar could smell the food being prepared. He sniffed the air and licked his lips.

"Gardar!" If Erica had been delighted to see Gardar again, then Torin was doubly so. "By Odin's breath, you are a sight for sore eyes. I doubted that I would lay eyes on you this side of Valhalla." He pounded him on the back. "I feared you were food for the fish, or that you walked into a trap or that perhaps the Scots caught up with you. But now my conscience is soothed. You are here. Just in time for the wedding."

THIRTY-THREE

There was the kind of excitement in the air that only a wedding can bring. All the women of the household took part in the planning of the festivities, including Nissa. If she wasn't friendly, at least she seemed to have put some of her hostilities aside, perhaps because she felt that once Erica was married she would no longer pose a threat.

Ragnar had gifted Erica with a wedding gown that he had obtained in Kaupang. Not to be outdone, Torin had given her a sleeping gown of silk. Though it was scandalously sheer, he jested that Erica would be wasting her time putting it on, for it would soon be removed. Touching the garment, Erica was again enchanted with the filmy, soft fabric.

"It is made from the cocoons of tiny wormlike creatures who spin the thread by order of the gods," Torin informed her with a smile. The color was aqua, a hue that matched the ocean and her eyes, he said.

The bridal gown was also of silk, embroidered with colorful threads at the hem and upon the bodice. The swirls of color emphasized Erica's breasts. Brightly colored ribbons, woven upon the ribbon looms by Ragnar's thralls, decorated the sleeves, hanging down from the shoulders of the garment so that they would billow in the breeze.

After a morning meal of fruit and cereal, Erica proceeded to the bathhouse with two female thralls whose duty it was to bathe her, wash her long red hair, anoint her with fragrant oils, and chant incantations over her. To pacify her own God and ascertain that he would not be angry with her for joining in such pagan customs, Erica closed her eyes and made the sign of the cross. Leaning back in the tub, she lost all her anxiety as the warmth of the water caressed her.

How strange that her people had always called the Norsemen unwashed heathens, she thought, enjoying the steam of the sauna. She had learned just how false that statement was. Among the Vikings she had found that cleanliness was expected.

She remembered the time, which seemed so long ago, when Torin had interrupted her in the bathhouse in Alba. Though she had fought against it, she had been attracted to him the moment they met. Now they would belong to each other, at least according to Viking law.

Stepping out of the water, Erica found a fire kindled and remembered that fire as well as water was a purifier. She stood before the blazing flames as the two slave women toweled her dry.

Torin, anxious to see her, stuck his head inside the bathhouse but was issued a stern reprimand by the oldest of the thralls. Shooing him out, she chattered excitedly as she slipped a robe over Erica's form and secured it with a rope around her waist. They brushed her hair until it gleamed with magenta highlights. Today Erica would wear her hair hanging down her back, its bright waves gathered within a gold circlet. But after today she would wear it in a bun, covered with a kerchief whenever she worked among the other wives in the hall. Among the Vikings, married women hid their hair, but Erica was of a mind to change that custom.

"Are ye really going to marry the Viking?" Geordie asked as if he had somehow hoped otherwise. His eyes were moody, his mouth set in a frown.

"Did ye think that I would change my mind, hinny?" It hurt her heart to cause him any pain. "Ye know how much

I love Torin, and besides, I wanted to be wed before we returned to Alba lest Uncle Coinneach make good on his threat to marry me to Malcolm MacKinnon."

Picking up a kid goat that had wandered into the bathhouse, Geordie scratched it behind the ears. "Are ye not afraid of what Uncle will say when he finds out that ye married without his approval?"

For a moment Erica's emotions were fragile, and she nearly shattered at the thought of never being able to see Alba again. "Nae, I do not care what he says or what he thinks," she asserted, but the truth was, she really did, and the thought of being ostracized from the clan forever made her edgy and nervous despite her bravado.

"But what if he says that ye cannot set foot on Mull or Ulva again? What then?"

"Then . . . then I'll find a way to have ye visit me here." Gathering him into her arms, kid and all, she squeezed him tightly. "Oh, Geordie, please understand." Somehow she had to make him understand. "I'm not choosing Torin over ye as ye may think."

He looked up at her. "What are ye doing, then?"

"I'm reaching out for the dream I had since I was old enough to walk and talk. Though I didn't really know it, I was never happy in Alba. Not really. I didn't belong." She stroked his hair. "I'm too independent and set in my ways to always do what others tell me to do. Ye know it, too. Like marrying the MacKinnon not because of love but because Uncle Coinneach tells me so. That doesn't happen here. Here the Viking women are independent. They choose their own husbands. And I have chosen Torin."

Unlike in Alba, where they followed the Christian faith and were married unto the death no matter how they were treated, a woman in the Northland could sue for divorce if her husband beat her or was unfaithful. While their husbands were away on expeditions or raids, women ran households and farms and were openly praised for their accomplishments.

"But Erica, ye aren't one of them." He stepped back, pacing up and down. "Ye are a Scot to the bone like me." Geordie struggled to understand how his sister could forget all the years she had lived among the MacQuaries.

"Ye forget that I am part Norse, too, as I was reminded over and over again."

"By Iona and those of small minds," Geordie replied, laughing as the baby goat chewed at his sleeve as if trying to nurse. "But there are those who always loved ye, like me!"

"Aye, I know, and I will love ye until I die and miss ye with all my heart, but I owe it to myself to be happy."

Geordie was reflective. "I do want that, Erica. I want it with all my heart." Hand in hand they walked back to the hall. "I'll miss our mock sword fights most of all," he exclaimed. "But then I suppose it will not be long until I fight with the real thing."

"No it will not be long. . . ." Strange, she thought, how quickly he was growing. It was almost as if he had grown up during the past few weeks. Perhaps he had.

Sweeping into the room, one of the thralls prodded Geordie out the door, led Erica to her bedchamber, then slipped a soft pleated silk chemise over Erica's head. Over the chemise the wedding gown was draped, two large brooches holding the loops of the gown at the shoulders. The short sleeves of the chemise peeked out from under the gown. Around her neck Erica wore the Raven's Eye pendant, which had brought her much more than just luck. It had brought Torin into her life.

Securing a golden chain from which many keys hung, one of the thralls whispered, "Your badge of honorable wifehood." The keys were those to Torin's storehouses and wine cellars—and his heart, or so he had insisted. The chain of keys was suspended from a brooch that was three triangles intertwined. Torin had called it the *volksknot* and said that it represented the three different worlds the Vikings believed in, and a way to travel between all three.

Three other chains were hung upon the gown, and from them dangled a knife, scissors, and a container for needles. Erica had noticed the same kind of chains upon the married women of the hall. Now having this token of her married state upon her made her feel for the first time as if she truly belonged.

Keeping to the shadows, the slave woman hurried to Herlaug's wooden house. Ignoring his outraged look, she swept through the door holding her hand out, palm up. "You said you would pay me if I found out anything of interest."

"I did?" Holding a silver bowl filled with raspberries and blackberries in one hand and a silver dagger in the other, Herlaug was amusing himself by spearing the fruit, then picking it off the point of the dagger with his teeth.

"You promised! You said that it would behoove me to be your eyes and ears in Ragnar's household. You even said that you might free me if I spied well for you."

He raised his brows as if remembering. "It's coming back to me. . . ."

Folding her arms across her chest, she was defiant. "Today I have learned something that is worth that silver cup filled with gold."

"Ragnar is dead!" He speared five berries with one fell swoop and licked them off with his tongue, wincing as he cut his lip.

"No, he is getting much better thanks to the potion the red-haired woman has been giving him."

"Better?" Venting his anger, he hurled the dagger to a target an inch above her head. "By the gods, I swear he is the hardest man to kill that ever there was. But I'm certain that you will find a way to hurry it along! Or you will rue the day that you were born!"

Without even flinching, the thrall reached up and pulled the dagger out of the wood. "And you will rue the day you harm a hair on my head, for I will keep my lips sealed and you will never know what I have learned." Once more she held out her hand and this time with a grunt he filled it with coins.

"Tell me." His expression seemed to say that her information had better be interesting.

"What if I told you that the woman Torin is marrying wears the Raven's Eye around her neck? What would you think then?"

"The Raven's Eye?" He toyed with the tip of the knife as he thought the matter out. Was it possible? No, it couldn't be. Or could it? "The Scotswoman must be. . . ."

"Ragnar's daughter!"

"And Torin thinks to undermine me by marrying her so. That outcast, that whoreson, that bastard thinks that he will become jarl. But not if I can help it!"

Erica made an impressive figure walking gracefully along in her flowing dress, the hem of the dress sweeping the ground, the ribbons at her sleeves floating behind her. Torin's eyes swept over her, taking in her beauty.

"If I said that you were the most beautiful woman I had ever seen, would you believe me?" Dressed in a bright-blue tunic embroidered with gold, tan trousers, and leather boots, he looked handsome.

"I would say that ye were a flatterer." The ceremony was to be out of doors on the hillside overlooking the ocean. Torin told her that many festivals and ceremonies were held there. Now, carrying branches in their hands to portray fertility—Torin a branch of the ash tree, the symbol of man, and Erica the branch of the elm, to signify her woman-hood—walked together down the mountainside.

"And I would say that he was truthful," Ragnar insisted, coming up behind her. He put his arms around her and kissed her on the cheek, his beard tickling her ear. "I am to be the one to escort you to the waiting *skuldelev*."

He took her arm and led her down the rocky path to the shore, where a small boat decorated with ribbons and all manner of brightly colored banners awaited. Four thralls sat upon chests to work the oars. Kissing her again, this time upon the forehead, Ragnar helped her into the boat, then took his leave of her to meet her farther down the shoreline, where both he and Wolfram would be waiting.

The breeze was cool, whipping Erica's hair around her face as the small ship moved up the shoreline. She could see the throng of well-wishers watching her from the rocky beach, and she held her head up proudly. From the crowd came whispers that she looked like a goddess as she floated along the fjord in her silken gown.

At last the ship reached its destination and Erica stepped upon dry land. As promised, Torin and Ragnar were there to meet her. Torin grasped her hand.

Beneath the branches of a tree, Ragnar recited the vows. It was his right as the patriarch and jarl. Torin and Erica repeated after him, and the thought ran through Erica's mind that in some ways this ceremony was not all so different from the Christian rites.

Erica drank from a goblet of wine, which was then passed to Torin, and she thought of her uncle Coinneach. What would he think when he found out that she had married Torin, a man who had for a short time languished in his dungeon. Would he banish her forever, or just until his anger cooled?

"May Thor smile upon you always and bring many children to your hearth," Ragnar intoned. Erica blushed as she looked up at her soon-to-be husband.

Torin held out three rings to Erica and slipped them upon her fingers. "Three rings means that I am a very rich man," he said softly. "But never have I been richer than at this moment when I have before me my greatest treasure, my wife."

Erica's eyes were filled with love as he bent to kiss her before the assembled crowd. Picking her up in his arms as if to carry her back toward the hall, he told her that this was the sign that he had claimed her as his mate for life. After carrying her a short distance, he set her back down and they watched the rest of the ceremony apart from the others.

Animal sacrifices were made then, and Torin and Erica ran back toward the longhouse that Ragnar had gifted them with, amid cheers and ribald comments. Sitting in two large chairs, Erica and Torin held court as if they were royalty, accepting congratulations from those who wished to share their joy. Then there was singing, dancing, and general merrymaking.

Torin joined in the singing, and Erica was surprised by his fine voice. She had never heard him sing before. "There are a lot of things you do not know about me," he whispered, nibbling her ear. "But you will soon find out."

Looking up at him, Erica felt a tremendous swelling of emotion, and an overwhelming longing for the others to leave so that they could be alone. At last, when it appeared that moment was never going to come, Torin turned upon the throng with mock anger.

"Out! Everybody out." Though they argued stubbornly, they all left, except for Geordie. "Your sister will be safe with me, Geordie. I give you my word."

"You do not want me to stand guard?"

Torin shook his head. "But I will tell you something that you can do. You can take Olaf with you and stand guard over the ship. We sail tomorrow. I wouldn't want anything to happen that would ruin our plans."

"Guard the ship?" Geordie was pleased that Torin trusted

him with such an important mission. Hurrying out the door, calling out to Olaf, he left Torin and Erica alone.

"At last!" Taking her hand, he led her toward the bed. Pulling her wedding dress down around her waist, he planted a kiss on her shoulder, then ran his mouth down the length of her bare arm.

Torin worshipped his wife with eyes and hands and lips, undressing her ever so slowly and savoring her beauty. If it was possible, she was even more beautiful tonight. He touched the swell of her breasts as Erica moved closer to him, shuddering as he caressed the peaks with gentle fingers. She reached up to tug at his tunic, longing to feel his bare chest next to her skin.

"I feel as if this were our first time together," Torin breathed, reaching up and helping her undress him.

Erica ran her fingers over the hardness of his chest with its golden thatch of hair, wanting to bring him the same quiver of fire that she felt. She was rewarded when she heard his soft intake of breath.

Torin made love to her with an intensity that made her forget anything else but the moment; then, when she had melted in his arms he made love to her again, unleashing all the power and virility of his passion. There was only this moment, this man, and her overpowering love. This was what she had always imagined her wedding night would be like, and she knew in her heart that as long as she lived, she would love him.

THIRTY-FOUR

Muted rays of sunlight fluttered through an opening in the tiny shuttered window of Torin and Erica's new house. From beneath the window the sound of the first cock's crow reminded Erica all too jarringly that morning had come. She stretched her arms and opened her eyes as her hand made contact with solid flesh. Torin. Her husband! Though once she had dreaded the word, she treasured it now.

"Husband . . ." She said it aloud, snuggling against the warmth and strength of his body.

The sound of his steady breathing made her heart begin to pound wildly as she remembered last night. Her senses had responded to him immediately. Beneath his hands and mouth, her body had come alive and she had been lost in a heat of desire she had never believed possible. His hands against her aching breasts had warmed her through the fabric of her gown. Never had she removed her garments so quickly or so frantically. A pain had formed so taut in her belly that she had feared she would explode with want of him.

Torin. Despite the heat of their passion, he had been gentle with her, hurrying nothing, taking his time. He had savored the silk of her flesh, his fingers sliding over her skin so tenderly that she had tingled with a prickly fire. But when he had touched the softness between her legs, she could wait no longer. Arching upward, straining against him, she had moved her legs apart and he had entered so smoothly, so easily that she wondered if she were but dreaming. But 'twas no dream. The heated lovemaking that had followed had been too gloriously real.

"And just think, my dear wife, we have the rest of our lives to enjoy such pleasure," he had whispered in her ear.

"Husband," she said softly. Oh how jealous Iona would be.

Rising up on one elbow, she looked at him now with aching tenderness. He looked so much younger and more vulnerable when asleep, not at all like one of the fearsome Norsemen who had terrorized first Eire, then Alba. He snuggled up against her, his powerful body sprawled across the bed as if he didn't have a worry in the world. His face had the calm peace of a contented man.

Closing her eyes, she smiled. Cooking and weaving had always been things that she hated, but somehow all that had changed. She wanted to be a good wife. That did not mean, however, that she would be content to stay behind while he sailed around in his ship. She was determined to accompany him.

Suddenly Erica's eyes opened wide. What was it that had pulled her from the mists of her reverie? *Smoke.* She was sure of it. And where there was smoke there was fire.

"Torin . . ."

"Mmmmm . . ." His hand moved lightly over her hip and down her leg as he awakened. Weeks of frustration and worry just seemed to have melted away. She was his.

"Just think: I'm going to wake up every morning and find you next to me," he murmured, nibbling at her earlobe playfully.

Erica pushed him away. "I smell smoke."

He yawned. "From the cooking fires."

"No. I haven't started a fire yet, and since we are the only ones in the house . . ."

Jumping out of bed quickly, Erica donned her pleated

chemise. She could smell the odor of burning wood; it made her choke.

"The house . . . the house is burning!" Without even thinking, she ran in the direction of the fire, looking for something that could be used to put it out. Seeing a pitcher of water, she hurled it at the fire.

Torin thought quickly. Yanking the blankets off of the bed, he beat at the flames. "Get out of the house, Erica. It's too dangerous."

"No!" Picking up a blanket that had fallen on the floor, she fought the fire too.

"Go. Alert the thralls. I can't fight this blaze alone." He also knew she would be safer near the main house.

Erica was anxious to get help, so she didn't argue. Opening the door, she hurried down the path to her father's house. She did not see the eyes watching her, nor did she see the smile curve Herlaug's lips until he was upon her.

Though she did not like him, Erica was relieved that he was nearby. She pointed. "The house. Torin is trying to put out the fire, but he needs help."

Something about his expression made her nervous. It was as if he were scrutinizing her. "I can see the flames," he said, holding his ground.

"Help him. Help us!"

Herlaug didn't move a muscle; he just kept staring at her with those cold, cruel eyes as if reading her mind. Erica sensed that he knew something, but what? Had he guessed her identity? Did he know? She was infuriated by his refusal to help Torin fight the fire. "Well, if you won't help, I'll find someone who will," she said. Turning around, she moved toward the jarl's hall, but before she could take as much as a step, she was set upon from behind.

"Now!" Hands grabbed her, holding her immobile. Startled, she fought against her assailants, but she was outnumbered.

"Do not struggle; you will only make it worse for yourself," a woman's voice mumbled.

"She'll be worth a lot of silver," she heard a man say.

She started to scream, but a gag was stuffed into her mouth. Erica turned her head and was surprised to see one of the female thralls who had dressed her for her wedding standing there. Suddenly it all clicked together in her head. This woman had seen the pendant. She knew who she was. And she had told Herlaug.

Though Erica couldn't speak, her eyes pleaded with the woman, *please don't do this to me,* but the woman had no pity. Remembering the scissors and small knife that hung by a golden chain from her gown, Erica tried to talk her assailants into letting her go back for her clothes, but Herlaug was much too smart for that.

"Are you going to kill me?" she asked as a collage of faces danced before her eyes. Geordie. Torin. Her father. She didn't want to die. They needed her. That thought made her fight all the more, but the more she struggled, the more they tightened their hold on her.

She looked Herlaug full in the face. The smug smile made her hate him so much that it nearly made her choke. The truth came to her in an instant.

"You set the fire!" He had known that Torin would try and protect her by sending her away from the danger.

"I did." He was blatantly sure of himself. "I wanted to get rid of you and also eliminate Torin. You must admit that it is a very clever plan."

"What are you going to do?" Her eyes darted back and forth as she tried to think of a way to escape. Perhaps they were going to sell her as a slave. No. Torin would rescue her! But Torin didn't know. . . .

While Herlaug and the women discussed their plans, Erica freed one hand. Reaching up, she yanked the chain that held the pendant. The necklace clanked as it hit a rock on the ground, but her enemies didn't notice the sound. Silently Erica prayed that Torin would find it, and that somehow it would lead him to her.

The others had seen the smoke and hurried to help. Now side by side with the thralls, Torin threw bucket after bucket of water on the blaze.

"How did this happen?" Ragnar growled, coming up behind him.

"I don't know," Torin coughed out as he choked on the smoke. "My only worry at the moment is putting it out."

Stripping off his cloak, Ragnar joined the fire brigade fighting the fire alongside Torin. At last it was out.

"Ragnar, where is my wife?" Torin scanned the cooking area anxiously. He liked to keep Erica in his sight, particularly since they were leaving this morning.

"I don't know," Ragnar answered.

"But I sent her for help. I thought she would come back with you."

"The last time I saw her was last night." Ragnar was just as worried as Torin. The distant howl of a wolf did little to soothe their fears.

Cupping his hands around his mouth, Torin yelled out, "Erica!"

Ragnar joined him in calling out her name, but there was no answer.

Gripping him by the arm, Ragnar scowled. "It wouldn't be the first time that wolves—"

"No." He couldn't believe it. "The fire would have frightened them away." The fire. Suspicion nagged at his brain. First the fire, and now Erica had come up missing. He stiffened. "Where is Herlaug?"

"My brother?" Ragnar shrugged. "I do not know."

"Something tells me that he is at the bottom of this," Torin growled.

Ragnar's angry grumble to "Cease this talk; I will not

have you say such things," proved that he did not suspect his brother of any wrongdoing. But then, it was always that way.

As they moved down the path, Torin wiped the soot from his face. "There is something that I must tell you. Erica is—"

"Look!" Something sparkled on the ground. Bending down, Ragnar picked it up, gasping in disbelief. "The pendant!"

Torin tore it from his hand. "Let me see!" With trembling fingers he examined the Raven's Eye. "Erica treasured this with all her heart. She wouldn't have lost it unless—"

"Erica treasured . . . ?" Suddenly Ragnar grabbed him by the shoulder. "What's going on?"

Torin choked the words out. "Erica—is—your daughter!"

"My daughter? But how . . . why . . . ?"

"There will be time to tell you the story once we have found her," Torin rasped. Hunkering down on the ground, he carefully examined the dirt for footprints, marks, or anything that might give him a hint as to which direction Erica had gone.

"Listen!"

At first Torin was too preoccupied to hear the faraway sound, but as he raised his head he heard it too. "A horn." The horn that announced the arrival of a ship was being sounded again and again. "Geordie!" He was trying to tell them that someone was going to steal the ship. He was using the signal that Torin had instructed him to use.

"Come on!" Hurrying to the lodge, Ragnar armed himself with his battle sword. Torin did the same.

THIRTY-FIVE

The tranquil air of the inlet gave the deceptive appearance of peace. Suddenly Ragnar, Torin, and a band of ten Vikings appeared as if out of thin air. With a nod of his head and a cry of "O—O—Odin," Torin jumped over the side of the ship. Wading in waist-deep water, he led the raid.

From the ship Erica watched in amazement as her husband and father came aboard. With axes and swords raised high, they looked like the kind of Vikings that terrorized the monasteries and castles. Before the men accompanying Herlaug had time to know there was any danger, the tiny band of Norsemen had attacked.

Shouts rent the air. Herlaug barely had time to look up before he was cornered. As if in slow motion, Erica saw Torin raise his sword.

"No!" Ragnar didn't want any harm to come to his brother, no matter what he had done. "Tell them to surrender, brother! Tell them now, or I will stand aside and let him do what he so wants to do."

Being caught red-handed didn't mean that Herlaug wouldn't lie. "These aren't my men, Ragnar. I heard a scream and followed the sound. I am as innocent in this as you." Even so, the minute he raised his hands, the others put down their swords.

"It's not what you think. . ." Herlaug pretended innocence.

"That will be decided at the *thing*," Ragnar said angrily. At the gathering, testimony would be given and Herlaug's guilt or innocence determined.

"Torin!" Erica ran forward, throwing her arms around her husband. "I don't know what I would have done if ye hadn't found the necklace."

Gently he stroked her hair. "It was Geordie who saved the day. I would never have guessed that Herlaug would be so bold as to steal my ship. I would have thought he would go by land. The horn gave him away. I told your brother to blow it in case something went amiss." He nodded toward the stern, where Ragnar waited. "He knows."

"I'm glad." The secrecy had nearly driven her crazy. " 'Tis his right to know." Though she didn't tell Torin, she had decided to tell Ragnar before they sailed. Now, taking her husband by the arm, Erica walked toward her father.

"I think deep inside I knew," Ragnar whispered, suddenly reticent, "for I took to you like a fish to water."

"Ye—ye are not disappointed that I am not a man?" Looking him right in the eye, she searched for any sign that he regretted her gender. There was none. "Ye wanted a son to follow in your footsteps as jarl . . ."

Ragnar looked toward Torin, then at Erica, then at Torin again. "I wouldn't be a bit surprised if I soon had grandsons on whom to bestow that honor." He grasped her hand. "How is your mother?"

She hung her head, hating to have to be the one to tell him. "She's . . . she's dead."

"No!" Her words struck him like a mortal blow.

If Erica had ever doubted that her father had cared deeply for her mother, she didn't have any such qualms now. Looking at his face, she could see that he was crying. Grinding his teeth, he was trying to hold back his tears.

"When? How?"

"After ye left, Uncle Coinneach forced her to marry her cousin, for he said it wasn't right for a woman to live alone. Geordie was the result, and then a few years later she was with child again, but she and the baby both died."

"I'm sorry!"

"Mother was a wonderful woman." Erica bit her lip to keep from crying. "But now we have each other."

Torin watched as Ragnar slowly, gently put his arms around his daughter. "So many years. Why does it take a man so many years to understand?" He looked askance at Torin. "Why didn't you tell me?"

"I wanted to keep Erica safe." He explained his suspicions regarding Ragnar's brother. "I think Herlaug was behind the kidnapping of Geordie in some way." Taking Erica's necklace out of a small sack tied around his waist, he handed it to Ragnar. "I fixed the clasp, but I think it only right that you have the honor."

Lifting her hair off the back of her neck, Erica waited. Strange how naked she felt without the necklace. "I know about the other pendants, Father," she said.

"There is much to tell."

Father and daughter decided to have a long talk when she and Torin returned from Alba.

"The ship is ready to sail." Torin issued a gentle reminder. "We have much to do before we go."

"Sail?" Ragnar shook his head. "She can't leave now." Seeing the look of determination on Erica's face, he gave up any thought of argument. "Go to Alba, then, but when you return we will have a long talk, you and I."

THIRTY-SIX

The wind sang in the taut sails of the Viking ship as it glided over the waves, leaving the Northland far behind. Watching as the ship nosed its way through the sea spray, Erica thought how strange it was that although she was going back to Alba, it didn't seem at all as if she was going home. Perhaps that was because after all that had happened, she now felt as if Torin's homeland was where she belonged.

"You don't have any regrets, do you?" Torin asked, misunderstanding her stoic gaze. The thought of Erica changing her mind and deciding to stay in Alba was troubling. Having known so much coldness, so much pain, he had learned to hide all his deep emotional scars. When he was with her, however, she helped soothe away his loneliness and emotional isolation.

She was an unusual woman. He was learning just how unusual. Brave, loyal to her companions, she had a sense of honesty and generosity that deeply touched him. Passionate, giving herself to him without reserve, she was the kind of woman a man dreamed about.

"Regrets? Only for all the precious time that has slipped away," she whispered, smiling as he put his arm around her waist. She put her head on his shoulder. "But now that we're together and I have made my peace with my father, I am perfectly satisfied." Except for the thought of leaving Geordie.

Torin seemed able to read her mind. "The boy will be fine. I'll make my peace with your uncle Coinneach so that we can come back to Alba from time to time. Ragnar told me that he hopes to establish trade between the two lands."

She looked across the deck to where Geordie sat face to face with Olaf, who was quickly becoming his friend. Using a barrel as a table and sacks of barley as chairs, the two boys were peacefully engrossed in a game of draughts.

"If only the men of our two lands could be as open-minded as those two boys, I know that peace would be more than just talk," Erica reflected. More than anything, she wanted an end to the quarreling between the Vikings and the Scots. Perhaps then she could truly have peace of mind.

"I think young Geordie is beginning to feel more comfortable around me," Torin whispered against her ear. "He grinned at me this morning and told me that Vikings really aren't so bad."

She pointed toward a miniature Viking ship that lay on the ground at Geordie's feet, whittled out of wood by Ragnar. "Father was quite taken with him, especially when he found out about my mother. He says he sees a lot of her in the laddie. He gave him that ship as a memento of his time spent among the Vikings."

The roar of the ocean, the sound of waves lapping against the ship, the cry of seagulls as they circled overhead were all the memento Erica needed. Taking in a deep breath of the salty sea air, she knew that from now on whenever she felt the wind in her hair, she would think of her adventurous time upon the sea with Torin beside her.

As for Torin, he had had enough seafaring for a while. He confided to Erica that he was anxious to return home so that they could rebuild the house that Herlaug had burned to the ground.

"Herlaug!" The very sound of the man's name angered

Erica anew. He was as skilled as a bard at weaving a tale of his innocence. "I was expecting him to insist at any moment that it was *I* who had abducted *him!*"

"Ragnar has always been lenient with his younger brother." For just a moment Torin looked grim. "He sees only what he wants to see, but that is the way with us all sometimes. Herlaug escaped the full brunt of his deserved punishment this time, but one of these days he will go too far."

"When we get back, I'll have a talk with my father. I'll warn him to beware. In the meantime, all I want to do is be with you."

"Oh, that we were alone," Torin sighed. As she moved against him he felt a rush of blood through his veins that sparked an arousal through his body, a hunger that made him all the more anxious to return to the Northland, where they could begin a new life together.

Closing his eyes, he remembered their wedding night. The word *passionate* had been created just to describe his wife. She loved Torin like no woman had ever loved him before.

He loved her. He admired her. He cherished her. He wanted her. Oh, how he wanted her. He wanted to touch her, commit her body to memory—wanted to be with her forever. Never in all his life had he felt so blessed, so content. As they stood together with the wind blowing in their hair, the taste of the sea air on their lips, they both experienced the greatest peace they had ever known.

PART THREE

HOMECOMING

THIRTY-SEVEN

The island of Ulva seemed to rise up from the mist of the clouds as the *Sea Wolf* sailed inland. Home. That was what Geordie called it as he stood at the side of the Viking ship, watching Alba come closer and closer. To Erica, however, it didn't seem like home at all. Her home was with Torin.

"But oh, how I am going to miss ye, hinny," she said to Geordie as she ruffled his hair in her usual sisterly gesture. She felt a twinge of remorse that it would be a long time before she was able to ruffle his hair again.

"And I'm going to miss ye!" Though it was unmanly to cry and he knew it, Geordie clung to her, wetting the front of her gown with the moisture from his eyes. "And Torin"—he swallowed a sob—"I'm going to tell Uncle Coinneach that the Vikings are not the heathens he has said them to be, despite what they have done to us."

"My father told me that he wants peace," Erica whispered. "Now it is up to Uncle Coinneach."

Though Erica feared what her Uncle might do to Torin, though she had wanted him to hide the Viking ship among the rocks while she saw Geordie safely to the castle, he had staunchly refused. He had fled from the MacQuarie stronghold once, but he would not run again. It was a time for grown men to come together and talk peace.

The ship touched the shore at dusk. The helmsman guided it to the land, bumping into the rocks. The Vikings preferred to run the ship aground, so it was not a gentle end to the voyage. When the ship was safely moored, Torin lifted Erica up in his arms and carried her to shore with him. Geordie tagged after them carrying a helmet, sword, and the carved sled that Ragnar had given him as a farewell present.

Looking about her, Erica was struck by how strange it seemed to be home. It was so green and fragrant with the smell of wildflowers. A mist hung over the land, bringing with it a dark-blue, pink, and purple sunset.

"Are you certain that ye want to go through with this, Torin? I could take Geordie back—"

"And take the chance of being punished for letting me out of that dungeon?" He shook his head. "No. I cannot take the risk of losing you."

Jeanne was the first person Erica laid eyes on as she walked through the door. She looked up from her loom, her eyes wide with amazement as she saw who stood before her.

"Erica! We thought . . . we feared . . . but the Lord has answered all our prayers and now, here ye are." Though they had never been close, Jeanne threw her arms around her.

"I'm just here for a while."

"For a . . . a while?" Jeanne gave a start as she saw who had accompanied Erica. "Oh, dear Lord!"

"Torin is my husband."

Jeanne's eyes were the size of saucers.

"We were joined by Viking law." Jeanne began to speak, but Erica silenced her. "I know what ye are going to say, that we were not joined together by God's ceremony, but I tell ye there is a deeper commitment than the words spoken to bind two people. That is the love one feels for another in the heart."

"Ye love him?" Eyeing him up and down, it was obvious that Jeanne understood why. "But what will Coinneach say?"

"He will have to understand——" Her words were cut off as Geordie ran through the door. Jeanne gave him the same hug that she had given Erica.

"Ye have grown! I swear ye are a head taller!"

"Nae, I'm just standing straighter. I learned that from Ragnar. He says that a man should keep his shoulders back, his head up, and his eyes focused on what lies ahead."

"Ragnar, is it?" Jeanne looked at the sword and helmet Geordie held and she shuddered. "Ye should put those things away before your uncle sees them."

No sooner had the words been spoken than the two women saw through the tiny window slits in the door that Coinneach and his men were returning. Erica felt a small flicker of fear. Could her uncle ever understand her decision to marry Torin and stay in the Northland?

"Erica!" Coinneach's mouth opened wide in shock as he walked through the door and saw her. "Is it really you?" His steps faltered. He looked as white as a ghost. "I thought . . . thought that the Vikings took ye and young Geordie!"

"Geordie was kidnapped by rebel Vikings under the liege of Ragnar's brother, Herlaug. Torin and I sailed after them, and as ye can see we have brought him back." She told him the story as quickly as she could, her eyes lighting upon Torin from time to time because she could not help it. "And then Herlaug abducted me and was going to sell me into slavery, but once again Torin came to the rescue."

Coinneach MacQuarie looked upon Torin with gratitude. "Then it is thanks I should be giving." He reached out to Erica, taking her hand. In that moment he noticed the rings upon her fingers. "What are these?"

"Rings."

"I can see that with my own eyes."

Erica knew the best way was to tell him and tell him quickly. "While I was in the Northland waiting for Torin to make repairs to his Viking ship, we . . . we were married."

For a moment Erica feared that her uncle was going to explode. "What about the MacKinnon?"

"I didn't want to marry him."

"Didn't want!" His eyes bulged in his head; his face turned red; his mouth twitched. "Ye were forced against your will; that's what ye mean!" For just a moment it appeared that he was going to throw himself upon Torin, but somehow she managed to calm him down.

"I love Torin. I think I loved him from the very first, but then I think that ye knew that I would, or at least ye feared it."

"What has love to do with anything? I promised ye to the MacKinnon's son. Ye will make me look like a foolish old man." He seemed to ignore the fact that in Erica's heart the matter was final. "Now get your things together. Perhaps it isn't too late to help me keep my word."

"I cannot marry the MacKinnon. I am already married."

"Bah. By Viking law? They have no laws. They are heathen. They worship false gods. How dare ye speak to me of their laws?"

Erica repeated. "I am married, and I love my husband very much." She felt Torin squeeze her hand.

He grabbed at his chest; his face grimaced in pain. For a moment Erica feared that her words had killed him.

"Uncle, please understand. I am happy in the Northland. I've found Torin and my father and—"

"Ye are blinded, just like your mother. But ye will come to your senses in time."

"My mother loved Ragnar until the day she died!"

"She was a Viking's harlot and so will ye be, but then they say, like mother like daughter!" He winced at his own words, but then as if he couldn't help himself, he cried out, "Better for me that ye had not come back here. I would rather have thought that ye died!"

"Uncle Coinneach!" Erica looked at him in stunned disbelief. "I am happy. Can't ye be happy for me, too?"

Though he had been quiet all through his uncle's tirade, Geordie stepped forward. "Please, Uncle. Torin could have hidden and Erica might have led me to the castle and then taken to her heels, but they were brave to come here when they knew in their hearts that ye would be bitter. But please, let Erica be happy—and—and at least listen to Torin."

Coinneach's eyes were cold as he looked first at Torin, then at Erica, then back at Torin again. "I should banish ye. Cast ye out so that ye can never return."

"Nae!" There was such finality to such an action that Erica cringed. "There is no reason to punish me."

Coinneach ignored her. "And I should return the Viking to the dungeon where he belongs!"

"Ye wouldn't!"

"I would!" Calling out to his men, he told them to surround the Viking.

Torin was shoved and pushed along a familiar pathway. *Fool.* He should have listened to Erica, but he had hoped that there could be an end of the bad blood between them. He had come to Alba to be a peacemaker, but now it appeared that once again he was going to be a prisoner.

THIRTY-EIGHT

He was back where he started, Torin thought angrily. Back with the rats and the spiders! The dank stench of the dungeon assailed his nostrils as he was once again shoved inside. "I swear, Coinneach MacQuarie, you will regret this! I will see that you pay."

"I am going to marry my niece to the MacKinnon if it is the last thing I do! When she is far away from here I'll let you out."

It was a promise that tore at Torin's heart. "After Erica was married," Coinneach had said.

"She is my wife. You have no right."

"I have every right."

"You had better hide yourself when I am let out, for I will see that you pay!" In furious anger, Torin lashed out, only to be kicked back down into the dark hole. The clank of the door put an end to any other threats.

It was a tiny, cramped cell, with a stone-and-iron-barred trapdoor that could be locked from up above. Torin was familiar with the dungeon. There was no way of escape; of that he was certain.

Coinneach had vowed to keep him imprisoned until Erica was safely married, to use him as a pawn if necessary to keep his niece in line.

"If ye conduct yerself like a good little lassie and ye are

bedded with your husband, then I will set the traitorous Viking free."

"Then I will do as ye ask. Have I any choice?" Erica had looked at Torin then, love shining in her eyes. "Aye, I will marry the MacKinnon, but not for love. My heart belongs to you, Torin. Now and forever, my own dear love!"

"My own dear love," she had said. She was going to marry another man to save him! "No-o-o-o-o-o-o-o!" The cry that tore from his throat was like that of a wounded animal. Sagging to the ground, he grasped his knees, hugging them with his arms as he had when he was a small boy and his mother had died. Even the years of being an outcast had never hurt like this. Rocking back and forth, he sought to fight the demons that tore at his heart. Erica belonged to him!

Torin seemed to lose track of time as he languished in the dungeon. It was dismal, uncomfortable, and humiliating. It was a disgusting hellhole. But the discomfort he felt was nothing to the ache in his heart.

"Erica!" Her eyes haunted him, her voice seemed to whisper in his ear.

"Torin!" It was Erica's voice, he had not been imagining it. A circle of light appeared above his head as the grate was opened. He stood up, reaching up as if to caress the face he saw hovering above his head.

"I begged my uncle to let me see ye one more time. Be— before the wedding." She stretched out her fingers and brushed his with the poignancy of a kiss. "To tell ye that I love ye."

His voice was choked with misery. "Don't marry the MacKinnon, Erica."

"I must!"

"For my sake. But I don't care what Coinneach has threatened to do to me. Please! Don't—"

"Torin!" She whispered his name in a long, drawn-out sigh, wishing oh, so desperately that she could be with him. More than anything in the world she wanted his arms around her, wanted his lips touching hers, but it was not to be. "I—I came to wish you happiness. I—I want that for ye, Torin."

"I'll never be happy now. Not without you!"

She forced a laugh. "Aye, ye will. Ye know very well that ye are a handsome laddie with all the lassies chasing after ye. Ye'll soon forget me." Just the thought made her die a little, but she forced herself to laugh again. "I know that ye will."

"Never!"

"I want ye, too. I do! Uncle Coinneach is sending me away after the ceremony, to a castle farther south. Just in case I get ideas."

"No!" Standing on tiptoe, he clasped her hand with urgency. "Oh, if only I could get out of here."

Coinneach's face replaced Erica's at the opening. "Get out? I wouldn't be thinking it to be very soon. So sad that ye will miss the wedding, Torin, but then I am being very careful just who I invite. Bad enough that the MacKinnons will be present!" He laughed, but not for long.

"The MacLeods! They are outside our walls!" It was a cry that sobered Coinneach.

"The MacLeods!"

Like a swarm of raging ants, the MacLeods were climbing the hill and marching across the boggy meadow, crossing to the MacQuarie land, which bordered their own. In their bonnets they wore a sprig of fur club moss to tell any who might wonder that they were a mighty clan, the MacLeods!

The droning, pounding, fearsome sound of the bagpipes made no secret of the marchers' intent. Had there been any misunderstanding, the bloodcurdling war cry that sliced through the night soon announced what was to come.

"Let me out of here! Let me gather my men together. We can help you win. Please . . ."

Torin thought his plea had fallen on deaf ears, but then Coinneach's face appeared at the opening. "Will ye help us? And not turn on us?"

"I give you my word."

THIRTY-NINE

It was either fight or back down. Erica knew that her uncle would choose to fight for his honor even though the MacQuaries were seriously outnumbered. Even so, she held on to Torin's arm, hoping to delay the inevitable.

"Be careful."

"To arms! To arms!" Coinneach dashed Erica's hopes with his call to war. He glowered at Torin as his clansmen stripped every sword, shield, and dirk from the wall. For a moment, Torin suspected that the chieftain was going to put him back down in the dungeon.

"I told you that I would stand by your side and I mean it. You have my word."

Coinneach MacQuarie mumbled a profanity, then turned his back as Torin grabbed for any weapon available. He settled for an old relic of a sword. Brandishing it, he looked around for Erica. Above all, he would allow no harm to come to her.

Shouts rent the air. Ignoring the clashing and slashing of swords in the bloody and violent melee, he fought his way to her, thrusting her against the wall to protect her with his body. With a growl of warning, he wielded his sword, wounding his opponent.

"Go. Get the others!" When he hesitated, Erica took the sword out of his hand. "I can take care of myself. I taught

Geordie how to wield this." She neglected to tell him that
the sword she had used to teach her brother had been
wooden. It was the first time she had fought with a real
sword. It was heavy and cumbersome.

"No!"

Torin didn't want to leave her, but Erica was insistent.
"My uncle and the others will put up a valiant fight, but we
will lose," she said. "Hurry. There will be no chance for
peace if all my clansmen are dead!"

He thought a moment; then, realizing that there was no
other choice, he moved toward the door. "I'll be back as
soon as I can."

"I cannot believe I would trust a Viking," Coinneach
grumbled. "He will not come back. He'll sail away. I should
have kept him locked up underground."

"He'll be back." Erica was never more certain of anything
in all her life. She watched as bands of armed men assembled to fight, hacking and thrusting at each other. The clang
of sword against sword echoed down the hill. Anxiously her
eyes moved toward where her uncle was engaged in combat
with a MacLeod half his age.

"Go. Get yerself a place to hide. Do not be stubborn,
lass."

"I'm not helpless. I can defend myself." She grabbed a
shield from the wall, using it as best she could to protect
herself while she lashed out with the sword.

Erica was amazed at the strength she suddenly possessed.
Conscious only of the frantic need to come to the aid of the
MacQuarie fighters, she held her adversary at bay, then
watched him fall.

More and more MacLeods poured through the door. Erica
didn't know how long they had been fighting, but suddenly
it seemed an eternity. It was two to one. She looked over
her shoulder. If ever they needed help, it was now. Even
Geordie had joined in the melee. Where was Torin?

"Look—Erica—over there!" Geordie pointed.

Erica watched in wonder as Torin's Vikings swept down the hill like an avenging thunderstorm. With swords and axes swinging, they fought against the MacLeods with a ferocious anger.

Still there were those who were fearful that the Norsemen's swords would be turned against them. "Vikings! Take cover."

In answer to the shout, some of the younger men gathered together, running in terror toward the safety of the hall.

"The Vikings!" came the shout again as the frightened crowd peered from behind the doors of the hall. A cheer arose as they saw that those they called heathens had come to fight with them.

Side by side, Torin and Coinneach fought wildly, knowing the tide of the battle had turned. The MacLeods, who had been the aggressors, now signaled a retreat.

The MacLeods had waged a relentless battle that was brief but destructive. In the aftermath, chairs and tables were overturned, the room strewn with wounded and those who would never rise again; but clearly the MacQuaries were the victors.

"We have won!" Sheathing his sword, Coinneach MacQuarie smiled triumphantly. He turned to Torin. "I owe ye a debt of gratitude, Viking. Ye kept your word. I'll not be forgetting. . . ."

From her place at the doorway, Erica watched as the MacLeods marched back in the direction from which they had come. Her heart was thumping wildly in her breast. They had been saved. All was well.

There was a huge celebration in the hall later that night as Viking sat beside Scot in the bond of newfound friendship.

"I never thought I would be happy to see the Vikings," Coinneach said with a laugh. "But surely ye have saved

more than our pride today." He pounded Torin on the
back as if there had never been ill will between them.
"Tell the others of my gratitude, and that as far as I am
concerned there is now friendship between us."

"Do you mean that, Uncle Coinneach?" Erica pressed
the issue. "Torin wants to establish a peaceful coexistence
between our clan and his people. He wants to establish
trade."

"Trade?" Coinneach shook his head, all thought of
friendship forgotten for the moment.

"I've seen for myself the wondrous goods that the Vikings have brought back from ports in the East. There
is a cloth that feels as soft as the petals of a flower, and
spices . . ."

"We have weapons, and items for less destructive purposes that you will find useful." Torin didn't want to
plead. The Scots would profit a great deal from the Vikings.

"I will not answer now." Coinneach pulled at his
beard. "Let me think about it."

"What about your niece?"

"What about her?" For a moment it appeared that the
old hostilities were going to resurface.

"I love her and she loves me. What will it take for
you to recognize her as my wife so that she isn't torn
apart inside by your anger?" He would do anything that
Coinneach asked. "She loves me, but she loves Geordie
and she loves you. Don't punish her for following her
heart."

Coinneach had a faraway look in his eyes, as if remembering another place, another time. At last he rose
to his feet. "Would ye agree to be married by Christian
vows to Erica?"

Torin nodded. "Erica and I are already married by my
people's laws, but if it would make her happy, then I

agree." Surely Odin would not be too jealous of Erica's god.

"Then let us begin," Coinneach announced. Behind his hand he said to Erica, "I wonder if I can convince the MacKinnon to take Iona?" He laughed. "I'd better hurry that wedding as well, before he finds out about her temper."

Erica laughed as she threw her arms around her uncle. It was as if her nightmares had suddenly turned to dreams. What more could she possibly wish for?

FORTY

A Highland wedding was an elaborate and lengthy affair with a lot of ritual attached to it. Erica was led to the bath-house, where a tub of steaming water awaited her. A pile of thick woolen towels were spread on an airer to warm before the fire, and as she stood still, several of the women stripped off her gown.

"Oh, how I envy ye," one of the younger girls said, making no secret of her attraction to Erica's bridegroom.

"He is as bonnie a man as was ever seen on Ulva or Mull."

Jeanne wrinkled her nose, "but ye cannot say the same for the others."

"Oh, I don't know. The one with the tawny hair isn't too bad."

Stepping into the water, Erica sighed with pleasure as the pleasantly warm water surrounded her. She lay back as the women soaped her hair, but though she tried to relax it was impossible. Even the soothing cocoon of water could not slow the pounding of her heart or make her forget the coil that was forming in her stomach. Two ceremonies. No one could deny now that she and Torin belonged together.

"Oh, the men. What devils they are." Rinsing her hair, Jeanne related that already there was wagering going on as to how soon Erica would find herself with child.

"Most of the men are betting on a son. They say the Viking looks virile." Jeanne handed her a towel.

"He is!" Erica answered, closing her eyes and remembering the last time they had been together.

The chatter ceased as two of the older women arrived, carrying Erica's dress of a pale yellow material. It was artfully decorated with embroidery, and she could nearly imagine in her mind's eye a woman's form bent to the task, sitting before the hearth fire. A white tonnag pinned with an elaborately worked brooch of gold, a belt of leather, and several pieces of brass, intermixed to give the semblance of a chain, emphasized the trimness of her waist and completed her attire. As was the custom, she was barefoot.

" 'Twill be a sunny day, a perfect day to be wed."

"And ye have the perfect laddie."

The young women chattered and laughed with as much exuberance as if they were to be the brides. They combed and brushed her hair until it shone with a red fire. Unmarried lassies bound their hair and wore a snood, but married women left their hair to hang free. As a symbol of her newly wedded state, therefore, Erica's side hair was braided, her back hair left to flow down her back.

"Ye look bonnie, Erica!" Even Iona had to compliment her cousin.

"Like some regal queen."

Erica stood before the large polished-steel mirror, studying her reflection. Though seldom conscious of her looks, she was critical now, pinching her cheeks to make them pink, licking her lips to make them shine. Then she walked down the stairs to make her grand entrance before all.

"Ach, niece, ye truly are a wondrous sight." Standing beside Torin, Coinneach MacQuarie was all smiles. Taking a large cup from the hands of a young male servant, he held it forth to Erica. "Drink!"

The cup was adorned with a sprig of rosemary and colored ribbons and looked like some pagan offering. As she took a sip of the spiced wine, Erica could not help but wonder if some ancient Celtic tribal bride had held such an object in her hand. Handing the cup to Torin, she smiled, forgetting for the moment the trauma of the fighting. She told him that the cup had been handed down for generations, all the way from the first chieftain of the MacQuarie Clan.

"We will give it to our son when he weds," Torin exclaimed, to be rewarded by a hearty slap on the back from Coinneach. With a nod of his head, Coinneach signaled it was time for the merry-making. Rising to his feet he flung back his chair, leaped upon it and raised aloft the bridal cup as a whirling, high-stepping, jubilant, laughing group of revelers gave vent to their joy. Erica was pleased to see that Torin's Viking crew joined in the celebration.

It was Highland custom for bride and groom to ride pillion on the back of a strong gelding; thus Erica walked beside Torin to the stables, mounting behind him on a long-haired Highland horse for the short ride to the castle chapel on the other side of the courtyard. On the back of the horse, in a leather pouch was placed the marriage money, guarded by two strong Highlanders who walked on each side of the animal. A troupe of musicians playing harp, flute, and bagpipes followed. Erica smiled to see that Gardar had been included.

Torin's hands were gentle as he helped Erica dismount. He motioned for the Viking crew to follow, but because the chapel was small and there were too many of them to fit inside, they made arrangements to wait by the front door. Erica suspected that some of them were uneasy about going into a Christian holy place, perhaps because it reminded them of some of the raids and the destruction they had done.

"Wait, then. We won't be long," Torin said.

Entering the chapel, Erica stood tall and proud as she took the lighted candle the priest held forth. The holy man asked the standard questions as a matter of formality: if she was of age; if she swore that she and the betrothed were not within the forbidden degree of consanguinity, if her parents consented to the marriage, if the banns had been posted; and finally and most important of all, if she and her groom both gave free consent to the match.

"Then come forth, daughter, to be joined in this holiest of vows."

Erica walked down the aisle to the spot where the priest waited. There she knelt at her future husband's feet in a gesture of submission.

"Rise!"

Together they faced the priest and repeated their solemn vows. The priest sprinkled her with holy water and recited an intricate mass. The ceremony unfolded so quickly that Erica hardly remembered what she had said. It was just babbled words in a foreign tongue. And all the while, as she clutched tightly to her rowan cross, she said a prayer that this marriage would mean peace between the MacQuaries and the Vikings for a long time to come.

The joining of right hands concluded the transfer of a gift, Erica's womanhood, and potential motherhood for Torin's protection and loyalty. Torin then slipped onto three of his new wife's fingers, one after another, the ring that signified marriage—a blessed circle of gold that would protect her from assault by demons.

"With this ring I thee wed, with this gold I thee honor, and with this dowry I thee endow," he said aloud, remembering the words Coinneach had told him to speak.

"A token of love and fidelity," the priest intoned.

The final phase of the ceremony was enacted. The groom received the priest's kiss of peace, then bent to transmit that kiss to his bride.

Returning to the hall, bride and groom presided over the wedding feast that consisted of cold mutton, fowl, and all the usual dairy produce, scones, cheese, oatcakes. Whiskey was drunk and the couple toasted by all.

After the feast, a riotous dance ensued, the bridal couple taking the lead in the wedding reel. This time the Vikings took part, and Erica was amused to see Iona dancing first with one Viking, then another.

Torches illuminated the steps of the dark, winding staircase that led to the bridal chamber. A chattering, drunken throng accompanied the newly married couple up the winding stairs and to their room.

The key element to the wedding was the blessing of the bedchamber and the bed to dispel any curse that might have compromised the couple's fertility, and to wipe away any taint of female adultery. Then bride and groom took their places in bed under the watchful eyes of a circle of close relations. Coinneach looked on, waiting expectantly.

" 'Tis custom that he see us in bed together before he leaves us, so there can be no denying that we will consummate our marriage," she told Torin when he seemed ready to protest.

"But they will leave?"

She laughed. "Aye, they will give us our privacy."

Once witnessed together in bed, the couple was to be left alone. The nuptial bed, a crucial element in marriage, symbolized what was at stake: power in and over private life. The Highland belief was that honor, marriage, and a person's very being were for the sake of the clan—the betterment of all.

The priest talked of death or annulment, in which case the surviving party to the espousal was not free to remarry a brother, sister, or other relative of the other party. Relations by affinity were forbidden to the fourth canonical degree, and relations of consanguinity were forbidden to the seventh degree. Then he intoned, "Have joy of each other. . . ."

Torin lay silent for a long time, recuperating from the tension of the moment. Then, with the greatest of tenderness, he slowly, leisurely began the love play that would culminate in the satisfaction of his greatest desire.

Murmuring Erica's name, he buried his face in the silky strands of her hair, inhaling the delicate fragrance of flowers in the luxurious softness. His lips traveled slowly down the soft flesh of her throat, tasting the sweetness of her skin. Then, with impatient hands, he quickly loosened her garments.

It seemed his hands were everywhere, touching her, setting her body afire with a pulsating flame of desire. Erica gave in to the passion he inspired, writhing beneath him, giving herself up to the glorious sensations he was igniting within her. When at last she was naked, her long flaming hair streaming down her back, he looked at her for a long while, his face flushed with passion, his breath a deep-throated rasp.

"I love you. You are my greatest treasure. . . ." With reverence he touched her breasts. Gently. Slowly. Until they swelled in his hands.

His exploration was like a hundred feathers, everywhere upon her skin arousing a deep, aching longing. Erica closed her eyes to the rapture. Without even looking at him she could see his strong body, blue eyes, and tawny hair, and she thought again what a handsome man he was. Yet it was something far stronger that drew her: the gentleness that had merged with his strength. She touched him, one hand sliding down over the muscles of his chest, sensuously stroking the warmth of his flesh in exploration. She heard the audible intake of his breath, and that gave her the courage to continue in her quest.

He held her face in his hands, kissing her eyelids, the curve of her cheekbones, her mouth. "Erica. Erica." He repeated her name over and over again as if to taste it on his lips.

"I am glad that I please you, for you please me, too, so very much." Her fingertips roamed over his shoulders and neck and plunged into his thick, golden hair as he kissed her once again, a fierce joining of mouths that spoke of his passion. Then, after a long, pleasurable moment, he drew away, drawing the shirt over his head, stripping off his trousers and tunic. When he was completely naked, he rolled over on his side and drew her down again alongside him.

The candlelight flickered and sparked, illuminating the smooth skin on his chest as she reached out to him. Her hands caressed his chest, her blue eyes beckoning him, enticing him to enter the world of love that was familiar, yet nonetheless seductive in its intimacy.

Erica was shattered by the all-consuming pleasure of lying naked beside him. A heat arose within her as she arched against him in sensual pleasure. Her breath became heavier, and a hunger for him that was like a pleasant pain went from her breasts down to her loins—a pulsing, tingling sensation that increased as his hand ran down the smoothness of her belly to feel the softness nestled between her thighs.

Erica gave way to wild abandon, moaning intimately, joyously as her fingers likewise moved over his body. She shivered at the feelings that swept over her.

The light of the three candles illuminated their bodies, hers as smooth as cream, his a muscular form of darker hue. He knelt down beside her and kissed her breasts, running his tongue over their tips until she shuddered with delight. Whispering words of love, he slid his hands between her thighs to explore the soft inner flesh. At his touch she felt a slow quivering deep inside that became a fierce fire as he moved his fingers against her.

"Love me, Torin," she breathed.

Taking her mouth in a hard, deep kiss, he entered her with a slow but strong thrust, burying his length within the sheath of her softness. He knew at that moment that love was the true meaning of life, the only thing on earth that was truly worth obtaining. Closing his eyes he wondered how he could ever have thought that anything was as important as this.

As they came together, spasms of feeling wove through Erica like the threads of a tapestry. Without him she was incomplete; joined with him she was a whole being. Feverishly she clung to him, her breasts pressed against him. Their hearts beat in matching rhythm even as their mouths met, their tongues intertwined, and their bodies embraced in the slow, sensuous dance of love. She was consumed by his warmth, his hardness, and tightened her thighs around his waist as she arched up to him, moving in time to his rhythm.

"Torin!" It was as if he had touched the very core of her being. There was an explosion of rapture as their bodies blended into one. It was an ecstasy too beautiful for words. *Love,* such a simple word and yet in truth it meant so much.

Languidly they came back to reality, lying together in the aftermath of passion, their hearts gradually resuming a normal pace. Torin gazed down upon her face, gently brushing back the tangled red hair from her eyes.

"Sleep now," he whispered, still holding her close. Tomorrow they would set sail for the Northland, but tonight belonged to them.

With a sigh she snuggled up against him, burying her face in the warmth of his chest. He caressed her, tracing his fingers along her spine until she drifted off.

FORTY-ONE

Torin's arm lay heavy across Erica's stomach, the heat of his body warming hers as they lay together. The sound of his breathing brought a sense of peace and fulfillment to her. They were married. Not by the laws of just one people but by two: Scot and Viking. No one could deny them happiness now.

Whispering his name, Erica stroked the expanse of Torin's shoulders and chest, remembering the heated passion they had shared last night on their second wedding night. His skin was warm and roughened by a thatch of hair on his chest. Against her breasts it always felt more pleasurable than she might ever have imagined in her maiden days. Oh, how she loved being married to *him*.

"Erica?" Torin cherished the blessing of finding her cradled in his arms, her mane of bright-red hair spread like a cloak over her shoulders. He felt an aching tenderness and drew her closer.

She snuggled into his arms, laying her head on his shoulder, curling into his hard, strong body. She shuddered to think that she had come so close to marrying the MacKinnon.

"Are you cold?"

"Nay. I was just thinking of how close we came to being parted forever. I suppose ye might say that we owe the

MacLeods a debt of gratitude for showing up when they did. It gave Uncle Coinneach something to think about except how angry he was with ye."

"Even if the MacLeods hadn't come, I would have found a way to reclaim you. I never would have lost you!" His hand moved lightly over her hip and down her leg as he spoke. She was his! Now and forever more.

"My heart would have broken if Uncle had had his way. But now I will wake up every morning and find ye next to me," she whispered, nibbling at his earlobe playfully.

He was her husband. She belonged to him. The very thought made her feel happy and content. Torin was everything a woman could wish for and much, much more.

Slowly he began the caressing motions that had so deeply stirred her the first time they had made love. He touched her from the curve of her neck to the soft flesh behind her knees and up again, caressing the flat plain of her belly. Moving to her breast, he cupped the soft flesh, squeezing gently. Her breast filled his palm as his fingers stroked and fondled. Lowering his head, he buried his face between the soft mounds.

"There is nothing like a woman's softness."

"Unless 'tis a man's strength." She was not content to be only the recipient of pleasure, but felt a need to give it as well. With that desire in mind she moved her palms over the muscles and tight flesh of his body.

A long shuddering sigh wracked through him. "Oh, how I love your hands upon me!"

Reveling in the knowledge that she could so deeply stir him, she continued her exploration, as if to learn every inch of him. In response she felt his hard body tremble against hers.

"Ahhhh . . ." The sound came from deep in his throat.

Stretching her arms up, she wrapped them around his neck, pulling his head down. Her mouth played seductively on his, proving to him how quickly she could learn such passionate skills. Then they were rolling over and over in the bed, sinking into the warmth and softness. Erica sighed in delight at the feel of his hard, lithe body atop hers. Her entire body quivered with the intoxicating sensations. She would never get tired of feeling Torin's hands on her skin, of tasting his kisses.

A loud pounding at the door interrupted their pleasure.

"By Odin's beard! Who would disturb a man in his marriage bed?" Torin's oath was muffled by Erica's hand.

"My Uncle Coinneach would if he had something on his mind." She caressed his body with hers, holding herself so tightly against him that there wasn't room to move a feather. "If we ignore him he might go away."

That was Torin's hope, but alas, it was not to be. A resounding bang, bang at the door signaled someone's steadfast determination to intrude.

"Erica?" There could be no mistake. It was Coinneach MacQuarie's voice. "I know ye are in there." The statement was punctuated by a belly laugh. "Tell your new husband that I would have a word with him!"

Torin gently nipped at her ear. "I hope he hasn't decided to put me back in the dungeon."

"Were he to do that he would have to put me there too, for I will never be parted from ye." She traced the line of his collarbone with her index finger.

"Erica!" Coinneach's tone was insistent.

Erica looked toward the door, then at Torin, then back at the door again. There was no way she could ignore her uncle. "My husband is asleep."

"Asleep? I wouldn't be surprised." She could hear a chuckle. "But it's morning, Erica. I have business to attend to, and that business involves your new husband. Tell him—"

"Tell me what?" Torin could not hide his annoyance. He could never imagine Ragnar intruding upon a couple just recently wed. But then Erica's uncle seemed to be full of surprises.

"That ye should be down to my chambers within the time it takes a cow to blink," Coinneach answered. "We have some negotiating yet to do—that is, if ye still want to be trading."

Groaning, Torin bounded out of bed, his ardor cooled. Hastily donning his trousers, leather shoes, tunic and belt, and trunk hose, he went to the door and yanked it open. Coinneach MacQuarie was not there, but the sound of his footsteps could be heard as he walked down the stairs. Grumbling beneath his breath all the while, Torin followed, but it was not Coinneach MacQuarie who greeted him as he turned the corner.

"The hounds!" Torin tried to placate the two russet-hued wolfhounds that guarded the door and were now growling at him. Bristling and baring their teeth, they gave warning of what they would do if he made a wrong move. "Easy . . . easy . . ." Torin carefully moved past the two animals.

"It seems that no one has informed the dogs that the Scots and Vikings in Mull and Ulva are no longer at odds," exclaimed a voice.

"Gardar!" It was obvious that he had been dallying, for his clothing was askew and there was a sheepish look on his face.

"Am I to assume that there will be another wedding?" Torin asked, playfully nudging his shoulder.

Gardar blushed. "She's already said yes . . . but—but—"

"She will not come with you to the Northland."

Gardar nodded. "I . . . I . . . would like to stay here."

Though Torin was disturbed by the thought of losing his friend to the Highlands, he understood Gardar's feelings. "Perhaps I can reach an agreement with Erica's uncle and make you part of the agreement." When Gardar looked puzzled, he said, "Wait and see."

Torin motioned for Gardar to follow him, but when they

started to walk, the two wolf-hounds growled menacingly. "Perhaps they haven't been fed," Gardar quipped, hurrying after Torin as he walked toward a door that led to a large chamber. Inside, Coinneach MacQuarie sat in a large high-backed chair, gazing intently ahead as if Torin and Gardar were not even there. At last he spoke.

"We are happy unto ourselves here in the Highlands. My people are self-supporting, proud, independent, and at the same time interdependent. We're like a family who do not welcome strangers. We are secure and well fed. Life here is essentially simple and pastoral."

Torin interrupted. "I have no doubt that you are content, but if you but open up your heart and your mind, you could increase your contentment twofold."

"And increase our population as they have in the north of Alba, with foreigners elbowing their way amongst us?" Coinneach shook his head. "That is not what I want. We are isolated, and if we lack worldly goods then so be it. At least we are free men."

"And so you would remain. Upon my word of honor, neither Ragnar nor I will seek to bring others here. We want to trade and not colonize."

Torin knew that Ragnar was as much a merchant as a marauder and conqueror. On his raids, his battle sword went hand in hand with the tiny scales he used to measure the silver that represented commercial gain.

"So ye say." They looked upon each other, each judging the other as a determined man. "There is a river of bad blood between us."

Torin nodded. "I hope that together we can build a bridge to span that river—if not with friendship, then at least with some measure of understanding."

"Understanding . . ." Coinneach was silent for a long time; then he sighed. "Aye. There's been enough blood spilled to last my lifetime."

"And enough to last mine."

Boldly he assessed Torin. "I think that ye are a man I can trust, for ye kept your word and came to our aid when the MacLeods attacked. But what about the others?"

Torin cleared his throat. "There is always the danger of betrayal." He thought about Herlaug. "Even from within, but we can offer you timber for ship-building as well as iron for making tools and weapons to strengthen your men when there is battle to be done." Folding his arms across his chest, Torin Rolandson held the older man's eyes without wavering. "I will protect the Highlands as if they were my own homeland."

"Aye, ye love my niece; that I can plainly see. I trust ye, Viking, but I have my worries. . . ."

Gardar, who had up until now kept silent, spoke out. "Times are changing. Though I have no reason to love the Vikings, I know that they are like the tide. No one can hold them back. But there is always much to be learned, even from one's enemies." His eyes met Coinneach's as if to remind him of what the Scots had done to the Picts. "I have learned that firsthand."

Coinneach swore violently. "I repeat. We are the Lords of the Isles; we do not need anyone. Do ye understand?"

"Then you have changed your mind. We will talk no more about it." Torin turned his back as if to walk away.

"Do not leave just yet. I've not finished with my say." At his gesture, two guards came as if from out of nowhere to block the portal, but he waved them away. Once again he scrutinized Torin. "What is it ye want from us?" There was a semblance of a smile on his lips. "Aside from our women, that is?"

"Cloth." He pointed to Coinneach's breacan. "The weave is tight and the cloth colorful."

Coinneach puffed out his chest with pride, as if he had been the one responsible for the cloth. "Our women make use of the plants on Ulva and Mull for the dye. 'Tis their secret."

The initial resource upon which the Norsemen's commerce was founded was a substance known as amber, a clear fossilized resin of pine trees that had died long before Torin was born. The sea washed it ashore in chunks. The Viking women loved the golden play of light on the strings of amber beads that they wore on their bosoms. It was rendered even more valuable by the fact that when rubbed it took on a highly magnetic charge, a property that seemed magical.

"For your cloth we will trade you amber." Though Torin didn't have any amber with him, Gardar did—a necklace of amber beads that he wore around his neck for protection.

Examining the amber, Coinneach grunted. "This and something more."

"Amber and wood for your ships."

"Agreed!"

Torin continued. "We are a people who love things from the sea. I remember the day that I went with your hunting party. . . ." *When they were going to kill me,* he thought but did not say. "You told me then how abundant the fish are here."

Again Coinneach reveled in his pride. "Aye. Salmon, brown and sea trout, eels and crab . . . and oysters . . ."

"In trade for furs for clothing, skins from whales and seals for ship ropes, and whale bones and walrus ivory carved with intricate designs."

"Pagan?"

"For Christians we have carved crosses."

Coinneach's frown slowly turned to the semblance of a smile "So, let us begin with this trade agreement Ragnar proposes."

Pulling up another chair, smaller than his own, Coinneach motioned for Torin to sit beside him. Though Gardar could likewise have sat in a chair, he was more comfortable sitting on the floor beside Torin, listening intently as the two men came to an agreement. He smiled when Torin told Coinneach that he, Gardar, would act in his stead and see to the managing of the agreement, and would be keeper of the scales for those times when trades involved the exchange of silver, coins, or other precious metals.

It seemed that Torin had won everything he had wanted but then suddenly Coinneach blurted, "I always wanted sons but I was denied. There is Geordie, of course, but were anything to happen to the laddie there would be chaos. Thus, my only hope of carrying out my line is through the next generation." The thick fingers of his left hand clenched and unclenched the wooden armrests. "I'll put it to ye bluntly. One of the terms of Erica's marriage to ye is that any male issue ye may have will take on the MacQuarie name."

Torin bolted up from his chair. "My son take on your name!"

"That's what I said." Coinneach's fingers curled into aggressive fists as he raised his hand. "Peace has its price. I am not simple-minded. Ragnar gets his daughter; ye get yer bonnie wife; ye both profit from trade with us. What about me?" He paused to take a deep breath. "I expect to profit from this union between my niece and you as well as does Ragnar."

Torin looked toward the door, fully expecting to be carried to the dungeon at any moment. Odin strike the Scot! He had been tricked, for there had been no mention of such an arrangement before the wedding.

Obviously taking notice of Torin's expression, Coinneach's tone softened. "It is not an unusual request. If ye will ask your wife, ye will learn about our system of fosterage. Sons grow up at the hearth of another to learn their ways and strengthen the clan."

Torin paced up and down the chamber in agitation. Even if what the MacQuarie was requesting had been done before, Ragnar would never agree. Torin slammed his fist into the palm of his hand to vent his anger. He wanted to scream out, to decry it as an outrage, but he fought to retain his composure, for the alternative was devastating: to lose Erica forever.

"So, you think to punish Ragnar, is that it?"

Though Coinneach didn't answer, his clenched jaw answered for him. His stiff-necked stance clearly said he would not back down on the matter. "But in the doing you punish Erica and me as well." Were they to have a son, Erica might be forced to choose between living in the Northland with her husband and living in Alba with her son. Even so, Torin finally agreed to the terms.

A soft, whispering breeze caressed Erica's flushed face as she stood atop the castle battlement walk, where she had retreated the moment Torin told her what her Uncle Coinneach had said. She couldn't quite believe it. She remembered the priest once telling her the story of Solomon, King of a land long ago and far away. Two mothers claimed that a child belonged to them. They were fighting over the wee babe, asking Solomon for his advice. Now her uncle was fighting her father's right to a child that had yet to be conceived!

"The child will be mine! I will be his mother."

And yet, that was the way of things. A woman's fate was never in her own hands but in the hands of those she loved and trusted. *Uncle, how could ye?* To him it was all so simple, just like a chess game. If that made her little more than a womb to breed a future contender to be the MacQuarie tanist, well again, that was the way of clan life.

Erica drew in a deep breath of fresh air, then let it out in a sigh. Her emotions were in turmoil. No, she wasn't going to let her uncle dictate the fate of her child. She wouldn't allow him to manipulate her life, her child's life, and Torin's life this way. It was time to take a stand.

FORTY-TWO

Though the chamber entrance loomed in her path like the most unwelcoming portcullis, Erica knocked decisively on the door.

"Who is it?" a voice thundered in the silence.

"Erica. I would speak with ye, uncle."

Furled brows showed his impatience at being disturbed as Coinneach MacQuarie opened the door. "By God, lass, what could be so important that ye would interrupt a man's peace and quiet?" He took one look at her and stepped back. "Why such a fearsome face?"

"I have something that needs to be said."

Words exploded from his lips. "Save your breath, lassie. If your fine husband has already told ye about what I want for your bairn, then so be it. I have made my decision. I have spoken."

"Your decision!"

For just a moment his face was completely blank of expression; then he grimaced. "Aye. My decision!"

"Then let me tell ye that I have made a decision on my own."

"Ye . . . ye have?"

"One that complicates all your plotting and scheming," Erica blurted out, looking him directly in the eye. "Since ye see so fit to tell me what I will do with my own bairn, I will tell ye a thing or two. With all my heart I want to be a mother and to bear not just one, but many children of my husband's seed. But—"

The MacQuarie's face tightened. "But what?"

" 'Tis time that ye didn't have your way." She took a deep breath. Her knees were shaking; her hands were trembling. "So . . . I will be forced to make a sacrifice. The gravest one that any woman can make." She closed her eyes and took a deep breath, then opened her eyes again, looking him in the eye. "If ye insist on being so petty and selfish, on trying to seek vengeance because my mother loved a man not of your liking—if ye seek retribution on my father by taking my future son—then . . . then I will have no children at all!"

"What?" He was stunned. "What nonsense is this?"

"There are ways for a woman to keep from bearing a child. Every midwife knows them."

"Ye wouldn't! It is against God."

"If ye can only think of yourself and your anger, if ye think to hold my child over my father's head like a game piece in this cruel game of yours, if ye care not a whit for my dear husband and his feelings, then as God is my witness, I will!"

He held up one hand, palm out, fingers toward the ceiling. It was a gesture he always used to intimidate and silence any opposition. "I will not have a slip of a lassie talking to me that way. I am the chieftain of the MacQuaries. My word is law!"

Though once she might have cowered, Erica let her rising tide of bitterness consume her. "Ye may be the MacQuarie, your word may be law on this isle, but even the mighty chief must bow to a greater power."

His face turned red; he balled his hands into fists. "Niece!"

Erica's eyes glittered in the candlelight. It shouldn't be like this, she thought. When she had a child it should bring her uncle's clan and her father's Vikings together, not pull them apart.

"All my life I have known that ye regretted that Iona and I were born female. Ye let me know it by every look, every word ye said. I also suffered because of my Viking blood. Do ye think I would put my own child through that?" She took a deep breath. "Ye have Geordie. One day he will make a fine chieftain. He will have sons. Perhaps Iona will as well. Ye do not need my child!"

There was such a fearsome pressure pushing at her chest that she feared she couldn't breathe. Then, without warning, Erica burst into a storm of tears. "Ye can be cruel, uncle. Cruel."

Coinneach was unnerved by her tears and regretted his outburst. Touching her shoulder he softened. "Eri, do not cry. It's just that . . . that . . . I cannot get used to sharing ye with Ragnar. I loved your mother and he wounded her."

"It was a long time ago. He has made his amends with me."

Dashing the tears from her cheeks, she spoke. "And mayhap he has reason to be angry with ye as well. But no matter what is between ye, I will not let it affect my life. Not any longer! If that means that ye intend to banish me, so be it!"

He was visibly taken aback. In all his life no one had ever talked to him this way. "Ye would have me banish ye?"

Her voice was little more than a whisper. "I want to be happy. I want to feel loved. Why is that so much to ask for?" She took his hand. "All my life I felt an emptiness. Now, with Torin I am fulfilled. I wake up each morning grateful for the day and for him. Why would ye want to take that from me?"

"I didn't . . ."

"But ye will if ye do not let me live my life the way that I choose, where I want—how I want to raise my own child— without your anger hanging over my head." She paused. "I have four men in my life that I love with all my heart. My husband, my father, my brother, and ye. I cannot be forced to choose between them."

He hung his head. "And ye will not!"

"Then ye will not take my son?"

Though he struggled with the words, he answered, "Nae." He gathered her into his arms. "I want ye to be happy, Erica. That is really all I ever wanted. I'm sorry if I was blinded by my anger. But I am an old man and I'm set in my ways."

"We all are!" She blinked away her tears. "I would like for Geordie to visit the Northland and for Torin and me to visit here many, many times to come." She tugged at his beard. "And for ye to visit us in the Northland, too."

He grinned. "I wonder what old Ragnar would say to that?"

"I don't know, but it would be interesting to see." Together they walked arm in arm down the stairs. Erica could only hope that when she left Alba behind, it would not be an ending but a beginning.

FORTY-THREE

The days that followed were a time for atonement. A time for explanations. A time for healing. A time for peace. A time for love.

Standing at the window of the castle, looking out at a bright, multi-hued rainbow, Erica could only hope that all the ill feelings and bitterness had at last been laid to rest.

"What are ye thinking about, my love?" Coming up behind her, Torin brushed a lock of her flaming hair from her eyes in a gesture that always stirred her.

"About everything that has happened." She turned slowly. "Do ye really think the fragile peace will last? Uncle has a terrible temper, and from what I know of my father, he does, too." She sighed. "Do ye really think that they have learned?"

"I do!" Taking her face in his hands, Torin looked for a long time into her eyes. "I am so proud of you. But would you really have carried out your threat not to have a child?"

"I was bluffing. I prayed he couldn't tell. I would never have taken the life of my unborn bairns. Any child I would have with ye would be much too precious to me." Even so, it had been the most rash, daring thing she had ever done in her life. But was it really over? Was all the killing and the anger really buried?

"Oh, Torin, how I love you," she whispered,

"And I love you. It makes a man believe in happy endings."

She smiled. "Then I believe in happy endings, too." Looking out the window, she saw that the land looked fresh and green, so peaceful. And up in the sky the rainbow could still be seen. "Look, Torin, how the rainbow arches across the clear blue sky like so many ribbons."

"A rainbow." Torin smiled.

"It's said that there is a pot of gold at the end. Shall we try to find it when we sail back to the Northland tomorrow?"

Torin bent his head and kissed his wife. "I've already found all that I want and need right here with you." Never in his life had he been happier, and he knew in his heart that the same could be said for the woman he so deeply loved.

The Viking ship, loaded with cloth, oysters, eel and salmon, sailed through the turbulent waters past the tip of Alba and headed "home." Torin brushed back strands of Erica's red hair as they blew in a swirl around her face, a gesture he had lovingly repeated many times while on the journey. Reaching out he held onto his wife to warm her and shield her from the wind blowing from the sea.

"What are you thinking?" he asked softly, kissing her forehead.

"How pleased Ragnar will be with all the goods ye are bringing to him from Alba, and I am content that all has turned out as it should," she sighed. "My father and I have a lot of memories to share with each other."

Feeling content standing beside Torin, Erica lay her head against his chest. If only they could stand like this forever, gazing out at the sea, heedless of worries, feeling only the joy of being together. If they could forget about Viking and Scot, about Herlaug's treachery and only think about the joyful things of life. Then she would have asked for nothing more.

The blaze of the sun cast a glow upon the water, looking like flames of a fire. "It reminds me of the midnight sun that we have in the Northland," Torin whispered. "Endless day. Summer sun shedding eternal light. That is how my love is, Erica. And Loki take any who would seek to part you from me."

Look for the next novel in
The Vikings series
—CONQUEROR—
coming from Zebra Ballad in June 2002

Gwyneth, daughter of an English lord, is haunted by the memory of her first love, a golden-haired Viking whom her father had enslaved when she was little more than a child. When she helped him escape, he gifted her with a silver pendant shaped like a dragon. It is her most treasured possession, which she wears even on the day she is to marry, Before the ceremony is carried out, however, the Vikings attack. Selig Boldheart seeks vengeance on the man who once cruelly sold him into bondage. He informs Gwyneth they will spend her "wedding night" together, for he does not want her beauty to go to waste.

Gwyneth does not recognize the Viking, for he has changed, but he recognizes her because of the Dragon's Tear pendant she is wearing. The pretty child has grown to be a beautiful woman. Shaken by the encounter, he determines to leave her alone and try to atone for the heartache he has already brought to her. Little does he realize that he has unwittingly kidnapped his one-time rescuer. Now he holds his greatest prize of all as hostage, Gwyneth, the daughter of his greatest enemy—or is it she who holds his heart captive?

About the Author

KATHRYN HOCKETT is the pseudonym for the mother/daughter writing team of Kathryn Kramer and Marcia Hockett. The award-winning authors live in Boulder, Colorado, and have published thirty-six historical romances under three pen names, some of which have been translated into German, Italian, Dutch, Hebrew, Chinese, and Romanian. In their spare time the authors design historical costumes for their collection of over four hundred dolls.

BOOK YOUR PLACE ON OUR WEBSITE AND MAKE THE READING CONNECTION!

We've created a customized website just for our very special readers, where you can get the inside scoop on everything that's going on with Zebra, Pinnacle and Kensington books.

When you come online, you'll have the exciting opportunity to:

- View covers of upcoming books
- Read sample chapters
- Learn about our future publishing schedule (listed by publication month *and author*)
- Find out when your favorite authors will be visiting a city near you
- Search for and order backlist books from our online catalog
- Check out author bios and background information
- Send e-mail to your favorite authors
- Meet the Kensington staff online
- Join us in weekly chats with authors, readers and other guests
- Get writing guidelines
- AND MUCH MORE!

**Visit our website at
http://www.kensingtonbooks.com**